I0551709

KRACKEN

RAY ELLIS

Kracken

By Ray Ellis

Copyright © 2015 Ray Ellis

All rights reserved as permitted under the U.S. Copyright Act of 1976, no part of this publication may be reproduced, distributed, or transmitted in any form or by any means, or stored in a database or retrieval system, without the prior permission of the publisher. The characters and events portrayed in this book are fictitious. Any similarity to a real person, living or dead is coincidental and not intended by the author.

First Edition eBook: 2015
First Edition Paperback: 2015
ISBN (ePub): 978-1-938596-19-3
ISBN (Paperback): 978-1-938596-20-9

Cover Copyright © 2014
Cover photography & design by Stephanie Blaser
https://www.facebook.com/StephanieBlaserPhotography

Published in the United States of America
NCC Publishing
Meridian, Idaho, 83642, USA
www.nccpublishing.com

Many of the designations used by manufacturers and sellers to distinguish their products are claimed as trademarks. Product names, brands, and other trademarks referred to within this book are the property of their respective trademark holders. No association between the author and any trademark holder is expressed or implied.

20150216 20150221

Dedication

I'd like to dedicate this book to the two women who were Nonna to me, my great-grandmother Viola K. Johnson and my grandmother, Winnie Lee Cockrell. They are both now enjoying the bounty of God's presence even as they were first faithful to sow the seeds of His love into my heart.

"The man who does the right thing when the right thing needs to be done, regardless of the cost to himself; history judges this man as great."

Anonymous

Before...

Late 24th Century Old Calendar, the year 135 in the New Reckoning.

The lighting technician looked up just as he slid the last panel shut, a smile brightening his already exuberant expression. "M-M-Mr. Stone—"

"I told you to call me—"

"I m-mean Mr. Mike. Excuse me, sir." The man rose and dusted his hands on the pant leg of his trousers and grasped Mike Stone's outstretched hand. "This is going to make you the most powerful man in The Company, sir."

Mike smiled as he looked past the edge of the wall and took in the sight of over twenty-five thousand people who had gathered to hear his announcement and to witness his rise to power.

At the podium stood Ted Waters. Though several years Mike's elder, he served as the junior partner to Mike Stone on the Gliese 581G project. He turned in a broad gesture; his hand extended toward the side of the stage where Mike stood just out of sight. "Ladies and gentlemen of the New Earth Order, join me in welcoming the man who has made this all possible. Who, by his single-minded drive, imagination, and sheer determination, has opened new regions of space for not only our exploration, but also our expansion and settlement. Help me in welcoming...Mike Stone."

Outside the hall, a summer storm raged. Flashes of lightning illuminated the translucent ceiling, sending a strobing effect over the heads of the attendees. Arriving at the podium amidst applause, Mike raised both arms. He absorbed the praise, then pointed to the ceiling. "Now, we can't let a little something like lightning dampen our celebration." Smiling, he rubbed the side of his face with a knuckle while manipulating a series of small controls on the podium surface with his free hand and instantly the ceiling shimmered and became opaque.

The crowd erupted into greater applause. In the wings, Ted Waters watched and his face darkened. From above and behind Mike, a giant avatar, matching Mike's every movement and expression, emanating from the ceiling, flickered and came to life.

The room faded to black and silence enveloped the hall. After a moment, the sound of Mike's voice began to rise, echoing in the cavernous space, as if coming from a great distance. Overhead, the image of deep space and the planets of the galaxy zoomed into view. Following the commonly recognized spatial bodies, rose the image of a single planet, at least twice the size of Earth. The image continued forward until it filled the screen.

Mike stood with his feet spread shoulder width apart, and after first lowering his face, he thrust both arms above his head in triumph and roared.

The auditorium erupted into applause.

"Ladies and gentlemen," Mike announced, "I give you Yargon!" The view changed as it followed the camera down through the atmosphere; clouds appeared then sped by as the view crashed through a jungle canopy.

Spooked, a flock of giant birds with strange and colorful plumages, rose, screaming in protest. As the descent slowed, the view opened to kilometer after kilometer of verdant plains stretching out in every direction as gentle streams and wide mouthed rivers poured in from unseen sources.

On the stage, a light, as if from a star, bluish white in color, cascaded from the rafters, illuminating Mike where he stood. His charcoal colored suit and bone scarf reflected the light from his athletic frame. Applause and cheers filled the chamber. Mike relished the moment—his ascension to greatness.

Off stage, Samuel smiled and turned to look back at Ted Waters. Samuel froze. The look of cold hatred on Ted Waters's face burned as if it were a living thing. Locking eyes, Waters did not speak but stared at the younger man. Then without uttering a single sound, he turned and walked away.

Chapter One

The village square was busy. Moist streets and the smell of sweat and dirt, mixed with the aroma of raw sewage, hung heavy in the air. Dirty-faced children played in the streets, and escaped animals ran under foot. Skipp Langg had come to find the needed components to finish the project that he was working on.

Skipp stopped, pretending this time to study a set of sonic amplifiers. He looked back the way he had come. The lone figure stopped as well. Now he was sure he was being followed. He rubbed his chin. He wasn't sure by whom or why, but he was sure whoever it was or for whatever reason, it wasn't good.

Tossing his raven-colored braid over his shoulder, Skipp used the occasion to scan the area more thoroughly. Nothing. *Where are you guys?*

He grimaced and spoke into his wrist communicator, "Jonas! Jay! Anybody!" He let his gaze travel over the sea of faces, studying them. He looked at the walls again. He swore. *Signal must be blocked.* His gaze shifted upward, tracing the canyon-like walls of the buildings in the inner city.

Since being let go by The Company, Skipp had made his home in the underground; the subterranean world, which had evolved in the abandoned subway systems that ran for over 4700 kilometers in length and more than 2.5 kilometers beneath the city streets. After years of no contact, Jonas had left a video message, calling in an old debt, urging Skipp to meet him that afternoon in the city. Now he was wondering if coming had been the best decision. He called again; still no answer.

Closing the connection, Skipp glanced over his shoulder again and then burst into flight, hoping to draw his pursuers out into the open. As he did, he realized his plan had worked, if only too well. Lowering his head, he simply ran. Rounding a corner, he came to a skidding stop; he had run into a dead-end alley.

Skipp turned—too late. Behind him, blocking the mouth of the alley stood four very large men and one smaller figure whom Skipp took to be their leader. With slow, purposed steps, the men made their approach.

"Jonas," Skipp called frantically into his wrist-com. "Jonas, now would be a good time to show up." Despite the cool breeze and damp weather, beads of sweat rolled down Skipp's aquiline face.

The group was near enough now that Skipp could see their faces. The five figures continued to close the distance between themselves and Skipp, fanning out in a half circle as they advanced. Suddenly, one of them pulled a handheld energy weapon from his pocket, an IMR/S457-Agitator. The weapon banned from legal sale had long been outlawed, even for military use. The energy beam did more than just kill its victim but was designed to torment as well. The beam attacked the central nervous system, disrupting the brain's electrical activity, increasing the body's core temperature. This would cause the brain to swell simultaneously, triggering violent muscle spasms. Finally, due to increasing pressure and contractions, the victim's heart and other vital organs would simply implode.

As the man leveled the weapon on Skipp, he smiled, exposing broken, yellowed and missing teeth. "After all I he'rd about you, I thought you'd be smar'er than this." He gestured with the weapon indicating the alley. "To allow yerself to be trapped in a blind alley. Too bad though." He began to laugh. "You don't get to learn from your lil'l mistake."

Skipp could see the man's dirt encrusted finger tightening on the trigger. "Wait!" It was all he could think to say.

"What, you want to beg first? Not that it'll do ya any good." The man continued laughing. "Hey, boys, he wants ta beg fer his life. Shall we let him beg or should we just kill em?"

"Oh, let him beg first. Who knows, he might even make me laugh, too," the second of the large men said. Then turning a fiery gaze on Skipp, he said, "I'm not as easily amused as my friend is though."

Skipp's words came quickly, "You don't have to do this. How much you getting paid for this? I'll double it." His hazel-blue eyes dancing all over the alley looking for something—anything that might be used in his defense. "You have me at a disadvantage." He managed a nervous smile. "At least tell me who you're working for. A man should at least know why he's being killed."

A third man spoke, "Our client just wants him dead. Didn't say nothing about keep'n him pretty. I say we have some fun first."

"Wait, fellas," Skipp said slowly, lowering his hands.

The third man grabbed Skipp by his collar and threw him against the wall. Skipp slid to the ground, the side of his face landing in a thin puddle of rancid water. With his hands beneath him, Skipp worked frantically to remove his wrist communicator. Just as he pulled it from his wrist, he was kicked hard in his side. Along with a burst of air forced from his lungs, he felt several ribs crack.

As he lay there fighting for breath, Skipp could see his attackers. The smallest of the group stood back; Skipp assumed he was the lookout, though why they would need one, he couldn't figure out. No one would interrupt them. Trying to force himself up, his breathing became labored; each intake brought with it a stab of searing, white-hot pain.

"Come on, get up, pretty boy. You're not done yet," the man said as he jerked Skipp from the ground and held him level with his face. Skipp's feet dangled several inches above the ground. "Look at me," the man bellowed into Skipp's face, flecks of sour spittle spattering him.

Skipp winced before staring defiantly at the man. Taking a breath, he settled himself then spat in the man's face. He grimaced. He knew this was going to hurt.

Roaring like a mad bear, the man flung Skipp all the way across the alley, slamming him off the far wall like a child's play thing.

This time Skipp was expecting it; in fact, he hoped that it would happen. He was ready. Twisting as he flew, he managed to absorb the impact on his side. Lying on the ground, he finished connecting the new components to the energy cell in his wrist-com.

Staggering to his feet, Skipp defied the men. "So, you gonna let this brute beat me to death and cheat you out of using your toy." Blood ran from Skipp's nose and mouth, his eyes swollen nearly shut, each breath coming rough and ragged. He stepped toward the men, antagonizing them. "Go ahead," Skipp yelled at the man, then closed his eyes and lunged forward. "Shoot me!"

The man fired.

At that precise moment, Skipp pressed the activator switch on his wrist-com. There was a bright flash and an accompanying blast, which threw him backwards, slamming him into a row of partially filled trash barrels. He felt the air rushing out of his lungs as his world suddenly began to grow dark.

Moments passed.

Struggling to his knees, Skipp willed himself back from the brink of unconsciousness. Grasping desperately, trying to catch that elusive first breath, he celebrated the fact that he wasn't dead.

Skipp looked up to see all five of the would-be assassins struggling to regain their footing. Overcome by the intensity of the optical burst, and unprepared for the backblast, the assailants had momentarily lost consciousness. Skipp made a mental note of the unexpected bonus and continued his struggle toward the mouth of the alley and freedom.

Willing his legs to obey, Skipp began in his best imitation of a man running but looking more like a common drunk after too many last drinks. Slowly, strength returned and just as he staggered past the last of the fallen men, he felt a hand close around his ankle.

He fell—hard.

With his body not fully recovered, he landed face first onto the murky pavement, his ribs screaming in protest. Dragging his breath through gritted teeth, Skipp turned to see the business end of another weapon, an optical neutralizer pointed directly at his head. Then the barrel swung away.

The cloaked figure turned and fired on the four other men, who in their weakened state, realized too late that they, and not Skipp, were the intended target. The men fell backwards, moaning and screaming, enraged and in pain. Their optical nerves seared, blindness claimed them.

The fifth and considerably smaller of the assailants turned his attention back to Skipp. The weapon leveled at him, directing Skipp to the back wall of the alley. The assailant stood, blocking any possible chance of escape.

As the assailant removed the hooded mask, Skipp realized to his amazement, that the fifth man was actually a woman, a fact lost to him during the earlier stress. "What?" A look of unbelief and confusion washed across his youthful face. "What are you doing here?" was all he could manage.

"Looks like I'm saving your rear end," she said smugly. "And good thing, too, you were about to run into the rest of this squad. There's Mercs all over the square."

Skipp could see, now that she had taken off the too-big-for-her mercenary's uniform, that although not a pretty girl, she had a strong athletic body and a confidence that gave her a certain attractiveness. Remembering himself and feeling slightly embarrassed at being saved by a female, Skipp tried bravado. "Well, I had everything under control. I was just about to—"

"—Get yourself killed and ruin an entire day's work for me," she said waving off his comment. "I saw these guys tracking you and was just about to make contact when you decided to run into this blind alley." She couldn't help smiling.

Skipp could feel his cheeks turning red. He looked away, pretending to check the burnt-out wrist communicator. "Not that I'm not grateful, but who are you anyway? So, I suppose I'm your prisoner now?"

She laughed. "Prisoner? You *are* full of yourself, aren't you? No, Skipp, you're no prisoner of mine. Jonas sent me in here to find you before these guys did. You almost messed that up."

At that moment, a chirping noise came from her pocket. She answered her communicator with a crisp military tone, "Julie here."

"Who is—" Skipp had tried to ask, but was stopped by an upraised hand.

"Copy. Setting position now. ETA?"

A rope ladder fell along the back wall, causing both Julie and Skipp to look up. Above the rim of the building, just over the rooftop, they could see Jay waving and speaking into a communicator. "How about right now," said a voice with a Caribbean accent and a widening smile.

Behind them, the four men began thrashing wildly, a barrage of profanities flooding the quiet of the alley. Julie stopped to kick aside the discarded weapons, taking the IMR/S457-Agitator with her. "How did you get past those guys," Skipp asked, stepping aside and offering her first up on the ladder.

"No way, pretty-boy, up you go," she said, tucking the weapon in her belt. "I didn't go through all this just to watch you get whacked while I'm climbing a ladder. Now store your chauvinistic attitude and climb the rope."

"Some people call it chivalry, but—"

"You know, I really don't care what you call it. Move your hiney before I carry you up."

She was smiling, but something about her stance made Skipp believe she was serious, and looking at her, he believed she could.

Chapter Two

Two weeks earlier...

Catching a whisper of voices on the wind, Mike Stone slowed as he approached the place he had called home for the last eight and a half years. Lightning flashed and a clap of thunder shook the foundation as he stepped up onto the porch, the thin board yielding beneath his weight, as he escaped the storm. It was then that he understood who the voices were.

"What are you doing here?" Mary Stone asked from just inside the thin walled building; her voice sounding forced, lacking even the slightest trace of warmth. "You've come to take Mike away again, haven't you?"

Standing in the shadows and looking through the window, Mike watched his wife pace back and forth across the small living room but could not see to whom she was speaking. She wore her long blond hair pulled back out of her face and tied off in a loose ponytail. Wearing a simple pullover and jeans, practical and functional for a full-time mom, Mary was sure of herself and what it was she believed.

The voices continued. "After seven years of-of nothing, you just show up here?" she barked, hardly breathing. "You've got some fool venture on your mind, and you want to take my husband along with you." She ran a hand through her hair and turned to face the person to whom she was speaking. "Well it's not going to happen! Not this time, Jonas!" Cradling her forehead in her palms, she finally took a breath, her face red with exertion.

The man, Jonas Sulk, looked up, compassion and worry etched in his aged features. He raked strong hands through his salt-and-pepper hair and pulled his hands across his grizzled chin. "Mary, I—" he began.

"Please, Jonas, just leave," she deflated. "If you care for the children or me at all, just leave. Leave before he comes home. I'll tell him you stopped by, but that…that you couldn't stay." Mary's vision drifted to the corner of the room to where her sons sat leaning against each other, eyes wide and hands clasped.

Feeling he had heard enough, Mike made his way into the house with soft measured steps. With a breath of movement, he stepped into view.

Silence engulfed the room.

With a start, Mary turned to see Mike standing behind her. The boys, ages seven and almost five, erupted from their seats and swarmed their dad, hugging him around the waist and knees. "Dad!" Relief and excitement filled their young voices.

From down the hall the sound of a baby's cries floated toward them. Sissy, as they referred to the 18-month-old baby girl, had finally been awakened by her brothers' screams.

"Honey," Mary stammered, "I didn't hear you come in." She fumbled awkwardly, brushing loose strands of sweat-moistened hair from her face. She left the room in quick steps and soon returned holding her daughter.

A knowing smile crept across Mike's face as he stood gripping his sons on their shoulders. He reached up and wiped rainwater from his face, the muscles in his forearms flexing with the movement. Turning to focus on the man sitting on his living room sofa, Mike's smile evaporated. He stiffened, and then flexed his jaw. A wash of anger coursed through him.

"Let me get you something to eat, sweetheart," Mary said, positioning herself between Jonas and her husband.

Mike pushed past her, ignoring the chubby arms of his daughter stretched towards him and stalked forward to stand over Jonas. "I knew you'd come looking for me someday," he said as he closed the distance. "But why now? Why here?" Mike waved his hand indicating not only the house, but his entire life as well. "What's so important that you'd come all the way out here to try and grab me up in the middle of the night?"

Mary turned toward the kitchen then looked back at her husband. "Coffee?"

Jonas sighed as a burst of nervous laughter escaped. "It's good to see you, too, old friend." He stood slowly, his palms extended toward Mike. "I was just telling Mary that I can't believe it's been seven years already. Three kids; you're a real family man now."

"Yeah, a lot's changed since then, but I don't think you were talking about my children judging from the way my wife was carrying on." Mike's gaze never left Jonas's face. He stepped closer. "So, what's really going on?"

"Nothing," Mary said, coming back into the room and offering Mike a cup of black coffee she'd retrieved from the food replicator. "Jonas was just about to leave when you walked in." She turned and looked pointedly at Jonas as she spoke.

Not taking his eyes off of Mike, Jonas exhaled a shallow breath. "Look, you've got good reason to hate me, all right. I admit it. I was wrong. When Waters and The Company came after you, I should've stood up to him. I should have said something."

"The truth!" Mike erupted. "The truth would have been just fine." Then in a low, tight voice, "Honey, take the kids and put them to bed. I'll come down and tuck them in when I'm finished here."

Mary looked at her husband, fear darkening her attractive features. Behind her, the boys became quiet, stiff with increasing anxiety. The baby began to cry. "Mike…" was all Mary managed as she ushered the children to their rooms, whispering a silent prayer as she looked over her shoulder, unsure of what was happening or rather what might.

"You're right," Jonas continued, taking a step back and bumping into the sofa behind him. "I should have been there for you and I wasn't." Jonas smacked his lips and worked his tongue, trying to draw moisture into his mouth. He stumbled over his words. "Mike, I didn't come out here to argue with you, nor did I come just so you could beat my face in."

"Why did you come?" Mike hissed through clenched teeth and stepped forward again, closing the distance further. "Just why did you come out here? I don't remember leaving a forwarding address after you guys kicked me out! After you stole my life."

"Mike, I need your help."

Silence.

Then Mike began to laugh, a deep guttural laughter born more of frustration than mirth. So unexpected was Jonas's request that laughing was all he could do. His emotions spent, he stepped back and sat down—hard and missed his intended seat.

The thud vibrated the floor, and Mary came rushing back into the room, worry and fear etched into her face. She looked from Mike to Jonas expecting to see her husband and their once close friend locked in mortal combat. Instead, Jonas was sitting where she had left him, with a sheepish look on his face, and Mike was on the floor where he'd landed after missing his intended seat.

Looking up at Mary, Mike shook his head from side to side in a slow sweeping arc. "So that's what this is all about. Old Jonas here"—he lifted his chin toward Jonas—"needs *my* help, and you're afraid I'm gonna go running off behind him." He chuckled under his breath as he regained his feet.

"Don't the two of you make a pair? You come marching out here from nowhere and think you can just count on old Mikey Boy to pull your fat out of the fire one more time." He was staring at Jonas. Then in a slow purposed turn, Mike looked at his wife. "And you, what were you thinking? You think just because this android"—he pointed at Jonas—"shows up, I'm just gonna run off and leave you and the kids and go trekking behind him?"

Mike closed his eyes as if suddenly tired. He sighed and shook his head again. "Tell ya what"—he took in both of them with his gaze and with a sweep of his hand—"I'm going to bed. You two can work out the details and let me know when you've come to a decision. Goodnight." He stood, turned, and started down the hall.

"The Company—he is going to do it again, Mike. Ted Waters is doing it again. He's about to hurt a lot of people, Mike, and I'm not going to let him do it. This time I'm standing up to him." Jonas took a deep breath, letting it out in a rush. "You can walk away from me if you want, and I suppose you got a right to, but this time who's the one too afraid to do anything? Who's the one too scared to even try and make a difference?" Jonas had spoken without considering what Mike's reaction might be, the words coming louder and with more passion than he intended.

Mike froze. His shoulders tensed.

Jonas started again, purposefully slowing and quieting his voice. Forcing a control he did not feel, he raised his hands toward Mike, palms forward. "Mike, he's gonna do it again. Only this time, though, it's not just you; it's bigger, much bigger. Help me stop this madman before he does to someone else what he did to you." Jonas sat back down and the room fell again into silence.

Mike turned slowly, catching Mary's eye. Together they stared at Jonas. The silence compacted.

Mike slumped, leaning his shoulder against the wall. Suppressed memories forced themselves back into his consciousness: how The Company, the resurrection of the old United Nations, had risen from the ashes of the world's nation governments. He remembered his own appointment as the head of planetary selection and development and the steps he'd gone through. Site selection, population base, climate control, planned topography, and the proposed economy, ripped through his mind with gale-like force. Then, abruptly, the memories ended with his fall from power and fame into obscurity.

Jonas's voice, hoarse with tears and emotion, broke in on Mike's reverie. Jonas inhaled deeply and then let it out in one long controlled exhalation. He stared at the floor, seeing nothing. "About a year ago I was working out in the Gliese System, deep-space recon. All pretty routine stuff until I came across a derelict ship. It was just stuck out there, locked in orbit around one of the natural satellites near the edge of Corot 27b.

"I ran an I.D. check but nothing returned. No serial number, no company stock number—nothing. I thought maybe she had been used for a drug run and left adrift. We find them like that sometimes. Anyway, per procedure, I boarded her to see what I would find; you know, see what had happened.

"What I found couldn't have been further from what I expected. The ship was filled with children or mostly what was left of them. There were twenty or thirty, young mostly—the oldest, fifteen or sixteen at best. The place stunk. It smelled of decay and waste. Apparently, environmental control was shutting down." Jonas's voice quivered as he described the effects, limited exposure, and malnutrition had had on the young victims.

He was, again, lost in the nightmare as he relived the account. Sweat beaded and rolled down his forehead, his eyes glassing over as he described how he had scrubbed and scrubbed trying to rid himself of the odor of human waste and the sickly sweet scent of the dead. He spoke as if he'd forgotten he had an audience.

In spite of himself, Mike stepped closer. "What makes you think Waters has anything to do with this? Was it even a Company ship?" His voice still had an edge, though the tone had softened.

"I quit," Jonas said as if Mike hadn't spoken. "I've left The Company. It wasn't until I reported the ship to The Company that all the weirdness started. The Company..." he said the words as if they soured his mouth. "They shake your hand and pat you on the back, but they don't do a darn thing. They just sit there in their comfortable offices and do absolutely nothing. It's just like when it happened to you; the same answers—non-answers."

Taking a breath and slowing, Jonas began again. "There was this kid, a little girl." His voice grew small. "She was maybe eight, about the age of your oldest boy, but she only weighed about fourteen to fifteen kilos...bones mostly. She was so weak she could hardly speak—but her eyes.... She had the largest brown eyes and so sad." Jonas swallowed and looked up first to

Mary and then to Mike. He swallowed again, his Adam's apple rising and falling with the action.

"She only mentioned one name—Kracken. I don't know who this Kracken is, but he scared this child. Even saying his name brought her fear. I could see it in her eyes." Jonas spread his hands out in front of him, his forearms resting on his knees. He looked up at Mike and then at Mary, tears brimming his eyes. "She was begging for me to help her." Tears broke free and began a jagged streak across his drawn, weathered features. "I made a promise. I promised her I'd help her. I promised her," he repeated, his usually strong voice reduced to a squeak.

Mary pursed her lips and took notice of how tired and worn Jonas looked, as if he hadn't had a decent night's sleep in over a week. Even his usually clean diction had deteriorated.

Taking a breath, Jonas continued, "After clearing de-con—." He looked up at Mary and shrugged. "Sorry. I meant after I cleared decontamination and filing my reports, I decided to check on the little girl. But when I got to medical there was no record of her ever having been admitted. At first, I thought it was just a mistake because I didn't have a name. I figured she had been signed in under the Jane Doe clause, but there was nothing. Even the nurses had been changed. I didn't recognize anyone in the place. Needless to say, I was ushered out in a hurry. The next day, I'm logged off the crew; no explanation, no nothing. I got days off, and the next thing I know, I'm reassigned." He rubbed his eyes and collapsed back, sinking into the cushions.

"What about the ship?" Mike asked. "What did they say about that?"

"The more questions I asked, the more I looked around, the murkier things got. I checked salvage records—nothing… everywhere—nothing. It just wasn't there." Jonas looked at Mike and Mary, allowing the weight of what he had just said to settle. "Don't you see? The Company knows. Why else would they try to cover up the whole mess? Mike, it's *you* all over again. Waters is doing it again, only this time there's a variable Waters hadn't counted on. Me.

I mean, if you decided to help, we can stop him."

Chapter Three

Mary looked from her husband to the man that, only moments earlier, had walked out of their past and was now crying on her sofa, his face buried in his hands. She knew that if they heeded Jonas's plea, it would drastically change their lives. Change her life. Looking at both men but speaking to her husband, Mary cleared her throat. "What are you going to do?" She had asked the question, not entirely sure she wanted to hear the answer.

"I-I don't know," Mike said, facing her and taking hold of her hands. Confusion played across his masculine features. *Could this be my chance...my way back in?* But he asked aloud, "What's the right thing to do?" Mike looked down the hall to where his children lay sleeping and then looked back into the upturned face of the woman who had stood by him through the worst time of his life.

She had left her position as a spec analyst at The Company and joined him as a social outcast. He smiled and brushed her cheek with his knuckle. He stared in the azure pool of her eyes and lifted a blond lock, letting it sift through his fingers. She had never given up on him, even when he would have given up on himself; she had loved him in spite of it all.

Now looking into her face, he saw fear. For the first time in eleven years of marriage, she was really afraid—afraid of what he would do. "I'm sorry, Jonas. I'm not your man." *No, not my risk to take.*

"But Mike..."

"Hey, I feel bad about the girl, but I've got kids of my own now, and they have to come first. I'm sorry. I just can't…"

Jonas rocked forward, thrusting his hands toward Mike. "Mike, haven't you heard a word I've said? The Company is doing something bad, and I mean on a large scale. I have done some checking already, and I'm not liking what I have found. Just let me show you what I've got—"

"Maybe you weren't listening, but I said I can't help you!" Pausing, Mike rubbed his hand roughly over his scalp, exhaling hard. "Maybe you'd better do like Mary asked and just leave." His words were firm but lacked a certain conviction. Inside, he warred with what he should do—what he *wanted* to do, but he owed Mary too much. He had promised her he would never leave her, and that was at least one promise he intended to keep.

From where Mary stood, she could see her husband's face, could read the silent language of his body, and she knew he was turning Jonas away not because he wanted to, but because he knew *she* wanted him to.

Mary began to feel guilty. She had known—rather had felt— almost before Jonas had appeared, that Mike would be going, leaving her to do something; she did not know what.

Was this what you had been warning me about, Lord?

Mike had been restless and irritable, constantly retreating to his study and looking at old plans when he didn't think she was watching. She fought the urge to grimace.

No, please, God, don't take him from me…not now.

Had it not been only this morning that she'd prayed and asked the Lord to do with her—her family, her husband, as He pleased? Would she now renege on that prayer? She looked at the table where she had left her electronic reader that contained her copy of the now hard to locate Bible. Closing her eyes, she turned away from it. She would not—she could not—give into what Jonas was asking.

Jonas stood, shaking his head, beaten. He walked with slow leaden steps toward the door. "I'm sorry to have bothered you guys." An intense sadness settled on him and his shoulders sagged. The door slid open silently, as he triggered the embedded sensor and the room suddenly filled with noise of the storm. He stepped out onto the porch, and looking back, he said, "Mike, I'm sorry I didn't stand up for you back then…when you needed me…I…ah, well, I…ah…I'm sorry." The door closed behind him, and once again, Jonas Sulk found himself alone.

Lightning flashed and the rain continued to fall. It seemed to Jonas that the wind had grown colder, the night darker. He stopped and turned his face upward, facing the storm. "What now, Lord?"

As he stepped from the porch, his feet sunk in the mire that had formed where the path had been. Pulling his jacket close around his neck and stuffing his hands deep into his pockets, he walked into the darkness, back toward the heart of the city.

Mary paused before closing the drapes, having reactivated the transparent mode. She watched as Jonas retreated, swallowed by the shadows of the night. She turned her back to the window and smiled a weary smile at her husband, the light of it failing to reach her eyes.

"Hey, babe," Mike began, a forced cheerfulness in his voice, "I'm not feeling much like eating. I'm gonna do a little something in my study, and I'll be on to bed later."

In spite of his wet clothes, Mike's hug was warm, strong, and safe, and Mary hated it. "Night, babe," he said, kissing her forehead as he turned and walked away.

I'm sorry, Lord, but I can't let him go…not now. Mary lowered herself onto the arm of the sofa, leaning against the deep cushion of the backrest, letting it support her. She looked around her home: pictures of the kids on the entertainment center, children's clothes and toys littering the floor. With a deep sigh, she closed her eyes. For the first time since Jonas had shown up, Mary really took notice of the rain falling hard on the thin roof. Without opening her eyes, she reached out, laid her hand on the face of the e-reader, and sighed.

Time passed. A brilliant flash of lightning startled her. Moments later, the corresponding thunder caused the walls of the modular home to shudder. She sat up, looking at the brightened view through the large front window, and just for a moment, Mary had perfect clarity. In that one moment, she had seen as clearly as if it had been noon; and in that moment, she knew what she had to do.

Alone in his study, Mike allowed his eyes to play over the note that Mary had left him—another one of those sayings from that Bible she was always reading. Setting it aside, he pulled a large roll of dust-covered pages from beneath his desk. Depressing the activation coil embedded in the document, an image shimmered and came to life; a huge yellow sun began to glow. As Mike looked on, his face illuminated by the soft light, worry lines appeared etched in his dark features. Planets and other spheres began their slow orbits through the depicted Gliese System, and at its extreme edge of the document, Yargon rose into view.

Cursing, Mike slammed his fist onto the writing surface and the page powered down. Pushing back from his desk, he looked around the room. Awards from his previous life still hung, prominently displayed on the wall. Mocking him.

A moment later, the walls were bare, trophies discarded haphazardly in a box on the floor. Silhouettes of various geometric patterns, sun-damaged into the walls, began to fade as embedded sensors detected the removal of the frames and began to adjust the pigments to match the surrounding surface.

Thunder shook the house again, and Mike turned to face the large window. Outside, lightning flashed and he turned angry eyes toward the sky. "You happy now? I'm here okay…just leave me alone." He cursed again and outside the world burst into brilliance. Mike crumpled the note from his wife and dropped it into the recycle bin. A slight hum and the paper disappeared. He looked back toward the window. "I don't need you...I never have."

Chapter Four

Iona Bowers had been thinking about *him* again, about how her life had changed, when the summons from Ted Waters drew her from her reverie. Her coppery hair cascaded over her shoulders, hanging neatly half the length of her back. With green eyes that burned with cold fire and flawless skin smooth over hard muscles, Iona moved with the lithe grace of a jungle cat. She was beautiful by any man's standard; a detail of which she was well aware. Years spent cultivating her image, she was attractive as a rare and exotic snake and just as lethal. She was as cold and aloof, earning her the nickname, "Ice," though never addressed as such to her face.

She cursed and then rebuffed herself. "After all these years, you're still pining after Mike Stone like a starry-eyed schoolgirl. Get over it! Get over him."

But she had not.

Riding the lift-car to the eighty-first floor of The Company's main building, Iona studied her reflection in the beveled-mirrored doors as they began to slide apart, and just for a moment, she disliked the person she saw. As the lift doors opened, her walls of mental control, rigorously prepared, slipped solidly back into place.

Her shoulders squared, Iona entered the corridor gracefully, taking no notice of the anxious glances or of the elaborate furnishings adorning the synthetic causeway. Ornate statues of struggling figures, bold and arrogant in both victory and defeat, made of imported marble, polished brass, or other rare materials, stood like sentinels on either side of the elevated path.

Underlings looked up from their desks as she passed or stopped midstride and watched, afraid that she might notice them, worried that she might not. Situated at the end of the hall was a set of large French-style wooden doors, a luxury in a city made chiefly of plasti-steel and glass. The dark mahogany seemed to leech light from the corridor, which was an oppressive reminder of the man whose name and title lay carved into its ornate face that read, "Ted Waters," and beneath that, "CAO, Chief Administrations Officer."

As she made her way to the end of the hall, the tap-tap-tap of her stiletto heels were absorbed by the acoustic dampening floor. No one spoke to her or even acknowledged her presence, and that was just how she liked it.

She stopped before the double doors. A soft blue light flickered over her face, changed its hue to a golden-amber, and then settled on her eye and scanned her retina. "Iona Bowers," a computer voice greeted her. "Mr. Waters is expecting you." She stood in poised silence as the doors swung open and then stepped through as they closed quietly behind her.

"Look at them," a male voice said to Iona.

Ted Waters stood with his back to her, staring out the wall-sized window. The vista that was Millennium City, formally Uptown Manhattan, seemed to go on forever in every direction. Much of the Hudson River now channeled underground and what had been New Jersey was now encompassed within the new city. With over a hundred million people, Millennium was the largest city on Earth, rebuilt on the ruins of old New York just after the final skirmishes of the last world war over a hundred years prior. "We built this city brick by brick, layer by layer. Reconstructing it from the fragments left after the rebels and religious fanatics had finished killing each other. Feral dogs!"

Iona had heard the speech before—many times. She watched as Ted Waters stood motionless in the charcoal gray suit that was his staple, his hands clasped behind his back. She admired that he maintained his excellent physical condition, looking only a third of his sixty-plus years.

Waters continued talking, taking no notice of her. "They are small-minded individuals, fighting amongst themselves without the foresight to see beyond their own petty issues. They are animals, ignorant as children, threatening the very structure of civilization itself with their insignificant ideals." He shifted his gaze, but still looked out of the window. "We saved them from themselves."

Iona stood quietly, knowing better than to interrupt, knowing that Ted Waters would acknowledge her when he was ready.

"The Company brought an end to the chaos, and in its place inserted order. We have taken control, removing or reducing the variables of their meager existence giving them stability and peace."

He turned to face Iona. He walked over and sat behind his oversized desk. "In the old world, more than a few generations back, my family were shepherds; did you know that, Ms. Bowers?"

Iona still said nothing; she was not expected to.

Waters continued, more talking at her than to her. "People are like sheep. They need a leader—a shepherd." He spread his hands toward her. "I provide that service; I am the shepherd.

"I protect and care for the sheep, and in turn, the sheep produce a certain standard of living for the portion of society"—he smiled sardonically—"that provides that care. By this industry, the shepherds enjoy a certain standard of living. A perfect balance." Waters finally looked directly into her eyes, "Ms. Bowers, that balance has been disturbed."

The office felt dark. Even though the curtains stood opened, very little light seemed to filter into the room. A feeling of heaviness lingered in the office like the smell of a burnt meal after the ruined repast had been discarded. Smokey-bronze light fixtures built into dark leather wall coverings, set against a blood red carpet with over-sized elaborate furnishings reflected the man whose office it was. His throne-like desk sat in the center of the space, very large and made from rich, lunar marble, its subtle veins of dull color teasing the eye with suppressed hues. The large leather chair, with its polished brass spike mounted at the intersection of the shoulder blades, above the juncture of the intercostal nerves, stood in stark contrast to the dark leather wall coverings.

Recessed into the top of the desk were three holographic-monitors. One of the monitors kept a constant vigilance on the foyer and hall, immediately adjacent to the office. Another shifted through the battery of cameras located throughout the building's many offices and corridors. The third, activated only when alone, Waters used to spy on any number of people that he felt might need to be *observed*. His was not a business of trust.

Ahh, so this is why he needs me. Another one of his messes needs cleaned up. Iona finally spoke. "You summoned me," her voice soft; it was not a question.

"You know what I want, Ms. Bowers. Did he make contact with Stone?" She was not surprised that Waters kept watch of the situation, but was surprised he had acted so soon.

Waters's voice was low and neutral in tone, but Iona knew that he was never truly neutral about anything. "Yes, he did," she answered. "But I'm not sure what will become of it. He left alone."

"So, Stone did not join our Doctor Sulk. Good. I do not have to remind you just what is at stake here, Ms. Bowers. I allowed Stone to walk away before only because it served the purposes of The Company at that time. Whether he serves this institution better by his continued life or his death, is still to be determined."

A pang of fear shot through Iona. She shifted her weight and motioned toward the seat in front of Waters's desk in an attempt to hide the sudden shock of sensation.

"But of course..." Waters said studying her, his eyes void and penetrating; he was thinking, figuring her into his plans. He watched as she moved forward and settled in the plush seat in front of his desk.

Iona sat, quickly recovering, shields back in place. "Yes, sir," she said smoothly.

"Our past makes us who we are, Ms. Bowers. It is the substance of our character. I am hoping that your past serves you well."

Anger coursed through Iona. She looked out the window, diverting her eyes. She hated being played with, but she did understand her position.

"I see you do understand my meaning, Ms. Bowers," Waters said, standing and walking around to the front of his desk. Sitting on the front edge, he stared down at her. "I am trusting that any, shall we say, familiar attachment you once felt for Mike Stone has been dealt with appropriately. I would not want you confused on this matter."

Suddenly, he smiled a cold dispassionate expression. "I almost envy you," he said thoughtfully. "Revenge is a wonderful thing." Waters stood and walked toward the window, his back to her, his hands once again clasped at his waist.

Realizing she had been dismissed, Iona smiled as she rose and walked toward the doors, which swung open quietly as she approached. Pausing just long enough to be sure Waters was watching her, she said, "You have no idea, sir, just how wonderful it can be."

Ted Waters turned away, fires of lust, whether of desire or hatred, Iona was not sure, burned in his eyes. She knew, even now he didn't entirely trust her, but for now, he still needed her.

She moved with agile grace, every step measured, a body in complete harmony with itself. She could feel him looking at her, knowing that he wanted her...wanted to control her and enjoying the fact that he never would.

Hours later after finishing a punishing workout, Iona prepared to reward herself with a hot bath. As she entered her high-rise apartment in the heart of downtown, she spoke into the air, "Computer, bath." She could hear water running and see steam as it wafted up from the sunken tub as she approached the bath.

"Do you require additives for the bath?" the computer asked, its voice coming from the in-set wall speaker closest to Iona.

"No—I mean yes, something soothing," Iona responded a bit distracted.

"May I order a masseuse for you before the bath? It will aid the relaxation process."

"No, just the bath. Download the files on Mike Stone, a former Company employee, PS&D division, and run a cross reference between him and Dr. Jonas Sulk, also a former employee. When you have the information, initiate display." Slipping out of the black spandex-type bodysuit she wore during her workouts, Iona eased into the hot water, her movement activating pressure jets that targeted their massaging force along her neck, shoulders, and spine. Extreme ultraviolet sensors, EUV's, scanned her body, evaluating the tension and adjusting the revivifying forces as needed. "Ahhh," she sighed.

"I thought you might enjoy the massage after all," the computer voice said matter of fact.

"You know me well." As Iona settled back into the foaming bath, images and printed data appeared on the vented-glass wall opposite her. Cool air expelled from hidden flues near the ceiling, keeping the steam from collecting and the image clear. "Audio on," Iona said and instantly sound filtered into the room.

As the monologue and images streamed in, Iona laid her head back, relaxing into the jetted water. Images of Mike as he announced the discovery on the planet Yargon, his arms raised in triumph, his appearance flawless. She bit her lip and slipped beneath the water.

It was four in the afternoon. Two weeks since Jonas had visited their home, and Mary found herself standing outside his apartment and hating herself for being there. The door slid open. "I want you to know I hate you, Jonas," she said, walking past him. "I hate you for destroying everything I've worked so hard for." Taking a seat, she looked up at him.

Stunned, Jonas looked past her for the children, then stepped away from the door, allowing it to close quietly behind him. The apartment was neat, but then everything Jonas did was neat. Two bedrooms with attached baths, a living room, and an adjoining dining area, which was separated from the kitchen by a chef's island, summed up the space. "Sorry about the mess. I wasn't expecting company," he said awkwardly. "If you'd called earlier, I could have cleaned up a bit."

Mary looked around, but didn't say anything; the place was clean. *No children live here, that's for sure.*

The bone colored furniture and chrome accents at first gave the apartment a sterile feel, but warm pastel wall hangings and paintings of long ago landscapes, with their rich greens and browns, brought to it a balance it would have otherwise lost.

"Get you something to drink, coffee or tea maybe?"

"Yes, tea, herbal if you have it."

"Mary, about the other night, I'm sorry. I didn't intend to cause any trouble between you and Mike, but I still need his help." He smiled wryly. "I won't lie. When I saw it was you on the monitor, I was hoping you had come here to tell me that Mike had changed his mind."

She sighed and looked around the apartment again before settling her gaze back on him. "Jonas, I still hate you. I hate you because I know you're right, and that makes me feel…well let's just say, I know I was wrong." She looked away, unable to meet his gaze. *Okay, Lord, here I go.* She exhaled. "What exactly did you have in mind, Jonas?"

Jonas smiled. "Privacy," he spoke into the air and the wall-to-wall window that looked out over the city shimmered into opaqueness of gunmetal gray hues.

Mike looked up to see a pair of booted feet approaching him from beneath the far side of the hovercraft. He was not expecting anyone. Sliding quickly from under the vehicle and grabbing a large wrench, he stood up, the weapon hanging near his side. Since the unexpected visit from Jonas, he had been more aware that The Company was still out there and that Ted Waters had not forgotten his name. "May I help you?" he said.

"Mike Stone, planet builder?"

Hearing the voice, the Caribbean accent, Mike dropped the wrench and froze. "Jay? What the—Jay? What are you doing here?" Laughter erupted from both men as they drew each other into a rough embrace slapping shoulders and backs.

"How are ya, mon?" Jay, christened Joseph Fredrick Truee, stood an easy six feet, six inches with hands the size of mitts. His dark skin matched the deepness of his rich baritone voice, his accent betraying his Caribbean heritage. "Do ya always greet ya guest with a club in your hand, mon?" His words had the slow singsong pitch of an islander.

Self-conscious, Mike eyed the wrench lying at his feet. "What brings you back to the city, so far north from the islands at that? I thought you had retired, vowing never…how did you put it? 'Aaa, mon, dis soul's never gonna leave de island no more.'" Mike finished with a flourish, doing his best to imitate Jay's mannerisms as well as his accent.

"Well, da't was den. Not a bad place you got here."

"It's not much, but I manage to provide for Mary and the kids." Mike looked at his friend and watched as Jay surveyed the extent of his kingdom.

Jay's eyes finally came to rest on Mike and he sobered. "Some bad things are happening, mon, don't ya know? It seems like something ought to be done about it. I was hoping Jonas would've talked to you about it already, but since I found you here, I'm guessing I spoiled his surprise. He wanted to tell ya himself."

"Oh," Mike said, cleaning his hands on the soiled rag he had hanging from his back pocket. "So that's why you're here. No, your timing is good." Holding his hands beneath the infrared scanner, he turned them over allowing the sonic vibrator to clean them. "I spoke with Jonas about two weeks ago. He showed up at my house on the night of the storm. Upset, Mary," Mike said, smiling at the memory. "Have a seat. Get you a drink?"

"Thanks, cola if you got it." Jay dragged a steel drum around and sat on its edge. "So you know then. Good. I'm so glad to have you with us. This is a mess, I tell ya. We sure gonna nee—"

"I told Jonas no."

Jay fell silent, his hand frozen in midair as he reached for the soft drink. "What?" It hadn't really been a question, more like white noise expressed in unbelief.

"I told him no," Mike said, repeating himself, walking to the far side of the shop. "Look, it's not that I don't want to help, but I have a family of my own now—three kids. Besides, it would tear Mary apart." Mike lowered himself onto an antique stool, eyes downcast.

The stool, left over from an age when things were made of wood, creaked and moaned as Mike rocked back and forth on it. The smell of hydraulic fluid, combined with the sweet smell of acetone and ionized wiring filled the air as a thick silence hung between the two old friends. "You know, Mike, when Waters burnt you, he burnt all of us. He only let Jonas stay on because they needed him for his expertise in analysis, but now that he's walked, they'll come after him, too. The way I figure, Waters won't let any of us live, and that includes Mary and the children."

Mike jerked upright and looked at his old friend, anger flashing. Memories of struggles fought side-by-side, bittersweet memories contended in his mind. "Jay, what do you want me to do, just leave my wife and kids and run off to who knows where and do who knows what? You were there. You stood with me. I made a promise to stay with her…that I would not leave her. You want me to break that?" He swung his head in a slow sweeping arc and rested his palms on the workbench. "Besides, Jonas didn't even tell me what it is he thinks I can do. What help can I be?"

Jay didn't speak, but instead stared at his friend, hoping Mike's conscience would work on him in ways persuasion could not.

"Besides…" Mike stood abruptly, turning his back on his friend. He paced away, creating distance. "You got Skipp in on this, too?" Taking the silence as a yes, he continued, "What does he have to say about all this? What's his take?"

Jay hefted his bulk from the rim of the metal barrel, allowing it to rock back and forth until it settled with a decreasing thrum against the gen-x-nanopolymer flooring. An explosion of air burst through his full lips as he released a deep sigh. Forcing his massive hands across his face, he turned and looked at Mike. "We haven't been able to locate Skipp. We know he's on the planet, but it's been a while since we've had any contact. Even now, Jonas is trying to find him." He laughed as if to reassure himself. "I'm waiting on a call now."

"So, Jonas, that's it, that's your plan?" Mary asked. "Okay, let's say I tell Mike it's okay—that I don't mind if he goes. Say I tell him I think he should help you, then what? How're you planning on getting to the far side of the system? I don't think Waters is going to give you a Company vessel."

"The Quest."

Mary sat the insolated tumbler down with a crisp thud. The beverage warmed by its interaction with the sunlight, splashed amber liquid over the web of her hand. "The Quest? How? If you've got the Quest then—I thought Joseph had retired back to the islands. You haven't gotten him mixed up in this, too? His father would never allow it." Mary had intended it as a statement, but it had come out more of a question.

Jonas smiled, handing her a small towel. "Jay, as he prefers to be called these days, was the first person I talked to. Without a ship, this whole thing would be finished before it started. Once Jay understood what had happened, and that there was a chance to get one up on Waters, he was eager to join. Not that his father was very happy with that idea," Jonas said, chuckling at the memory. "He would have been happy just to keep his son on the family's plantation...bringing back a forgotten lifestyle as he called it." He smiled and the corners of his face wrinkled with the gesture, brightening.

"I bet he wasn't," Mary said and took another drink of her tea. She was about to argue this new point when she saw the clock on the wall, then double-checked her personal chronometer as if she didn't trust what she had seen. Interrupting herself, she said, "Wow, I've got to go. Mike will be home soon. I'll get dinner ready for the kids, and then I'll talk to him." She stood, being careful to place the small cup on the vapor coaster; the stationary unit designed to evaporate excessive moisture. "You come by later; I won't stand in your way. But, Jonas...you'd better be praying."

"Thanks, Mary, I am." Jonas said, walking her to the door. "I promise to take care of him."

Again, he was smiling. *I hope I'm not making promises I can't keep.*

Matching his smile, Mary offered a wry smile of her own, "I still hate you, Jonas Sulk. I'm glad to see you again, but I still hate you." She hugged him and kissed his cheek, turned, and walked away. The door slid shut behind her.

Jonas thrust his fist in the air and mouthed enthusiastically, "Yeah!" Then he walked over and checked his message board.

The next day, Skipp joined the small group, comfortable in the aphotic atmosphere of Jonas' apartment. "So," Julie asked as she settled into a seat, "what was that you hit us with back there in the alley? Good thing I was behind that big guy, or it may have put me out as well. As it was, I got the wind knocked out of me."

Everyone turned their attention to Skipp. Jay looked up from the holographic star map he was studying.

"Yeah, what was that?" Jonas asked, coming out from a backroom. "From what Julie says, it was rather potent."

Jay echoed the question as he pushed back from the table, rocking in his chair and earning a stern look from Jonas. He lowered the chair back to the floor. "Can it be adapted to the Quest's systems?"

Enjoying the spotlight, Skipp pulled up his sleeve exposing the ruined wrist-com. "Oh, just a little something I'd been kicking around for a while," he said, smiling. "I was getting components for it—that's why I agreed to meet you in the first place. Never had a chance to test it 'til the alley though. Thankfully, it worked," he finished proudly. Then sobering, "Good thing, too, or I'd be…" He stopped, not finishing the thought.

Just then, coming in from the backroom, Mike joined the group. "So you gonna tell us how this thing works, or are we just supposed to guess?" He sat, joining Jay and Jonas at the table, perusing the ship's specs but still listening to Skipp.

"Well, it's simple, really," Skipp started.

"No lecture dis time," Jay said, a smile in his voice. "Keep it simple for de simple."

"Anyway," Skipp continued, feigning annoyance, "the way the shield works is by creating a barrier that reflects energy back out, like a mirror reflecting sunlight." Greeted by looks of confusion, he stood, scanning the room. "Mike, throw me that towel."

Mike complied.

"Okay, it's like this. Now pretend my arm is a directed blast of air, you know, confined." He motioned with his hand thrusting it into the towel he held draped over his opposite forearm. "Now, if this blast of air is concentrated enough, it can penetrate like the air hammers used in drilling."

Heads nodded as they followed his explanation.

"Now, suppose I put this towel up in front of that blast—"

"You get a hole ripped in it and a shot in the chest," Jay said laughing.

Skipp threw the towel, hitting Jay in the face.

Everyone laughed.

"Now, this towel, or in the real world, the shield reads the energy blast, or in this case the concentrated air and configures itself at the molecular level and deflects the blast out and away."

"So how did you program the shield thingy for that particular weapon in the alley?" Julie asked, as she absentmindedly rubbed the bruised shoulder she'd gotten during the fall.

"That part was pure luck. Like I said, I hadn't even had a chance to test it yet, but I figured I had nothing to lose. They were gonna kill me anyway."

"Well, lucky for us it worked," Mike said.

Jonas shot him a sideways glance. "Mary wouldn't call it luck." He saw Mike look back at him and shake his head. Jonas smiled.

"No, she'd have a more inspired description of that, wouldn't she?" Both men smiled. *Truce.*

"Okay, let's get to work," Mike said to the group at large. "Show us what you've got, Jonas."

Jonas spoke into the air, "Computer, privacy, audio, and acoustic." Silently, blinds shimmered and solidified, sealing themselves against the edge of the windows, and the room slipped into a deeper gray of darkness. A soft hum began to reverberate from the four corners, the subsonic wave blocking electronic listening devices. Almost like a slow sunrise, a soft illumination filled the room as embedded lights came on to counter the lack of sunlight.

Jonas turned to Julie first. "You don't have to stay for this part, you know. I don't think Waters knows you're involved yet."

"You know the old saying, 'in for a penny—'"

"In for a pound. All right," Jonas added. Turning back to the group, he said, "As you know, this all started when I found a derelict ship and its only survivor was a little girl whose name I later discovered to be Amanda. No family name."

"How'd you get that?" Mike interrupted.

"You don't spend twenty years in an organization without developing some friendly contacts," Jonas said, smiling. "Anyway, both this girl and the ship suddenly disappeared, and when I began to ask questions, it was made plain that questions on this particular subject were not to be asked. Eventually, the attacks became personal, but that's a different story."

Mike locked eyes with Jonas. Personal or not, he would find out what happened. Jonas would tell him.

All of them had stories of how they had crossed or been crossed by The Company—by Ted Waters and had everything they held dear threatened, turned upside down, or simply taken from them.

Jay, grounded after serving as The Company's lead pilot; Skipp, labeled as a liability and his electronics lab sealed and his projects confiscated; and now Jonas, finally, discredited like the rest. They also knew of people who had suddenly just gone missing. Mike rubbed rough hands over tired eyes and sighed.

As Jonas continued talking, Mike's mind began to wander, to drift back to his own story.

Sitting in his office on the 70th floor of The Company's central office, a younger Mike Stone began shutting down his office in anticipation of a long weekend with Mary. This was to be the weekend when he finally met her grandmother, Nonna.

Both he and Mary had been working long, hard hours just so they could take off a few extra days for the World Day celebration. This was the celebration where the world's various governments had finally come under universal command and the last of the rebels were overthrown. Over a century later, those governments had combined under the auspices of The Company.

As Mike began closing out the figures and double-checking what should have been routine plots on the Samarian development, he had noted a series of discrepancies. Red flagging the entries, he sent memos to the various section leaders. He cc'd a copy to his then junior assistant Ted Waters's office. Thinking all was well, he took off for the planned weekend. Little did he know then....

Mike shook himself and looked around, wondering if anyone had noticed his drifting. *That's when my life ended.* He rubbed his eyes as if awakening from sleep.

"Hey, Mike, you still wit' us?" Jay called. "You look like you've seen a ghost, mon."

Mike laughed. "Yeah...you guys. But back to business. So how does all this tie into The Company? What does Waters have to do with a derelict ship and a load of sick children?"

Murmurs rose as others voiced similar questions.

"Jiyst." Jonas's single word response silenced the room.

A narcotic used to stabilize brain chemistry in psychiatric patients, but sold on the streets for its pheromone-releasing agents and mind focusing effects. The drug stimulated the anterior cingulated cortex, the mind's creative region, while simultaneously increasing awareness and stamina. Whatever the user focused on while under the influence of jiyst, he became more focused and more absolute in its accomplishment.

"Jiyst? Since when did The Company get mixed up with narcotics?" Mike asked incredulous.

"It was one of the planetary mining projects The Company was into about ten to fifteen years back," Jonas said, building a context. "The Samarian Project."

"Samarian," Mike said startled.

"Yeah, I remember that," Skipp added. "Planetary survey looking for heavy metals and fuel alternatives, if I recollect." He ran his hand through his hair, reworking his braid. "Man, I was just out of school slaving as an intern with The Company."

"More like planet raping," Mike blurted, rising suddenly. Walking over to the closed window, he stared at the opaque shutters. In a subdued voice, he spoke over his shoulder. "We were supposed to be bringing in ore samples to see if it would be worth The Company's investment. That's when I discovered a fully operational mining colony.

"Apparently, it had been in operations for years. When I brought it to Waters attention…well, let's just say that's when my world began to turn crazy." Mike grew silent; no one spoke.

Finally, Mike turned to face them. They were waiting for him to finish. Looking into their eyes, he looked for judgment or condemnation or even pity. Instead, he found understanding. "It was the weekend that Mary and I went off together. World Day, ten years ago. I thought she'd never speak to me again. They came after me, arrested me right in front her family. I didn't even know what I was being charged with. I remember seeing the look of horror and shame on her grandmother's face as I was dragged away. Neighbors, news teams, police cars everywhere. It looked like one of those drug busts you see in the old movies." Mike looked from face to face, still feeling shame, but knowing that his friends understood—that they would not condemn him.

Mike continued, "I never told you guys this, but Waters came to visit me. Offered me a deal…if you want to call it that. Told me if I accepted the charges and agreed to just go away, he would make sure I never went to prison." He looked up again.

Mike walked back over and sat at the table where he had left Jonas and Jay. "I stood up in court, knowing that what I was going to swear to was a lie and that everybody I knew and loved would be watching." He laughed, small and sad. "I still didn't even know what the charges would be. When the clerk of the court read the list of charges against me, I went numb. They accused me of criminal negligence, misappropriation of Company materials, and aggravated homicide. They accused me of killing those families…of killing those children. I looked around the courtroom, but all I can remember seeing was Mary. She was there and the look on her face…"

Chapter Five

Hot tears made silent treks down Mary's cheeks as she watched another squad of officers pull up in front of her house. The men offered no explanation for entering and searching her home, at least none that made sense to her. She stood clutching her baby daughter protectively. Anger swelled.

"Mommy, what are these men doing in our house?" M2, her oldest son said, resentment and fear shading his young voice. "They can't just come into our house." Then stepping toward the uniformed men, he said, "I bet you wouldn't do this if my daddy was home!" The boy yelled at the men as they ransacked the house. "Get out of our house!"

Mary corralled both her boys to her. "Quiet, Son!" she said a little too harsh. "Just ignore them; they'll be gone soon."

The boys said nothing. Travist hid his face against his mother's thigh. Sissy, the baby, beginning to react to the tension, stiffened in her mother's arms and let out a strained cry.

Suddenly, M2 blurted, "I don't care who you are or who you work for, this is our house, and you got no right just coming in here! Get outta our house!" he said, stepping away from his mother's grasp.

"Michael Stone!" Mary screamed after her son, pulling him back against herself. Mary pivoted her hip forward, preparing to defend her son if the need arose.

The men stopped and looked around, their hands dropping to the holsters at their sides. The officer that appeared to be in charge turned and stared at Mary, his gaze shifting between Mary and her son, a dark smile pulling at the corners of his mouth.

Mary stared at the man's hardened features. A wash of emotion swept the man's face. Was that relief or fear?

"I'm glad you at least seem to understand who's in charge here, Mrs. Stone." He looked again at the child. "I wouldn't want to see any harm come to the boy. A little manners won't hurt him none neither."

Seeing that her child was not in any immediate danger, Mary relaxed and used the family nickname again. "M2, I didn't say you were wrong, it's just that these men are bigger than we are." She had spoken to her son, but her gaze never left the face of the man standing in the middle of the small living room.

Around them, the shelves had been emptied, their contents strewn about the floor. Her Bible lay face down on the floor next to the cushioned chair where she'd been reading to her children. Pictures and paintings were removed and thrown about; furniture had been pushed or pulled from their normal placement leaving silhouettes and color-voids on the walls and floor, the sun damage already beginning to fade.

"And there's more of em' too, Mom," M2 said, the scowl still on his face as he stared at the men in house.

Stepping toward Mary, the officer raised his hand to strike her.

Mary stiffened, preparing to receive the blow.

The boys screamed. "No!" "Mommy!"

"As you were, lieutenant." A stern voice came from just outside the front door. The blow stopped mere inches from Mary's face.

"But she—"

"I said, as you were. Besides, I really don't want to see you get beat up in front of your men by a woman holding a baby." Iona Bowers walked slowly into the room. Just inside the door, she stood, feet spread shoulder width apart, and her hands hanging relaxed by her side. She looked coolly into the face of the officer. He trembled with rage at the perceived offense to his authority.

With great effort, the man brought himself under control. "Yes, ma'am."

Taking his obedience for granted, Iona said dismissively "Wait outside," and walked past him without so much as a second glance in his direction. Finally turning her attention to Mary, she said, "So this is what you've come to." She looked around the small home, a sneer turning the corners of her lips. Iona smiled; it was not pleasant.

Mary looked down at her children. The baby had gone from fussy to crying, twisting and pulling in her arms. Travist stood hugging her leg, his tear-streaked face pressed against her thigh. And M2, how he reminded her of Mike, stood heaving angrily, his small hands fisted, stared after the uniformed men.

Mary watched helplessly as the officers first violated the privacy of her home, opening and checking cabinets; even pulling clothing from the closets. Finally, after what felt like an eternity, they left.

Feeling violated and very much alone, Mary turned to face Iona. "So, Waters sent you to do his dirty work again?" Then shifting the crying baby in her arms, she stooped until she was face level with her sons. "You guys were great. Now be a big help to Mommy, go to your room and start cleaning up the mess those bad men made. Mommy has to talk to the lady." She kissed each of their cheeks and foreheads before dismissing them.

"Well, Mary, is this really the best you could do?" Iona said, indicating the modest home. She drew a manicured finger along the wall, checking her hand for dust. She rubbed it clean on the back of the sofa. "Doesn't seem like much for the once best and brightest The Company had to offer." Her words dripped with sarcasm and were intended to cause pain.

Mary did not respond.

Iona walked around Mary, appraising her. "I can't believe just how much you've let yourself go." Iona's voice was silky, her tone condescending. As she moved, her hair poured over her shoulders like fountains of liquid fire, green eyes sparkled with barely contained energy. Wearing a black body suit beneath a short emerald jacket, she stood in stark contrast to Mary, who was in sweats and one of Mike's old shirts. She had been relaxing with her children just before being broken in on.

They were friends once. They had shared a deep and rich history, once. Now all that existed between the two women was jealousy, hatred, fear, and pity.

Iona stared at Mary, loving her position of dominance. "You thought you'd beaten me, didn't you?" She laughed.

Mary still said nothing.

"Everything you worked for, I have. I have your living quarters. Of course, I had to have it redecorated. I even have your old office." She sighed. "What? You got nothing to say? Oh, I've dreamt of this day. The day when little Miss Mary Perfect, with everything just so, would have to come begging to me." Laughter erupted from her. "Everything you ever worked for, I have; it's all mine."

"I have *his* children," Mary said snidely and regretted it the moment she did. "I'm sorry," she said reaching out toward Iona.

Anger swelled in Iona. "How dare you?" She stepped menacingly toward Mary. "How…dare…you!" She slapped Mary, the blow catching her full across the face. "Don't you dare pity me."

Mary turned with the blow, positioning her shoulder between her daughter and Iona. "Iona, I'm sorry. I didn't mean that." She adjusted the baby in her arms, nuzzling her neck, and she spoke around the agitated child. "You and I were friends once, closer even…" She hesitated, kissed the baby's face and looked back to Iona. "Mike chose me. It doesn't mean that we—"

Iona stepped toward Mary. "Sorry? Oh, you will be sorry. Before I'm done, Mary Stone, you will be very sorry." She spun and stalked out of the house.

"Oh God!" Mary cried, sinking into the chair behind her. "Oh, God, I keep saying the wrong things." Her emotions broke on her like waves crashing onto shore. Curling her legs beneath herself, she rocked absentmindedly, hugging her daughter to her breast and silently wishing her husband was with her to comfort her. The baby, quieted, rested her face against her mother's.

Looking upward, Mary cried softly, "Lord, Jesus help me. I can't do this by myself. I'm not strong, Lord. I'm just not."

Looking out the opened door, Mary watched the small parade of vehicles float away. She spoke again, "I'm scared, Lord. Help me not to hate her." Turning, she saw her sons who had come upon hearing her cry. Then with silent tears, they embraced and sat quietly, staring at the russet sky.

Iona settled in the rear seat of her company hover car. "Isolation." She spoke to the computer control panel.

"Full or partial," the computer voice answered.

"Full."

The windows shimmered and went black, creating a one-way mirror effect, the interior filling with a soft amber glow. Iona sat unmoving, waiting for her heart to stop racing. She stared at the small house and could see Mary just inside the door, holding and rocking her children with her. She bit her lip and looked away. "Drive."

"Destination?" the computer queried.

"I don't care. Drive!" The hover car lifted from the surface of the street and began accelerating away from the house.

Some hours later, Mike turned to his wife and focused closely on her face, studying her features. He was still amazed at just how beautiful she was and never more so than when at her selfless best. She spoke, but her words were lost to him as he surveyed the tossed house. Anger swelled at the thought of his family having been threatened and his home violated.

"Are you listening to me?" Mary asked, lifting her face from his chest and looking up into his.

"Um, yeah, sure," he lied.

Mary smiled and squeezed tightly against him. "I don't believe she will actually hurt us. I think she was just trying to scare us more than anything," Mary said sounding hopeful.

"She hit you! You have always tried to see the good in her." He inhaled and then released it, fighting for control. "I don't know, but-but this was why I didn't want to get involved in the first place. I didn't want trouble with Waters finding you and the kids back here unprotected." Standing abruptly, he walked to the far side of the small living room. Turning back to face his wife, he said, "I don't have your kind of faith." He raised a hand at the objection he knew she was about to offer. "Sure, I believe in God and all, but I just don't see how believing in Him is gonna make any difference here. Fear is the only thing people like Waters and Iona Bowers understand. Fear and power. If we're going to fix this, we are going to have to do it ourselves." Seeing Mary's hopeful expression and knowing he would disappoint her again, he turned away, looking unfocused and forlorn through the open window. *What have you ever done for me, God? Nothing.*

Coming up behind him, Mary rested her face against his back. Grasping him by his shoulders, she kissed them. "I don't pretend to know or understand everything that's going on here, but I do know this, God is good." She could feel him tense beneath her fingers. "God is good," she repeated, "and Waters is an evil man. Everything he touches turns bad. Iona wasn't always like this. She used to be our friend."

Mike turned to face her, his eyes boring into hers. "Iona's no victim, Mary. She chose her path just like everybody else. She gets off on hurting people."

Mary smiled mischievously. "There was a time when you thought she was all that. What changed your mind?"

Taking the bait, Mike smiled. "You." He pulled her close and kissed her deeply. He breathed in the fragrance of her hair and kissed the softness of her face and neck. "You changed all that; you changed me. You're the only woman I'll ever love; that I've ever truly loved."

Sobering, Mary rested her face against his chest. She whispered softly, "You know you have to finish this. Waters won't just let us go this time. He made that plain when he sent

Iona out here. He's not going to stop. We—you have to stop him."

Holding her tighter against him, Mike said nothing. Together, they stood in silence, feeling the burden of leaving his family alone and unguarded but knowing Mary understood that this was the only path he could take. He held her tightly, desperate in the embrace. Leaning into the warmth of her, doubts assailed his mind and heart. This was a task he had to do and one he was sure he couldn't.

He looked at his wife. Once again, he was drawing her into a bleak and uncertain future. Only this time, the children that might die were his own.

Ted Waters looked past the papers in his hand and stared into the face of Iona Bowers. "It would seem that your visit did not have the desired effect. Stone is still meeting with his band of meddlers and, at this very moment, is making plans that might be costly to me and this corporation."

To her credit, Iona matched his gaze. She neither looked away nor challenged him; she just looked back at him. "I think that, with time, Mary will begin to weaken, and if she weakens, Mike will fall. She is his foundation," she finished coldly.

"Time is the one commodity that we do not have in great abundance, Ms. Bowers. Although I appreciate your subtleness in the matter, I feel that a more profound statement needs to be made. Something that will get Mr. Stone's attention and let him know that this is a matter—a situation—in which he would rather not be involved."

"What did you have in mind? I can have my team ready in an hour."

"Oh, that will not be necessary, Ms. Bowers. It is already done." Waters turned his attention back to the papers.

Iona rose, dismissed, and left the office.

Having kissed Mike good-bye earlier, Mary decided to take the children out for a simple dinner rather than contend with the emptiness of knowing Mike was gone. Just as she locked and secured the door behind her, the com-panel began buzzing. Mary turned and faced the closed door to their home, her hand hovering just above the security pad. She looked back at the excited children strapped in the safety restraints in the family transport and then back at the panel's flashing lights, indicating an incoming transmission.

"Come on, Mom, you promised," M2 called out from the front passenger seat plaintively. "You said we could leave right away."

"But what if it's your dad calling?" Mary asked her son, smiling at him.

"If it's Dad, he'll call your personal com if you don't answer in the house. Come on, Mom," he finished with a plea.

Travist, the younger son added in as well, "Com' on Mom," encouraging her to ignore the buzz-chirp of the com-panel.

Looking at her children, Mary decided they had been through quite a lot these past few weeks and that they deserved to just get away. After first checking the baby's seat restraint, she climbed into the transport and sealed the door behind her. "Just in case," she said, smiling at her children. She activated the call forward and had the incoming call routed to her transport's com-unit. She activated the panel as she glided the transport into the electro-magnetic field embedded in the roadway beneath traffic lanes. "Audio only," she said and winked at the kids. The boys smiled and then began to giggle.

"Hello," Mary said happily.

"Is this Mary Stone?" an unknown voice asked.

"Yes, who's this?"

The line went dead. The next moment, an explosion rocked the entire area. The concussive blast picked up and carried the family transport vehicle as if it were nothing more than a raft caught in rough surf. The vehicle careened sideways across an open parkway and crashed solidly into the deep grass, leaving an open gash in the manicured surface.

Burning debris fell from the darkening sky, igniting vehicles parked along the street and shattering windows in houses up and down the roadway. Trees and shrubbery erupted in brilliant multicolored conflagrations.

Looking back from where they had traveled, Mary could see that their home had been destroyed.

"Oh my God! Oh God! Oh God!" Mary yelled reaching for her children. Inside the vehicle, all was pandemonium. The children screamed.

"Mommy, Mommy, you're bleeding," one of the children yelled.

"Mommy's gonna die," cried a terrified voice.

"Nobody's gonna die," Mary said, trying to sound calm. The edges of her vision began to soften and blur, darkening. She could feel a hot stream and knew it must be blood flowing down the corner of her forehead. With bruised, trembling fingers, she explored the cut. It was deep. "Now, see, it's not so bad. Are you guys okay?" she asked, lifting the crying baby from the restraint seat. She forced a calm she did not feel into her voice. "M2, pass Mommy the first-aid kit. It's in the front panel."

M2 had the kit opened and extended it toward his mother before she finished asking. "Here you go, Mamma. Here you go," he said excited, fear in his voice. Sissy continued crying.

Outside, emergency vehicles began screaming past them en route to the heart of the blast zone. From all over, people were crying and screaming in pain and despair. Bodies, broken and battered, were strewn on the street. The smell of burning ozone and silted dust wafted out of the charred neighborhood. What was once a rather poor and run down housing area, now looked more like old footage from one of the bombed out cities of England during the German blitz of the 1940's of Earth's old calendar.

Mary could feel her head growing light; she knew if she did not stop the bleeding soon, she would pass out. Opening the med-kit, she did her best to clean the wound and apply a compress. Wrapping the bandage tightly, she again tried to encourage her children. "Hey, M2, why don't you pray for

Mommy? Pray like Mommy taught you, okay." She tried to sound cheerful.

The child began to pray.

More emergency vehicles sped by, and soon someone, a man, stood knocking at the door of the transport. "You guys all right in there?" he asked.

As the door to the transport opened, the man took quick stock of the situation. Only the woman appeared injured. "You're gonna be all right, Miss. I'm a medic. Let me get a look at that cut." He turned his attention to the kids. "Your mom's going to be just fine."

Mary was grateful that the man had come when he had. She closed her eyes and began praying under her breath. "Oh, God, please help us. I know Waters is behind this. Don't let him find us. Don't let him win."

"What's that? What did you say?" the man asked leaning close to her. When she didn't respond, he turned and yelled over his shoulder. "Ed, over here, we've got one for transport."

With energy born of desperation, Mary sat up and pushed the man away. "No, no hospitals. Just bandage the cut, and let me go."

"No way, lady. You need to see a doctor about this cut. It's pretty deep and-"

"I SAID NO HOSPITALS," she said more forcefully, her breath coming in ragged gasps. "Look, I don't want to be mean or sound ungrateful, but there's a lot of people out there who need your help. Can't you just give me something for the pain, and I'll see to getting myself to my own doctor. Okay?"

Just outside the hovercraft's open door, the emergency transport vehicle glided to a stop beside them. The driver called out, "Hey, we got one for transport or not?"

Her eyes pleaded in quiet desperation. "Thank you," Mary said, taking the man's hand and sitting up, "but I'll be all right."

He looked at her long and hard. "Look, lady, I don't know what's going on here, but you need help." Reaching into his bag, he took out a small aerosol can and sprayed the cut on Mary's head.

Mary sighed. Instantly, the wound began to cool and the throbbing headache ceased.

"This stuff won't last more than a few hours, and its effects wear off with prolonged use." Standing up to leave, he looked at her, and seeing a look of uncertainty, he then looked at the children. He tossed her the can of spray. "Reapply this in about two hours. Keep that compress in place and you should be okay. But if you don't get to a doc, you're gonna have a nasty scar." He smiled reassuringly and jumped from the vehicle.

Mary sat listening to the men as they talked just outside her vehicle's door..

"Thought you said you had one for transport over here," the driver said impatiently.

"I was wrong."

"So much for that God of yours leading you, huh?" The driver began to laugh scornfully. "What was that you said? Oh, yeah, led by the spirit. Ha, you'd do better using a scanner like everybody else. There's a reason that old religious stuff went out." The man began to laugh again.

Mary looked out as the transport pulled away. She could see the unnamed medic looking back at her, and a small smile bent the corners of his mouth as a familiar look brightened his eyes. The look Mary identified with, a look of confidence, a look of faith.

"We've gotta go, now!" Jonas said, pulling Mike away. Orange flames and black oily smoke still roiling from the crater where moments earlier the Stone's home had been.

"Mary!" Mike's anguished scream died in his throat. "My family. He killed my family…"

"And he would have killed you, too, had you been here. Don't you see, the only—"

"No! He's going to pay for this. If I have to wring it out of him with my own hands. I swear to you, Ted Waters is going to pay for this!"

"Mike…" Jonas started, but words failed.

"My family, he killed my family. My baby, she wasn't even two years old."

"Mike, let's go." Jonas said, grabbing him by the shoulders and dragging him away.

With an anguished groan, Mike turned and allowed his friend to pull him away as uniformed officers began pouring into the scene, some offering assistance, others scanning the crowd searching faces, searching undoubtedly for Mike and members of his crew.

Grabbing Mike's shoulders, Jonas forced his attention from the guards and onto him. "Don't let their deaths be in vain. Waters was trying to kill you; he may even think you're dead. Let him."

Mike turned and looked at his friend, his eyes barely focusing on his face. "He killed my family. Just like those families on the Moab colony. He's doing it again."

Jonas let his friend talk as he continued leading him away from the area. Finally back in his transport, Jonas closed the hatch. "Computer, privacy screen." With virtually no sound, the windows shimmered and then settled. The view, merely dimmed from the inside, blocked all but the most intense visual scans from without.

"I'm gonna try to contact the guys using a tight beam transmission. If I use short bursts, we should be able to keep from being scanned by Waters's people." Jonas knew Mike wasn't listening, but preferred conversation over the heavy, stilted silence.

Mike stared out the window.

Jonas checked his chronometer, verifying schedules against the time. He reasoned Jay would be working on the Quest and, therefore, the easiest to contact. "Jay," he said crisply, transmitting the signal. The big man's troubled face filled the screen. Mike's workshop visible in the background. "Get everybody. Now!"

"My God, mon, have you heard what's happen'?" Jay interrupted, anger and grief thickening his accent. "They hit Mike's house."

"I know—we know," Jonas said, lifting a hand to silence his friend. "Mike's here with me. We just left the house."

"Oh, good. Thank God. Mary and the kids are all right then," Jay finished in a rush. He leaned back into his seat, relieved.

Silence rushed into the gap, filling it.

Drawn by the silence, Jay looked back at the vid-screen and began shaking his head. It was then that he saw Jonas's expression. Looking past Jonas, Jay saw Mike sitting slumped against the bulkhead, and just as quickly, his grief returned, and redoubled for the false hope that had preceded it.

"Jay," Jonas's voice broke in, "pull it together. There will be time for grief later. Right now we need to move. This signal won't last much longer so I've got to say what I need to before Waters locks onto us. Get the team together. We need to move. Now!"

"What? After what they did? The only place I'm going is to Waters's office."

"You're talking nonsense, and I don't have time for it. Besides, you dying won't bring back Mary and the kids," Jonas winced and looked back at Mike. Thankfully, it didn't appear he had heard. "Now, get the team together and transmit on the secure line only. We need to go. Do you understand what I'm saying?"

"But, but," Jay said through tears.

"Not now, Jay. I need you with me on this, big guy. Reel it in for now."

Jay nodded and straightened. "I'm with you. Skipp and Julie are in town, back at the market square. Skipp said something about picking up components for that deflector grid or something or the other," Jay said still sounding distracted.

"Meet us with the Quest, and then we'll get Skipp and Julie. I'm sure Waters is onto them. I'll get us to the rendezvous. Meet us there. We need to be in the air within the hour. Any more than that, that'll be pushing it. Jay, get it done."

"We'll be there."

The Quest was sleek, deadly, with twin ion cannons on the bow and stern. Armed with duel laser rifles on both the port and starboard sides, the ship could escape earth-normal gravity from a hot start in 28 seconds flat. The ship's shielding was built to withstand the battering of a small asteroid storm, and flying with the nav-com at full throttle, it could come through the storm unscathed.

With upgraded heat shielding, the Quest could withstand a direct blast of ion fire at a rate of over 2273 degrees Kelvin for over 30 minutes sustained. Being a small troop transport, The Quest was enhanced with fighter capabilities.

The ship's running lights began to flicker in soft emerald and white patterns as the engines heated up. The sapphire blue hull stood in stark contrast to the T.E.C., tantalum energized cells, plated engines.

Tantalum, a once rare mineral discovered in abundance in near space, used to coat the hull, had an almost organic responses to heat. As joules released into kinetic energy, the shields absorbed the heat in a not so crude imitation of photosynthesis, which then transformed it into source energy, strengthening its own molecular structure.

Large enough to carry fifty people plus the eight-man-crew compartment, the Quest quivered with power as she rose effortlessly on vertical thrusters. Jay nosed the craft upward and pulled hard on the helm. She jumped, and a moment later, the ship was leveling out in the stratosphere. "That's it, girl. You're a fine lady," Jay said proudly.

Reaching the edge of the city core, Jay brought the ship in quick and low and sat her down just north of the hill ridge, within the green of the city's only remaining section of trees and grass. He shut all but auxiliary power down, hiding the ship from line of sight from casual view. Now began the part he hated most, waiting.

The roar of the engines was near deafening; the blare of the loud speaker only adding to the assault on Skipp's already strained eardrums. Julie tensed.

The voice rang out again, "Skipp Langg, you have been identified as a threat to the normal operations of The Company. You were seen in the vicinity of the market square when four SFP officers were assaulted. You are ordered to come with us for questioning. "

"You gonna stand here gawking all day, or you gonna get that cute fanny of yours moving," Julie said, her jaw taut. "Or will I have to carry you this time too."

Skipp turned to run. "What do ya mean, 'too'? You didn't have to carry me."

Julie pulled a hand blaster from her jacket and blasted the ship's speaker grid. "Really, you wanna talk about that now?" Julie fired again. She knew the hand blaster wouldn't harm the ship, but the flare and smoke and the pilot's overreaction would give them a diversion while they ran. "Head for the gate. We'll try and make it to what's left of the central woods north of us," she yelled over her shoulder, continuing to fire.

Running for over ten minutes, ducking in and out of doors as they became available, Skipp felt his heart would burst, his blood pumping, coursing past his eardrums like waves crashing on shore, but he could not stop. Julie wouldn't let him.

Behind and above them, the patrol cruiser stayed hot on their heels. Skipp began yelling into his wrist-com. "Jay…we need evac…now!" he cried, gasping for breath. "Where the heck are you guys? Could use some help." His lungs burned.

"We're right here," a voice came over the open com. "Wouldn't want any of the good people 'round here getting hurt by any of the falling debris," Jay answered from the cockpit of the Quest, having collected Jonas and Mike.

Skipp and Julie continued running. Leaving the crowded streets behind, they headed for the open fields and the cover of the forest beyond.

"What falling debris?" Skipp panted. "What are you talking about?" He exhaled and slowed as he came over the top of the rather large mound that bordered the city on its northern perimeter.

"Keep moving," came Julie's voice, tense, but calm. The open field and the thinning forest lay before them. She knew that if they didn't make it to the cover of the trees before that patrol cruiser could lock onto them, there would be no need for questioning. With that in mind, she grabbed Skipp's arm, pulling—dragging him along behind her.

Sweat dripped down Skipp's face, stinging his eyes. Stumbling, dirt, grass, and small rocks clung to his exposed skin. "Get up!" He looked up at Julie who stood over him, scanning the sky.

Julie readjusted her grip on Skipp's arm. She could hear the whine of the patrol cruiser coming behind them and knew they would never make it to the tree line before the SFP cruiser had a clear shot at them. Shoving Skipp ahead of her, she spun, drew her blaster, and renewed firing.

Above them, the sky exploded, the concussive wave driving them backwards into the dirt and grass. The wave of heat and furnace-like blast rolled out from the explosion, lifting and throwing Julie on top of Skipp, driving them both into the moist soil.

A thundering crash rocked the earth beneath them, followed by a dense shower of mud and burning fuel. Then just as suddenly, from behind them, came the shrieking sound of the twisting and tearing of metal as the hull of the Security Force Patrol cruiser crashed to the ground.

"Get down!" Julie shouted, flattening Skipp with her body.

After the briefest of pauses, a thunderous explosion erupted from the crater created by the downed patrol cruiser, thrashing about like some giant monster in its death throes.

Then silence.

They both looked back to see the Quest bursting through the cloud of oily black smoke rising from the crash site of the patrol cruiser.

Julie laughed sardonically.

"What?" Skipp asked, puzzled by her outburst.

"For a minute there I thought I hit an unshielded fuel line or something."

This time Skipp laughed with her. As they chuckled, their eyes met and abruptly the laughter stopped. Suddenly aware that she was straddling him, Julie became self-conscious and quickly scrambled to her feet.

Skipp noticed the flush of color in her cheeks, but chose not to mention it, acknowledging the effect her nearness had had on him as well. Instead, he turned his attention to Jay. "Think you can cut that a little closer next time? We almost got cooked down here."

Jonas's voice answered him instead, "Well, you might still get your chance. I'm reading two moderator class ground to space aircrafts coming in hot and low to this location. From the looks of them, they're fighters. If they catch us on the ground—" he was saying, but was cutoff.

"There won't be a fight," Julie finished for him.

"You're right about that. Look, there's a clearing about a hundred and fifty yards beyond those trees just north of your location. You guys hightail it over there, and we'll swoop in and grab you."

"Got it," Julie said, running before she even closed the com-link.

Standing and looking after her for a moment, finally realizing she was gone, Skipp took off as well.

———————————————————————————

The Quest hovered just above ground level and lowered its forward boarding ramp. Not breaking stride, Julie threw her backpack through the open hatch and dove in after it. Rolling and coming up in a crouch, she could see Mike behind one of the struts taking aim at the incoming aircraft.

"Here they come," Jay said over the com.

Julie, taking the opposite position inside the hatchway, turned and began firing at the incoming ships. She fired, though she knew her hand blaster would have even less effect on the moderators than it had on the cruiser. "Hurry! Run!" she screamed to Skipp, who was still some distance from the Quest.

About fifteen yards from the ramp Skipp fell, hitting the ground hard, forcing the breath from him. He felt his legs go weak.

Without hesitation, Julie jumped from the door ramp. She ran to help him and, gathering him up, turned for the ship. She had almost made it inside when the first volley erupted from the assault ships.

The Quest rocked as the laser impacted the hull. "Get that ramp closed!" Jay yelled even as he began the ascent.

Another volley hit, rolling the Quest hard over port. Just as she rolled, exposing her underside, the second of the attacking ships began strafing, diving at them with the sun at its back, blinding Jay as he looked for a route of escape.

The maneuver caught everyone off guard, and a single laser split the starboard side shields, piercing into the ship's hull.

"Whew," Jonas said amazed. "These are not the typical patrol cruisers we saw earlier. These are the big guns. Waters wants us pretty bad."

"These are the new X-1 Executioners," Jay cut in. "These babies have laser capabilities and sealed pilot compartments making them space-worthy, upgraded shielding as well. In a word, they're designed to pursue, overtake, and destroy. They were made for the fight.

"Now that we've downed the patrol cruiser, the X-1 pilots won't bother asking us if we want to give up. It's all about revenge at this point." Jay looked over at Jonas and grimaced.

Jonas nodded, acknowledging that the fighter pilots would have orders to fire on their own discretion. "They won't be trying to disable the Quest and take survivors on this one," he said.

"Hold on to something," Jay said stiffly. From a stalled hover, the Quest had settled in, he pushed the ship into a power climb and rolled her over to her starboard side. Powering the Quest into a climb, he accelerated into a barrel roll. Coming out of the roll, he continued into a split-s, twisting and turning. He was now inverted and accelerating back toward the two ships still firing at them.

The Quest's shields, now at full power, deflected the incoming laser blast, redirecting it without injury to the ship. The errant blasts careened earthward, scorching trees and open fields as they struck whatever lay along their new trajectory.

Firing proto-lasers at point blank range, the Quest tore between the two crafts. Turning to Jonas, Jay said through clenched teeth and a slight smile, "Hey, doc, watch this."

Jonas, seeing what Jay intended to do, rerouted energy from life support in the unused passenger compartment, adding it to the shielding.

Just as the X-1s came around, setting up for another attack pass, Jay pulled the nose of the Quest straight up. He began a climb that would have them in orbit in only a few seconds, had that been his true intention.

Just as he had hoped, both of the X-1s accelerated in pursuit, following him into the climb. And as the chase vehicles accelerated, closing the gap between them, Jay killed power to the engines allowing the Quest to fall backward into the path of the X-1 fighter cruisers.

Jonas added more power to the shields.

The X-1 pilots were taken by surprise. Confused. It appeared the Quest had stalled, and was in a free fall, tumbling nose over tail, en route to a fiery crash. Both jets arced away on opposite vectors in order to avoid what they thought would be a mid-air collision.

As the X-1s cleared, Jay brought the Quest level, bringing her ion cannons online and firing before either of the ships had a chance to recover. The canon fire tore through the first ship, then, just as quickly, Jay targeted the second and fired. The enhanced laser blasts ripped through the ship's lorication as easily as if they had been made of paper.

The initial blast caused the armored shielding of the ships to crack like the shell of a hardboiled egg dropped on a firm surface. Followed by the secondary and larger explosions as the weapons magazines erupted, both ships exploded into mere pieces as they showered the earth with their fiery entrails.

"That was for Mary and the kids," Jay hissed. Slapping the console in excited relief, Jay set the autopilot, unstrapped himself, and headed back for damage assessment. The ship shook slightly, nosed upward, and climbed into the darkness of space.

The door to the forward cargo hold slid open and Jay walked through, sliding as he did, falling into the slickness of pooled blood. Lying on the floor across from him, Skipp sat holding Julie; her eyes still open, as she tried to speak.

"Hush," Skipp said. "Save your energy. You're gonna be just fine."

She smiled. "Liar." Her hands fumbled at a section of metal support strut sheared off by the X-1's laser blast and now extruding from her midsection. The laser had cut into the support. The strut had broken free and skewered her. The impact shattered her pelvic girdle, and the strut continued traveling upward until it protruded from her right side just below her rib cage. Blood oozed a lazy fountain from the wound.

She grimaced and sucked in a shallow breath. "Before I die, Skipp, tell me...tell me the truth. Don't lie to me." A weak smile pulled at the corners of her mouth. "Did you feel it too? There was something special with us, right?"

"You bet there was. I was just afraid you wouldn't go for a gadget geek like me." Hot tears dripped from his face onto hers. He touched her face and left a bloody streak where his finger alighted.

"Never had a guy cry over me before," she gasped, convulsed, and stilled.

"Help me!" Skipp looked up in desperation, color draining from his face. "We've got to get that bleeding stopped. Apply direct pressure around the wound."

Jonas knelt beside him. "It's too late. She's gone," he said, taking control, giving orders.

Skipp buried his face in Julie's short hair and pulled her to himself. "She saved me."

Mike had stood off to the side transfixed by the scene. Unable to move, tears welled then breached his eyes. Tears for Mary, tears for his children—tears for himself.

Chapter Six

Ted Waters turned his back and cursed. "Incompetents. Incompetents surround me. It was a simple job: kill the Stone woman and her children and bring me that computer brat, Langg."

The more he talked, the angrier he became. The angrier he became, the more Iona enjoyed it. "Ted—Mr. Waters, it's not so bad," she said soothingly. "With Mary dead, Mike is of no further threat to you. Besides, Skipp Langg may not even have the information you're looking for."

She walked toward Waters and leaned against his desk, stretching her long legs out in front of her, crossing them at the ankles. The skintight pants complemented her athletic build, and the short black jacket accented her womanly figure.

Ted Waters turned and stared at her. "We lost two good ships on this little assignment, and one of those was a new prototype."

"I know, the X-1 Executioner, but you also lost three pilots and four footmen," she said testing him.

Waters regained his composure, tugging softly but firmly on the sleeves of the smoky-gray blazer. His eyes were cold and focused. "Ms. Bowers, I would appreciate it if you did not remind me of the incompetence of my employees. The question set before me now is: How much does Stone know, and what will it take to stop him?" He placed a hand on each of her thighs and pulled her toward him.

She leaned forward and looked into his eyes unblinking. "I'm your best chance at stopping Stone, and you know it," she said matter fact, a smile adding a sheen to her eyes.

Reaching forward, he dropped his hand on the desk between her thighs. She heard a soft click and the murmuring hum of a fan. A small compartment opened in the surface of the desk; moist air rushed upward, tingling her face as it brushed past her. Waters retrieved a cigar from the humidor and held it up to his nose enjoying the aroma of it.

Without taking his eyes from her, he said, "One of the few pleasures I allow myself. Even so, it too must be controlled— kept within perfect tolerances. Not too dry, or the flavor is lost. Not too moist, or it will waste away corrupting itself."

He looked from her to the cigar. "Good things—fine things—have to be taken care of, or they lose their value." He sniffed the cigar again, and then dropped it into the recycle- trough set in the floor near his desk.

As the cigar fell through the mouth of the receptor, a soft orange light began to glow, emitting a small spark and then powered down. When the process was finished, the cigar was gone, disintegrated.

Waters looked at her. "When a fine thing goes bad, it cannot be redeemed; it must be eliminated." He pushed her leg away from him, turned, and sat behind his huge desk. "Go after Stone. Do whatever it takes to stop him."

She stood, preparing to leave when his huge hand grabbed her around the waist, turning her back to face him. "I do not want to see The Company's name attached to this. Do you understand me?"

Stepping toward him until she stood between his knees, Iona smiled softly. "I understand." Then taking a half step toward him, deeper into his personal space, she spun and walked away. Again, she could feel his eyes scouring her, studying her every move, trying to decipher her. Again, she smiled as the doors slid solidly shut behind her.

Knowing that he would still be watching her, Iona kept walking, looking neither to the left or right, not trusting herself—her emotions—until she was out of his line of view. As she covered the distance from the massive doors to the lifts, Iona knew the office staff was watching her as well. Muted greetings went ignored as she passed, not conceding to reward their unwanted attentions.

As the door to the elevator closed, she exhaled and leaned against the wall. She knew she couldn't let down yet, not even here. He would see. He would know.

Yes, she had wanted to see Mary in pain, to see her hurting as she herself had hurt. She wanted to see Mary cry, bowed in a deep sense of loss of *something*—someone special; but she had not wanted to see her dead—or the children.

Anger swelled. Iona lifted herself from the wall. She squared her shoulders and stared with dispassionate disinterest at the camera she knew lay hidden within the wall.

The Quest dropped out of hyperspace just as she entered the Gliese System. The alarm on the nav-com, the navigational computer, roused the men from their sleep.

Still groggy from too little sleep, too much trauma, all of which had occurred in too few hours, Mike made his way from the crew compartment. He silenced the alarm. Standing, he stared out into the aether of space and, not for the first time, contemplated Mary's ideas about an all-loving, all-powerful God. *Right.*

But even more pressing at the moment was his reconciling as reality a universe that did not include Mary or his children. That they had been savagely ripped from him by a madman's ploy just to make a point. He stared, lost in thought, and slowly his contemplation turned to fury.

"You'll pay for all of this," Mike said aloud, thinking of Ted Waters, anger making his words tight and brusque. Tears spilled from his eyes as thoughts of Mary returned. So did thoughts of her God.

Forgive... the whispered memory seemed to suggest.

"What's that, old boy?" Jonas said, joining his friend. Rubbing the sleep from his eyes, he didn't want Mike to know he'd overheard his grief's expression.

Startled, Mike turned, wiping at his face.

"I—ah," Jonas started uneasily. "I…ah, yeah." He leaned toward Mike and bumped shoulders, as close as he would come to an actual hug. Then leaning back, he joined him in silence.

After a moment, Jonas began again. "She was a great woman. Waters won't get away with this."

Mike swore. "You're right, he won't. I guarantee you that much." He turned back toward the porthole, his vision blurred. "I swear to you, Ted Waters is gonna pay for the life of my family."

"Whoa, buddy, slow down there. Justice. We want Waters to pay in court for what he's done."

Mike turned and stared at his oldest friend.

"Simple revenge is not our way, we're better than that…better than Waters." He sighed. "Besides, I don't think Mary would want that for you. You know how she was—about what she believed."

Mike began shaking his head, waved a hand at Jonas and turned back toward the porthole. "I can't…I can't go there."

"Hey, I'm not—I'm not pushing here. It's just that if you're going to do this, I think you should at least be honest with yourself. Mary wouldn't want the revenge; she wasn't that way. It's not how she believed."

"Well, Mary's not here to tell me what she believed, is she?" Mike snapped. "And you know why she's not here—'cause Ted Waters killed her! He killed my…" Mike slammed his fist onto the console. "He killed my children."

An awkward silence, like a stifling humidity hung heavy between them.

"Look, Mike, I don't have the answers. All I know is that if we're going to stop Waters, we need you—now. Focused."

Mike turned and faced his friend, his features clouded, his fist clenched. Then exhaling, he relaxed. "Okay, okay. You're right. This is not the time, but…"

"When the time comes, I'll be right there with you, my friend, and we'll make sure Waters gets everything he has coming. But we'll do it the right way."

Mike stared back at him.

"The way Mary would have it done," Jonas concluded. *God, I'm not as good at this as Mary was, but we...he needs your help. Bad.*

Again, Mike relaxed, dejected, and slumped against the bulkhead. He turned back to the porthole, an emptiness growing in his heart and lost himself in the vastness of space.

Just then Jay walked in and looked from Jonas to Mike. "Somebody take your lunch money?" He laughed, pleased with his joke.

Jonas chuckled; Mike continued looking out the window.

"You know, Mike," Jay began, "I wasn't at all sure you and Mary would help us after what happened with you guys—with The Company, I mean. You took a big hit. Stripped of your commission, your holdings seized, and now Mary and the kids." He settled in at the pilot's station. "Waters has done everything he can to you." Jay was busy adjusting the trim on the helm; he hadn't noticed Mike's pained expression. He continued, "I just don't know...why does he fear you so?"

Mike didn't like talking about those days at the best of times, and this was far from even a good time. He cursed himself for having actually believed in The Company and what it stood for and for having trusted Waters.

Whenever Mike thought back to the things he had done, the avarice, the pride, he felt the beginnings of shame. Now all he felt was anger. He looked from Jonas to Jay. "To be honest with you," he started to no one in particular, "if it hadn't been for Mary, I would've lost it a long time ago." His voice lowered, "She believed in me—in us. She kept telling me that our love had been a *gift*, something worth fighting for. She wouldn't give up on me, so I couldn't." Aware that he hadn't, that he couldn't answer Jay's question, Mike shook his head.

Jay looked up from the computer console, his large hands frozen mid-motion, and for the first time since walking in, he took actual notice of his fellow crewmen. The conversation melted and silence dripped between them, warm and strangely comforting.

Thinking food would be a safe topic for discussion, Jay said, "Anybody for breakfast? I'm starved." He saw a look pass between Mike and Jonas, and he understood that something had happened, that something had been said. He knew their relationship went way back. He also knew that in life there were just some things you didn't want anybody else to know. Entering various commands into the computer, he satisfied himself with the task of cooking.

Moments later, the smell of hot pancakes and bacon did little to disguise the fact that the food they were eating wasn't *real* food. Made to look and feel like the real thing, all shipboard food was generated from a gelatinous protein compound stored in the ship's tanks. Dietary computers, affectionately referred to as di-coms, fashioned menu selections according to the eater's choice.

Even the coffee was fake, though it tasted good. In fact, the flavor was almost perfect, made from the same gelatinous mixture. The brew was thinned and various accents added so instead of a simple caffeine boost, the drinker got an amino acid dump; a kind of chicken soup in disguise, tasting good and good for you.

Finally, Skipp joined the three men. Making his way to the science station, he pulled up the ship's stats, running a systems check. "I…" he started, took a breath, let the sentence drop. "I checked Julie's body in stasis. She'll be okay there until we get back."

The men acknowledged him with a tilt of their heads and assorted grunts. "Join us," Jay said, finally speaking around a mouth full of pancakes, waving his hand toward the table.

"Yeah, I think I will" Skipp answered slowly and meandered toward the di-com. "Where are we anyway?"

"Just entering the Gliese's inner system, about two hours out," Jonas answered from navigational control.

Skipp distractedly punched in his breakfast request. "Well, the ship handled beautifully, all systems in the green. No power drop-offs," he commented.

On the ship's forward screen, Milcah, the System's largest star and so named due to the straw colored light it produced, rose into view. The orb was huge compared to the Terran system's Sol, which would hold 1.3 million earths in its core.

"How close can we get to that before our shields overheat?" Mike asked, pointing to the forward display screen.

"It's actually cooler than our own sun. As long as we stay at least two hundred million kilometers out, we should be just fine," Skipp answered.

"What's the gravitational pull on us at that distance?" Jay asked, heading back to helm control. "That big ball's not gonna reach out and grab a hold of us, is it?" Then without waiting for an answer, he disconnected the automatic pilot. "Computer, release helm." A slight shudder ran through the ship as Jay nosed her in a slightly wider arc away from the system's sun.

Smiling at Jay, Jonas finished a mouth full of omelet and said, "Judging from the size of that thing, I figure life would be unbearable on any of the system's planets except those at the extreme outer fringes. It'd be too hot." He cleared his throat and continued, "But the proximity might cause tremors on the planet...you know, small quakes from time to time."

Mike, turning to Skipp, called, "Look for any signs of artificial life anywhere within the system."

The Gliese System had been the first planetary system where human life had seeded and taken hold. Designated for hard element acquisitioning by means of mechanized mining, the outlying planets should have been free from human settlements.

The Quest approached the last planet in the system, 581, originally selected for colonization. But the plans—Mike's plans—had gone very wrong. The initial sweep revealed enormous planetary instability, earthquakes accompanied with constant volcanic eruptions. After a more exhaustive study of the scan, Skipp knew he found the planet he had been looking for.

The fifth planet in the system, Yargon, was named after Dr. Julies Yargon. Yargon, discovered eighty-five years prior by the renowned astronomer and designer of the astro-nautical charting program, shown blue on the screen, indicating a large water supply.

As they established a standard equatorial orbit, they could see dense jungles bordering dry deserts. "Only one settlement showing on initial scan," Jonas said, setting his empty breakfast tray aside. "Whoa, what's that?"

"What'cha got?" Skipp leaned over Jonas's shoulder.

"Unless the computer is messed up, we've got large groups of animal life down there as well as significant lower life forms," Jonas answered.

"That shouldn't be. There shouldn't be anything down there but a mining colony," Mike said, turning to face the scanner. "When I was taken off the project we had just seeded lower Earth life-forms. Maybe small mammals by now, but nothing larger than rabbits and field mice. The indigenous life forms were benign at best. What has Waters been up to out here?" he asked into the air.

"I'm showing several different large land creatures of some sort in both the jungle and beneath the surface in the desert regions. This place should be empty. I mean, no indigenous life forms were recorded in this sector," Jonas said, looking up from his scans. I wonder what else Waters had lied about."

"This was supposed to be cut, back before Moab-Six initiated," Jay said over his shoulder.

"Yeah, but Waters was in charge of that for a while too, and—" Skipp began before being cutoff.

"Wait a minute, guys," Mike said, settling everyone down. "The only thing we know for sure about this planet is that we don't know anything for sure. I say we just go down there, and then make our assessments. I want a full record of this. We're going to show everybody back on Earth what Waters is doing out here."

"And why he is trying so hard to keep it a secret," Skipp added.

"You're wrong about one thing, Mike," Jonas said. "We do know that the ship of children came from here and that Waters is somehow responsible. What we have to do is uncover that connection and make Waters pay."

"This is strange," Jonas said, looking up from his station again. "There's not one significant body of surface water." He brought the image up on the main screen. "Look."

There were complex river systems running back and forth through the jungles, crossing themselves at several points, but no oceans or seas, not even large lakes. The rivers, small and large, ran kilometer after kilometer twisting and turning, doubling back on themselves with no apparent fountainhead.

To Mike's mind, it didn't make sense. It would stand to reason that if there were rivers, there would be oceans or seas. At least there should be a snowcap to start the flow at the river's head to account for the water flow. But there was nothing of the sort. The whole system just simply refuted logic. "Jonas," Mike said from the con, "figure this out. Tell me how this can happen." He thought to himself, *it has to be either artesian, artificial, or some strange combination of both.*

By now, Jay and Skipp had taken a greater interest in the scan of the planet below them. Mike looked around and knew the men were just as confused as he was. "Any bets, gentlemen?" Mike asked.

Jay answered, "I bet it's a good place to be away from."

"Look at that jungle." Skipp exhaled. "I've never seen anything like it. And just look...look at that desert. Anybody want to try and explain how you can get a jungle that lush and wet to butt up against a desert as severe as that? No steppes, no grasslands—no transition phase...just change. I'm telling you, I know weird and that's weird. Something strange is going on down there!"

"What is Waters up to?" Mike whispered to no one in particular.

Jay turned to face the crew. "You know, I didn't see 'dat little girl you found out here, and those other little ones that didn't make it, but I gotta know what Waters is doing down there and how those kids figure into it. You know, no matter, it can't be good. This far out, nobody knows about it. The kids show up and they hid the whole incident away like it never happened...then they rail you out, doc. There's a whole lot of wrong going on here."

"Just looking at this place gives me the creeps." Jonas had spoken for them all.

The men fell silent, staring at the planet that now filled the view screen, willing it to reveal its secrets.

"Better go into stealth mode. Waters is going to have this planet on alert. We don't want to get shot down without first finding out what this is all about," Mike said, returning to the conn.

"Shields to full?" Jay asked. "Don't know about you, but I'm none too keen on getting shot down at all."

Nervous laughter floated around the bridge.

"Shields up. Take us in," Mike ordered.

Mary sat, staring at her non-functioning console. The screen on the transport vehicle was black. Thankfully, navigation still functioned in manual control, and she was able to escape from the scene of the explosion. Accelerating rapidly, Mary directed the transport vehicle out of the city. Desperately trying to put an appreciable distance between her kids and the mess behind them, she sped away. Mary felt only then could she stop and try to find some sense of direction, make some kind of plan for her next step.

Mary drummed her fingers on the steering control handle and then ran a trembling hand through her hair. *Think, Mary, think-think. What do you need to do first? First?*

She sighed as the tendrils of an idea began to take form in her mind. The first stop had to be the depository. She needed to be off the grid; she needed cash. She knew it wouldn't take long before *they* knew she and the kids hadn't died in the explosion, but she didn't want to make it easy for them to find her again.

"What happened, Mom!?" M2 asked, comforting his baby sister as best he could.

"Mommy, why did the world blow up, Mommy?" Travist, the younger son, asked, his voice sounding fragile.

Although unhurt, Sissy became irritated and fussy, agitated by the sudden excitement and resulting tension. The noise and the crashing of the cruiser had left them all shaken.

"I don't know, baby," Mary answered distracted. "We've got to get off the road and try and contact your father." Mary turned around and looked at her children, fear and anxiety clouding their small faces.

"You know your dad was going to join us, so he'll just have to meet us at the hotel now. This is all part of a game," she hedged. "We're gonna stay in different hotels, and daddy is gonna try and find us. Like hide and seek."

Travist's face brightened with the wonder of a game, the fear and stress of the explosion all of a sudden seeming not so bad.

M2 caught his mother's eye, and although he wasn't willing to call her a liar, he knew something was not quite right.

Mary saw the light of recognition dawning in her oldest son's eyes and, just as quickly, an understanding passed between them. She rested a hand on his leg, and a wave of sadness darkened her heart as she witnessed her son's maturation increasing and pieces of his childhood slipping away.

Hours later, the transport floated quietly into the parking lot of an old-fashioned motel. The ancient business was a leftover from a period long past with the office on one end and all the rooms facing a common square. Grass and weeds sprouted up where the asphalt had long ago cracked and spread apart. Faded lines still showed where old-fashioned gas engine cars had once parked.

Mary shut the engines down and the transport settled softly on the ground. Sitting, staring at the blinking vacancy sign, the chipped and peeling paint mirrored her feelings of brokenness and desolation. Dropping her face to the backs of her hands, tears dripped from her chin. Looking at the blinking sign again, she shook her head slightly; this was the kind of place she had driven by thankful to God she could afford better.

After paying for a room with one of the recently acquired gold coins, Mary looked down at her daughter sleeping in her safety carrier. *Something to be thankful for.* Travist was just awake enough that he could walk to the room under his own power. M2 carried his sister.

She pressed the keycard against the door reader embedded in the ancient frame. The lock popped open with a dull buzz-click. She sighed.

Looking around the small room with its two full-sized beds, M2 asked, "Where's my bed?" I don't want to share a bed with him." Travist had already curled up near the head of one of the beds and was sound asleep.

"Please, M2," Mary said, her voice heavy with fatigue.

"But, Mom, he kicks, and he always winds up on top of me. I'm gonna hit em' if he does."

"Nobody's hitting anybody, please," Mary said, laying her daughter down and checking the child's diaper before finally sitting down herself.

She rubbed at her head; the cut was starting to ache. Mary sagged against the headboard, the muscles in her neck and shoulders feeling like twisted cords. Closing her eyes, she massaged her neck, loosening the smaller knots forming at the base of her skull. Weariness pulled at her. Her lip trembled. *Mike, where are you?*

Looking at his mother with sober eyes, M2 asked, "Head hurting, Mom?" He came over to her and laid his head on her shoulder, his small arm encircling her protectively.

Mary turned toward him and hugged her son. "Come on, let's get you in bed."

"Do I have to brush my teeth tonight? Travist didn't brush his."

Realizing that she hadn't brought anything with her from the house, Mary ruffled the boy's hair and shooed him off to bed. "You can brush them in the morning. Now go to bed." It didn't take long before all of Mary's children were sound asleep, and now that she was alone, she felt her resolve finally weaken. She cried.

Sitting on the cold linoleum covering of the bathroom floor with its cracked tiles and years of floor wax heaped in the corners, Mary let her mind wander back over the events of the day. She knew in her spirit that Waters was responsible; she also knew that he had intended to kill them all. Suddenly, grief and sorrow overcame her and she collapsed down, racking sobs tearing through her gut.

After a few minutes had passed, Mary pushed to her knees and climbed slowly to her feet. She was exhausted, but too worked up to sleep. Despite her agitation, she decided that she had to rest and headed for the small bed where her daughter lay sleeping.

Stopping by the small sink, Mary splashed her face and dried it with the rough towel, which hung with stiff pleats from the wall. Freshened, she made her way out of the small bathroom, and then gently lowered herself onto the bed. The worn bedspring groaned in protest. Looking at her sleeping children, Mary began to do something she hadn't done all day. She began to pray in earnest.

Soberly at first, but as she spoke, her emotions broke. "Oh, God, why? Why? Where's Mike? Is he okay? Does he even know we're alive? How do I let him know we're okay? Why has this happened to us?" Her anguish had turned to anger and as she poured out her heart, confronting her fear that she might never see her husband alive again, Mary began to resolve herself to life without Mike.

Looking at nothing in particular, Mary sat wearily, leaning against the headboard, hot tears falling steadily into her lap. At that moment, she looked down at the partially opened nightstand. Opening the drawer, she found an old yellow-paged Gideon's Bible. The cover was stained and damaged where someone had used it to put out cigarettes.

Slowly, she opened the book and the faint odor of dust billowed upward. A smell of dampness accompanied the opening as an old tissue tilted and hung from the pages. Repulsed, Mary shook the book, causing the soiled paper finally to fall to the floor.

She turned the pages, carefully examining them. Then a familiar passage caught her eye, Isaiah 40:11:

He shall feed his flock like a shepherd: He shall gather the lambs with His arm, and carry them in His bosom, and shall gently lead those that are with young.

Mary remembered being a little girl and her grandmother Nonna explaining that God, through His Son Jesus, would gather all those who loved Him, and that He would provide a safe place for them. She found herself wondering if this was true, if it applied to her situation now.

Mary looked around the small room, grayish even with the lights on, and again took account of her children. "I don't know if that is literal or not God; or if You intended this for me, but I'll take anything right now." She brushed away her tears, and hugged the dirty book to her breast and enjoyed the warmth of the memory. Suddenly sleepy, Mary snuggled down next to her baby and fell into a dreamless sleep.

"Hallo…housekeeping," an older and heavily, German accented voice called through the closed door.

Mary rolled over, surprised to find that she had slept in her clothes. Slowly, recognition dawned as memory surged. She looked at her still sleeping children and then at the clock, an old analogue model that seemed as old as the hotel, and the hands indicated 10:00 a.m.

"Hallo-hallo, housekeeping," the German accented voice called out again. "*Frau…mam*, it's checkout time. Do you want me to come back?"

Mary made her way to the door and peeked through the security hole. She could see the middle-aged blond woman with her hair tied back and wearing a faded housekeeping uniform. "No, ahh, we'll be right out. Give us a minute, please," Mary said, rubbing sleep from her eyes.

"Makes no difference to me mam, but you're gonna have to pay the *gebühr spät*, the late checkout fee," the woman said as she pushed the cart down to the next set of doors.

Mary began waking her children, and fifteen minutes later, she was loading them into her transport. She checked to make sure the kids were strapped in and then secured her own restraint. Beside her on the floor was the worn Gideon's Bible taken from the hotel room.

Chapter Seven

Nine-year-old Albert Steins sat quietly in the waiting room of the Children's Guardianship administration building, C.G. for short. A bright child, Albert's eyes had once shown with hope that his mother would recover from the degenerative nervous system disease. Those eyes were now darkened by hope expired. Having never known his father, for the last two years of his short life Albert Steins had been alone.

He sat, with anxious eyes, looking through the large window at the two men inside the main office and wondered what they wanted with him. Like the other children at the C.G., he had been told that one day someone might want to take him to a new home, a place where he could be a part of a brand new family. Albert wasn't so sure he wanted this; families were places where you got hurt, where people left you...abandoned you. At least here, he had nothing to hope for, and with that, nothing to lose.

He wondered if the man in the fancy suit was one of *those* somebody's. He had just about reached the limit of his reserve of patience when the big door swung open, and the two men walked out into the foyer.

Footsteps echoed in hollow tones from the high ceilings and ancient wood floors, as the men came closer to where Albert sat waiting. Dust motes swam through blond shafts of amber hues as the late afternoon sun streaked through the single pane window high overhead. One of the men Albert recognized was Mr. Payne, the administrator of the Children's Guardianship.

The other, he had never seen before. The man was tall with short brown hair combed straight back coming to a point just above his collar. He wore what looked like a very expensive suit. Albert thought that the man had to have lots of money.

As the two men came closer, Albert found himself thinking that if this man did take him as part of his family, at least having lots of money could be much better than living at the C.G.

Mr. Payne spoke first. "Albert, stand up and come here, boy," he said in his crisp, cold tone. "This is Mr. Adams, and he has informed me that he would like to be a father for you, if you didn't have any objections."

Paul Adams knelt down and spoke to Albert face to face. "Now, tell me, Albert, what do your friends call you?"

"Gibb," the child answered shyly. Looking into Mr. Adams's eyes, Albert took an involuntary step backwards, all the warmth of hope suddenly draining from him. He could not explain what it was he felt. It was just that looking into this man's eyes made him feel very uneasy.

"Speak up, child. Don't be rude," Mr. Payne said, his arms folded over his boney chest.

Either unaware or ignoring Albert's reaction, Paul Adams kept right on talking. He was smiling and appeared to be very excited and happy at the prospect of having Albert as his son. Maybe a bit too happy.

Mr. Payne called out for one of the many custodians that worked in the building. "Bring me the boy's bags."

Albert's eyes danced up to Mr. Payne's face. *The decision that I'm leaving has already been made. I'm not wanted, not even here.*

Albert didn't have many bags, two to be exact. A few articles of clothing, the book his mother read to him at bedtime, and a picture of his mother.

The sound of Paul's voice drew Albert back to an awareness of what was happening to him. "Tell ya what, you call me Paul, and I'll call you Albert. I don't much like the way Gibb sounds. Sorry, kid."

Albert didn't answer but picked up his bags as he was expected. He thought he should be happy, but instead he was afraid. He couldn't say why he was scared, but he was truly afraid of this fancy-dressed man and what this new situation meant for him.

For reasons he could not have explained if asked, gripped by a sudden panic, Albert turned and sprinted toward the dorm where the children slept. He had just made it to the double doors leading to the quad when Mr. Payne grabbed his shoulder. Skeletal fingers sunk deep into the brachial plexus at the juncture of Albert's neck and shoulder, jerking him to a hard stop. Searing heat coursed through him. He dropped his bags, spun, and collapsed to the floor in a spasm of pain. The larger of the two bags broke open as it hit the floor. His mother's book bounced free by the impact, slid across the smooth surface, jamming itself under a huge planter that stood against the far wall.

Albert was pulled back through the foyer to where Paul Adams stood waiting for him, still smiling that stupid too-good-to-be-true smile. Realizing any complaint he had would not be recognized, Albert simply gave up. He kept quiet and wondered what this strange man could possibly want with him. Whatever it was, he knew it wasn't any good. Therefore, in silence, he decided he would watch and wait.

"Albert, what is your problem, boy?" Mr. Payne demanded. "You should be very happy that Mr. Adams has decided to take you as part of his family. You know full well that you have nothing, no one." He suddenly stopped as if remembering himself. He cleared his throat and continued, "Now, if you don't want to spend the rest of your life living here in this hall, I suggest you grow up and take advantage of this opportunity that has come looking for you."

Then turning his attention back to Paul Adams, Mr. Payne changed his hard expression to one of coolness and entreaty. "Please excuse the child." He smiled and cleared his throat again. "He's still a little upset over his mother's recent death. Well, not too recent," he added quickly, sounding apologetic.

Paul didn't answer him, but looked at him coolly.

Payne began to sweat. "He's been with us over six months, and it's been two years since the woman's death. He should be over his grief by now." Again, Payne smiled weakly.

"Not a problem," Paul clutched Albert's shoulder tightly. "I'm sure the boy will do just fine."

Albert chanced a look up at the man whose hand was on his shoulder. He was still wearing that stupid smile. A few moments later, Albert found himself in the back seat of a shuttle. It was then that he realized he had left his mother's book back in the hall. He knew it would be pointless to ask Paul to go back for it.

"How old are you, kid?"

"Nine." Albert's voice was a lot softer than he had intended. He didn't want this man to know just how scared he really was. He was wondering if he could chance asking about his mother's book.

The transport's communicator chirped. "Adams here," Paul answered.

Albert listened closely to the one-sided conversation, trying to figure out what was going to happen to him.

"Yeah, I got him."

The other person spoke.

"Payne was his usual adequate self. No, no problems."

There was another pause, then, "ETA in about..."—he looked at his chronometer—"five point five hours. Yeah."

Ending the communication, Paul continued questioning Albert. "So you got any family left? Your mama was all you had, right?" All traces of friendliness now gone from his voice.

Albert didn't know that the man who had just adopted him was the second in command of The Company's energy reconnaissance commission and a very dangerous person. What Albert did know was that he did not like Paul Adams and he sensed, contrary to what had been said, Paul Adams did not like him either.

The commission consisted of three people, one of which was not aware of his precarious position. The second was Ted Waters and the third member, appointed from the transportation management section, was Charles Ada; appointed without his approval or knowledge. An exorbitant salary had been routed to Ada's accounts along with a suite of luxury apartments in several of the city's finest high-rises. All this was done quietly over the past few years, and all of it done without Ada's knowledge.

These were facts of which Charles Ada would only be made aware if The Company needed someone on whom to attach ownership of some of its less desirable activities. Plausible deniability.

But Paul knew nothing would go wrong. Since he had taken over the position, production had doubled. He prided himself in this. He prided himself on being able to make the hard decisions, of being cool under fire, of anticipating Waters's needs. If there was one thing Paul Adams was sure of, it was himself.

Paul began thinking. It was, after all, his idea to use the children. Nobody would miss them, and nobody would care if they were lost. The truly beautiful part of his plan was that there was no shortage of this type of child to use. "Raw supply." Paul turned, looked at the boy in the rear seat of his transport and laughed.

Albert cringed.

Speaking more to himself than to be heard, Paul laughed, "Payne, the poor sap. He's probably patting himself on the back for helping yet another abandoned child find a loving and caring home."

Again, the leaden fear gripped Albert's stomach. His breaths coming in short, ragged gasps. Albert curled into a ball trying to squeeze that funny feeling out of his stomach. He tried to think how he could get out of this situation. He had lived on the streets before; he could do it again. Despair settled in on him, and he began to cry. He hugged the picture of his mother to his chest and collapsed into a restless sleep.

A short time later, the shuttle came to a stop; the sudden jolt waking young Albert from the milky swirls of his dreams. His chance to run had slipped past him. Looking around, he knew whatever trap he was in had just closed behind him. He was caught.

They were in an underground garage. Albert knew this because he had been in one like this with his mom back before she...he left the thought unfinished.

Looking around at the dark gray walls, Albert felt himself sink within himself. Inside, he promised, for his mother's sake, that he would survive. He was not sure how, but he would survive. He had to.

Opening the hatch to the shuttle, Paul pulled the child through as if he was nothing more than baggage. Snatching the two bags from Albert, Paul threw them in a dumpster and pushed a switch on the side, starting the burn cycle. The doors slid shut with a rusty clank and the swoosh of the natural gas flame ignited. Burning at well over 850 degrees Celsius, the bags were soon reduced to dust. The timer clicked off, the fan buzzed on, and the remains were sucked away. With a resigned click, the heavy metal doors slid apart, again revealing an empty blackened interior.

Paul looked down at the stunned child and sneered, "Where you're going you won't be needing those." Then he walked off obviously expecting Albert to come after him.

Tired and alone, Albert was too afraid not to follow. As they walked away from the dumpster, he wondered if his life would ever be *normal* again. Tears streaked his face. He was stunned and angry, but found comfort and strength in that he'd been holding the picture of his mother when Paul had taken his bags.

Once inside the elevator, Paul pointed to a corner. "Sit down and keep quiet, kid." The threat was implied, not spoken.

Albert did not want to anger this man and really wasn't sure he wanted to see any part of this building, wherever *here* was. He had seen this type of man before in the C.G.; and Paul impressed Albert as the type of person who enjoyed hurting other people.

The elevator stopped. A computer voice spoke from the speaker in the wall. "Seventy-fifth floor. Please display proper ID." A panel in the wall slid aside, and a small screen extended forward. The screen, about twelve inches square, flickered and then glowed with a warm pink light.

Paul placed his right hand palm down onto the screen. The voice spoke again. "Paul Adams, identified. Please report to the office of the president immediately." The panel went black and the elevator doors opened.

"Oh, sure," Paul said softly, "Waters, you want the job done but don't want to get your hands dirty." He looked around. "I can't take this kid in there with me."

Albert looked around, too, and wondered whom or what Waters was and why it made Paul act so weird. He was, however, glad Paul was not taking him with him.

Paul looked around as he walked the short corridor to the executive offices. He needed somewhere secure to drop off the kid. Looking up, he saw the bronze nameplate: Iona Bowers.

"Any port in a storm," he said to no one. *With any luck,* he thought to himself, *she wouldn't be in.* He wasn't lucky.

"What do you think you're doing?" Iona demanded. Standing quickly, the force of her movement sent papers scattering off her desk onto the floor. She was apparently in a bad mood, which wasn't at all unusual.

Noticing the child standing behind Paul, Iona hesitated ever so slightly before allowing her anger to rise. "Get this..." She stumbled over her words trying to find one that would fit. "...this child out of my office before I throw both you and it out the window."

Albert stood absolutely still.

Now it was Paul's turn. "Come on now, babe, I gotta go see the boss. I can't go taking this kid in there with me. He'll kill us both on the spot and then dock my pay to have the carpets cleaned."

She advanced on him. "If you call me babe one more time, I'll kill you myself. Now get out of here," she said turning her icy gaze to Albert. "But I'm telling you, if you leave this thing here more than fifteen minutes..." She left her sentence hanging. She turned the cold fire of her eyes back to Paul. "Do you understand me? Now get out of my sight before I change my mind."

Walking backwards toward the door, Paul slowed. "Love ya, babe—err', Iona," he said, quickly correcting himself. "We've got to do lunch sometime...soon, you know, for old time sake." The file she had been shaping her perfectly manicured nails with just moments before, now hung quivering in the door between Paul's index finger and thumb. Calmly, with deliberate movements, Iona opened her center desk drawer and pulled out a letter opener. Looking at Paul, she said, "I won't miss a second time. The door snapped shut as Paul left the room.

Turning her attention to the child, Iona spoke slowly, "I don't care why you are here or what Paul has planned for you, but don't touch anything and do not talk to me." She lowered herself back into her seat, waving the letter opener at Albert, emphasizing her words as she spoke. *Why did it have to be a child? Why now? Mary....*

Albert simply nodded but said nothing, swallowing and following the arc of the blade as it danced in her hand.

Lost in her work, hours passed before Iona became aware of time's passage, her anger faded. Suddenly, she remembered the child Paul had dumped in her office, invading her private world. Pushing back from her desk, she set out to find what havoc the child had created. Deciding that for whatever the child had done, he would pay severely.

She walked into her adjoining private lounge, suspecting that the child may have favored it's more homey appearance compared to the highly professional area of the main office. Thinking she heard him behind her, she turned, determined to put such a fright into the kid that he wouldn't move a muscle or dare make a sound until Paul came back to collect him, which for Paul's sake, she thought, had better not be very much longer.

Finally, finding the child, and to her surprise, he had not done any of the things she had imagined. Instead, she found him tucked beneath a large settee curled back against the wall, still holding the picture of a woman in his arms. *His mother?* She noticed now that he was asleep, that even now he somehow managed to look at peace.

The concept struck her. Turning away from the scene, her breath caught in her throat, and she sagged against the wall. "Peace," she said softly to herself. "When was the last time you had real peace?"

Looking through the open doorway, Iona was stunned as she saw her reflection in the mirror across the large office. Her red hair hung loosely down her face, and she thought she looked...vulnerable. "Peace," she said as if tasting the word. "Now there's a novel thought."

Just the idea of being at peace seemed foreign to her, that she somehow could possibly have a measure, even a small measure of the tranquility, portrayed on the sleeping child's face.

Staring into the mirror, Iona's thoughts drifted back to an earlier encounter with Waters, and she felt the red-hot anger building again, but this time, instead of focusing on the child, it turned to Waters himself. Something weird was happening to her. It was funny, she thought, but this vulnerable little child was having a very strange effect on her. *Was it that Waters had ordered Mary and the children killed?*

Without thinking, she crossed the room, lifted the child, and laid him atop of the settee, covering him with a throw. Looking at the woman in the picture, she said barely above a whisper, "It must be nice to have someone to love you."

She didn't know the woman in the picture the child was holding, but she envied her. Apparently, she had loved the child so much that the memory of that love could still soothe him. The idea that the boy could take comfort from an old-fashioned, worn-out, paper photograph overwhelmed Iona, touching something inside her; she did not know what.

Jealous? Yes, she was jealous of the woman in the photograph. Suddenly, a new feeling started growing somewhere deep inside of her. For the first time Iona began to feel shame for what she had become, for the things she had done. Memories of her own childhood came flooding back, bursting through her well-placed barriers.

Forced by hunger to sell her body for food and a dry place to sleep, she had learned then that power was the key to security; and she had sworn she would never be powerless again. Now she had power, but she asked herself, what had she lost to get it?

Hot tears dripping from her chin surprised Iona, and she considered her position of power and all the success she had gained and felt suddenly empty. She felt something else as well.

A second feeling she wasn't accustomed to feeling; Iona was confused.

Mary…the children…dead. Waters.

She brushed at the tears. Where were all these feelings coming from? What did they mean? It seemed her encounter with her past had had a greater effect on her than she thought. She knew seeing Mike Stone again would be hard, but she had not counted on the effect seeing Mary would have on her. *This would definitely take some sorting out*, she thought to herself.

In her line of work, feelings were a liability, and loving someone was just plain stupid. It gave your enemy a tool to use against you. Iona had made many enemies in her climb to the top, but until now, she had never thought of them ever being able to touch her. Before now, she had not been vulnerable. Up until now, she had been cold, distant, and aloof. But all that was before Mike came back into her world, or rather, she entered back into his.

She sat motionless, just watching the sleeping child. As time slipped by unnoticed, she found herself taken by the soft curl of his lips, and the way they quivered slightly as he breathed. His skin was a light, golden brown. She reasoned that he was of a mixed heritage; although she couldn't be sure which. The soft loose curls framed his face as he slept, and Iona had to admit that the child was truly beautiful.

Thinking of what Paul had wanted with the child, her mood suddenly darkened. Knowing Paul, she knew it was not good, for the child at least. She determined that she would not allow Paul to hurt this child. She would make up some lie; tell him a story, anything to get him off her back and out of her face.

Without stopping to think about possible repercussions, she spoke into the air, "Computer."

"Yes," the mechanical voice replied.

Iona continued, "Contact Paul Adams."

After the briefest of pauses, the computer's voice answered, "Paul Adams is no longer in the building. He was confirmed off premises at 1933 hours. No point of destination has been logged. Would you like to contact him via the net?"

"No," Iona said as she stood and walked toward her desk, running a hand through her hair.

"Would you like to leave a message?" the computer intoned.

"No." Iona answered, then quickly changed her mind. "Yes, yes, I would."

The computer beeped its readiness to record.

Iona paused, reminding herself to stay true to her established character. Taking a breath and setting herself, she began, her voice cool and controlled. "Paul, perhaps I didn't make myself clear when we spoke earlier. Since it was you, however, who imposed yourself into my day, and it was also you who left this, this child," she said it as if the word tasted bad in her mouth, "in my office. But it was *I* who once again had cleaned up your mess. You can find what's left of it in the recycler." She ended the transmission abruptly and released a breath she did not know she had been holding.

Massaging her temples, she thought, *The easy part was over. Now for part two.* All she had to do was figure out just what part two was. Turning, and to her surprise, found a teary-eyed Albert standing in the open doorway.

Chapter Eight

"Okay, Jay, let's see just how rusty you've gotten, big guy." Jonas smirked.

Short, nervous laughter, unguarded and familiar, swept through the men. With knuckles tightened and pressed back into their seats, the crew of the Quest held on as Jay nosed the ship downward and began a power dive.

Jay piloted the Quest in through the planet's atmosphere. Her shields hardly challenged by the friction-generated heat. She glided in low over a jungle canopy so thick it looked like carpet suspended above the ground. Undulating patterns revealed the rolling hills hidden beneath the roof of leaves and varied colored branches. Exotic woods of oranges, greens, and umber and blood reds broke through on occasion; their arms reaching for the sun's warmth. Giants, dwarfing the remaining trees of Terra, their shadows cast several lengths beyond the forest's edge. The roar of the engines startled large colorful avian, not too unlike those found in the tropical regions of Earth, from their resting spots high in the jungle ceiling. The birds burst from the trees, desperate to escape this strange intruder that had come unwelcome into their domain.

In the distance, granite monoliths rose above the jungle like islands of stone in a sea of greens and yellows. Black and gray smoke rose languidly as if from seething pots hidden within the peaks and chutes. In the lower levels, steam layered in sickly yellow sheets, hung heavy on the horizon before misting and thinning on the air.

Jonas looked back at his screen, confirming his hunch, before sharing it with the group. "Gravity's gonna be slightly higher than Earth's. Say point 05."

Skipp came over to look at the readout for himself. "What's that mean in standard?"

"Means you're gonna weigh slightly more than you're used to." Jonas leaned back so the younger man could get closer to the screen.

"Here we go." Jay flew a crossing pattern over the jungle, looking for a suitable landing. The jungle did not cooperate. The canopy, too thick for penetration, offered no point of entry for getting the ship beneath its cover. Landing there was out of the question.

"How do you feel about walking?" Jay asked over his shoulder. Met by quizzical glances, he explained the problem posed by the forest. Minutes later, he directed the ship out across the desert's aureate and russet hued sands.

Sighting a small outcropping of rock about two hundred meters from the jungle's edge, Jay brought the Quest in for a landing. As the ship nosed over the lip of the large flat surface of the rock formation, a cloud of dust swirled up nine meters, casting pebbles and fist sized rocks into the air. The ship's engine exhaust blasted the stone face, pitting deep crevices in the crystalline surface. Dancing eddies of rock, dirt, and newly formed glass, created by the intense heat from the Quest's hovering engines, contrived together to create a mystical cloud on the otherwise barren platform. The stone protested, mini fractures spreading like webs from beneath the feet of the ship's landing pads as the Quest settled.

The ship creaked and moaned as the struts positioned themselves, readjusting to the effect of being planet-side and the direct impact of the gravity field. "Hey, if anybody saw that entry they'll be out looking for us now. I don't like much sitting out here in the open," Skipp said, looking up from his station.

"Can you hide us?" Mike asked.

Jay smiled. "Yeah, I can do it, but it's gonna be tricky."

"What?" Skipp came to stand behind the large pilot. "What are you planning? I don't like that smile, at all."

"I'm gonna bury my baby."

After unloading the needed equipment, the men stood on the edge of the jungle watching Jay work.

Using the automatic piloting control, via his wrist-com, Jay brought the ship's systems online. The vertical-thrust engines screamed to life and the Quest rose slowly off the rock ledge. Jay's brow furrowed with concentration, his lips moving in silent verse as he spoke, willing the ship to obey him.

"Shields," Jay ordered. A shimmering wave, like a heat mirage, rippled over the surface and enclosed the ship. Jay moved her out over the sand roughly fifty meters from the edge of the sands. Nosing the ship down, he held her at precisely a 30-degree angle. Warily, he increased the thrust to the main engines while decreasing the hovering thrust at the bow of the ship. The Quest began a slow power dive. Moving ever so slowly, she appeared to burrow her way beneath the dusty yellow sand.

As the ship disappeared from view, the men all cheered and clapped Jay on the shoulder. "Ain't done yet," Jay said, not taking his eyes from the bubbling surface of the desert floor. "Gotta reset the escape angle just in case we got to get outta 'ere in a hurry. Know what I mean?"

Once satisfied with the depth and egress trajectory, double-checking the scans of the ship's systems for possible leaks in the seals, Jay killed the power to the Quest's engines.

The roar of the engines fell away like the sound of a thunderclap far off in the distance. An airy silence reclaimed the desert as a constant, but soft wind swept smooth where the ship lay buried beneath the sands. The dust settled, and as the breeze died away, all traces of the Quest simply ceased to exist.

The men turned toward the jungle, peering into its emerald and black depths. Skipp said, "I'm getting a faint energy pulse coming in from just north of here." He eyed his scanner pad screen curiously. "Looks like it couldn't be more than an hour's hike into the jungle." He looked off in thought and confirmed his readings. "Yep, straight toward that mountain," he said, pointing to a high peak off in the distance.

Hours later, the men were soaked from river crossings and footsore. The lack of acclimation, to the heavier than Earth's normal gravity, was finally taking its toll, forcing them to stop.

Jay cleared his throat, and after getting Mike's attention, he smirked. His voice slow with fatigue, Jay said, "Hey, Skipp, was that an hour Earth time," he panted, "or local? 'Cause we've been out here for a while, mon, and I ain't seen nothing but jungle and swamp." He paused long enough to smile and catch the expression on Skipp's face. "Now, tell me if I'm missing something or not?" Then he added with a laugh, "Jungle and swamp."

Jonas answered in Skipp's defense, "We had no way of knowing the jungle would be this dense. It's not like we've been here before, you know." His voice betraying fatigue as well.

Mike didn't mind the guys razzing each other. It kept their minds off just how tired they really were and that helped the morale. Mike also noticed that Skipp had been unusually quiet for some time now, and to him, that was like a five bell alarm.

"Skipp," he called out.

"Huh?" returned the somewhat distracted response. "What was that, Mike?"

"I was just about to ask you the same thing. I couldn't help but notice"—he paused—"you look kind of preoccupied. What's on your mind, kid?"

"Oh, nothing really. It's just that since we started into the jungle, I've been kind of keeping track of our location, using the ship as a point of reference. You know, like the ancient sailors using the North Star. Well, only in this case it would appear that the North Star keeps changing its location. Either the ship has been moved or none of our electronics are working well enough to guide a disc across an empty room."

Coming to think of the Quest as his own, Jay didn't like at all the idea that someone, or something, could be messing with his ship. It made him very, very uncomfortable. "Are you sure the ship's been moved? Maybe it's just that fancy notepad of yours short circuiting or something," he said hurriedly, his accent thickening along with his stress.

"That's just it," Skipp said frustrated, "I'm not sure. The readings keep changing. Look at this," he said holding up his notepad so that Jay could see it.

Just as he turned to allow Jay a better view of the screen, a roar tore through the silence as a huge unidentified something knocked Skipp off his feet. The notepad clattered to the moss and dirt-covered ground stopping a few feet from him. All Skipp knew was that it was huge, moving fast and, judging from the impact, very strong.

Skipp landed on the ground with a thud. Looking up, he saw what looked to him like a gorilla, but with a leathery hide and protruding canines. The beast, on its hind, stood a full three meters tall with large muscled arms and barrel chested. As it moved, its muscles seemed to glide beneath taut skin, veins appeared gorged and swollen, and iridescent patches reflecting mottled light.

From the creature's jaws, protruded four three-inch canines, easily seen as it howled and roared. A dark purple and green drool dripped from its bared fangs. Skipp looked up into the animal's angry face and judged it to be a carnivore or at least omnivorous, a thought which brought him no peace.

Drooling, the beast began to roll Skipp's limp body into the jungle, backing away from the screaming group of men, challenging them for the rights to its quarry.

As the strange beast looked hungrily at Skipp and backed further away from the men, Skipp began to regain his senses and screamed to distract it.

The animal looked down and raised doubled fists preparing to strike Skipp. At its feet curled onto his side, Skipp cowered, lifting his arms to protect his head.

Taking advantage of the distraction, Jay yelled and launched himself at the animal's gut. The beast roared and lashed out with a violent backhand, just missing Jay's head as he ducked beneath the animal's attack, catching it full in the stomach with his shoulder.

This startled the creature, though it didn't appear hurt. The beast stared at Jay as he bounced off its torso, then crouched. The animal seemed confused by Jay's action, that something it obviously considered food would attack it, rather than running away. The animal pounded the ground with fists and claws, roared and leaned toward Jay, answering the challenge. It launched itself at Jay, mouth agape and claws extended.

Surprised by its speed and agility, Jay couldn't move quickly enough to escape the violence of the attack. He stood crouched, waiting, frozen in his stance. The animal landed on top of Jay, its fangs bared and its roar deafening. One large claw, covering Jay's chest like a vice, pinned him to the ground, the other raised, claws unsheathed. Bellowing its triumph, it prepared to deliver the killing blow.

The smell of ozone and burning flesh filled the small clearing as the heavy silence overcame the woods. A hole the size of a small ball opened in the animal's chest. The eyes went vacant and arms slackened and dropped heavy to the ground. It collapsed, trapping Jay beneath its bulk.

Jay strained to free himself. "Can you get this thing off of me!"

Mike and Jonas lowered their laser pistols; the double blast had torn through the animal's chest, cauterizing a cavity through it as it burned through. The beast was dead before it fell.

Mike ran over to where Jay lay straining. "You do a fool thing like that again and I'll shoot you instead of the—of the, whatever this thing is. You understand me, mister?"

"Understood, Skipper. Now, can you get it off me?" Jay said, sucking in precious breath through clenched teeth and bruised ribs.

"You gonna be okay?" Mike asked, pulling Jay to his feet and turning his attention to Skipp who had rejoined the group with Jonas's help.

Skipp nodded.

"Good thing you can walk. We better get out of here, and soon by my guess," Jonas said. "This one's a female and I'm assuming it has a mate of some sort nearby. And sooner or later he's gonna come looking for his lady friend. Get my meaning?"

"Wow!" Skipp breathed. "If this is a female, I don't want to be anywhere near here when the male comes looking for her. Sticking to the norm, I mean, the male could be twice as big." Then adding as an afterthought, he said, "And more aggressive."

"Skipp," Jay broke in, "shut up and let's get out of here."

The men laughed like tired and haggard soldiers, and then hurried away from the place where the fallen beast lay dead.

The jungle grew thicker and thicker the further they traveled and still they found no trace of anything capable of either sending the energy pulse that Jonas had detected, or the power fluctuations Skipp was now reading on his pad.

"So far," Mike said frustrated, "instead of answers, all this planet's offered is questions and more questions."

As the sun began to set, the men prepared to spend their first night in the jungle. After the experience earlier, they didn't feel any better about sleeping on the ground than they did about sleeping in the trees. But in the end, caution won out over indifference, and they climbed a tree to bed down for the night. The trees here grew tall and wide; the enormous branches provided ample space for a campsite.

Mike surveyed the surroundings. "Jay, get a line on that lowest branch. We'll set up a hoist and get our camp off the ground for tonight."

"A step ahead of you, boss." The twang of the rope snapped and echoed through the woods as Jay fired an anchoring bolt up into the tree, setting the hook in the massive trunk above one of the mammoth branches. Though climbing was difficult, balancing their supplies on makeshift lifts, the electric harness made the ascent quick work, and soon the camp was set.

Although no one said so, the men were glad the trunk provided enough space for them all to camp on the same level. Having everyone close by made them feel better about sleeping in this strange world.

Muttering more to himself than to the others, Skipp said, "Maybe I'm just being overly sensitive, but just for safety sake, I'm gonna rig a perimeter alarm." Using the energy cells of the crew's wrist-coms and battery packs from the hoist, Skipp set up an energy wave fence.

Jay looked over his shoulder. "So how does this thing work?"

"Well, it's not very complicated really. The wrist-coms are set to the same low energy frequency. If anything comes between one or the other of them, the frequency will be broken and create a feedback and—"

A loud screeching pierced the quiet of the jungle, startling the men, causing them to cover their ears as they grabbed their side arms and scanned for intruders.

"Whoa, gentlemen, that's just the alarm," Skipp said, resetting the wrist-com nearest him.

As humidity settled over the men, the small heating coil provided a ring of soft light against the encroaching darkness. Light faded to darkness, and the men found themselves serenaded by a wide array of night songs, unfamiliar and beautiful noises, all of which served to remind them of the intense alienness of this strange world. When night settled, fatigue overtook them and they succumbed to sleep.

As the sun crested the curve of the planet, the men awoke to find themselves surrounded by a brood of small furry and inquisitive creatures. About the size of a small bunny, the animals' eyes were large, round, and seem to look everywhere at once. Each had a unique hair pattern on their faces that, combined with their larger than normal eyes, gave them the appearance of constantly smiling. Clad in the varied colors of the jungle, the creatures showed no fear of the men.

What struck the crew most acutely was the soft giggling sound the animals made as they rummaged through the men's gear. They appeared harmless, but were insatiably curious, as was tokened by the fact that they had sampled the supply of provisions the men brought with them. Most of those supplies, picked over and half eaten, now lay strewn about on the jungle floor beneath them.

"So much for your alarm system," Mike said trying not to laugh. "Those critters, whatever they are, have made a mess of everything."

"Now wait a minute," Skipp started in his own defense, "you can't blame me for this. I told you last night that the fluctuations were wreaking havoc with the electronics."

The guys all looked at Skipp without the slightest hint of sympathy, gracing their unshaven faces. All they could see was their food, picked over by these eccentric visitors of the night, was almost all gone. Not to mention all the gear that would have to be re-packed. In spite of giving Skipp a hard time, they all helped clean up. Most weird was that Jay didn't give Skipp too hard of a time during the entire process.

Once the gear had been gathered and some simulacrum of a breakfast eaten, the men determined that the situation wasn't quite as bad as they'd thought. With a look toward the mountain, the journey through this mysterious jungle resumed.

Chapter Nine

The sun continued its climb toward its zenith, casting greenish shadows beneath the emerald canopy. Soft, spongy ground interlaced with vines and crisscrossed with animal paths led to and from various breaks in the trees. Above the men, the chattering laughter of the Look-looks, so tagged by Jay due to the animals' large eyes, accompanied them, hidden behind the thick foliage. Every once in a while a large brightly colored bird would swoop out of the branches, snapping at insects, only to be captured by a larger animal and taken as prey.

"Harsh world," Mike muttered.

Skipp wiped his face and tossed his head, throwing his ponytail back across his shoulder. "Yeah, kill or—"

"Get eaten," Jonas finished for him. "I know Skipp has been monitoring the scans, but have any of you taken particular noticed how dense the jungle has been?"

"Yeah, what about it?" Jay said between hacking at a series of vines hanging across their path.

From behind him, Jonas inhaled, filling his lungs and allowing the air out between pursed lips. "It's the CO^2 levels; they are about twice that of Earth."

"And..." Jay left the sentence unfinished.

Jonas wiped sweat from his brow. "CO^2, Carbon dioxide naturally occurs. It's a gas registering at ah...about a concentration of 0.078 percent by volume," Jonas said as if that explained everything.

When the older man didn't continue, Jay stopped and turned to face him. "So professor, what does that mean to me?"

"It means that you can expect the dense growth to continue. With the CO^2 levels being so high, the greenhouse effect on this planet is off the scale. I would guess almost anything could grow in this climate."

Silence reclaimed the group and they continued their trek. Soon afterwards, the men came to a granite wall with a small clear stream flowing near its base. In stark contrast to the heat and humidity of the jungle, the water was ice-cold and refreshing. Swarms of insects dogged the men as they walked, attracted by the salts and sugars in their sweat. Daring birds darted in, enjoying a feast on the flying pest, assisting the men in their fight against the biting bugs and flies.

The stone ridge extended several hundred meters straight up and for many kilometers to either side, bringing their immediate progress to a halt.

"Jay, what's the range of that harness of yours?" Mike asked, stepping back and looking up at the precipice.

"Twenty-three meters, max. Cut that to eighteen to nineteen-five, if you're counting on penetrating that rock face," Jay answered, dropping his pack and starting to unload his gear.

Kneeling to take a drink from the stream, Jonas splashed its cool wetness over his face, allowing it to run down his back, soaking his shirt as he did and plastering his salt and pepper hair against his skull. Catching a quick breath, Jonas dunked his head beneath the frigid surface, cooling his entire body instantly. Coming up for air and wiping water from his face, he saw a shadow at the base of the wall. Sputtering, he pointed. "Hey, what's that?"

"What?" Mike said turning to him.

Jonas lowered his face toward the surface of the water again. "It looks like a cave...just at the waterline—"

"Hey," Jay interrupted, not sure if Mike intended to attack the cliff or explore the opening.

"The problem is," Mike said, continuing his survey of the rock face, "we don't want to be stuck out in the open climbing that thing." He nodded toward the rock face. "Who knows who can be watching us?"

Skipp looked up from his scanner. "Wait. I don't think we're going to have to climb that at all."

"Yeah, and why's that?" Mike asked, frustrated at being stuck. He looked at Skipp, and swatted a fly that had landed on his neck.

"It seems to me that going through the door would be a heck of a lot easier than climbing over the roof," Skipp said pointing his scanner toward the opening.

The opening at the base of the rock on the far bank was more of a hole than a door and stood only about 1.2 meters tall and half again as wide. The entrance lay covered over by a piece of deadfall that, over time, had molded and come to share the same brownish gray tones as the cliff itself.

Wading out into the water, Jay lowered his 1.9-meter frame into the passage. "There's a path leading down from the rock face, running parallel to the stream." Jay scooted back until he had worked back out of the opening. Turning and resting his back against the wall, he looked up at his team. "The path continues going slightly down. I could only see so far. No light—deep, deep dark."

After hiding the bulk of their gear, the men decided to explore this new mystery. Since the morning visitors, the cave had been the only thing of interest they had encountered since the day before.

"I'll check it out and see if it's safe." Mike started lowering himself to the mouth of the cave.

"Ay, mon, I don't think you should be going first, let me," Jay said to Mike, catching him by his shoulder.

Mike ripped his shoulder from the big man's grasp. "What the—" Mike stopped, turning away from Jay. "Get your hands off me." Mike knew his behavior was out of line, but the idea of getting Ted Waters made him anxious and irrational, he reasoned.

"Think, mon. You're the team leader. It's because of you we're out here. We can't have you going in there first. What if something happens?" Jay met his gaze.

"That's right! What if something happens, and I'm sitting up here nice and safe. Again, look, I wasn't home when they went after my family, and I'll be—" Mike swore and stepped toward his friend, then swallowed the rest of his thought. "I...if I'm staying topside while one of you takes the risk with me safe behind!" Mike had screamed the words at Jay. By now, he was standing face to face with the larger man, tensions in both men escalating.

Jay took a deep breath, stilled himself, and stepped back.

Jonas inserted himself in the conflict. "I don't see it, Mike," he said calmly. "The way I figure, God spared you from the bomb. He must have a reason for you coming here. Don't throw that away by being stupid. One of us should go first," he said. "This mission needs you."

Stomping toward Jonas, Mike exploded, "If God did this to me, then both you and God can—" He stopped, taking a deep breath. Then almost spitting the words at Jonas, he continued, "Mary believed in God and look what it got her. It got her killed—her and my children. No thank you, Jonas. You can have all the God and Jesus you want. I'll take my chances with my mind and a full blaster pack." With that, he turned and stormed toward the cave opening.

Stepping out into the water, Mike slid through the opening on his stomach. Inside, on the smooth stone path, Mike stood to his feet holding a hand-lamp above his head, awed by the shear immensity of the cavern.

Fresh air flowed freely through the cavern, and the path was well worn, as if used often. Mounted in the wall were torch racks as well as the remains of simple thatch torches that still smelled strongly of pitch. Being the team leader, he thought to himself, it had been his right to go first. No, it had been his duty. "I will apologize, but not for what I said," he said to himself.

Standing in the quiet coolness, Mike felt bad for how he had spoken. He knew both men would—had put their lives on the line for him. He decided he would apologize to all of them when he went back out.

Back outside, Jonas laid a hand on Jay's shoulder. "Let him go, Jay. You won't change his mind, not now."

Jay grunted something unintelligible and turned away.

"He feels responsible. It's the whole honor thing. I'm not sure how it all ties in, but it's the same reason he left The Company in the first place. Mike felt responsible for those settlers dying, and now with Mary and the kids, he couldn't take it if anything happened to one of us while he stood by watching."

Jay turned looking after Mike, exhaling sharply. He let his shoulders relax, but all he said was, "Yeah," as he walked past Skipp who stood quietly at the opening of the cave, looking behind Mike.

At that moment, Mike called out, "Hey, this place is huge. Get the gear and come on in. The path leads further into the mountain, and it looks well used."

As the other men prepared to join Mike, the ground suddenly began to sway. First gently, and then with each passing moment it grew in intensity. Large portions of the rock face snapped with ear splitting blasts and began to splinter and break away, crashing violently to the ground sending the men scrambling away for safety. With a thunderous roar of utter power, the rock face gave way and crumbled like a waterfall of rock and stone.

Where the opening to the cave had been moments before, now lay a heap of boulders, stone, and dirt, six to eight meters thick. Dust hung heavily, choking the air as small stones and even smaller pebbles continued falling, seeking the lowest point.

As soon as the shaking stopped and the dust cleared enough to see, Jay threw himself on the pile and began digging furiously at the small mountain of debris blocking the mouth of the cave. He had been digging for almost thirty seconds before he allowed himself to be pulled away by Skipp.

Sinking to his knees, Jay looked at his bloodied fingers, now bruised and cut, as if embarrassed by their inability to perform the task he had demanded of them.

Skipp spoke first, his voice weak in the heavy fog like silence. "There's nothing we can do for him now. No way could he live through that." He paused not sure what to do with the strange empty silence. "We should make our way back to the ship—to re-group."

Jay sat, unmoving, leaning on the small mountain of rock and dirt covering the mouth of the cave. He didn't speak, but stared at the pile of cold stone.

Jonas cleared his throat. "What now?" His voice sounded small in the silence.

No one spoke.

Jonas met the gazes of both Skipp and Jay. "We can't quit. Not now, after all we've come through. After Mary—the kids—and now...now Mike. Don't you see? We can't let Waters get away with this?"

Neither man answered.

Jay stood and turned to face the two men. "Well?"

Skipp tried to answer. "I just thought...I just was thinking that—"

"No," Jay said, his voice soft, but menacing. "You weren't thinking; you were talking. But you weren't thinking. 'Cause if that was what you call thinking then you're just confused about why we came out here in the first place."

Jay walked over and looked down on Skipp. He draped a hand on the smaller man's shoulder. "Tell me what ya feel, buddy. Right now, what's ya gut telling ya to do?"

Jay's voice was soft and strained, and his breath slow and raspy. This was as sober as either Skipp or Jonas had ever seen him. A man afire, devoted to a single idea. Skipp and Jonas looked between each other and nodded. They both knew there was only one way Jay would leave this planet without the answers for which he had come. Dead.

Without speaking, Jay grabbed his pack, turned and walked away. "Where you going?" Skipp called after him.

His answer wasn't complicated. "Inside."

Chapter Ten

Albert was confused, but he knew better than to argue with his current situation. Something had changed. This woman, who had earlier threatened to throw him out of her window, was now talking about how she might care for him.

He wasn't sure about her, but he could tell already that it would be easy for him to grow to like her. In this brief time, Iona had already proven more motherly than anyone else in the two years since his mother's death. He smiled at her, and she smiled back; a funny awkward smile, like she wasn't used to smiling in that way.

Iona had tried to explain to Albert that when she took the time to look at him, to see him, she just couldn't let anything bad happen to him. She had said she wasn't sure if she felt love for him, but something inside her told her it was a good thing she was doing.

"Now we need to get you out of here." Iona tousled the boy's hair. Looking around her office, she counted her options and slowly a smile pulled up at the corners of her lips.

A half hour later, Iona stood on the underground loading dock of The Company's main building. The huge garbage scow hovered above the oil-stained surface of the garage floor as the odor of diesel and other fuels hung heavy in the air. She waited with strained patience as the constant beeping accompanied the backing of the robotic ship. After a few minutes that seemed to take forever, the scow finally pulled out, leaving her alone in the garbage bay.

Iona ran quickly to the door of the garbage chute. Opening it and holding her breath, she ducked her head inside. There, still sitting on the bench used for lowering garbage from the upper floors, sat Albert.

"Wow, that was cool, can I do it again!" Albert's eyes were bright with excitement and the thrill of the ride.

Taking the child by his hand, she sighed. "Maybe some other time." She looked around. "Let's get out of here."

They were out of the building and in her private shuttle, driving, but without a defined destination. She couldn't go to her apartment, knowing it would be bugged. *Funny, how knowing my apartment was bugged never bothered me before.*

Time passed and Iona was suddenly aware she had stopped driving, noticing a vaguely familiar landscape.

"What happened here?" Albert said in an astonished voice. "It looks like a warzone."

Iona continued looking, forcing her brain to focus on the still smoking crater, barely visible in the predawn light.

Whether he serves this institution better by his continued life or his death, is still to be determined. Waters's words shouted in her memory.

And with a sickening clarity, she recognized what was left of the Stone family's home. Looking into the hole, unshed tears brimmed in her jade colored eyes. Seeing the child sitting wide-eyed beside her, she was overcome by a sudden wave of guilt and shame. Thankful for the early morning darkness, Iona managed to hide the tears that finally streaked down her face.

Albert, however, awed by the chaotic scene, was paying little attention to her. Instead, commenting on every detail of the carnage he could make out despite the dusky gray light of early morning. "What we gonna do now?" he asked in childish innocence.

"Well, little man, there's only one place I can think to go. I haven't been there in years, but maybe she'll still let me—I mean I don't think she'll turn us away."

"Is it your mama?"

"Not quite."

Mary rubbed weary eyes as she stood, unknotting cramped legs and a tired back. Laughing to herself, she remembered when driving all night used to be considered fun. Looking at her children still sleeping in the family transport, she sighed and turned her face to absorb the warmth of the rising sun.

Magenta streaks effervesced against wisps of gold and pink, like clashing titans battling for the honor of escorting the sun from his nighttime chamber. The colors played off Mary's face, revealing soft freckles and bringing out the rose-hinted highlights hidden in her long blond hair. Far below the lip of the cliff, the sounds of the surf crashing against the rocks rose like whispers against her ear.

Taking the pilfered Bible, Mary sat with her back against the grill of the transport. Opening the book, she looked up. "Okay, God, it's time You and me had a talk." She looked back inside the transport to make sure her children were still sleeping.

Finding her way to the book called Psalms, Mary allowed her fingers to play over its pages as if she could feel the energy from the life-giving promises the book offered. She allowed her mind to wander back to a time when, as a little girl, she had found herself afraid or frightened, and her grandmother, Viola, would recite passages from the Psalms to calm her. Racking her mind, she tried to remember the one her grandmother quoted most often. Something about lights and lamps at night.

Flipping through the pages, she found herself in chapter 119, the longest chapter in the Bible. Coming to verse 119:105, she read, "Thy word is a lamp unto my feet, and a light unto my path." She closed the book. "I could use that light right about now, Lord..." she said with a sigh.

Feelings of being overwhelmed threatened to wash over her. "Oh, Jesus," was all she could manage. And for long seconds, no sound save her crying, disturbed the early morning silence.

When she found her voice again, she prayed for Mike, asking for his protection and that he, too, would have that special light shared with him. She looked out over the varied colors of the ocean, set ablaze by the burgeoning sunrise. Feeling drawn to its majesty, she walked toward the ocean and sat on the side of the road.

"Does he even know we're still alive?" Mary asked toward the sky. "Oh, God...oh, God, why? Why us, Lord?" She covered her face with her hands. "I can't do this. Jesus, it's too much. It's too much." Silence overcame her.

I am with you.

Startled, Mary looked up. Brushing tears away, she wasn't sure if she actually heard the voice or if it had been inside her head, but she accepted it as real and held it as a promise nonetheless.

Turning her back to the water and looking back over the valley that stretched out behind her, she had the sudden desire to go home. Not back to the bombed out remnants of the pre-fab in the community park, but to Nonna's house. Full of resolve, she stood quickly, dusting sand pebbles from her trousers and smiling to herself. She hurried back to the transport.

M2 stirred as his mother sealed the hatch behind her. "Where are we, Mom? Are we home yet?" he said sleepily.

"Almost, baby, almost."

Paul Adams knew he was in trouble. He had dealt with Iona enough times to know she wasn't a woman of idle threats. So when he retrieved his messages, and found out that Iona said she had the child destroyed, he was frustrated but not surprised.

Iona had said she had the boy thrown into the incinerator. Although cruel, he had judged it not outside of her capabilities. After all, he reasoned within himself, he would have done the same thing. Besides, it was a better end than the one he had planned for the child. He found himself wondering if he could somehow use the loss of the boy to talk Iona into having dinner with him. He didn't think he had any real chance of her saying yes, but he reasoned, what did he have to lose except maybe his pride. Also, he thought, walking on his pride had become a way of life for him a long time ago. He smiled and called Iona on the computer link. He tried to compose himself as the screen finally came to life.

"Iona, darling," he said, trying to be as casual as possible. "You do know how much extra work you've caused me? Getting that kid took a great deal of effort."

Iona's green eyes glowed with cold fire as her gaze bore into him from the computer screen. "Ask me if I care," she answered in her usual cold manner. "I told you before you left your problem in my office that I didn't want your extra baggage." She looked back to a notepad in her hand and then back to the screen. "I've got problems of my own." She reached as if to terminate the call.

"Wait, wait," Paul said hurriedly. "You know Waters. I had to take care of something that the boss...well, that couldn't wait." When she didn't interrupt, he continued. "At least you can have dinner with me to make up for the extra work you cost me. I had to talk to the headmaster at that school for over an hour to convince him to let me have another kid, and..."

Paul was still talking, but Iona hadn't heard him past the phrase "another kid." The heat in her eyes intensified. She sat back, watched him, and imagined the pleasure it would give her to kill him.

Never having noticed Iona's change of expression, Paul continued his monologue. "...No matter how you look at it, you hurt my project, which means, you hurt The Company's business. Now what do you think Ted is going to say about that?"

"He's gonna call you the fool that you are. Then he'll probably demote you after ripping out your throat for wasting company resources."

Paul stopped talking and stared at the screen.

Iona continued, "Okay, I haven't eaten yet. She looked at her chronometer. "Let's say, in an hour at the Up Towner. I'll meet you in the lobby."

"That'll be great, but it would be no trouble for me to pick you up. Let's say I—"

The screen suddenly went blank. Paul sat for a long moment staring at the darkened screen. Slowly, the realization that Iona had hung up on him settled in. Satisfied, he smiled anyway.

Across town in her apartment Iona finished cleaning, removing any trace that Albert had been with her. Thinking about her upcoming dinner with Paul, she began to plan. Iona reasoned that the best way to get the information she wanted about Paul's dealings with Waters, and just what that had to do with Albert, was to get Paul simply to talk about himself. She also knew that time and just the right amount of distraction was all it would take to make that happen.

The restaurant stood in the center of midtown. Its dining room on the 109th floor rotated a full 360 degrees, offering the full panorama of the city. One floor up on the roof, laser lights and holographic images pulsated, along with dancers driven by the sometime subtle and sometime manic bass rhythms. Known as star dancing, the holographic dancers and lasers interacted with the partier's by reading their biorhythms and generating pulse energy through sound and light waves.

Combined with the rhythmic beat of the drums and lights designed to engage and alter the brain's alpha waves, the dance floor produced the euphoric state of mind that was very in vogue with the up and in crowd. It was in this crowd that Paul Adams was most at home.

Over dinner, Paul was charming. Iona could see why some women found him attractive. He obviously kept himself fit and synthetically altered, including a dermal pigment-shifted tan and surgically perfected teeth. The way he always looked directly into her eyes when he spoke to her, he could have made her feel like she was the only person in the room. His conversation was seasoned just right with compliments: not so much as to seem insincere, and not so few that it seemed he had to remind himself that she was there.

No doubt, Iona thought, as she smiled demurely, he was a real charmer and used to having his way with his women. Unfortunately, for him, she was not one of his to play with; she knew what lay beneath that thin skin, flashing eyes, and flickering tongue. She also knew that it would be hers and not Paul's will imposed tonight.

As she knew it would, the conversation turned to work and Paul bragging about himself. "So how's the Stone case coming? I'd be glad to work with you if you need a hand," Paul said, reaching across the table and brushing the backs of her knuckles.

She let him hold her hand and leaned forward watching as his eyes found the neckline of her low cut top. She had picked this particular top with him in mind; the tight fitting thin material clung to her womanly figure, leaving little to the imagination. As she leaned toward him, Paul's gaze traveled to the V of her neckline and stopped.

"I don't know. It's so hard sometimes getting the crews to remember that I'm more than just another woman. I have to be twice as hard on them as the average male super." Suddenly, Iona withdrew her hand and sat back, fixing a slight pout on her face and looking frustrated.

Paul stood and walked to Iona's side of the table and pulling the empty chair closer to her, he sat. Taking a moment, he looked over her again. He noticed the ankle length black skirt and the span of tan leg extended through the thigh level split.

She seemed not to notice his taking inventory of her, so Paul continued and chanced laying his hand on her upper thigh. Iona breathed slowly and turned to look at him. "It's so hard being a woman and being a supervisor sometimes. Unless you're being an absolute monster, nobody pays any attention to you. Sometimes I just want to be a woman. Not—well, you know as well as I do what they call me."

Paul scooted his chair closer now so that he straddled Iona's seat between his knees. "I know what you mean," he whispered.

Iona leaned toward him as if to kiss him, brushing his cheek with hers. She whispered into his ear, "Dance with me."

Moments later on the dance floor, the two moved flawlessly to the entrancing music. Holding her close and whispering in her ear, Paul asked, "Stone case getting to you?"

"It's not so much that..." she said, resting her head against his broad chest, "there's this new situation I've been hearing about, something to do with kids, and Waters hasn't let me in on it. I'm beginning to think he's cutting me out."

"New situation?" he asked stiffly.

Iona could feel him tense slightly and hugged herself to him tighter, rubbing his shoulders and back as if her mind were a thousand miles away. "I just don't like being left out. I've given too much to this company—to Waters." She pushed away from him and looked up, meeting his eyes. "You understand what I'm saying, what I'm offering?"

"I think so, but I'm not sure."

Pulling away from him, she turned and walked away, speaking over her shoulder, as the crowd of dancers collapsed into the increasing gap opening between them. "I thought so. Just as I thought this evening would be a waste of my time."

"Wait," Paul called after her. "It's not like we can talk here," he said gesturing with his arms, indicating the crowd.

She stopped, but did not look back, allowing Paul to catch up to her.

Slipping his arm around her waist, he said softly, "Let's get out of here."

Iona allowed herself to be pulled close to him. Away from the flashing lights of the dance floor into the white light near the exit, Iona could now see a slight yellowing of Paul's eyes. Surprised that she hadn't noticed it before, she cursed to herself. But unless she'd missed her guess, surgically enhanced teeth and skin were not the only chemical accessories Paul had in his system.

As they left the restaurant, Iona became angry for not having seen the signs earlier. Paul was good at what he did and just a bit too exact, hyper, and uniquely vigilant. What was plain now was that Paul Adams was a user of jiyst, maybe an addict.

The drug stimulated the mind's creative region, while simultaneously increasing awareness and stamina to the exclusion of everything else. Now with his mind intensely focused by the drug's effect, Paul's full attention was on Iona.

The downside of long-term exposure to the drug was that it often resulted in damage to the cerebellum, resulting in a debilitating disease known as Wernicke-Broca Syndrome. The disease resulted in a condition where the sufferer lost his ability to understand and use language, virtually trapping him inside a world of meaningless sounds yet bound in silence. Eventually, all higher cognition ceases and the user is reduced to a vegetative state.

Paul brought the transport to a soft landing on the shore of the lake. The city lights made a fantastic backdrop against the blue-blackness of night. Lights of many different colors, themed designs, and intensity brightened the horizon and reflected on the glassy surface of the water.

A steady breeze brought the fragrance of fruit trees and other flowering shrubs, sweetening the nighttime air. In the midst of this, Iona watched as Paul broke a vial of the shimmering purple dust that was jiyst.

After offering Iona a hit off the vial, Paul snorted all of the contents and settled back to allow the drug to take full effect.

Iona knew she could be in trouble. Users of jiyst were known for sudden violent sexual behaviors, a fact that served to drive its use in an industry known for its impassioned violence.

Paul made his way around the transport and grabbed Iona by her shoulders, pulling her top off her shoulder, exposing the bare skin; the iridescent body spray sparkled in the soft reflected light from the city. He leaned down to kiss her exposed shoulder.

"Paul," she began softly, "tell me why you needed the boy. Are there more like him?"

"Yes," he murmured, continuing his advances.

"But…but what does Waters want with them?" She leaned into him, snuggling into his kisses, pretending to enjoy his nearness.

"Yeah, Waters thinks he has it all figured out. He gets me to do all the dirty work, and he keeps his hands—not to mention his name—clean."

Working up her nerve, she kissed him. She pushed away from him, playing coy, buying time for herself before the next touch. "But what does Waters need them for?"

Smiling and obviously influenced by the jiyst, Paul attempted to follow her when a sudden flash of pain stabbed through his head, ending with a burning throbbing behind his eyes. He stumbled. "Hey, no fair," he said, regaining his composure. "Come here." His words starting to slur.

"There will be time for fun later, but tell me about the kids. What is Waters getting out of this?" Iona could feel that time was running out; she could feel her nerves tense as she watched the ragged disintegration of a jiyst overdose beginning its deadly spiral.

With surprising speed, Paul covered the space between them. Catching her, he pulled her close to his body, the smell of the drug rancid in his skin. "I said come here," he said, but it sounded more like 'com-sher'.

"You want to know what the connection is," he continued, regaining control of his speech. Paul reached into his jacket pocket and pulled out another vial of the powder. Holding it up to the light he smiled. "Power."

"Jiyst?" she asked, feigning confusion. As the missing elements began to fall into place, Iona finally understood why Waters needed the *disposable children*, children like Albert.

Snapping the vial between his fingers, Paul held it up to her face. She turned away from the deceptively sweet odor.

"Power, Iona. It's all about power. Whoever controls the flow of jiyst controls the power, and right now, Waters controls the flow. But it was my idea to use the kids. Throwaways. Nobody will miss them, and when they're done, you simply get more." He smiled, tilting back his head and inhaling the contents of the second vial.

Iona could feel his grip tightening on her arm. "You're hurting me," she hissed into his unseeing eyes.

Instead of letting her go, Paul grabbed her with his other hand and stared not so much at her, but rather through her. The sclera of his eyes now yellowed with the effects of the drug. "Moab," he said laughing sardonically. "That wush my idea toooo." The slurring thickened. "Stone never knew whaaa happened." Suddenly he released his grip on her and clutched his head, screaming in pain.

Too stunned to run, Iona stood staring at him; it was her undoing. He grabbed her again, and this time there was no doubt to his intentions. Pulling at her blouse, the material ripped away in his hand exposing her skin to the sudden coolness of the night.

Talking too loud, Paul began to ramble. "That's right, I had your boyfriend defrocked, and now I'm going to have his lady. I'm going to do to you what he never had the guts to do."

Iona figured she had heard enough and planted a crossing back-fist squarely to Paul's temple, dropping him to his knees.

The blow caught him off guard; but with pain receptors dulled by the drug, he was back on his feet before she could create any distance between them.

"This is going to be fun." He lunged for her.

Iona knew she could not survive a match of strength versus strength. Accepting Paul's weight unto herself, she rolled backwards, sending a knee strike crashing into his groin as she did. Behind her, Paul landed hard; she continued her roll and regained her feet, ready for the next assault.

With a cat-like response, Paul recovered and pounced at her, growling wild and unstructured in his attack. This time he swung a sweeping right hook that Iona barely ducked. As he followed up with a jab, she stepped inside the blow and delivered two quick elbow strikes to his face and a palm heel strike to his chin, standing him up straight. Stepping away from Paul, Iona delivered a spinning heel kick that landed solidly in his temple.

Screaming out in pain and rage, Paul dropped to his knees grabbing his head. His words deteriorated into none syllabic gibberish. At the realization of what was happening, he forgot his plans for Iona. Paul stared at her, his rage replaced by fear. Either the second vial or the blows to his head or maybe a combination of it all had pushed him too far. He pleaded with her even as his reasoning failed.

Iona stood over him, and grabbing a handful of his hair, she jerked his head back. Exposing his throat, she drew back her hand preparing to deliver the killing blow.

Paul looked up into her face, but clearly did not see her. Nonsense syllables overflowed his spit-flecked lips in an incessant flow.

She lowered her hand, released his hair, and turned to walk away. As she closed the door to the transport, she could hear him still rambling in the jiyst-induced non-words mixed with cries of fear and desperation. Beside her on the floor, she saw two more vials of the purple powder. Piloting the transport out over the water, Iona ripped open the tops from the cylinders and poured them out, watching as the reflective light sparkled on the powdery midst as it fell innocently onto lapping waves.

Taking Paul's transport back to midtown to where she had left her own, Iona activated the EAN; the electronic aid notification system, directed emergency services to citizens who could not get themselves to the services needed. Once the EAN activated, she directed the transport back to Paul's location.

If he was lucky, she sighed, tucking loose strands of red hair behind her ear, they won't find him. Death was preferable to what passed for life once the drug's damage settled into the Wernicke and Broca areas of the brain.

Chapter Eleven

"Penthouse." Iona's voice sounded distracted and distant to her as she leaned heavily against the lift's interior wall.

"Good morning, Ms. Bowers, and welcome home. Shall I start a bath?" The computer voice intoned from hidden speakers.

"Yes, the usual."

Moments later, Iona walked into her penthouse apartment, greeted by the low soothing sounds of a Latin guitar. The lights were set to thirty percent illumination and a soft fragrance of jungle fauna wafted through the room.

Dropping items of clothing as she walked, Iona was ready as she stepped into her spacious bath. The wall facing the city, transparent from the inside out, offered a spectacular view of the early morning cityscape. Following her, a house-drone, a small robot equipped with arms and various sensors and screens, picked up her soiled clothing and deposited the items in the appropriate bin. The unit also performed small household repairs as needed.

Settling into the foaming bath, Iona allowed her mind to wander back over recent events. Her thoughts took her back over the last few days, to the seemingly random event of Paul's unceremoniously depositing Albert into her office.

Finally, her thoughts settled on the last time she had seen the child, and a mixture of sadness and joy clouded her already overloading mind. Iona knew that if push came to shove, Nonna could at least hide Albert with members of her underground church; it had given her heart a measure of peace.

"But why?" Albert had asked her, unshed tears still in his eyes. "But why can't I just stay with you?" He clung to Iona's hand.

"Because it's not safe. And don't worry, the place you're going is not like that children's home. It's my Nonna's. You'll like Nonna."

Albert had not been convinced, she knew, but she also knew he couldn't stay with her. As she settled him into his seat on the public carrier, her feelings for this young man were starting to overwhelm her. "I'll be there as soon as I can. I promise."

"When will that be?"

Her tears threatening again. "Soon…I promise."

I promise. The words echoed in her mind as she lay in the warm semi-darkness. Knowing that before she could leave, she would have to go back into The Company headquarters to find the information she would need to uncover Waters's part in the drug scam and the misuse of the children. *But how many children?* She had no way of knowing.

Iona forced her thoughts back under control and considered the task: *Figure out what Waters was up to, stop him, and then get back to Albert.* It was a promise she wasn't at all sure she would be able to keep.

Mary brought the transport to a smooth stop in front of the grand old house. The two and a half-story Victorian was ancient even before the last reconstruction movement, only managing to miss being torn down because it was so far off the main road.

The house sat on a small hill overlooking a shallow creek that ran from north to south at the base. With the nearest neighbor over a mile away, the farm provided a quiet and peaceful respite against the harried pace of city life.

A flower garden occupied the front yard of the stately home, sat fully exposed to the evening sun. A small heavyset older woman, with several braids rolled into silver balls, set by a series of old-fashioned bobby pins, was busy weeding and planting. She took to the chore with the comfortable pace of a daily routine.

Hearing the vehicle stop, Viola looked up from her work. Hooding her eyes, she squinted against the morning glare. She brushed rich soil from her hands and then cleaned them on her apron.

Getting out of the transport, Mary waved for the children to follow her. Standing silently, she watched the woman now studying them. "Grandma—Nonna," Mary said feeling more relief and joy than she expected.

"Mary? Is that you, child?" Viola started toward the younger woman, replacing her tools on her handcart. "Mary, oh, thank God it's you. I've been pray'n, child, ever since I saw the news. I knew the Lord would protect you and my babies. I just knew you were all right."

Moving with surprising agility, Viola made her way to Mary. The women fell into each other's arms, amidst tears of joy, and for long moments neither spoke. They stood just holding each other and enjoying the nearness. Mary rested her face against her grandmother, enjoying the familiar fragrance of fresh earth and baked breads.

Behind them, a child's voice broke into their joy. "Mamma?" M2 stood beside the transport, holding Travist's hand. The baby carrier sat on the ground in front of them.

"Oh, my," Viola gasped and, releasing Mary, hurried toward the children.

M2 stepped back involuntarily, surprised by the sudden attention. He looked from the rapidly approaching woman to his mother standing behind her brushing tears from her eyes. Whether of sorrow or joy, he could not tell. With the confusion of the last two days still weighing heavily in his young mind, M2 was not sure how to react to this new development.

Viola stooped, placing a hand in the small of her back and positioned herself on the children's level and hugged them all at once. "You must be Little Mike," she said looking at M2. "And that makes you Travist." Viola turned her face to the younger boy. "And look at this baby girl. Mary, shame on you for not bringing my babies here sooner." Though the rebuke was serious, it was softened by the sheer joy of being together.

"Who are you?" Travist asked, squinting, his youthful face basked in open curiosity.

"I'm your Great-Grandma Viola." She scooped up Sissy in her arms. Slowing as she rose back to her full 1.5 meters, she allowed a kink to unknot itself in her back. Nuzzling the baby's neck, she was rewarded with giggles and laughter.

"Nonna, you shouldn't be lifting that baby. Let me take her," Mary said, reaching for the laughing child.

Suddenly pointing toward the front porch, Travist asked, "Who's that?"

Everyone turned to look in the direction that Travist was pointing. Standing on the front porch and rubbing sleep from his eyes, stood a young child of about nine years of age.

Having enjoyed the special attention and nuzzling, Sissy reached a chubby hand toward Viola's face, inviting the older woman back for more play.

"Oh, that's Albert," Viola said, ushering her brood toward the house. "Iona sent him to stay with me for a while."

"Iona? Is she here? Have you seen her?" Mary demanded, anger and panic threatening.

"No, dear, I told you she sent him to stay with me for a while." Viola turned and looked at Mary. "Mary, what's wrong, child?"

Mary froze, the muscles in her neck alternately flexing and relaxing. Her breaths were short and shallow, her eyes flicking around the property looking for threats against her family. The color drained from her face.

"Come on, child, let's get these children out of this here sun." Viola pulled Mary by her arm and waved toward the sky. "What's troubling you, child?"

As they stepped up onto the broad porch, Albert suddenly stepped forward. "I know you," he said coming up to Mary. "They blew up your house. I saw it. I saw the hole. Iona, the lady that saved me, took me there. I saw your picture on the news-vid, too. I'm sorry about your house."

"Who's your mommy, sweetheart?" Mary asked him, not sure she wanted to hear the answer.

Albert looked down, scuffing the toe of his shoe against the porch rail. "My mamma's dead." He paused and, after a minute, sighed and continued. "The lady that saved me, she's not my mamma, but she acts like a mommy. Her name is Iona. Do you know her?"

Mary felt her knees weakened, and slowly she sank down to the porch. *Lord God, help me. It's not even safe here.*

Viola took Mary's face between her wizened hands and forced the younger woman to look at her. "What is it, baby? I thought you knew."

Leaning back at her desk, Iona terminated the transmission, letting the strength of the chair catch her. Relaxing into the gentle hum of the sonic vibrations, she allowed the burden of the news to sink in. She had a meeting in thirty-minutes with Ted Waters, and she had to be in control; she had to be Iona. Fatigue, both physical and emotional, gnawed at the edges of her control. It had been five days since she had sent Albert to Nonna's. She had to focus for his sake as well as her own.

She paused in a moment of contemplation and stillness. *It felt good to be thinking about someone other than herself, to love someone other than herself.* With that thought, she allowed herself a quick nap as the sonic vibrations emanated from the chair weaving its magic on the knotted muscles in her neck and back.

A quarter-hour later, Iona sat across the table from Ted Waters, her veneer back in place. The three other supervisors sat quietly, heads bowed, studying the folders open on the table before them. Across the table sat an empty chair before a closed folder where Paul Adams should have been sitting. Waters was all business. He always was. With him, nothing mattered but The Company. The Company first. The Company last. Always The Company.

He sat behind his large marble desk and stared straight into Iona eyes. She found herself wondering if he somehow knew what she had done, what she had become, then just as quickly, dismissed the thought from her mind, attributing it to nervousness on her part. She would have to be careful. *You need to keep control.*

As he stood, his black suit seemed to swallow any light that touched it. He moved with the heavy gracefulness of a prowling cat, like a predator that has sighted its prey and would not relent, but instead, would slowly stalk it until the moment of attack.

For the first time, Iona allowed herself to see Ted Waters for what he truly was—evil. The revelation that the man she had admired for so many years was a reservoir devoid of light and decency. The thought slammed against her with physical force. Candor compelled Iona to reckon herself in the same shaft of convicting light. Covering her face with a hand, she rested her elbow on the arm of the chair.

A shiver snaked up her spine, like someone throwing ice-cold water across her back on a hot, dry day. She was both ashamed of what she had become and angry with this man for nurturing that part of her. But even as she did so, she knew she had no one to blame but herself.

Guilty. I'm guilty. She looked away from him, staring out the window, forcibly bringing her thoughts under control.

Having repressed the feelings of sudden repulsion, Iona looked back at Waters. She slipped seamlessly into the familiar patterns. She smiled demurely, just a soft curl of the lip. He was telling her about a plan that he had to bring down the rising religious alliance.

The alliance, the fanatics as he called them, a group of loosely connected rebels that rejected the universal governance and centrality of power, had seriously undercut their authority and challenged the legitimacy of The Company. Iona smiled, thinking how his face would look when he found out that she, too, would be a part of the underground; if not religious at least rebellious, at least she hoped to be.

Unable to control herself, a small giggle slipped past Iona's lips. Turning away, she brushed at her eyes in an attempt to cover her slip. All eyes turned to her.

Suddenly, Ted Waters stopped speaking. Turning the whole of his attention to her, he sat down. "Maybe you would like to let us in on the jokulation that has so distracted you in the midst of my presentation." His tone was dry, his arms spread in a placating gesture. "If I am boring you, please let me know, and I will do my best to make it more interesting for you." With that, he stood quickly, throwing the file of papers he held in his hands striking Iona in her face. She winced, but to her credit, held her ground.

Waters stood, towering over her. "I do not care what you do on your own time, but if having dinner with Paul affects your job performance, then I suggest you skip all such engagements in the future."

She looked up at him surprised. The three supervisors had not so much as moved, but their eyes flickered from Waters to Iona and back to Waters before returning to the pages before them.

"Oh, yes," he continued. "I know about your outing this past weekend. Paul was an idiot, too stupid to know and respect his own limits."

She stared at him. *Did he know?* she wondered.

He was still talking. "The way I see it, we are better off without him, but if his loss is too much for you, I can arrange to have you replaced on this project. I trust I do not have to remind you that I own you and everything you are, and it is my business to know the business of those whom I own."

Iona's mind raced. *Control. Control. Just how much did he already know? Did he know about Albert, about her taking him to Nonna's?*

Waters's back was turned to her now. "You are mine to take or to throw away as I please." He paused to let the severity of his words sink in. Then he walked over to her and gently kissed her on her cheek.

She cringed involuntarily.

He smiled.

He stood over her, gloating, and said in a bitter tone, "Now pick up my papers and get out of my sight."

Iona knelt down and neatly stacked the papers, being careful to place them in numerical order and right side up, and then gave them to Ted Waters. He threw them on the desk and smirked as they fell once again into disorder.

As she walked out, he said softly from behind her, "The next time you come into this office, it had better be for business purposes, or it will be the last time you enter this office. Have I made myself understood?"

Without turning, she simply said, "Yes."

As Iona walked back to her office, she couldn't help but smile. She allowed herself to relax a little. He thinks my lack of concentration was due to my being upset over Paul; I'd gladly of killed the fool myself if he hadn't OD'd first. How absurd. She considered it all again and smiled. For the first time since she had met young Albert, she was beginning to believe that they could really beat The Company. That they could beat Ted Waters, for they were one in the same.

Mike fought to open his eyes, but had to squint against the blinding light and the accompanying pain that stabbed at his brain. He didn't know where he was; all he knew was that he hurt all over.

As the moments passed, he became more and more aware of his surroundings. The bright light turned out not to be the noon sun as he supposed, but the glow of a modest torch mounted on the wall of the cavern. Just ahead of him at the base of the wall and the foot of the path sat a small shelter.

Layers of soot, from torches long ago burned out, discolored the low hanging ceiling. The smallish shelter, not much more than a lean-to made of hide and branches, smelled of sweat and soiled clothing. There were no furnishings to speak of, just a skin of some sort thrown on the floor, which appeared to be covered with any number of small crawling mites and various critters.

The one thing missing were people. There was absolutely nobody around. The place echoed with oppressive silence as ghostly shadows danced wearily on the walls cast by the oily light.

Mike tried to stand up, but the swirling in his head convinced him to go slow. He decided that sitting up would be a better start. After a while, as his world and his senses came back in line, on legs that trembled, he ventured to explore the dark around the shelter. Looking up, he could see from where he had fallen. He was deep inside the mountain. "Jonas. Jay. Skipp..." he yelled, and waited for the echo to die.

He lifted his scratched and bloodied hand, looked at it, and then propped it against his forehead, trying to concentrate. The last thing he remembered was the ground beginning to shake and the ledge beneath him giving way. Mike shook his head as the memory snaked through his mind....

The rumbling, then the ledge jerking upward, flinging him in the air like a child's plaything.

The grinding, snapping, and breaking of granite, sounding like an explosion in the enclosed chamber.

Then falling.

The floor had opened and he had fallen through.

Mike shuddered. He looked up at the collapsed opening where he had entered the cavern. He realized that if the shelf had not broken when it did, dropping him into the darkness, he would have died, crushed by the wall of stone. He sagged against the wall. Tearing a strip from the cloth in the shelter, he wrapped his hand.

Mary and the kid's deaths would have been all for naught. Waters would have won. He inhaled; glad to be alive. For that, at least, he was thankful.

The thought gave Mike pause....

Thankful, to whom?

He shook his head. Now was not the time to debate whether or not there was a God actually worth thanking. Besides, if God were real, wouldn't that make Him responsible for Mary's death? He shook his head again. Now his need was water, and then he needed to find his crew.

"Anybody here? Hey? Anybody!" His voice echoing off the walls of the vast emptiness was his only answer. Mike stilled himself, forcing himself to relax. Turning in a circle, he allowed his eyes to travel over the interior, not focusing on anything in particular. Off to his right in his peripheral vision was a movement—

A shift in the shadows.

A muffled scraping as of rough cloth on stone.

Easing his laser pistol from its holster, he walked cautiously over to where he'd seen the figure cloaked in darkness.

"Come on out. I see you." Mike gestured with his empty hand, while holding the pistol down by his opposite thigh. To his surprise, a little leg slid out from the recess.

The body, to which the leg was attached, stood about 1.4 meters; the rest of the little girl of about five to seven years old followed. Her eyes wide with fear, her lip quivering as she began to cry.

Realizing he had the pistol in his hand, now aimed at the terrified child, Mike quickly put it away. "Ahh…what's your name, sweetheart?" he asked, approaching her slowly so he would not scare her any more than he already had.

She did not speak; she just stared up at him as tears made muddy ruts down her small face.

"Look," he said, "I'm not going to hurt you. I came here to help you and any other children that may still be here."

He smiled at her and knelt down to meet her gaze. Slowly and shyly, she reached up and touched his smile. Then taking her hand, she touched her own mouth. A look of wonder colored her small face. Mike wondered what evil had happened to bring this child to this state.

If there is evil, there must also be good, Michael.

"Not now!" Mike shook his head against the whispered thought. The child withdrew her hand and Mike cursed to himself for his loss of control.

As moments turned into minutes, Mike realized he had been with the little girl for over three hours and still she had not spoken. She watched him closely, however, jumping back if he moved suddenly or spoke too loudly. It was plain to him that the child had suffered some level of trauma. But the question remained, by whom, by what, and why?

Dense jungle gave way to a large clearing. At the bottom of the hill leading away from the forest at its base, a river rushed by in a noisy gurgle. Beyond that, gentle sloping hills reminded Skipp of his home in Southern North America. Though large, the clearing was not natural. Stumps of trees, like broken teeth and ugly gouges, scarred the otherwise pleasant landscape. Slag piles in various stages of burnings dotted here and there, and running through the midst of it was an actual path. The men walked in silence, still dealing, each in his own way, with the loss of Mike.

Skipp saw it first. It hung low and was made of vines intertwined with large and small branches, but definitely constructed by the hand of man. The makeshift bridge was the first real sign that man had ever been on the surface of the planet. They followed the trail that led to the bridge.

Looking beyond it, they could see a small settlement. Jay thought it looked a lot like the tent cities he had seen in old photographs of Earth's refugee camps. But here, the shambles were made of earth and prefab instead of fabric.

It was rather servile, scattered about here and there with the few hutches all facing a center court. Actually, to call the opening a court was to be generous—very generous. It wasn't really much more than a patch of cleared dirt pounded smooth by many feet over time.

Smoke rose slowly from the structure closest to the middle of the camp. Jay signaled Skipp and Jonas, and then pointed to his chest and gestured that he would approach from the left and Skipp from the opposite side. Finally, he directed Jonas to circumvent the camp and approach from the rear. Jay furrowed his brow; almost hoping that whoever was inside would resist and give him a reason to fight. He was itching to make somebody pay for Mike's death.

Jay moved out first, heading straight up the middle with Skipp and Jonas covering the flanks. They advanced slowly as not to rouse the occupants of the hutch. Reaching the door, Jay sidled up to the thatch-covered opening, making eye contact with Jonas and Skipp, then counted to three silently, mouthing the numbers as he did.

Jay screamed. A blood-curdling yowl exploded from deep in his throat as he kicked in the door, splintering it. Before the shards of wood had settled to the floor, he rushed in. Skipp dove through a side window rolling to one side clearing Jay's path. At the same time, Jonas, who had snatched open the back flap, ripping it from where it had been tacked above the door, came in from the rear. They poured into the small hutch in a flurry of shouts and screams with weapons drawn.

Inside, three children sat scared and motionless, frozen by fear. A female, about sixteen years old, a boy of about twelve, and a younger female of about five, hugged each other against this new danger.

The boy spoke first, although obviously scared. He tried to be brave. "D-d-don't hurt them. It-it was my idea," he stammered. "I-I m-made them d-d-do it. We were hungry."

Now the little girl spoke up, her voice sounding small and airy. "Please, mister, don't hurt my brother. I was hungry. We were not 'sp'ose to eat this cycle. I'm sorry." She began to cry. "We snuck off detail to get some food." Her tears flowed freely, both her hands and her face upturned in supplication. Clutching her with a trembling hand, the boy pulled his little sister close to him as if to protect her.

The older girl didn't move or make a sound. Her breath was slow and small tremors began, first in her legs and then moved steadily upward through her upper body. As she stood, unmoving, the apparent stolen rations burned over the open fire. She kept her eyes cast down.

"Wait, wait, wait," Jonas began, "no, no, no. It's all right." he said, trying to soothe the children. "Nobody's going to get in trouble and nobody's going to get hurt. We don't want to hurt you." He motioned for Jay and Skipp to put away their weapons. "We're here to help you."

The children did not respond. A deep, engrained fear kept them rooted to where they had stopped. They were afraid of the men, if for no other reason than that they were adults.

Jonas swung his weapon across his back and continued speaking to the children, softening his voice. Kneeling to face the little girl, he reached to touch her cheek. She cringed, but did not move away.

Encouraged, he continued. "We've come to help you. We've come to take you away from this Kracken?"

At the mere mention of the word, all three children dropped to the floor screaming. Covering their heads, they kept their faces to the earthen floor. Reaching forward with their hands, they grasped at the men's feet. The food forgotten, black smoke began billowing up to the low ceiling.

Now visibly shaking, the little girl began sobbing loudly. "Please don't take us! I'll be good. I'll be good! I didn't mean to get hungry. Please don't take us." Begging, she pleaded not only for herself, but for her brother and sister as well. She looked up, hoping against all hope that these strange adults would show them mercy. Refusing to be comforted, she digressed into gabbling.

Jay, usually not moved by such displays of emotion, shuffled uncomfortably, his large hands flexing and relaxing alternatively. Suddenly and without preamble, he reached forward and picked up the little girl, cradling her in his large muscular arms; he hugged her tightly against himself.

With the apparent discounting of her pleas, the little girl simply went limp; she lay across his broad shoulders like dead meat weight.

After long moments of constant reassuring, the girl lifted her head and looked into Jay's large face. Her tears slowed and her breathing turned toward normal. "Y-you're not t-t-taking us to the Kracken?" Her voice small, along with eyes, swollen from crying, brightened at the prospect of not being punished.

The other two children, more aware of their situation, held no such hope. Skipp unslung his pack and began to prepare foodstuffs to replace the burnt rations that had fallen into the fire. The older children still hadn't moved. Lying as they had, prostrated on the floor, their faces were hidden in their hands.

Skipp lowered himself to the floor. "Hey, it's all right. We're here to help you." He spoke softly as he brushed hair back from the side of the older girl's face. Smiling, he offered to help her to her feet. She took his hand and rose unsteadily, moving like a wounded animal; she acted more out of obedience than trust. Controlled by fear.

Seeing that no evil befell his sisters, the boy rolled to his side and sat up. A degree of his courage returning, he asked, "Who are you guys? You're not C-men, that's for sure."

"What's a seaman?" Skipp asked.

"You know, a C-man," the little girl said gesturing with her arms as if that should have been explanation enough.

"So what do these seamen do?" Jonas asked.

This time it was the older girl that spoke, albeit haltingly. "Anything they want," she said bitterly, her eyes cast down. "They do anything they want."

Jonas thought he could see a shadow, perhaps of shame, settle on the young lady, haunting her features.

She continued, "They're in charge. They run this place. So that gives them the right." She looked at Skipp and tilted her chin as if in spite of what he might think of her; and in that moment the men understood the nature of what her personal trauma had been.

"Yeah," the boy added, in his own way deflecting for his sister. "We work for them, and they work for the Water," he finished, taking his sister's hand.

Still with more questions than answers, the men, through silent accent, decided to allow the children to eat before beginning any further inquiry. Skipp paid extra attention to the young lady in attempt to show her a bit of kindness. He felt by doing so he could help her see that not all men were like those that had hurt her. Catching his eye, Jay spoke so only Skipp could hear him. "Be careful with her. She's been hurt."

Skipp arched an eyebrow, nodded, and then turned back to face the children. "So," Skipp began, "what are you guy's names?"

The older girl looked away. "I'm Andrea and that's Sally," she said in a soft voice. "And he's Peter."

"Well, happy to meet you, Andrea," Skipp said, smiling. "And you, too, Sally," he added when she reminded him that she was there as well. "How long have you guys been here, and how did you get here in the first place?" he asked light heartedly, trying to draw the children out.

Again, the now familiar shadow darkened Andrea's face. "We were taken to the Payne House after our parents died. That was about four years ago, maybe three and a half."

Peter took over the narrative. "Some time after that, some guy showed up saying he wanted to adopt us all together. That's what we were wishing and hoping for—that we could stay together."

Andrea looked up at Skipp, studying his face. She continued again. "Well, anyway, that was when the bad stuff started." She lifted her chin in the familiar defiance. "He did things to me. He said if I went along with him, if I didn't fight him, then he wouldn't mess with Peter or Sally." She looked at her younger siblings, grateful they were for the moment, safe.

Anger coursed through Skipp as he listened to her story. He exchanged glances with Jay and Jonas. Filled with rage for the girl, Skipp knew he could kill the men that had hurt her.

Andrea was still talking. "We stayed with him in his big apartment for a while, and then one night after dinner he brought us drinks." She stopped again to explain when Skipp looked askance.

"Sometimes at night, if we were good, he would bring us special drinks as a treat, or sometimes when he just wanted them to go to sleep," she said, nodding her head indicating her brother and sister, hers eyes downcast.

She stopped and looked up at him. "Well, when we woke up, we were here. We haven't seen him since, but in talking to some of the other kids that was pretty much how they got here too."

"Anybody for seconds?" Jay announced, breaking the tension that hung in the air. Skipp didn't know what to say, or if he should say anything at all.

The meal eaten, they all stood. "What now?" Andrea asked. The group began to move outside toward the earthen square, walking in silence.

"We lost a friend." Jay pointed to the big mountain. "We were hoping to find a way inside." Although clearly afraid, the children agreed to help.

"Did I hear you say there were other children," Jay said to Peter who had taken a liking to the big man.

"Yeah, there are others," he said with a hint of triumph in his voice, "but some got awa—"

"Shut up," Andrea scolded him. "We don't know these men. We don't know who they are!" Feeling somewhat vulnerable after telling Skipp her experience, she cut her gaze to him and added in a softened voice, "Sorry."

"Well, I'm telling," Sally said defiantly. "The last supply ship that came, I was just a baby then. We took over. Most of us got away."

"Took over?" Jonas asked.

"They stole it," Peter said, smiling.

"I was saying it," Sally said with strained patience. "Most of us got away."

"But some didn't," Andrea said sadly. "I lost my best friend in that deal." She ran her fingers through her hair in an unconscious effort, releasing her breath as she did. "At least, though, she's not still trapped here."

Peter added, "You mean, at least she didn't go to the Kracken." With the utterance of the name, an oppressive silence settled over the children; as if by saying it out loud, it would call the evil down on them.

Above them, the deep expanse of blue seemed to go on forever. Altocumulus clouds hug high on the horizon as flocks of brilliantly colored birds passed overhead. Suddenly diving from the sunward side, a giant hawk-like bird tore through the drove of birds. Their strange and terrible cries rose in pitch, echoed through the canopy of trees and died away in a sudden strangled squawk. A brief shower of iridescent feathers floated to the ground as the birds scattered and the hawk-like creature settled down to enjoy its repast.

A relative silence returned to the jungle.

Jonas picked up a number of the feathers and studied them up close. Holding it to the sun, he could see the multihued colors running like liquid through the rachis and barbs, the pigment shifted, matching the color and pattern of his palm. *Strange world.* Placing a number of the feathers into his bag, he placed one in Sally's hair, tweaking her on the cheek as he did so.

He couldn't help wondering about this Kracken and felt it was time the children explained what or who it was. Not wanting to assume too much on their fragile trust, he wasn't sure how to begin. Frustrated, he asked no one in particular, "So tell me about yourselves."

Sometime later, the three men and three children approached the mountain. They found themselves surrounded, again, by the lush jungle. Its strange fauna and exotic animal sounds were quite beautiful in an alien sense. The breeze, sweet with the fragrance of blooming plants and flowers, wafted past in steady ebbs, dancing along the granite base and through the trees. The sun shone warm on their faces.

The sky was suddenly alive with a dynamic show of flying creatures of many and varied forms and colors; not to mention the unfamiliar sound echoing as they performed their aerial ballet. Other land animals were just as strange and wonderful as were the fuzzy wide-eyed *murkurs*, as the children called them, that they'd shared their breakfast with earlier that day.

There were small blue rodent-like creatures that seemed docile enough, but as Skipp found out, were quite feral. What they lacked in size, they more than made up for with a nasty attitude. They had razor sharp fangs and a paralyzing poison they secreted with each bite. Only after several minutes, sensation began to return to Skipp's index finger where the creature had nicked him.

The men discovered from the kids that one bite from one of the larger creatures would be enough to completely incapacitate an adult human. The creatures, jhetvas, as they were called, due to their size, often ran in packs numbering between ten and fifteen.

Sally found Jonas's mispronunciation of the animal's names particularly funny. She repeatedly attempted to teach him the name correctly, which sounded more like Cha'faez when spoken correctly. After several tries, she gave up and decided instead simply to laugh.

Soon the laughter stopped. "Look at these." Jay knelt beside the trail pointing at a set of footprints of a very large creature. Judging from the size and depth of the track, the animal must have weighed two tons or more.

"Let me measure this," Jonas said, taking out his notepad and scanning the distance between impressions. He looked up and whistled.

"What?"

"I'm thinking, whatever made these was at least seven to nine meters."

"Well," Jay began, "let's just hope it doesn't eat meat."

"Oh, it eats meat all right," one of the children said.

They walked on in silence for a while until they reached a rather large stream, the water of which was crystal clear and unusually deep, like looking through a window into an underwater world. The stream's bottom sloped away into darkness. The crystalline water abounded with aquatic life; a large portion of which appeared to be carnivorous. Watching the current, they could see it flow right up to the foot of the mountain and disappear beneath its base.

Strange, Skipp thought, *for a stream to flow into a mountain and not out from it.* But he reasoned within himself that everything on this planet had been strange so far, so why not the stream as well.

"There," Peter cried out, pointing at the base of the mountain near where the stream disappeared, "that's how we get in. We go inside at night so we can be safe from the drags."

"What's a *drag*?" Skipp asked.

"They're big ugly creatures about this tall," Peter said, pointing up at a scar on the rock face, about two meters high. "They're strong and have really long teeth, and they got tough skin. Our sharp sticks can't even hurt them," he said referring to their crude spears. "They usually stay in the deep jungle, but sometimes they come down here to hunt. If we're not careful they'll carry off one of the smaller kids." He finished without taking a breath.

Skipp answered with a chuckle, "I think I had a run in with one of those drags yesterday. An experience I don't care to repeat," he said with a shiver as the memory replayed itself in his mind. "So tell me," he continued, "do these things ever attack out in the open?"

"No," the kids answered as one voice.

"Unless they're sick, or if the Kracken is in their regular hunting grounds," Andrea added.

Taking a chance, Skipp asked, "So, what is this Kracken anyway? Was that one of its footprints we saw back there?" Skipp purposely kept the tone of his voice light, hoping that this would disarm the kids, allowing them to talk about something they were obviously uncomfortable discussing.

Looking back and forth to each other, as if trying to see if it was okay, they appeared to come to a consensus.

"Well, all we can say is that it lives inside the mountain most of the time, and yes, that was one of its footprints we saw back there," Peter said.

"The truth of the matter is that none of us have ever seen it. All I know is if they take you to the Kracken, you never come back." Andrea swallowed. "At least not all of you," she finished with a shiver and hugged Sally to her side. The younger child had not uttered a sound since the discussion began.

Skipp shifted his gaze from face to face. What is it about this Kracken that has the children so afraid?

Jonas caught Skipp's eyes and nodded, indicating that he should continue with the questioning.

Skipp acknowledged Jonas with a tilt of his chin. "What do you mean 'not all of you' comes back?" Skipp continued.

Andrea looked at Skipp for a long minute as if she wouldn't answer, but then she cleared her throat and exhaled. "I mean, you're never the same. Your mind...it's all chewed up." She paused and looked down, tears forming in her eyes. "You're never the same. It's better that you die than..." her voice trailed into a strained silence. She looked away, making it plain that she no longer wanted to talk about it.

Skipp honored her silent request.

Jay nudged Peter and asked him again to explain how they managed to get inside the mountain. Peter raised and dropped his shoulders, and again, he pointed to the base of the mountain where the stream flowed into solid rock.

"You're gonna have to get wet," he said laughing.

"I hate this part," Sally said, crinkling her nose; her first comment in some time.

"Oh, stop complaining." Peter dismissed her comments with a wave of his boney arm. "You don't want to stay out here by yourself, do you?" he said with a sly smile.

"Of course not, you silly. Didn't say I wouldn't go in, just said I didn't like it."

"You two knock it off," Andrea interrupted. Walking between the two, she directed their attention back to the watery passage.

"Well, well," Skipp said, "who'll be first?" He looked around for volunteers. The men laughed, but began storing their gear and sealing packs against the water. The power sources activated, the small units began to hum and then fastened the openings against leakage.

With a whoop and a yahoo, Peter ran and jumped in the fast flowing water, sending a small wave of crystal clear water rushing over the pebble-strewn bank.

Soon, they all were under water and found themselves being carried by the swift current. The men were surprised that the water was warm. And inside the mountain, where there should have been cavernous darkness, a slight luminance glowed instead.

Beneath the surface of this warm subterranean river, the small troop rode the current right up to a sand and rock-covered shore.

Breaking the surface of the water, the men found a vaulted ceiling high overhead spreading away into darkness. The cavern had the feel and smell of industry, a light scent of smoke and oil hung in the air, mingled with the odor of unwashed bodies. Leading up from the water was a stone ridge that jetted out over the water. And on it rested another of the little hutches, the type that had been in the jungle clearing.

Once on the bank, they sat down to catch their breath. The air was warm and heavy with stale humidity. With no real air current to speak of, it felt more like a draft created by something being moved and then resettled again.

Jay yelled into the darkness and waited as the echo returned after a few moments delay. "Big."

"Looks like the whole mountain's hollow," Skipp sighed and whistled between his teeth.

"Nothing 'bout this place makes sense." Jay slapped his hand against his thigh and turned looking at the vastness of the cavern. Seeing the mountain from the inside gave them a new reverence for the overall size. Above them, the ceiling disappeared into darkness and appeared carved out of the stone. Around them, several entryways were cut into the walls where torches sat ensconced providing a greasy light to the immediate area.

Just over the horizon, created by an up swell of the floor, they could see a strange glow; its exotic illumination danced wildly off the curve of the grotto ceiling and high walls. The yellow-orange light made the walls seem warm and beckoning, almost hypnotic in its allure. Combined with a low steady hum, like the sound of machinery in the distance, the men felt compelled to investigate.

"What is that?" Jonas asked no one in particular. He started toward the light, Skipp and Jay falling into step along with him.

"No!"

"Ahhh, stop!"

"Don't. Stop! Don't go there!"

The children cried out and surrounded the men, pleading with them not to go near the strange luminescence.. They begged for a promise that the men would not go near the light, averring a horrible danger awaiting anyone who wandered into its glowing grasp.

Skipp allowed troubled eyes to travel from Jay to Jonas and finally back to Andrea. He began shaking his head, a slow unconscious motion. They needed answers and this represented their best chance. He turned to Andrea. "We can't do that."

"That's why we came here, darling," Jay finished.

Taking out his notepad, Skipp began running scans of the caves interior. "Hey, the interference is gone. My gear is all working. The jamming or static—or whatever it was, it's…it's gone." He began scanning the vault, projecting his scan toward the mysterious light.

Andrea called, "Please, Skipp, please don't go over there. That's where the Kracken lives. It's over there in the light."

Skipp softened his voice, speaking in reassuring tones. "Don't worry. We do this kind of thing all the time." He laughed to show her he wasn't worried.

She laughed, too, a weaker, smaller version; it was at best forced. She looked at him again and said softly, "I just wouldn't want anything to happen to you," and then added quickly, "I mean, any of you."

Sally giggled, beginning in a singsong voice. "Andrea gots a boyfriend."

Embarrassed, Andrea snapped at her sister. "Sally! The word is *has,* and I do not. Can't anybody be concerned about good folk?" Finishing, she stood abruptly and stalked off.

Skipp looked around dumbfounded. Raising his hands, palms facing outward, he waved them in a gesture of surrender.

An awkward silence filled the space between them.

Jonas spoke, finally putting an end to Andrea's torment. "Now, now, Sally, don't tease your sister."

Laughing through tears, Sally was barely able to breathe out her response. "Okay." Still giggling, she rolled to her side as another wave of laughter engulfed her.

Jay sidled over to where Andrea had stopped, sitting on a huge boulder that had come to rest alongside the path. "That was pretty uncomfortable back there, huh?" he said as gently as possible. He sat in silence beside her.

After a few moments had passed and she had given no reply, Jay continued, "Hey, that kind of thing happens. You-you just don't let it get you down. You know, keep your chin up."

She turned and looked at him. "I b-bet he thinks I'm some kind of dork or something, or even worse, some stupid little kid with a crush."

"You know, it's like my great Aunt Hattie used to say, 'in times like these, all you need is a good strong hug and a big bowl of ice cream.' Well, we don't have any ice cream, but I'll give ya a hug, and I'll owe you."

Laughing, they walked back to join the rest of the group.

Sufficiently scolded, Sally, though still tickled, kept her comments to herself.

Andrea walked over to where Skipp sat reviewing the scan results. "I'm sorry if I embarrassed you in front of your friends."

Skipp looked up at her and smiled. "No worries. Friends?"

"Sure," she said and stuck out her hand.

Laughing, Skipp pulled her to him and hugged her tightly around the shoulders.

After settling on a preliminary route of incursion, Jay finally decided that Peter would join the men and act as their guide; the girls would stay behind at the shelter and out of sight.

With the good-byes said and sufficient rations divvied, the small troop headed out, destined for whatever lay waiting in the eerie incandescence.

Finally, the men set off toward what they hoped would bring them to the answers they needed along with the proof that would bring Waters down. Jonas looked back, scowled, and shook his head as the girls tucked away into the shadow.

And now we need to get these children off this cursed planet, too. Lord, things just got more complicated.

Chapter Twelve

Closing his meaty fist with slow and deliberate motion, Ted Waters crushed the freshly cut rose; its sweet fragrance lost in the cloud of smoke that encircled his shadowed face. Taking the overly large cigar from his mouth, he pressed it into a sterling silver ashtray, one of many such trophies he'd won over the years for excellence in business. A faint green light illuminated the bowl of the asbak, and a moment later, the cigar vaporized and the remaining smoke and residue was drawn away through hidden filters embedded in the receptacle.

It had been a day and a half, thirty-six hours exactly, since he had his run in with Iona, and still it bothered him. He couldn't figure out what it was exactly about it that bothered him so, and that small detail niggled him even more.

Ted Waters did not like puzzles, and this was turning into one very large unanswered question. He prided himself on being aware of even subtle changes in his people; it was how he kept ahead of the game he played. And lately, he had noticed a change in Iona. However, right now he was feeling anything but ahead. In fact, he felt sure that he was far behind.

For Ted Waters, second place was the same as losing. Being the best of the losers was not an appealing thought. It was something Ted Waters could not—would not—do.

He sat smoldering, replaying every frame of his conversation with Iona. Over and over, he sifted the words, the expression, every nuance across the screen in his mind. He steepled his fingers and stared into the murky darkness. With practiced grace, he retrieved another of the cigars from the humidor, cut off the tip and lit it.

Seated at the large white marble desk, he activated the third computer screen; the one reserved for looking in on his employees. Typing in code alpha-1: Iona, he looked in on Iona Bowers. He watched her busy at her desk. Everything looked normal; she was hard at work as usual. She had dispatched two assignments ahead of schedule as usual. Still, there was something different.

What was it, he thought. Was it her hair, the way she sat at her desk? There was definitely something, and he was determined to study her until he found what that something was.

He zoomed in on her face, and then he saw it. He crushed the newly lit cigar in the recently emptied tray. He leaned forward and stared at the screen. A narrow furrow creased his brows. Iona was smiling. Just sitting there working at her desk and smiling.

Flicking off the monitor, he sat back sinking into the Corinthian leather, throne-like chair, allowing the short spike mounted to the upper middle of the backrest to grind into his back. The pain reminded him never to let himself become comfortable. He would use the pain to drive his passion in solving this little puzzle that had presented itself. With one last surge of pain, he activated a toggle on the desk and called for one of his few *trusted* informants.

With Ted Waters, the word *trust* meant that he had enough information—harmful information—on a person to guarantee that person's cooperation and obedience.

When the short, rather ordinary looking man, entered the office, he was given one simple set of instructions: "Examine Iona Bowers level alpha1-1a, and report back to me." The code was reserved for the most sensitive of cases. In the rare occasions where it had been necessary to be invoked, the investigation had often ended with the unexplained disappearance of the subject in question. And since there were no formal charges ever filed, there could be no trail leading back to The Company or Ted Waters.

The man looked at the face of the darkened monitor and then up at Ted Waters. "Any orders regarding disposal?"

Sitting back, Ted Waters activated the monitor and, again, stared at the small, almost insignificant, smile that played at the corners of Iona's mouth. He rested against the spike in the backrest, enjoying the *pain* and studying the face of the woman that he had handpicked to work alongside him. "What a shame it would be if I should have to replace her." He stared at the smallish man standing in front of him. "But have no doubt, if it comes to it, I will destroy her, absolutely."

Finishing her workload for the day and after readying her desk for the morrow, Iona set out to leave her office. *Strange*, she thought, *there was a time when there was no place she'd rather be.* But now, since Albert had come into her life, she couldn't wait to leave and go be with him. Again, she wondered if this was what love felt like. She went over the checklist in her mind, making sure she hadn't left anything undone. Scooping her final papers, she headed out the large mahogany door.

As her office doors slid open before her, Iona found her path blocked by none other than Jorge Trevino, the same man who had met with Waters earlier.

"Miss Bowers, how fortunate, I was just on my way in to see you."

Iona studied the man, and it was readily apparent to her that he had been waiting for her. She ran her eyes over him, a quick survey, studying his pockmarked face and his too small eyes that made him appear to wince whenever he spoke. By the way he was looking at her, she could tell he was about to ask her for something she had no intention of giving.

In fact, she smiled to herself, anything he asked for, she had no intention of giving him. She squared her shoulders and walked right past him as if he was not there. Either missing or ignoring the hint, he fell in beside her, escorting her toward the executive elevator.

"Hey, beautiful," he began, "what's your big hurry?"

"Trevino…" she said, stopping and looking down into his eyes, "I've had a long, hard day. All I want is to go home, alone, take a bath, and relax. Now with that in mind, what could you possibly want with me?"

Undaunted, Trevino pressed on. "I couldn't help but notice that you had a pretty good time out the other night with Paul. That was before he…well, you know, you were there. I was just wondering what are the chances of you and me hooking up? Maybe I could show you how to really have a good time." His eyes traveled slowly over Iona, smiling as he studied the curves of her body.

She could not believe his forwardness, but she knew whom he was and what role he played in The Company. His approach to her could only mean one thing, that she had been sloppy. Somehow and for some reason, Waters suspected her. Still, he could have no real idea of where her true loyalties lie. She would just have to be more careful; she would have to be Iona.

"Trevino," she said through clenched teeth, but refusing to meet his gaze; she looked over his head. "I don't date short men." The elevator doors opened and she stepped in, not looking back and hoping this interruption was over.

Refusing to accept his dismissal, he followed her into the elevator. As the doors closed, and before she could react, Trevino grabbed her, twisting her arm behind her back and forced her into the back wall. Arching her backwards from the waist, he whispered into her ear, his tone menacing. "I've had dames like you before, all talk and show and no action." He cursed and flecks of spittle spattered the side of her face. "If I wanted you, I'd take you right where you stand and there wouldn't be a blessed thing you could do about it." With his free hand, he compressed the nerve at the base of Iona's neck and jaw line. Leaning closer, he kissed the side of her face, her jaw and her neck and paused, holding his moist lips against her earlobe. The door chime dinged behind them, and he pushed her away then turned and walked away leaving her alone in the lift car.

Caught off guard and knees weakened, Iona stumbled into the corner and collapsed to the floor. Temporarily stunned, she could not move but could only watch the gloating smile on Trevino's face as the doors slid closed. Iona forced herself to remember the darkening smile and swore to herself that she would one day personally remove it.

From his office, Ted Waters watched the entire episode. Satisfied, he closed his eyes in quiet contemplation. Rising from his desk, he turned the monitor off and stood staring out over the city, looking but not really seeing. He smiled. His thoughts were as dark as the night that slowly claimed the city.

In the parking lot, Iona replayed the events in her mind. She had to be more careful, and she had to decide what it was she would do, rather, who it was she would be. Either way, whatever choice she made she didn't have much time. Bringing her cruiser to a hover, she headed out into the busy thoroughfare. Floating on the stream of air created by the cruiser, Iona set the controls to automatic and listened to the soft hum of the vehicle's engine and the gentle swoosh of wind.

Settling into the cushion of her seat, Iona allowed herself a quick scan, checking for tails. About four vehicle lengths behind her, a small unobtrusive one-man craft appeared to be following her. Taking the controls, she changed direction. She had been heading to her apartment, but decided now to go to the gym instead. Drawing her pursuer into the open would give her a better chance to study the would-be spy.

It had been said of Iona that nobody followed her without having first been asked to do so. Those who had, had found her a harsh receptionist. She'd earned the reputation of coldness.

That had been her safety net in the past. No intimacies. No liabilities.

Chapter Thirteen

Iona turned off the main road, leaving the dusty rain shower that had started as she wandered through the city. Keying on her computer, she activated her message-scrambler, a device she added herself, especially for times like these when she wished to communicate without Ted Waters's knowledge.

Taking a deep breath, she focused on the image of the woman she knew as grandmother who appeared on the screen. "Hi, Nonna," she said worriedly, "how's Albert?"

"Oh, hi, child. The boy's fine, but how are you doing? You don't look so good."

"I don't doubt it. I'm in trouble."

"Well, child, no matter what the trouble is, the Lord has an answer for you. Now, tell Nonna all about it."

"I can't—not yet, but…"

"Now, child, if you don't tell me, how can I help?"

"Not this time, Nonna." She took a deep breath and exhaled slowly as she ran a hand through her hair. "Nonna…it's about Mary and the kids…" Iona looked away, but then refocused on the wizened face on the screen. "Nonna, there was an explosion—"

"I know. Why, Mary and the children were fit to be tied when they got here."

"What!?"

"And that baby is so big now—"

"Nonna, Mary is there? With you? She's alive?"

"Yes, baby. She and the children got here some time ago. What is it, baby, you look troubled? First Mary and now you. What is going on with you girls?"

Iona swallowed. "Mary...? Did she tell you? Did she say anything—about me?"

"She told me there was some trouble, but she didn't go into details. Why don't you tell me? Are you girls fighting again?"

There was a long silence where only the sound of the rain was heard; that and the hum of the electronics. Iona looked around, checking to make sure she was still alone. "I've finally gone too far, Nonna. I don't even know how it happened; just one day I looked at me, and I didn't like who I was anymore."

"Is it Mary that you think can help you, baby?"

"Yeah...no. I don't know. I messed up, Nonna. I need Mary to...forgive me, Nonna, but I don't know if she'll be willing to after all that I did. I've been...well, I've been evil, and not only to her."

"Tell Jesus all about it, child," she said soothingly. "He understands your life, baby-girl, and He has a plan for you."

"You know, there was a time when maybe I would have jumped at those words, but now I fear it's too late for me. Not even Jesus will forgive me for what I've done, for what I've become. I've done too much—too many bad things. I don't deserve His or Mary's forgiveness, much less their help." Iona sighed in frustration. "And besides, I know the Lord doesn't want anything to do with me. I wouldn't even be asking if it wasn't for Albert." She added wistfully, as if speaking to herself, "There's something about that child that reminds me of how I was before you took me in."

"Baby," Viola began, "no matter what you've done or how wretched you may have become, God's grace is sufficient."

A large sigh escaped Iona and warm tears streaked her face. *Grace? Sufficient?* She decided not to deal with that just yet. "I don't know what I would do if anything happened to that child." She began to cry. "And, Nonna."—she took another breath and forced the words out in a rush—"I was part of Mary almost losing her entire family. How can she ever forgive me?"

"Oh, baby..." The sentence died in labored silence.

The two women sat staring at each other's image, not speaking, neither sure of just what to say. Iona could see Viola's lips moving and knew from long practice that the older woman was praying. Her heart took comfort in Nonna's prayers; somehow, they always seemed to make a difference. She hoped this time would be no different.

A shadow passed through the room behind Nonna, and then Mary's face appeared on the screen. "Iona?"

Taking the crude torch and holding the little girl's hand, Mike started walking, not sure exactly where it was he was going. He just felt compelled to do something, at least to be moving.

After walking for some time, with Mike doing all the talking, he stopped. "What's that?" He pointed toward a soft illumination that brightened the distant walls far up in the cavern. He stooped, bending down to speak to his small companion, trying to draw her out in conversation.

She did not answer, but only looked at him, her eyes open so wide that the white of her eyes showed on all sides.

When he started toward the light, pulling her along with him, she screamed. Fighting, pulling, and twisting her arm in his grasp, she tried to break his hold. She pulled frantically against his arm, like a wild animal; fear plainly visible in her large brown eyes.

"Hey," Mike began, dodging kicking feet and biting teeth, "what-what? I'm not going to hurt you!"

As if she didn't hear, the girl continued to fight. Tears washed her dirty face, as flecks of spittle careened from the open maw of her face.

Taken aback, Mike tightened his grip. Not sure why the girl panicked, but sure nonetheless that if he let her go, she would bolt. Mike held her firm. After a time of struggling, the child seemed resigned to the fact that she could not break free. She collapsed, surrendering to whatever fate this man had designed for her. She fell at Mike's feet, motionless and silent.

Overcome by the thought of what must be going on in his new friend's mind, Mike knelt down and picked up the little girl. Like a child asleep, he held her listless body in his arms, sat on the ground and rocked her.

Many times, Michael, I have longed for you to know Me, that I might calm your fears.

Mike shook his head, trying to free himself of the incessant voice.

Over an hour passed before the little girl even so much as moved. She looked startled to find tears on Mike's face. Reaching a small dirty hand, she touched them and looked into Mike's face, wonder covering her own.

For so long she had lived in this place; all she had known was cruelty and hardship. She tilted her head and looked into his face again. Lifting her feeble hand, she touched his cheeks, examining the moistness of his tears. The thought that someone would cry for her, especially a grown up, touched something deep inside this little girl. A flame of trust and hope, which had been snuffed out a long time ago, quietly flickered and came back to life.

Leaning her face against his chest and patting his shoulder with her small hand, she said softly, "Don't cry, mister. I'm all right."

Startled by the girl's voice, Mike hugged her close, a barely suppressed cry of joy escaping his lips. Realizing that she might not be able to breathe, he loosened his grip, and stood her up, looking at her as if for the first time. "Are you sure you're all right?" he asked with deep concern.

The little girl was so enjoying this new revelation that someone cared for her. Instead of pulling away, she clung to him as close as possible. When he finally settled down, she said, "Mister…"—and paused to see if he was listening—"will you hold me some more, please?"

"Of course I will, honey. Of course I will." With a mixture of joy and sorrow, Mike held the girl knowing that he would never hold his own children ever again. Silent tears burned hot streaks down his dusty face, and he slowly increased his grip around the child as his own pain began to grow.

For long moments, the two sat together, enjoying each other's nearness, each taking from the other what was needed and giving what little they had. "So," Mike said, speaking softly into her hair, "since you don't want to go toward that light, where would you rather go?" He set her off his lap and stood beside her.

"Come with me," she said, "I'll take you where I live. Only we have to be careful cause of the C-men. They're mean. I thought you were one of 'em at first, you being a grown up and all."

"Hey, I can't keep calling you little girl, what's your name?"

"Rosemary."

"Well, pleased to meet you Rosemary." Mike shook her hand. He whispered her name, repeating it to himself, committing it to memory. "So, Rose—can I call you Rose? What's a seaman?"

"They work for the Water," Rosemary said in a whisper as if she was afraid someone would overhear her. "They make us go down in the holes and dig up the spice called jiyst. Sometimes they hurt us bad. What's a rose anyway?"

Mike smiled in spite of himself. "A rose is a very pretty flower that grows back on Earth. You remind me of a rose."

"It's okay then, you can call me Rose." She smiled up at Mike and leaned into him, hugging him, stretching her arms around his broad shoulders.

"Where do these seamen come from?" Mike asked, trying to figure out what she meant by the name, and what connection they had to the rivers that seemed to crisscross the planet.

She pulled him down closer to her mouth and whispered, "If you don't do exactly like they say, then they take you to the Kracken." She visibly shuddered at the word.

Mike didn't want to cause her any more distress than necessary, but now he had a third mystery to go with the first two. What was a Kracken? He knew from ancient mythology that a kraken was a beast, held by the gods and used to punish the men of ancient Greece, but he had no idea what its correlation here would be. And who knew what old-time sailors had to do with any of this, but he had to get some answers.

The more he learned, the more questions he uncovered. Questions like, just what did any of this have to do with Ted Waters and The Company.

Too many questions and not enough answers. Questions without answers had been the problem since he decided to help Jonas. Now, all of that was about to change, he could sense it, and somehow little Rosemary was the key.

"Rose," he began slowly, "I was wondering if you would—"

"I know, you want to see the Kracken, right?"

Surprised by her frankness, Mike simply said, "Yeah, I would."

"Tell me, how come all grown-ups like watching that thing? The C-men like watching it, too."

Mike was sickened by the thought that she'd identified him with her tormentors. "Hey, I don't just want to look at it, I want to destroy it if I can." His tone had been sharper than he intended, and he was instantly sorry.

She looked up at him timidly. "But what if you can't?" Tears beginning to well up in her eyes, she spoke softly, "I just thought…" Her words trailed to silence. She looked at Mike, her lips moving, forming words, but not speaking. Instead, she collapsed against him and hugged him around his knees.

Realizing she needed to be reassured he wasn't mad at her, and that he wasn't going to change the way he felt about her, Mike picked up the little girl and hugged her tight, chucking her under the chin until she smiled.

Soon after that, they reached a broad stream that ambled lazily through a small crack in the rocks. "Through here," she said, "it's not very deep. You can walk in it if you can't swim."

He smiled at her being concerned for him. It made him all the more determined to end the nightmare that she and all the other children like her had been forced to endure. Once in the water, Mike found that the crack opened up into a rather sizable passage, easily allowing them to pass through.

As they broke the surface of the water on the opposite side of the cavern wall, Mike, dazzled by the brilliance, warmed his face in the sun as it filtered through the emerald canopy. Mixed with the sounds of birds and wind in the trees, angry voices carried on the breeze drifted toward them, pulling Mike to awareness.

Soon, the sound of crying and the lashing of a whip rang out, displacing the earlier more pleasant sounds. The two sounds echoed off stonewalls and through jungle fauna. Rose froze in mid-step. Squeezing Mike's hand, she buried her face in his side and began to cry. Her voice, a strained whisper, "It's the C-men, they're back! Oh no! Oh no, they're back!"

Mike secured Rose in a small clearing where the trees reminded him of those found on Earth like the strangler fig, hairy walnut, and mangroves converged. Mike knelt in front of Rose and held her small face between his hands. The ropes of the strangler fig-like tree hung like a curtain around them, sealing them from the view of the small path they had entered on. Mike forced her to look at him. "Stay here. I'll be back."

She grabbed his arm.

Mike kissed her forehead. "I will be back." As Mike crept closer to the sound of the falling whip, he suddenly began to understand what Rosemary knew—only too well.

A man's voice, stilted with callous disregard, spoke over the sound of crying. "Four more of you worthless whelps are missing," The angry voice continued, dripping with undisguised hatred. "I'm going to beat you one by one until either you tell me where the others are or until you're all dead. Don't matter to me one way or the other." Angry voice flicked his wrist and the whip jumped as if alive, snaking out and biting the exposed skin of a child's thigh. Another lash answered by another cry.

"You sorry excuse for…" Angry voice withdrew the whip wet with blood and began his forward motion. The whip froze mid-strike. "What the—" He turned and looked into Mike's burning gaze.

A shot fired.

Two more C-men who were laughing while holding the teenage boy that was being beaten, looked up in sudden surprise, then bewilderment, and finally fear. Their gaze traveled from the hot anger in Mike's face to their comrade lying dead at his feet; a fist sized hole still smoldering in his chest where the laser blast terminated his protest.

Before either man could recover, Mike slammed his fist into the face of the closer of the two. He was rewarded by a wet crunching sound as the man's nose collapsed beneath the blow. The man staggered back, drew, and fired his blaster while trying to grab his injured nose. The shot sizzled over Mike's head into the canopy. Hairy walnut like fruit, the size of softballs, began to rain down from the trees.

The third man, having replaced his fear with the instinct to survive, screamed and charged Mike, catching him with a shoulder to his mid-section. Both men tumbled backwards. Mike, allowing the momentum to carry him over, placed his knees against the man and pushed. The third C-man careened out of control and landed in a heap at the base of a fir. Mike rolled to his side and took the opportunity to catch his breath.

The C-man with the broken nose, turned toward Mike, cursed and fired his blaster at the back of Mike's head.

Mike jumped to his side, allowing the blaster fire to pass over him. Landing in a crouch, Mike returned fire, catching the man full in the face.

Knowing that now was not the time to celebrate this minor victory, Mike spun, anticipating an attack from the rear by the man he had thrown against the tree.

Bringing his pistol up in preparation to fire, Mike stopped, taking a moment to understand what it was he saw. The man, obviously in the middle of an attack, lay on his back clutching at his arm where it had been severed from just beneath the elbow. The man's hand still cinched around his own blaster, laying on the ground with the rest of his arm about two meters away.

Mike nudged the man with his boot. He screamed out in pain. The stub of an arm glowed red and smelled of charred flesh.

"His partner shot him," a voice said from near the edge of the path.

His anger spent, Mike turned and looked into the frightened faces of the children he just saved.

Turning back, he snatched the man to his feet. "So, you like hurting children?" Mike slapped the man across the face and then grabbed what remained of his arm, and squeezed. The man cried out.

Looking at the large green C on the man's shoulder patch, Mike cursed inwardly. C-men, of course Company men; these men worked for The Company, which meant they worked for Waters. *"The water"* he remembered Rose saying. It was all starting to make sense now.

Mike drew back and punched the man, once, twice, and then a third time. Each time he hit him, he saw Mary and his children and then their bombed out home. Drawing back to hit him again, Mike caught a glimpse of Rose and the terrified look on her face. He dropped the man and turned away. The man lay barely conscious at Mike's feet. Mike looked back at Rose, feeling slightly ashamed; he bent down and collected the man's weapons and the communicator from the clip on his belt.

Mike hurried over to the youth who, struggling for each breath, winced as he moved, trying to avoid further injuring the weeping lacerations from the whip. "Let me." Mike pulled his first aid kit from his pack and began to tend the young man's wounds.

The small group of about a dozen or so children stood huddled together and watched. None spoke or dared to interfere.

Then Rose approached and placed a hand on Mike's forearm. "Is he going to be okay?"

"I don't know. I think so," Mike said, washing the lacerations. "He's going to need more help than I can give him, though." He pulled out a canister and began spraying the cuts. The young man sighed and visibly relaxed.

"Wh-what was that," the boy said, pleased the burning had at least stopped for now.

"Just something to make the pain stop."

"Thank you."

The boy closed his eyes. Whether unconscious or just asleep, Mike didn't know. He looked up at the sky again, tempted to pray, but refused to call out to a God that would allow his family to die. Rubbing his face, he muttered to himself, "I need to find my friends."

Chapter Fourteen

A scream rang out and Mike turned to see the one armed man standing over him, a large stone in his hand. Mike dove to the side and rolled forward; coming up, he leveled his blaster and fired.

Two bolts of energy slammed into the man at almost the same moment. The sickening smell of ozone and burnt flesh filled the glade again and the last of the C-men fell dead beside his fellows.

Rose sat kneeling over the unconscious teen; her eyes squeezed tight, her finger still on the trigger of the recovered blaster. Tears streamed down her face.

Mike let out his breath through pursed lips, slipped the blaster from the girl's hands and then pulled Rose against his chest. "I've got you. It's okay. You can let go now." He kissed her forehead and stroked the back of her hair the way he'd seen Mary do with his own children.

One more reason to hate Ted Waters, Mike thought, as he surveyed the children.

The crowd of children backed away en masse, ripples of confusion on their faces. Who was this new adult, and would he turn his fury on them as easily as he had the C-men?

Mike stood, lifting Rose as he did. He whispered against her ear, "Are you okay?"

She nodded, but did not speak.

Mike looked at the small group of children. "I've come to help you; I'm a friend."

The children did not respond; fear still controlled them. The expressions seemed to ask why an adult would offer help. This was a new concept to try to comprehend.

"Come on," Rose said. "He's my friend."

In spite of their fear, Mike could sense the children wanted to trust him. He began gathering the children together, ushering them away from the gruesome scene.

As the small group moved away, jungle animals could be heard circling the camp, coming nearer. With the smell of fresh blood in the air, the camp would soon be filled with both predators and scavengers alike, fighting for the rights of the prey. Mike did not want the group there when that happened.

As the last of the children passed, heading into the jungle and away from the kill site, Mike lifted the sleeping youth and, as he did, he renewed his vow to stop Waters, no matter what the cost.

The children made their way back to the opening that led into the mountain. Mike followed them through the underwater passage. He found himself hoping the children's fears would be calmed by the security of a familiar place. Coming out of the water on the other side, Mike counted eighteen children, including Rose. "How many more of you are there?" he asked Rose.

"Only three more, but really, we don't know where they are," she said, standing near him, possessively.

"We went out on work detail, and they weren't there. That's all we know." Although Mike had asked Rose, one of the older boys answered. He had spoken in quick frantic defense of himself and his companions.

Mike could sense the children's intense fear, like something physical between them. Slowly backing away from him, they huddled together like scared animals drawing comfort from the proximity of the pack. Mike lowered the injured boy to a sleeping pallet and made sure he was still breathing.

"What's the matter with you?" Rose asked the group. "I told you he was my friend. Now come on, and stop acting like scared babies."

Mike had to laugh at the irony. In fact, the whole group was made up of not much more than babies and Rose, one of the younger, stood scolding them for acting like children.

"What's so funny?" Rose asked, a look of petulance coloring her cherubic features.

"You are." Holding her face in his hands, he said, "Standing there with your hands on your hips giving everybody the what for, acting like an old mother hen." He stooped and ruffled his fingers through her hair, winning a smile and a hug.

"I love you, Mike," she said into his neck, "I knew Jesus would bring us somebody."

Mike stiffened at the girl's words, but only slightly. Standing to hide his discomfort, he took Rose's hand. "What's next, since you seem to be calling the shots?" Mike asked lightheartedly.

Mike realized that, although hope survived in these children, it was a hope born of desperation rather than of the surety of confidence. "I need to find my friends so we can get you guys out of here. If I know them, they will have made it inside this mountain by now and on their way to check out the source of that light."

The silence returned.

"I don't know what it is about that light that scares you kids so much." He lifted his chin toward the faint illuminance. "But if I'm going to be able to help you, I have to know what's going on. Now, I won't make any of you come with me, but *I* have to go."

The resistance to trust began to weaken in the children, but they were still scared, and Mike understood why. One of the older boys, no more than fifteen, walked out from the group. "I'll take you," he said, swallowing hard.

Mike extended his hand and the boy shook it, clumsily, but he shook it. "What's your name, son?"

"Frank. The kids all call me Frankie," he answered, unable to meet Mike's eyes.

"Thanks, Frankie. I'm Mike and I'm going to get you guys off this god-forsaken rock."

"If you can do that, sir," he said enthusiastically, looking up to catch Mike's eye. "I'll go with you all the way to the camp."

At this, the children gathered around Mike, pushing and shoving trying to get close enough to touch him. Something had broken, a barrier split, and trust had begun to grow.

"My name's Bill," said a tall and ungainly boy of about fourteen.

"I'm Sara," said another.

"Me too, but my name is spelled with an h," cried another youthful voice.

Mike reached out touching as many of the kids as he could reach, trying to remember each name and face.

However, Rosemary turned and walked a short distance away. Folding her arms across her chest, she pouted. "Hey," she called out, "give the guy some room; he won't be able to catch his breath." She was not so pleased now that everyone was in on what she had come to think of as being exclusively hers.

Mike, on the other hand, enjoyed the moment of shared acceptance. The children's faces looking so trustingly at him, reminded him of his own children, and with that, came a stab of pain. He turned his face toward the light. His eyes narrowed as one thought burned in his mind: *Waters would pay.*

Then a warm breeze seemed to caress Mike's face, and in it, a still small voice echoed in his mind: *"Vengeance is mine."*

The men slid up next to the wall of the building staying to the shadows. The place was alive with activity. There was movement everywhere, mostly robotic in nature; cargo trucks loaded with huge shipping carts and automated machinery in a blitz of activity.

"What's in the carts?" Skipp wondered out loud.

"Those are what they send the spice out of here in," Peter answered. "They have us dig up the ore and then they refine it to get a spice called jiyst…"

At that, the three men turned abruptly, looking at each other. What would Ted Waters want with jiyst? Another piece of the puzzle. Another question.

Peter, unaware of the exchange between the men, kept talking, "…and then the ships get sent back to Earth, I guess. I don't really know what they do with it. They never say."

"That's as good a guess as any," Jonas added. "Skipp, can you get a reading on who's doing what over there. How much fire power do they have and where is it located…those types of things?"

"Yeah, let me know who I get to hurt first," Jay said, kissing the barrel of his laser rifle.

"I get the general idea," Skipp answered, forcing a smile into his voice for Peter's sake. Directing his notepad toward the area ahead of them, he began to read the scan. "There's a major energy reading coming from inside that main building; somewhere on the lower levels I'd say. I think it may be the source of the energy fluctuations we experienced on the surface," he said, pointing at the larger of the buildings.

"Good," Jay said solemnly. "Then that's where I'll start. When you hear da boom you'll know I've done my business." He smiled down at Peter, whose face was fixed with a look of determined concentration.

"There's also a large array of life signs down in that pit over there to the left," Skipp continued. "Looks like it may be a holding cell of some kind."

Peter's voice broke. "That's the hole. That's where you go when they take you to the Kracken." Looking away, he fell silent, his resolve weakened but held.

"If you'd rather wait out here, we'd understand if…" Jonas looked at him, trying to read his expression.

"No, I'm okay," Peter said finally. "If you guys can risk everything to help us, then the least I can do is face this," he said. stiffening his back.

Skipp continued his report. "Everything else looks pretty dead, just storage and bunk houses, that kind of stuff. Nothing we have to worry about.

"Okay, it's settled then. Jay, you take out that power source, and we'll get down to that pit and see about putting that Kracken out of business."

"Hey," Jay interrupted, "just because I've gotta take care of our electrical problems first, doesn't mean I don't want a piece of that Kracken thing, okay?"

"Okay."

After a while, Mike and the group of eighteen came to a small camp, not unlike the one they had left behind at the clearing in the jungle. Mike was startled as one of the children called out.

"Yooo-woo-woo."

He looked around, wondering what the significance of the call was.

After a few seconds passed, a responding call was heard. "Wooo-yoo-yoo."

Mike dipped his chin in approval. It was some kind of identifying signal the children had devised.

Up ahead he could see, coming from behind a large boulder, two children—girls: one a teen and the other much younger. The children all ran to meet the two new children, apparently surprised, yet relieved to find them there. The voices mixed into one confused chorus as they all tried talking at once, the noise echoing off the vaulted ceiling high above their heads.

Mike removed the straps he had made from bedding at the first camp and lowered the still unconscious youth to the ground. While checking the bandages, to make sure they had not come loose, he looked toward the head of the group, listening to the exchange of stories.

The new girls spoke over one another, beginning, interrupting, and finishing each other's sentences.

Breaking from the crowd, the smaller of the two new girls looked up at Mike as if she knew him. "You must be Mike," Sally stated.

"You've seen my friends?" Mike asked excitedly. Forgetting himself, he walked through the crowd of children and knelt in front of the child grasping her by her shoulders. "Where are they? Where did they go?"

"Don't hurt her," the older of the two girls said. She looked at Mike. "I'm Andrea and that's my little sister Sally you're squeezing."

"Oh, sorry," Mike said, letting go of the little girl. "I didn't mean to hurt you—her."

He stood and faced Andrea. "You said you've seen my friends?" Mike could not force the anxiousness from his voice. Those men were his responsibility, and his only hope of getting these children off this planet.

"Yes, they took our brother and went to the light."

Instantly, the crowd went silent, and again, the old doubt and fear darkened the children's faces. A rapid current of concern and fear flowed through the group of children, eating away at the foundation of the newly formed trust.

Leaning down to whisper to Rosemary, Mike asked, "What's going on?"

"I don't know," the child responded, her eyes wide, studying her friends. "Want me to go find out?" she asked starting toward the now frightened and confused children.

Angry voices rose from the group.

Frankie spoke up, addressing Mike. "They say three more grown-ups dressed like you took their brother into the light," he said pointing at the two girls who had recently joined them. "Why would these men take Peter to the light unless they wanted to take him to the Kracken, huh?"

Mike could sense a growing fear and knew if they were compelled by fear, a strong voice could compel them to act impulsively. He also knew that all that anger and pent-up frustration would be directed at him.

Before he could say anything in his own defense, a small voice cried out, silencing them all. Rosemary walked toward the crowd. "Hey, guys, don't forget it was Mike here who saved Matt from being whipped back at the clearing."

Mike could hear voices agreeing with Rosemary, but the bulk of the crowd was still unsure. The children wanted to believe that Mike was here to help them, but they had been abused and mistreated too many times to simply trust the words of an unknown adult, especially in the light of this recent revelation.

Rosemary continued urging, "…And besides, when he had me here in the inside before," she said indicating the cavern, "he could have taken me to the light then; but he didn't, did he? Come on, guys, let's give him a chance. Maybe he really can help us," she finished with a plea.

From the back of the crowd, the two girls, fighting to be heard, finally broke through. "Wait! Wait! Now wait a minute," Andrea said. "We never said that the other men were C-men. All we said was that they took Peter with them to go investigate the light. They were going to try and destroy it." Exasperation made her tired and she leaned against a boulder as she finished.

Taking this opportunity, Mike finally spoke to the children. "If I wanted to hurt any of you, I could have already done that by now. It's like I told you before, I only want to help you—to get you out of here."

The children began to quiet down.

Mike continued, "I came here with three of my friends. We were separated during that earthquake two days ago. I got stuck here inside the mountain and them on the outside. But I'm sure they would have continued looking for you guys, and if these two…" he said, pointing at Andrea and Sally, "say they met three strangers who said they wanted to find this Kracken thing, then can't you see they've got to be my friends!"

Facing the two girls, Mike asked, "What did these men look like? Did they give you their names? Did one of them carry an electronic notepad with him?"

"Yeah, that's the one Andrea has a crush on," Sally said adding emphasis to her sister's name. Turning to face the crowd, she displayed her satisfied grin, happy to be the one to share the news.

Andrea pinched the back of Sally's bicep and glowered at the little girl.

Grabbing her upper arm, she cried out and stepped away from her sister. "Well, you do?" she said, scrunching her face and rubbing her sore arm. This caused laughter to ripple through the small group, losing control of the smiles they had been trying to hide behind. Just as quick as the mood had darkened, it changed, now that they had a reason to believe again.

"What about teasing?" Andrea said. "You did promise Mr. Jonas you wouldn't do that."

"Wasn't teasing. Just telling him about Mr. Skipp," she said, poking her tongue at her sister's ever-reddening face.

"It's okay, sweetheart," Mike smiled at Andrea. "We'll speak no more of it. And you, Sally, stop it."

Andrea smiled in relief.

"Those are my friends. We came here together to see what was going on out here, and now that we are here, we're going to help you kids. We're going to take you somewhere where this Kracken and even Waters will never hurt you again."

The children cheered.

"How you gonna get us outta here, mister?" one child asked.

"We've got a spaceship hidden out in the desert. She's more than enough ship to get us out of here. But first, I've got to help my friends destroy that Kracken, whatever it is."

He paused and looked over the crowd. Dusty faces did little to hide the burgeoning joy that shone in their eyes. Though small and frail, barely clothed and not well fed, the children showed a remarkable strength of character that Mike found a mystery.

"What do you say we start off with one of you telling me what exactly this Kracken is," Mike asked the crowd at large. No one seemed eager to answer. Instead, they looked around exchanging glances.

"It's a beast," Andrea said.

"A monster," another voice added in.

"If you're lucky, they just let it kill you, but when they want to have fun, they just lock you in with it and release the gas," Andrea finished.

Mike did not say anything, but his face must have shown his confusion because Andrea began to explain.

"When the C-men just want to have fun or torture one of us for whatever reason, they bind the Kracken and lock you in the pit. Once the seal is set, they release the jiyst—"

"Jiyst?" Mike asked incredulously. *What would Ted Waters want with Jiyst and why a gas?*" He asked himself as understanding continued its dawn.

Andrea was still talking, "...the gas causes you to hear, almost feel the rage of the Kracken."

"They locked you in with this beast?" Mike asked rhetorically.

"Not me, but enough of my friends have been through it." Her face was stone, her eyes hollow.

"Can this Kracken be killed?" Mike asked, not sure if he intended to ask the question out loud.

"I don't know," Andrea answered vacantly.

The rest of the children were quiet. Rosemary leaned against Mike, resting her head against him. He cradled her in the crook of his arm, rubbing her shoulders as if warding off a chill.

Frankie, the older brown-haired boy, who had spoken up earlier, said, "The Kracken's a carnivore. It doesn't care what it eats—you, me, it makes no difference."

"It eats meat, and if it's made of meat, it can be killed," Mike said. "So, Waters uses the threat of the Kracken to keep you children working in the mines."

If Mike hated Ted Waters before, what he felt now was more akin to loathing. He would kill the man, and he would enjoy doing it. He would kill him for Mary and for each of his children; and he would kill him for these children. Finally, Mike decided he would kill him just for the joy of seeing him die.

Vengeance is mine, the voice echoed.

Mike stood abruptly. Rose looked up at him, a question in her small face. Walking away from the children, he clinched his fists, grinding them into his temples. "You will not rob me," he said through clinched teeth. "I tried it Your way, and you took Mary from me."

Trust me.

"You ask too much. I will have my vengeance," he spoke into the darkness.

Those who live by the sword....

"Enough," Mike screamed, silencing the voice in his mind. The gentle breeze, which had begun, died down.

"You all right, Mike?"

Mike jumped and turned toward the voice. Rosemary stood a short distance away from him, half hidden by an outcropping of rock. "You shouldn't sneak up on people, you know," he said.

"I didn't mean to. I was worried about you."

Mike rubbed his scalp roughly and exhaled. "Well, you might as well come on over here." He reached out his hand to the little girl. He sat down and she climbed up in his lap.

"You know," she began, "when I'm sad, I pray."

"Here?" Mike asked, pushing the girl away so he could see her face. "What do you have to pray about and who would listen?" He regretted the words almost as soon as he had uttered them.

Rose looked down and away from him.

He cursed himself for stepping on what little hope she had. "Hey, hey, I didn't mean that. It's just that, well…" How would he ever explain such a confused subject to a little girl? He hardly understood it himself. *If only Mary were here she…* He did not allow himself to finish the thought.

Rosemary was looking into his face, searching his eyes. "You hurt bad, huh, Mike? What happened?" she asked but kept talking.

Mike was grateful that he would not have to answer her question; the child had a way of getting to him with her straightforward manner and honest expectation. *How had she remained so pure in this pit?* he thought to himself.

"You know what," she said.

Mike wasn't so sure he wanted to know.

"There are times when I can almost see Jesus," she finished, answering his unasked question. She stared at him. She was serious.

Mike just looked at the child. "We'd better head back, so I can figure out how to get to my buddies." He stood, taking Rose by the hand and leading her back to the campsite and the rest of the children.

Once back with the others, Mike focused his attention on the light. "Seeing that I don't really know my way around yet, I'll need a guide to show me the way. So who's gonna help me catch up to my friends?"

The first hand up was Rosemary's. "No, no," Mike said, "things might get a little rough; I'll need somebody just a tad bit bigger." He ruffled her hair as he spoke.

"Hey," she protested. "I'm plenty big enough. Got you here, didn't I?"

"Nothing doing; you're staying right here. I'll go with him." It was Frankie. "That way I can keep an eye on him, and you can stay out of trouble."

Mike was taken aback by the open distrust revealed by the boy's statement. Seems he still had work to do in winning them over. No one else took notice as the children all laughed at the thought of Rosemary staying out of trouble. Mike understood from the exchange that her wandering off was a fairly common occurrence. *Lucky for him*, he thought, *she had wandered out and found him the day of his accident.*

"Good," Mike said. "I had hoped you would be the one to come along. I could use someone with your attitude about things." He met Frankie's stare, and he knew the child understood him. He slapped the young man on the shoulder and extended his hand.

"Mike Stone," he said.

The boy took the offered hand and looking around at the small crowd with hints of the pride he felt inside sparkling in his eyes, he said, "I guess we better get started, Mike."

"Okay, let's be off."

Then turning to the group, Mike said, "The rest of you get everything you need together and be ready to leave as soon as we get back. I don't know when that will be, so just be ready."

They didn't have much, a few rocks and trinkets they had picked up along the way, and for whatever reason, had attached some value to. There was not much about this planet to endear it to the children.

Rosemary stood at the edge of the camp looking after the two as they walked off; her little mind working as it always did. As she waved her good-byes, a smile stretched itself across her face. "You didn't say how far behind," she muttered. "And you didn't say not to follow." She yelled after them, "See you later." The smile growing ever larger as she waved.

"What are you planning," Andrea asked, walking up on Rosemary, her voice soft and lending itself to conspiracy.

Rosemary turned with a start. "Nothing. Leave me alone!"

"No use getting mad! If you don't tell me, I'll just go tell everyone you're up to something, and you won't get a minute to yourself."

"Okay, okay, just keep quiet, will ya? Well, I've always wondered what the Kracken looked like, and this is my best chance ever. Not to mention my last."

"So what're you gonna do, sneak up there or something? 'Cause that would be stupid," Andrea said, not believing that even Rose could imagine something that strange. Looking down and seeing the expression on the younger girl's face, Andrea almost laughed. "No. No, you can't be serious. Do you know what Frankie would do to us if he found out you left the camp after he told you not to?"

"So who's gonna tell him?"

"You've had some dumb ideas, but this one's the worst yet. Have you thought about what would happen if you got caught?"

Looking at Andrea with pleading eyes, Rosemary said, "So, you in or out?" She paused allowing Andrea to consider the offer.

"I'm out and so are you. You're not going anywhere near that light. You're going to stay right here with us until Skipp and his friends come back and get us. Do you understand me?" All pretense of conspiracy vanished; all that remained was Andrea; the older girl who sometimes bossed her around.

"You know," Rosemary began, "it's because of people like you that I wander off so much."

"Yeah, well one of these days a *drag* is gonna get you. Now get back to camp." Despite herself, Andrea smiled at the little girl as she sulked her way back to camp. Andrea looked down the trail, the way the men had gone, and then at Rose. She smiled and shook her head. *How Rose reminded her of herself.*

Chapter Fifteen

The air smelled heavy of hydraulic fluid and fuels along with the musky odor of a large animal, stale and heavy. A short distance away, the three men studied the compound as it stretched out, disappearing into the inky darkness before them.

Skipp checked back over his shoulder to make sure Peter had stayed hidden where they left him. *So far, so good.*

In the middle of the compound stood what had to be the command center. Everything seemed centered on it, with walkways and power lines connecting it to the other structures.

The building itself was not particularly impressive in its own right, but compared to the others, it was grand; the only building having multiple floors and made of stone. The surrounding structures looked temporary in nature, made of canvas and a synthetic siding fashioned to look like wood.

Power lines originated from the main building and stretched out like the web of a Zygiella orb spider or like arteries stretching out from a heart, connecting all the various points in the compound. "See that?" Skipp said pointing to the main building.

"What's up with the light show," Jay whispered. On top of the main building a single antenna array pulsated with a visible beam that disappeared through a chimney-like structure to the outside world many thousands of feet above it. "That's got to be the cause of the electronic interference that messed up my reading earlier," Skipp said. "That's gotta be the first target."

"Done." Jay angled himself toward the building.

All about the ground lay cables, 10 centimeters in diameter and synthetic piping half buried beneath the fine dust that seemed everywhere inside the mountain.

The sentries, such as they were, stood lazily off to one side of the main entry. The men leaned against the stone wall, laughing at an off colored joke. Neither man paid any attention to the large black man as he ambled toward the main door. "Anybody inside," Jay said nonchalantly, not slowing his stride.

"Just Old Fred," one of the men said, not looking up, and reached into his vest pocket for a cigarette.

"Those things will kill you, you know?"

"Hey, bud, when I want your opinion, I'll give it to you," the man answered, handing a cigarette to his partner.

At that moment, the second man looked up at Jay. "Hey, who are you?" He stood abruptly and moved his hand toward his gun.

He never reached it.

Jay hammered the guard on top of his head with his fist. The man's mouth slammed shut and several teeth chattering, exploded from pursed lips. He dropped where he had stood, the severed cigarette mixed with his blood pooling around his down turned face. Continuing his movement toward the second guard, Jay spun and backhanded the man against his temple. Finishing the move, he landed an explosive elbow strike into the guard's nose.

The fight was over. The eyes of the first man rolled back into his skull, his legs and arms twitching as his partner collapsed atop of him. Both men lay at Jay's feet. Neither moved.

Skipp and Jonas jogged over to where Jay was, dragging the unconscious men into the foyer of the building. "You enjoyed that, didn't you," Skipp said, looking at the downed men.

"You have no idea," Jay answered with a wry smile. "I've been wanting to hit somebody ever since we landed on this rock."

"What are you doing, doc," Skipp asked Jonas when he saw him removing one of the men's uniforms.

Jonas pressed a hypo against each man's neck. "It's a CSN and muscle inhibitor. It'll make sure these two don't wake up and start screaming."

"Somebody's got to stand watch at the door. Looks like you and I just got a new job."

Skipp looked from Jonas to the men on the floor. It was obvious Jay was too large to fit into either of the men's uniforms. That left him and Jonas. "What if they have lice or something?"

Jay took the load of explosives Skipp had put together and set off to find the main power source. "I'll be back, and when I do, be ready to run."

Skipp and Jonas donned the uniforms and assumed the guard position by the door. The uniforms were made up of gray fatigue-type pants and gray loose fitting shirts, cinched with a wide red web belt at the waist. The men each had a holster strapped to his side with a thigh strap securing the end of the holster in place. The uniform shirts had a green patch on the right shoulder with a white "C" in the middle overlaying a faded globe: The Company logo.

Skipp nodded to Jonas and touched the patch on his shoulder. "C-men, get it?"

Jonas nodded in return.

That symbol alone proved that The Company was behind the enslaving of the children, but the men still had not tied together the purpose of the operation as a whole. Skipp recorded scans of the base into his notepad for study later.

Voices approached from the darkness. Skipp and Jonas assumed the lazy posture the guards had held and pretended to be in deep conversation. Each man surreptitiously un-holstered his blaster and held it low, hiding from the view of the approaching men.

A group of about five uniformed men walked by and not so much as looked at the supposed guards. A fine layer of bright yellow-blue dust covered their uniforms. Jonas noted that the dust even covered their holsters and weapons, indicating a long period of non-use. The men disappeared down a corridor on the far side, and their voices faded into the darkness.

"That was close," Skipp whispered.

"Too close; Jay better hurry. I don't like sitting out here in the open like this," Jonas breathed through gritted teeth.

As if on cue, the front doors burst open and Jay ran out screaming, "Move it. We've been made."

White lights flooded the compound while at the same time klaxons screamed in alarm. Uniformed men appeared as if from nowhere, but none seemed on alert. That would soon change.

The three men ran, heading for the safety of darkness. Behind them, laser fire hissed through the air, barely missing them. The rock face exploded as blaster fire slammed into it, splinters of molten rock spraying the air.

Turning to his friends, Jay shouted, "Three-two-one, get down!" The entire mountain seemed to rock as the compound exploded. The central command building seemed to swell as if it was taking a deep breath, concaved then erupted into brilliant flames as explosion after concussive explosion rocked the cavern.

Super-heated gases from the explosions back fed through the main piping that connected the entire compound. As plasma mixed with highly charged ions, structure after structure burst into flames, taking out many of the C-men with them as they did.

Atop the central building, the communication array seemed to rise straight up like a rocket blasting off, before it swelled and then collapsed in on itself, crashing to the floor of the cave. As it fell, the transmission beacon began to flicker, fade, and seemed to implode before erupting into a cascade of sparkling, hissing magnesium.

The attack died down and became unfocused as the troops' mindset shifted from capture to survival mode. Men, set aflame, screamed as they fled buildings, seeking relief from the heat and burning. Some dove into the fine dust, rolling back and forth trying to extinguish the flames while others dropped and lay still where they fell, a listless pyre.

Jumping up, the three men ran for the deeper cover of darkness. As they did, a small group of C-men spotted them and broke away from the compound in pursuit. Layers of blaster fire and lasers cut through the air behind and over the three men as they ran.

"I'm getting too old for this." Jonas gasped out in between breaths.

"Peter," Skipp called out as they approached the place where he had told the boy to hide. "Peter," he called again, fear gripping his heart.

Coming around a bend, Skipp saw Peter. A C-man held him, pulled back against his chest; a blaster pressed painfully to his temple.

"Come on out here where I can see you," the uniformed man said in clipped tones. He held the child's throat with his other hand, the larynx compressed between his index finger and thumb. He began to squeeze his hand closed, reducing the gap between his fingers, shutting off Peter's air supply as he did.

To no avail, Peter clawed and scratched at the man's gloved hands. The boy's eyes began to bulge then rolled back in his head until only the whites showed. "All three of you. Now! Or the kid dies right here, right now."

Peter coughed and gagged as he continued to claw at the man's hand. Jay swore and stepped out from the shadows. "You hurt that child, you die," Jay said staring at the man through slitted eyes.

"Drop those blasters. Now kick them over here," the man said and smiled. Activating his com-link, he spoke into his communicator. "I got them."

Silence followed as he listened through his earpiece. Then after a small delay, he said, "Three, plus one of the kids."

Silence.

"Copy that."

The man looked at his captives and slowly squeezed his fingers together. Peter's face went white as his eyes rolled back and he collapsed.

Jay screamed and rushed the man. The blaster fired. A wave of white-hot pain tore through him. He collapsed. The C-man, having anticipating this, turned and fired on Skipp and Jonas in succession, dropping them where they stood.

The sweet musky animal odor was stronger here, Jay noted from behind closed eyes. The smell reminded him of horse and cattle stalls back on his father's plantation. Figuring he was being monitored anyway, Jay slowly opened his eyes only to find his hands trussed behind him, knotted to his feet. He moaned as the residual pain from the blaster resonated in his muscles.

Across from him, lying face down on the hard-packed dirt floor was Jonas and Skipp. Peter was nowhere to be seen. Jay wasn't sure if it was the smell or the feeling of wetness that got his attention first, but he became aware that he was lying in a shallow but foul stream. Of its makeup, he was not sure he wanted to know.

Walls rose on three sides, melding into the ceiling as if they had been carved from the stone. A dirt ramp led down into the pit on the far side which lay about forty yards from where the men lay bound. They were in a bowl-shaped depression, obviously man-made. Crude seats had been cut into the stone surface, and stadium lights, dimly lit, hung from poorly constructed poles and wiring.

Rolling, Jay managed to position himself away from the stream near to where Skipp and Jonas were starting to rouse. "Skipp, Skipp, wake up," Jay whispered loudly.

Skipp groaned and opened his eyes only to find that he, too, had been tied hands to feet, behind his back.

"Where are we?" Jonas managed. "And what is that odor?"

"Where's Peter?" Skipp asked, his voice tense.

At that moment, a spotlight shone down on the men, blinding them. "I see you have wakened. Good." It was the voice of the man that had shot them.

Jay trained his ear on the voice trying to locate the speaker, remembering he had a debt to pay him.

"Where's Peter?" Skipp demanded. "If you've hurt him—"

"I don't think you're in any position to make threats," the voice said. "Don't worry; you'll see your little friend soon."

As if on cue, the sound of a diesel engine roared to life and a small truck-like vehicle rolled toward the men from the right side of the arena. On the back of the flatbed, trapped inside a clear enclosure, Peter stood terrified.

One of the uniformed men approached the truck and taking a canister, lit it and set it near a vented window by the foot of the cage where Peter was. The incandescent flame soon died down, and an eerie bluish-yellow smoke rose lazily up around the boy and began encircling Peter's face and head.

"Jiyst—no-no, not the gas. Please!" Peter screamed and began to fight, trying to free himself, kicking and scampering about his transparent prison cell. As he screamed, he inhaled more and more of the smoke until he collapsed to the floor coughing and gagging, fighting for every breath.

Just at that moment, a grating sound, like stone dragging against stone, filled the small amphitheater. One of the three walls of the small enclosure slid slowly and noisily into the ceiling.

Jay could see that the stream he had been laying in originated from beneath where the wall had risen. From behind the ascending partition, a roar or animal's scream poured out into the arena and echoed off the stonewalls.

In a cage, not unlike the one Peter was in, stood a creature at least six meters tall, bipedal and mad with apparent hunger. The animal's skin was leathery, but it had fur along its shoulders and back. Its canines extended from both its top and bottom jaw and shone wet with saliva. Well-muscled and with claws sharp enough to gouge the thick synthi-glass of its cage, the animal stared at Peter with predatory focus. Huge droplets of puss-colored mucus dripped from its open mouth and ran in puddles beneath its grated floor.

Jay realized now what the nature of the stream he had been laying in. He smelled his sleeve and gagged.

The uniformed man backed up the flatbed of the truck until the two cages touched. Peter redoubled his screaming, as the men finally understood what it meant to be taken to the Kracken.

Under the effects of the jiyst gas, Peter's mind was completely open to the emotional energy directed at him by the Kracken. He could feel its anger, its frustration at being trapped, and its overwhelming desire to feed. He could feel its desire for satiation. He screamed in blind panic.

With its prey so close, the Kracken multiplied its efforts to break free of its cage and feed. Massive claws tore at the glass enclosure and with each blow, small flecks of synthi-glass broke free from the surface, and the rend grew larger.

The man's voice called down again. "I do believe you said you were going to kill me. Well, that's not going to happen. Once that Kracken breaks free from its cage, I'm not sure he'll want the extra work of tearing the kid out or just enjoy you guys without all the fuss. Either way, it'll be fun to watch."

"Why the gas?" Jay screamed at the darkness.

"Oh, don't worry," the taunting voice returned. "We won't be using the gas on you. I want you completely sober as you're being eaten alive." The man began to laugh. "We actually found out about the gas by accident, but once we found that the kids could feel the animal's emotions and lust, well, we just couldn't resist the entertainment value of it every now and again." His hoarse laughter floated down to the men.

Peter's screams filled the cavern as the Kracken tore furiously to get at him. The sound of splintering glass crescendoed above the cries, mixed with the bellows and roars of the Kracken.

"Unfortunately, I won't be able to stay for dinner," he chuckled. "With the loss of this one," he said pointing toward Peter, "and the one other we wrote off as an example, we are going to need to get the rest of the kids back to work, or we'll never make quota. You know how Mr. Waters hates failure."

The click of the P.A. system turning off was loud in its silence. The only sounds left were Peter's futile cries and the snarling growls of the Kracken.

"We've got to get out of here," Skipp said stating the obvious.

"Scoot this way," Jonas said. "Turn your back to me; maybe I can undo your knots."

Then the lights went out.

Chapter Sixteen

"Is too." Travist complained, his young voice cutting into the sound of the shallow brook, bugs, and gentle breeze. Scuttle clouds banked high overhead, and the boys played as boys do, running through the fields and grasses near the old house. In the few weeks that they had been together, the three boys had become fast friends.

Mary sat on the blanket, entertaining her daughter as flocks of anhinga, avocet, and dovekie flew overhead, their whistling squawking cries filling the air in their wake. Mary pulled a twig from the chubby hand so the child would not put it into her mouth even as she pointed and squeaked trying to imitate the bird sounds. Smiling at her daughter, Mary sipped distractedly from a large mason jar of Nonna's sweet tea. Her grandmother still made it the old-fashioned way by setting out a tall pitcher and allowing the sun to brew the tea long and slow, she added so much sugar you could see the white crystals collecting on the bottom of the container. Mary swore it was the boys' favorite part, as it had been hers as a child.

She sighed. *Today I am not a child, and this is anything but the good old days.*

Today she was an adult, a mother of three and her friend—her sister—was on her way to meet her, and things were not good between them. *Would they ever be again? Could they be?*

Looking at her boys, Mary envied them their childish innocence. She longed for the days when she and Iona could fight and still be best friends by dinner. Now she wondered if they could even be civil. In her heart, Mary truly feared that she hated her sister.

"Mary? Mary?" Nonna's voice rang out much as it always had.

Mary stood and turned to face her grandmother. "Over here, Nonna." Something about the way Nonna looked made Mary start toward the older woman. "What is it?" she asked, arriving at her side.

Nonna appeared calm, but she had that anxious look Mary had come to respect. With a cooing chuckle, Sissy reached for her great-grandmother, and Mary handed her to the older woman.

"It's nothing, I'm sure," Nonna began, adjusting the baby on her hip.

Mary knew when Nonna said it was nothing that it was usually anything but.

"I had a dream is all."

"About me? The kids?"

"Well…"

"Come on, Nonna, what was it? Did you dream something bad happened to us?"

"No. It was Iona. I'm afraid for her Mary."

Mary's face fell as she turned and looked away from her grandmother.

Viola laid a wrinkled hand on Mary's cheek. "Can't you forgive her, Mary? You know what the child went through; you know she didn't have as good a start as you did."

"Don't give me that. She grew up here just like I did. Oh, sure she had been abandoned and lived on the streets. I'm not making light of all the bad that happened to her. But, Nonna, sooner or later a person has to take responsibility for themselves. She has been doing whatever she wanted since we were kids, and everybody just made excuses for the poor orphaned girl. Even me.

"The only time I ever stood up to her was when it came to Mike, and she couldn't even take that. Wouldn't even let me have the man I loved. And now—and now she's working with the company that tried to kill my family, and you want me to just forgive her!?

"I can't. I won't." Mary looked away. She knew she had spoken too harshly, and she had no desire to hurt Nonna, but she was hurting herself right now.

"Oh, child," Nonna said and slipped her weathered hand around her shoulder, the child nuzzled between the two of them. "You know that's what they did to the Lord, too. And even Stephen, when he was being stoned, allowed forgiveness to cover his heart." She paused and adjusted her embrace around Mary. "Not you, child. Not you, but the Lord in you."

Mary allowed herself to be pulled into the maternal embrace. Maybe she was not as grown up as she thought. A hug still seemed to make things better.

The two women stood in silence. Mary cried and Nonna prayed. The baby wiggled to get down and stood, leaning against her mother's leg, tottering before trying to step away. Below them, down the hill, the three boys played like brothers. Their happy voices rang up the rise like the fragrance of fresh baked pies on a breeze.

"They even look alike," Mary said into Nonna's shoulder. She knew Nonna understood she was speaking of the boys.

"People said that about you and Iona when you were children."

"I know," Mary said in a whisper. She looked down into the upturned face of her daughter and tossed a soft curl that had fallen across the child's forehead. *How Lord,* Mary thought to herself, *can I forgive her?* Tears streaked Mary's cheeks.

How can you not? The voice seemed to answer from the breeze.

Ted Waters sat behind his large desk in semi-darkness. Filtered light fought through smoked glass windows as he reviewed the second of three files on his desk.

He dropped a personnel file on top of the one laying face up in the center of the desk. The name on the new file: Mary Stone.

He knew what the connection between Mike and Iona was: her attraction for the man. But something stood out about the way Iona reacted to Mary. It was more than jealousy. That he could understand. There was something more, and for the moment, it eluded him. He did not like not knowing.

He picked up the third file and opened it, set to the task of discovery. He reached for the over-large cigar and drew on it. The faint glow illuminated the area of his face around his mouth. Apple-brandy flavored smoke circled his head before gently being drawn out by silent vents.

He opened all three files, laid them side by side, and studied them. He knew the answer was in front of him. He knew with diligence, he would find it.

Mike came around the wall of the enclosure and wondered at the silence, Frankie close behind him. He had hurried once the explosions began, sure that it was his crew doing what they had come to do. But since the original eruptions, everything had grown deathly quiet.

Voices approached out of the darkness.

Mike pressed himself against the wall, pulling Frankie into a natural alcove alongside him. Mike lifted a finger to his lips then mouthed, "Somebody's coming."

A flashlight beam danced around the corner, rising and falling with each step on the man that held it. "Too bad we couldn't stay. I really wanted to see the big guy get his."

"Yeah," a second voice agreed, "he's the one that promised to kill you, isn't he?" They all laughed.

"Promises, promises. I guess vid-replay will just have to do," the one with the flashlight answered as the group of men passed the alcove.

Frankie looked at Mike as if to ask what the men were talking about.

After a moment had passed, Mike peaked out from the recess. Once he was sure the men had gone, he scampered down the path from which the men had come. It was then that they heard it.

Frankie froze. "It's the Kracken," he said through clenched teeth. "I can't go in there." He dropped to the floor and pulled his knees up to his chest. "I c-can't. I can't go in there."

Mike looked at the young man with a mixture of pity and exasperation. "Okay." Mike looked away from the cowering youth. After several moments, he softened. "Wait here," he said with a sigh and gripped the boy's shoulder. "Don't move or I'll never find you in the darkness."

Mike made his way down a hard-packed path made smooth by earthmovers and foot traffic. The sounds of a snarling beast rose to almost deafening, reverberating from the walls and ceiling of the enclosed corridor. Mike took a breath and held it for just a moment before allowing it to leak past his lips.

Bringing his laser blaster up, Mike looked at the weapon in his hand and wished he had brought the laser rifle Jay favored rather than just a hand blaster. He readied himself.

With one last check, Mike swung around the corner and came face to face with the Kracken.

The animal's attention was turned toward something Mike could not see, and he was glad that it appeared to be held inside some kind of enclosure. He knew his hand blaster would be no match for an animal of this size.

"Mike, Mike is that you? You're alive! How—never mind," Jonas called out. "Hurry, hurry, cut us loose."

Collecting the weapons that had been stored nearby, Mike ran to where his three friends lay hogtied, their hands secured to their feet with a synthi-cord. In rapid succession, he cut their bonds and pulled them to their feet. "Let's get out of here; that glass is not going to hold that thing much longer." He tilted his head toward the Kracken.

"No," Jay said and pulled away from Mike's hand. "Peter's in there."

"What?" Mike said in confusion. "That thing is coming out of that cage, guys, and we don't want to be anywhere near here when it does!"

"Give me your blaster," Skipp said and followed after Jay.

Jonas turned to Mike. "Peter's one of the kids that helped us. He's in that cage over there…by the Kracken! We have to get him out, now!"

Reaching the cage, Jay tried to calm Peter, now panic-stricken. The boy screamed and flailed, kicking and swinging his arms in wild arcs. His actions seemed to entice the already enraged Kracken.

Firing near the base of the cage, Skipp shattered the glass. Jumping through the hole, Skipp struggled through the shards of the frame, grabbed the teenage boy, turned, and ran.

Peter, still under the influence of the jiyst, fought against his would-be deliverer, broke free of Skipp and backed into the cage. He locked eyes with Jay just as the big man scampered through the hole and entered the cage. "I got you, buddy," Jay said as he wrapped the boy in his muscled arms, locking his arms down by his side.

Skipp took a hand full of the spice that lay on the floor of the cage, blew it into the thrashing boy's face. Jay looked at him startled. "What're you doin', mon?"

"I figured he's already under the influence of the spice, a little more won't hurt him. Maybe I can redirect his thoughts," Skipp said in explanation. Skipp grabbed Peter's face between his hands. Forcing empathy into his words, he directed the boy to calm down and follow him. Doing his best to feel the words he spoke, Skipp began to back out of the enclosure. Peter relaxed and allowed Jay to walk him through the shattered opening and toward the earthen ramp.

Mike yelled, "It's getting out! Hurry!"

Jay lifted Peter, who had gone limp, and slung him over his broad shoulder. They ran.

They fled up the ramp, and slipped into the shadows. The sounds of crashing and breaking synthi-glass and twisting steel washed up from the pit like the roar of a tsunami. Soon afterwards, the Kracken's roar careened up the passage and danced along the walls and ceiling, causing the floor to vibrate beneath their feet. It was free.

"Quick, in here." Mike directed them into the small alcove where he had told Frankie to wait.

Shortly after they were inside, the Kracken tore by, its roar and footfall breaking up the smooth path and shaking rocks and dust loose from the overhang.

The men held their breath as the sound of the beast died away in the distance.

"Peter, Peter." Skipp spoke into the face of the semi-conscious youth, slapping one cheek.

Peter did not respond.

"It's gonna take time."

All four men jumped and turned toward the sound of the voice. It had been Frankie.

"I'd forgotten about you," Mike said.

"No wonder, after how I acted," he said, shame coloring his voice.

"Maybe I would have acted the same way if I'd known what I was getting into," Mike said and grabbed the child's shoulder squeezing it. "I had no idea what a Kracken was before going into that pit." He shuddered.

Frankie doubted if any of these men would have cowered the way he had, but he was grateful for Mike having said so. "Let's get back to camp," he said in a shallow voice.

"Let's. Which way?" Jay asked.

"These are my friends," Mike said as he introduced the three men to Frankie. "Now lead the way."

Frankie led the group back out the way they had come, traveling quickly.

Sometime later, as they came over the last rise from the kids' campsite, Peter stirred and asked to be putdown. He stood on weak legs and looked around. He had wet himself.

Noticing the boy's shamed expression, Mike laid a hand on his shoulder. "Don't let that bother you, son. What happened back there stays back there. Okay?" He looked at both boys who seemed to understand.

"From where I'm standing, we could all use a dip in the stream," Jay said, lifting his tunic to his nose, and they all laughed their agreement.

Finally, coming into the circle of the torch light, the group of children fell on them hugging them and rejoicing. No one seemed to take notice of the foul odor lingering around the new arrivals.

"We're glad to see you, too," Frankie said, trying to take in everyone's face at a glance. "But we need to go. The Kracken is loose."

After the hellos and the group afforded a chance to wash up and change clothes, Mike called the swelling band together. "Pack up," he ordered. "The Kracken is loose, and the C-men are looking for you. We need to get you back to our ship and off this planet before either one of them finds us."

All traces of distrust that permeated the group earlier had lifted and in its place trust, confidence, and hope had settled. Rose stood close by Mike, holding his hand and looking at him with admiration and childish pride.

"Take only what you absolutely need," Skipp called out. "We have almost everything else on the ship, so don't worry about extra clothing."

The camp was busy with children rolling their few belongings into their bedrolls. Having anticipated the men's return, the camp was a flurry of silent action. In just a few minutes, they were ready to move.

Chapter Seventeen

"They're going where?" Iona demanded.

Her secretary looked up at her with startled eyes. Iona tried to find a connection with the girl, remembering she had been one of Paul Adams' hires and had dated the late executive. The secretary's long black hair lay across slender shoulders in thick rivulets. Her cheeks flushed with a combination of fear and frustration at the perception of stirring Iona's ire.

"When did they leave, and how come you didn't inform me of this earlier?" Iona asked, closing the distance between herself and the seated woman.

"Th-the f-fleet left last night," the girl stammered, "heading for one of the mining planets in th-the Gliese System Sector."

Noticing the secretary cowering away from her, Iona softened her demeanor. She took a breath, held it a moment, then spoke. "How many ships did they take with them, and what was the mission?"

The young lady relaxed visibly. "Five. They took five ships." Then she leaned closer to Iona. "The order said something about getting production back on line."

She continued now in a conspiratorial tone. "I thought Mr. Waters was going to kill us all. I could hear him shouting at that Mr. Trevino from out here in the foyer about some guy named Mike Stone slowing down production. I've never seen Mr. Waters so out of control. Have you? It was scary."

She looked around as if fearing she might be overheard. "Ms. Bowers, can I ask you a question, off the record, you know, just as women?"

Iona, standing with her arms folded across her breast, looked down at the young pretty face. *How old was this girl anyway— eighteen?* She could see the woman appraising her. Iona's long, red hair had been French braided and pulled over her right shoulder and tied at the end with a piece of forest green ribbon.

"Call me Iona." She relaxed for the girl's sake. "What's your question?"

"Is it true you dated Paul—Mr. Adams—before he died?"

"You might say that," Iona answered and wondered where this was leading.

"It's just that…I went out with him once or twice, and well, I thought it was pretty…all right. You know, dating one of the VPs, but now…well, he's dead. Anyway, he'd said some things to me when we were together."

"Like?" Iona encouraged.

"Like, maybe he was just trying to impress me, but he said something about taking over this department next quarter. He said Mr. Waters was going to promote him because of his increase in the profit margins in the mining division. He said something about using children because it was cheaper and…"

"I think you've said enough, young lady." A stern voice cut in from behind Iona. It was Trevino. Iona had forgotten that the queer little man had been following her. She cursed herself inwardly.

"Ms. Bowers, I think it's time you and I had that little talk." Trevino then turned his attention back to the still seated secretary. "I will deal with you later."

The girl seemed to shrink in on herself.

Without turning, Iona answered, "There's nothing I can think of that I need to discuss with you." She knew it would agitate him.

"Well, maybe Mr. Waters would be interested in your connections with Mary Stone and Viola Johnson." Iona could tell he was reaching, trying to get her to expose herself. She turned her attention back to the young lady who had stood when

Trevino made his presence known. "Let me give you some advice, sweetheart, if I may," Iona said wryly.

"Please do," the girl said, her voice filled with fear.

"Two things you should do right away. One, start looking for a new job, something away from The Company, and two, get that bruise taken care of."

"What bruise?" the girl started to say when she was knocked off her feet as Iona, beginning a series of spinning kicks, pushed her out of the way. The girl fell across her desk and landed hard on the floor. Iona continued spinning and kicking. Each kick landed with a solid thud against the temple of the unsuspecting and over-confident Trevino.

The man lay battered and unconscious on the floor at Iona's feet. Satisfied that he would not be able to inhibit her for some time, Iona decided she had to risk contacting Mary.

Iona walked past the young secretary sitting sprawled and confused. She activated her private com-line attempting to reach Mary at her grandmother's home.

She looked at the girl who was just getting back to her feet. "Come over here. What's your name, anyway?"

"Sasha Velt——."

"Sasha, take his clothes off." Iona pointed to Trevino's unconscious body on the floor. "And don't look at me as if you've never seen a naked man before. Hurry up."

After a few minutes of trying, Sasha had finished her task. "Now what?"

Iona put down the com-link, took the wadded up clothing, and dropped them into the incinerator. "Help me lift him."

Together the women put the unconscious Trevino in Iona's private bath. Running a nice warm bubble bath for him, she directed the computer. "Computer, add lavender fragrance and Ashwagandha; and keep the water at body temperature. I want him to stay asleep."

"Shall I prevent drowning?" the computer asked.

Iona paused in thought. "Keep him asleep, but keep him alive."

"Ending point?"

"Indefinitely."

"Understood and complying." A strong lavender fragrance began to fill the bathroom as the lights dimmed. As the door to the bath closed, Iona heard the computer voice intone, "Chemical sleep inducement added." The door sealed shut.

Crossing the office, Iona opened a floor safe and removed a small velvet bag. Opening it, she gave Sasha a stack of credit chips. "Now get out of here and don't ever come back. You've got enough credits there to live very comfortably for the next year." Closing the bag, Iona dropped it on her desk. "Take a nice long vacation and then get a real job; one where you use your brain and not just your body."

Sasha smiled an embarrassed smile. "Thank you Ms.—I mean Iona. Thanks." She turned and quickly left the office, the building, and Iona hoped, The Company.

Iona felt good about helping the girl. It was a feeling she could easily get use to liking.

The com-link chimed indicating a connection had been made. Mary's face appeared on the screen, angry and confused. Mary spoke first. "Iona, what are you—I mean—what do you wan—"

"Mary," Iona interrupted. "I know I'm one of the last persons you want to see right now, but I need you to know Mike is okay. He's alive. For now. Waters is sending a small fleet of ships after him at the mines on Yargon, but he's okay." She had rushed, fearing Mary wouldn't let her get it all in before disconnecting the call.

Mary sat opened-mouthed, staring into the video pickup.

"Mary? Did you hear me? Mike's alive."

Mary continued staring at the screen. Not sure if she dared believe what it was she was hearing. She shook her head. "Are you sure, Iona, because I couldn't take it if this was another one of your tricks?"

"I'm sure as of right now. But like I said, Waters is trying to change that. Look, Mary, I have to get out of here. My time at The Company is done."

"Oh, I see, this is really about you needing my help." Mary moved her hand to end the call.

"No, wait, Mary, listen. Let me talk. I don't have much time. I-I've done some things…to help you. Things that don't allow me to stay here. However, there is one more thing I have to do before I call it quits."

Despite herself, fear suddenly gripped Mary's heart, surprising her, because this was fear for Iona. "What are you going to do?" She leaned toward the screen.

"I've done enough to you already without pulling you any further into my mess. I won't do that to you, too. Mary, take care of Albert for me. If—if I don't make it back. Thanks."

———

Iona cut the line, and Mary sat looking at a darkened screen, overwhelmed by a combination of emotions: joy at hearing Mike was alive, fear at whatever Iona's plan was, and surprised to feel that love still lived in her heart for her sister.

"Nonna," Mary called, running into the older woman's bedroom. "Nonna, we need to pray."

———

On the roof in the fleet hanger, Iona found The Company's store of spacecrafts. She knew she had been detected by now, and soon the roof would be crawling with security with orders to stop her. Selecting a small one-man ship with combined hyper-thrust and a sleeper chamber, she began working through the preflight checklist.

The auxiliary engines came online filling the hanger bay with its low constant resonance. Reasoning within herself, as she checked fuel levels and the onboard diagnostics, if she traveled at full thrust while in sleep mode, she could reduce energy to life support and redirect it to the engines.

The hanger alarm sounded, echoing off the steel and concrete at deafening decibels. Iona leapt into the cockpit and slammed the starter sequence. The canopy began to close.

Checking the chronometer, she realized the fleet had almost a full-day's head start, but reasoned that she should be able to overtake them.

The canopy locked and sealed, and the hiss of pressurization filled the compartment. Just then, a lone guard burst through the bay doors and onto the flight deck, waving his arms directing her to abort the takeoff.

"Preflight complete," the onboard computer announced. "Destination?"

"Manual override. I'll do the flying myself. Shields to full." Blaster fire erupted into the flight deck just in front of the spacecraft.

The computer responded. "Shields are not normally required within the hanger. Suggest delay request until exiting Earth's atmosphere." Iona slapped the console, turning off the computer's voice response.

The tower indicator light began flashing. "Last warning," a voice intoned from the speakers.

Iona pulled back on the thruster control, and the ship lifted vertically from the flight deck, its landing strut folding into its belly. All around her, the screens went white with discharged energy as the security detail opened fire.

"Here's hoping Waters hasn't gotten around to deactivating my command codes yet." She angled toward the hanger's clamshell opening and fed power to the engines.

As she began to rise, the roof shielding started to retract. The alarm blared. "Security code override. Priority alpha-1-1: code-A." The computerized voice filled the hanger.

Out of every conceivable entrance, armed troops spilled out onto the roof surrounding the spacecraft and lining up to open fire.

Nursing a badly damaged head, Trevino stumbled through the door covered in a blanket stolen from the sofa in Iona's office. Pointing at her, he shouted, "Shoot! Shoot! Don't let her get away."

A shower of laser and projector fire engulfed the ship. Iona pulled back on the thruster control, and the ship seemed to jump forward and burst through the narrowing aperture. "Computer, systems check," she ordered.

A line of script began crawling across the screen before she remembered to reactivate the voice interaction capability of the computer. "Systems all green. Prepped for deep space flight."

"Weapons," she demanded.

"A full accompaniment of weapons are onboard and ready," the computer answered.

"Good, this one's ready to go," she said to herself.

"Clarify request," came the computer's voice.

"Disregard. Confirm manual control."

"Manual control initiated."

Activating the rear-targeting computer, Iona opened fire, strafing the roof with laser fire, assuring no immediate pursuit from that quarter.

All around the deck, men dove for cover as ship after ship exploded. Klaxons began shrieking fire alarms as yellow and white suppressant foam began spewing from overhead spouts.

Although she could not see him, she knew Ted Waters stood on the deck recording her betrayal. She almost wished she could have been there to see it. Almost.

Ted Waters stepped back through the door, shielding himself from the suppressant foam. "Get the ion cannon setup and return fire!" he yelled.

The troops hustled the portable ion cannon, called *the PIC* by those who worked with it, onto the roof. Waters ordered the weapon's use, knowing full well that to discharge it within the city would mean to destroy everything around its target for a .402 meters radius. He did not care. All he cared about now was destroying this one woman who had the audacity to betray him—to best him.

Behind her, the shield doors began to pulsate from red to orange to white, and Iona knew something bad was coming. She logged into The Company's mainframe and saw that the PIC was being brought online. She also knew that shielding or no shielding a cannon would devastate her ship and her with it. She intensified her fire.

Back on the roof, the shield doors began to waver and dissolve. At first, a small hole appeared, and then the entire shell melted and fell away. The iridescent beam of the PIC exploded through the newly formed opening and locked onto the heat signature of Iona's ship.

Watching the beam track toward her, Iona knew it was a race against time. Setting the ship's shields to maximum, and tucking her head for good measure, she added full power to its thrusters, and dove back toward the city. Iona knew she had but one chance and that was to make the PIC miss on its first shot and then escape before the large cannon could recharge for a second blast.

The small ship curled to its right and began a power descent heading for the heart of New-New York. Just as the ship broke past the spires of the Caster building, 150 floors of glass, steel, and alumi-glass in the heart of midtown, the blinding white blast of the PIC tore after it.

The building erupted and the ship jostled; the engines sputtered and failed. All around her the debris fell like rain as the structure began to melt and collapse in on itself.

Registering the blast on the ship's scanner, Iona pulled the ship in a hard bank to starboard and initiated the automatic restart. The engine flared to life, and she nosed the ship toward the horizon and gave it full power.

Iona suppressed a shiver as she saw the Caster building glowed white then blue and dissolve. Everything from the ninety-second floor and up was gone; people, furniture, concrete, glass—everything. What was left was a unrecognizable heap of molten slag.

Flying low through the man-made canyons of the city to gain cover, Iona maneuvered the small craft toward safety. She cursed. *Fighters.*

Just as she had feared, a small force of fighters now pursued her. Not wanting to open fire within the city's limits again, Iona took her craft lower toward the surface of the streets. The pursuing fighters, not capable of flying at the slower speeds, were forced to pull up and wait for more maneuverable crafts to come and replace them in the fight. Taking advantage of this lull, Iona doubled back on her route, being careful to stay low, using traffic to confuse her signal. Seeing an opening, and not wanting to wait and be boxed in, Iona gunned her engines and climbed toward the blackness of space.

Once out of the atmosphere, Iona set her course for the Gliese System and the planet Yargon. "Computer," she spoke into the silence. Once the computer responded, she directed it using her private scramble codes to contact Mary. When the connection had been made, she brought her up on what had happened. "Mary, Waters knows about Nonna. Get the kids and get out of there. If he gets the chance, he'll hurt you. Please, don't give him that chance again."

"Don't worry about us. Nonna can sneak us away with some of her *church* friends. You just get out there and warn Mike of what's coming their way." Mary ran her hand through her hair and busied her lip with her teeth. "If The Company still does things the way they have, the fleet will stop halfway out in order to refuel, check stores, and dump waste. You can still beat them to the planet if you hustle."

"No worry there. I'll hustle, all right. I helped start this mess, and I'm going to do everything I can to clean it up," Iona answered, a twinge of pain in her voice. She continued, "I've got a sleeper ship. It'll get me there. With the extra power from life support routed to the engines, I can get another two perc's out of the engines before they'll blow."

Mary felt chastened. "I didn't mean that this was your fault."

"I know what you meant." She smiled. "And we both know that it is. You get everybody out of there and into hiding, Mary. We'll find you when we can."

There was a long silence. When Iona spoke again her voice had changed, softened. "How's Albert? Is he okay?"

"Ask him yourself. He's right here," Mary said, her voice lighter than before.

Standing too close to the visual pick-up, Albert's face filled the cockpit screen of Iona's ship. "Hi," he said and smiled, his eyes and face visibly brightening.

Iona, caught off guard by her own feelings and moved by his expression at seeing her, sat unspeaking, simply staring at the small screen. Slowly, she reached out and touched the screen, engaging the automatic record sequence, wishing, instead, that it had been the soft face of this child that had worked his way into her heart. Fighting an urge to cry, she sat up and took a deep breath. "Hey there, big guy. Now you be good for Nonna and Aunt Mary, okay, and be sure to mind your manners. All right?"

"Oh, I will. Why are you crying? Is something wrong?" he asked in childish innocence.

"No, nothing's wrong. It's just something that grownups do when they're happy. Let me speak to Aunt Mary."

The boy pressed his hand against the screen, leaving a moist palm print on it before turning to leave the room.

Mary replaced him in the field of view. "Feels good, doesn't it?"

"Oh, yes it does," came Iona's enthusiastic but subdued reply.

"It's at times like these when you wish you could record everything. Look here, girl, now you've got somebody else here waiting for you, so be careful. That child's had enough disappointment for a lifetime."

"Don't worry, I will. Hey, Mary, I love you, too. See you later. I'm out."

As the transmission ended, Mary turned her attention to the children. "I knew—I hoped this day would come," she muttered to herself. "I just didn't think it would all happen like this." She sighed. "Oh, God..." Mary began and her words melted into tears.

Across the hall, Nonna sat in her favorite rocker with a knowing smile on her face. She closed her eyes and continued rocking, never uttering a sound.

"Okay, kids, let's get moving. We've got a lot of work to do and not a lot of time to do it in."

Mary and the kids started packing a few of their belongings into their bags and then added them to the pile already in the middle of the living room floor. Other than having to tell young Travist twice that he could not bring all of his toys, everything went well.

Now for the hard part.

"Nonna—" Mary began, but didn't get any further.

"Now, child, I've been on this hill for near eighty-seven years; don't see much sense in leaving it now."

"But you heard what Iona said. Ted Waters won't care that you're an old woman." She stopped after seeing the look on Nonna's face. "Sorry, but you know what I mean; he won't care that you're a senior citizen."

"Well, I am old and proud of it. But it's going to take more than Ted Waters to move me. Besides, I have Jesus here with me, and he won't let anything happen to your old Nonna that's not for His glory and my good. I've lived my whole life by that principle, and I'm not gonna stop trusting Him now."

Mary knew it was useless to argue with her grandmother on this point. They had this fight too many times before, and Mary had always lost. "Nonna, just promise me that you will be careful. Don't do anything that will get yourself hurt."

She hugged her grandmother's neck fiercely, cried softly on her shoulder, and was reminded again that a mother's hug always seemed to make things better. "Come on, kids, give Nonna a hug and kiss good-bye."

Mary stood as each of the boys took their turn hugging and kissing their great-grandmother. She smiled noticing how Albert fit right in with the others, giving and receiving love. She lowered the baby into Nonna's arms and stood again watching as the wizened woman held, rocked, and kissed the baby girl.

After seating herself in the transport, Mary allowed herself one last look around the old Victorian-styled house, letting her eyes linger on her grandmother as she did. The hatch slid shut, and Mary directed the transport down the long gravel drive.

Early the next morning, Viola found herself kneeling and praying as she worked in the rich soil of her flower garden when she looked up and saw the line of Company vehicles snaking their way toward her home.

She continued kneeling even after the vehicles came to a stop, fanning out around the property, and a number of uniformed men approached her.

"You Viola Johnson?" one of the men in uniform asked.

"Why, yes I am. Who wants to know?" she asked in return.

"I'm with The Company security office, and we're looking for your daughter, Mary Stone."

"Well she's not here. Are you the same people who blew up her house?"

The man was put off balance by the older woman's lack of fear and directness. "That's classified information." He cleared his throat. "We're still investigating that, but the best information is that it was some kind of domestic accident."

She made a sound in her throat, harrumphed, and turned back to her garden.

"We'll need to search your house and grounds."

"Not without a warrant you won't. This is still a free country last I checked," she answered without looking up.

Glad to be back on ground he understood, the man smiled dark and threatening. "That's where you would be wrong *grandma;* I do what I want to do." Then turning his attention to his men, he yelled, "Search the house. Look everywhere and into everything." It bothered him that she never looked up, never even stopped digging her flowers or pulling weeds.

Chapter Eighteen

The fleeing troops ran in desperate strides toward the river camp. Even though they could not see it, they knew the Kracken was behind them. They could hear its bellows as it cried out, announcing its freedom and its thirst for blood.

Once at the top of the food chain, it had been forced to perform, to beg for its every meal. Like the mythological creature for which it had been named, the Kracken now roamed the forest, as if loosen by the gods, to punish disobedient mortals. Only this time there was no benevolent deity to appeal to; this time it was truly man against beast.

Following Skipp's lead, the group trusted themselves to the beeps and chirps emitting from the notepad indicating a probable path. "I hope that thing is working okay now," Jay called out from beside him. "Now that the electronic interference has been removed, navigating should be back to normal."

Working their way in darkness, via the natural pathways through the heart of the mountain, the kids were as unfamiliar with the surroundings as were the men.

A dull roar began to fill the cavern. "What's that sound?" Sally asked, tightening her grip on Mike's hand.

"Sounds like water; maybe one of those underground rivers we saw flowing out of the mountain," Skipp called back over his shoulder. "No way of knowing how big or deep it is until we get there." He added a light tone to his voice, projecting confidence where he felt none.

"Check your pad. Is there another way around?" Mike said, noting the moisture buildup on the limestone surface. "Everybody, watch your step. Footings are getting a little slick."

As if to emphasize his point, one of the children fell, crying out as she began sliding down the increasing decline. Frankie dropped his pack and dove, sliding on his stomach, barely grabbing the little girl's hand before she disappeared over the edge. Breathing hard, he pulled her against his chest and held her there. "You're all right. I got ya."

As the rest of the group caught up with them at the ledge, the full sight of the river came into view. More than a stream, the muddied red and gray waters churned in an angry blast as it slammed against the rock wall and surged, curving deeper into the darkness beyond the reach of their lights.

The path, such as it was, narrowed to only a couple feet in width with the wall on one side and the churning water on the other.

The children cowered together, clutching to one another. Their murmured voices, mixed with the sound of the water, created a cacophony of unintelligent sound.

"Can we go back?" Jonas yelled over the din.

Mike shook his head. "We have no idea where the C-men are, and I don't want to risk running into that Kracken.

"You big kids grab one of the younger ones by the hand," Jay said. "We gonna take dis nice an' slow."

"What about the C-men?" a child's voice called out. "They'll catch us!"

Mike answered, "Don't worry about them for now. They don't know which way we went, and that Kracken is a lot closer to them than it is to us. So you just concentrate on staying on that ledge."

Jay reached down and grabbed Sally, as Rose had seemed to attach herself to Mike. Lifting the child, Jay put Sally on his broad shoulders. Pressing his back to the wall, he reached back, took a second child by the hand, and began sidestepping along the path.

A few meters below their feet, the water swirled angrily, flowing back on itself creating eddies and suck holes that seemed to gulp and breathe. The sloped ceiling, with its protruding stalactites, rained sulfur-colored droplets on their heads and added a layer of slickness to the sandstone surface.

Following the curve of the ledge, the river became a confluence and resulted in a more violent stream. The water gushed from the hollow mouth of an adjoining cave, illuminated by bioluminescent algae; it glowed as it poured through the yawning maw.

Heated by thermal vents deep in the planet's core, the algae thrived until it mixed with the cooler water from the surface. Where the hot and cold water met, steam rose in billows and dripped like heavy raindrops from the cavernous roof high overhead. Covered with the slimy remnants of the dead algae, the footing became more treacherous along the ledge.

Another slip. Another scream. The group continued.

The once dark waters now churned milky-gray as it rushed from the juncture where the two rivers combined and became one massive flow. The sides of the gorge grew shear, offering no beach, even as brackish water splashed violently dousing the slim path.

Up ahead, Jay raised a light. "This is as far as the path goes on." He turned his face back in order to be heard.

"How far?" Mike called back to him.

"Mike," Jay called out and the timber of his voice said trouble.

Skipp leaned out and scanned the path ahead, using his off-hand to shield the notepad from the spray. "Looks like a dead end."

"We can't go back!" Jonas yelled. "The path is too slick from our traipsing, and the children are afraid. Check again. Find an alternative."

Children began crying. The smaller ones whimpered, demanding that something be done. Their voices sounded small in contrast against the roar of the water.

Mike looked at Skipp. "How thick is the rock here?"

Loosening a length of cord from his pack and securing a large stone to one end, Jay dropped the line in the water, taking a sounding of the depth. He reckoned it to be about a meter deep near the edges, but deeper near the center. "Not too deep, but the current is still too fast for wading. I think I see where you're going with this, Mike," Jay said. "Skipp, can we blast a way out of here?"

Skipp's face was aglow, washed in the soft light from the notepad's screen. "The rock here is pretty porous," he answered. "We might be able to get through. It looks like there might be another chamber just beyond that far wall."

"That still leaves us the width of the river to deal with," Mike said absently. Rose clung to his arm and leaned tiredly against him. He looked down at the little girl, her face barely visible. He could tell she was afraid, but proud of her for trying not to let it show. Mike stroked her hair reassuringly as he spoke with the men.

"If Skipp can open us a door in that wall, I'll get us across," Jay said matter of fact.

"Okay, move the kids as far back as you can. It's gonna get hot in here," Skipp said, turning his attention to his blaster rifle.

"You mean hotter," Jay said as he stepped up next to Skipp and together leveled their weapons at the wall. The children scooted back along the ledge, Mike and Jonas doing their best to hedge them against the rock face.

The concentrated beams of fine energy bored into the base of the ledge on the far side of the stream. The water began to boil and pop as gases trapped in the stone heated and released into the water. Steam began to rise.

For long moments, nothing seemed to happen. Then a sharp snap and a cracking sound began to grow, filling the chamber. Suddenly, with a violent rending and tearing that shook the ground, causing a cascade of small stones and pebbles to shower the escapees. The wall collapsed and broke free.

A draft of wind sucked and grabbed at loose debris, pulling it through the newly formed hole. The river, now redirected, broke through and drained, decreasing its surface level but none of its velocity.

Across from them, a dark orifice opened, and the roar of the sucking wind sounded like a cry of a beast. Children screamed. They hugged one another as the gurgling noise of the river's draining increased. The water began to shallow as more and more ran off into the new depression.

Just then, Andrea yelped as she lost her footing and fell into the still violent stream. Instantly, Jonas was in the water behind her. Jay retrieved and then cast a cord to Jonas as he swam after the frightened girl.

Fighting and clawing, Jonas grabbed the girl. He fought against the surge of brackish fluid. The sour water burned his eyes and goaded at his throat. With exhausted fingers, he dug at the wet stone trying to find purchase. The current snatched at him and pulled on the limp form of the youth in his arms. Just as he tied the cord around his waist and wrapped his arms around Andrea, his grip gave way, and they were both swept through the dark opening in the wall.

Scratching and pulling, Jonas managed to wedge himself between two boulders on the far wall. Holding Andrea's face above the water's surface, Jay anchored the line as Skipp and Mike began to haul the two back through the opening, fighting to outlast the draining water.

After a short time that seemed to last forever, the water's current slowed as more and more drained away. Jonas found himself standing on solid, but slippery ground. He lowered Andrea to the surface, making sure she was steady on her feet before letting go.

Jonas patted her shoulder and then smoothed wet hair back from her face. Looking up, he gulped, sucking in precious air. Then turning his attention back to Skipp, he said, "As long as we stay south of the stream, we should be able get across here." He tried to make it sound as if his ending up on the far side had been his plan all along.

"Kind of like that Moses fellow at that—what was it called, Mike?" Skipp asked as he jumped down beside Jonas and renewed his scan. He laughed.

Mike looked up but didn't answer.

Skipp continued, undaunted. "Yeah, we can get through here, that's not the problem. The problem is that going this way will take us out on the opposite side of the mountain. It'll put us that much further from the Quest."

"Don't see where we have a choice," Mike said, stepping down in the riverbed. "Let's get a move on."

Peter finally felt strong enough to walk on his own.

Andrea knew something had happened to her brother, but also knew she shouldn't ask. He would tell her when the time was right, if it ever was. But for now, she decided she would just be with him.

The two walked in silence following their new friends, placing all their hope of escape and a chance of having a normal life in the men's hands.

"Remember back when we were talking about trying to escape?" Peter asked Andrea. He was not looking at her. His voice was barely a whisper. "When the first group had tried to steal that supply ship?"

She nodded, not wanting to interrupt him.

"The reason I voted no was that I was afraid of what might happen, that we would fail…that we would die." He turned and met her gaze in the low light. "I'm not afraid anymore. This time we will either get off this planet or I'll die trying."

Andrea couldn't answer; she didn't know what to say. She looked around her taking in the crowd of dirty, tired, and scared kids that made up her family. Then she allowed her gaze to travel over the backs of the men and, for the first time in a long time, thought that there might be some good in all of Rosemary's praying.

Up ahead, a gray light began to spill over the horizon. As they came closer, they could see that they had come to the mouth of a cave. The gray light of predawn greeted them.

"Never thought I'd be so happy just to see a sunrise," Mike said, inhaling deeply.

"What a choice: a musty cave or humid jungle," Jonas said chuckling. After so long in the cave, the smell of the woods was fresh and invigorating. The hurried breath of the wind through branches replaced the constant splashing and gurgling of the river they'd left behind.

"I'm just glad we didn't have to swim all the kids through some narrow hole in the wall just to get them outside," Jay said from behind them, off to their side.

Mike and Jonas nodded their heads in agreement as Mike turned and faced the group. "Get everybody together in small groups, and we can take a break. I want everybody rested before we try and tackle that jungle."

The group broke up into clusters of threes and fours, all gathering near to each other. Soon the children were all deep in the sleep of exhaustion and severe fright. Too tired to eat, the camp was washed in silence, except for the deep breathing and snoring. The men took turns keeping watch.

As the sun arced in the mid-morning sky, the day was already warm. Flies, gnats, and biting insects were beginning to swarm. "I think its best that we stay near the base of the mountain where we can. We don't want to tempt the drags to attack," Skipp said, slapping at an insect on his arm.

"Yes," Andrea said, coming up next to him. "The drags would never attack a group this size without the advantage of surprise. They like the trees."

The hours passed. They continued along the base of the mountain, needing still to travel half its circumference. Heeding Andrea's warning, Mike chose to keep the group clear of the dense foliage of the interior jungle.

Soon they arrived on the bank of the widest river they had seen up to this point. Having exited the mountain opposite of their camp, the children were no more familiar with this part of the planet than were the men.

Like the other rivers, this one too flowed from the mountain, but unlike the others, this one became a thundering waterfall just after clearing the base of the mountain. The water poured with a clamorous roar into a boiling cauldron of gray foam and misty spray some 15 meters below them.

Tired and hot, Mike slapped the side of his thigh. "We won't be able to walk across that." He grimaced in frustration.

Skipp ran a hand across his forehead, and holding up the notepad, he spun, scanning the area. "Yeah," he exhaled the word in a hollow breath. He locked eyes with Mike and then with Andrea. "Looks like it's into the jungle after all."

"Bring the group in tight," Mike ordered. "Jonas and I'll take rear guard. Jay, you and Skipp run point."

The big man unslung his rifle and moved toward the front of the group. "And if anything gets in our way?" He patted the barrel and smiled down at Rose.

"We blast it," she squealed in response, pumping her arm for emphasis.

"We blast it." He laid a hand on her shoulder and squeezed.

Some of the children edged near the cliff and peered over its rim, drawn by its magnetic beauty. Jagged rocks stood like teeth in the rainbow mist at the foot of the falls, and beyond that, miles of forest trimmed with a yellow band just below where the earth and sky met—the desert.

The children knew they would have to go back into the jungle. Every one of them had a personal terror, a story that included a friend having not returned from its dark interior. Fear and panic began snaking through the group, passing from one retelling of a story to the next. A heavy foreboding began to replace the sense of well-being the children enjoyed since coming out of the mountain.

Some began to cry. Others seemed to stiffen their resolve and were determined to go through. Still others simply gave up and sat down, refusing to move.

Peter's voice rang out above the din. "Shut up! I am so sick of your whining. You know we can't go back, and you know we can't stay here. So pick up your gear and let's follow these men to their ship. Either that or stay here and become food for the drags or maybe the Kracken. Either way, we're leaving."

Silence claimed the camp. In the background the thundering roar of the falls rumbled. Mike exchanged looks with his crew, all of them doing their best to suppress smiles.

Peter brushed away angry tears. Sweeping an arm across his chest, taking in the entire group, he squared his narrow shoulders. "Mike and the guys are leaving, and me and my sisters are going with them. If you want to stay here, fine. If you want to go back and work the mines, go. But when they leave, we leave, and if you want to stay behind, then you're, you're—" he didn't finish the statement, but grabbed his gear and stalked toward the jungle.

Mike looked at Jonas and the guys, picked up his own gear, and started after Peter. "I guess we're leaving."

"I guess so," Jonas laughed.

Without another word, the group got up and fell into step. Rosemary went forward and walked with Mike, but Sally took her place beside Andrea and her big brother.

Chapter Nineteen

After giving the children their various instructions, Mike called Andrea and Peter over.

"We're missing somebody," Peter said.

Confused, the men looked at each other. Peter called Frankie, who had been standing a short distance away looking on. Springing up, Frankie ran over, stopped and looked at Mike and then sat down beside Peter.

Mike looked at the young man, dipped his head in acknowledgement and began discussing their plans for escape.

Jonas smiled at Mike's choosing to include the older children in the planning meeting, knowing that it would help calm the group as a whole.

Back upriver, the Kracken washed its face and drank deep of the cool water. It had eaten and, for now, was content. Back in its hunting grounds, it roared declaring its dominance, a challenge to any that would dare. The creature lifted its massive head, nostrils flaring, as it tasted the air. The scent of the human's was heavy on the trail in the dust, clinging to the leaves. It would catch them, and in its own animal way, would remove them from its territory. It would hunt. It would track the humans until every one of them were gone, dead, or fled away, but out of its realm.

Stepping gingerly out into the water, it started to cross the river, leaving what was left of the C-men's camp. Standing in the middle of the river, the water running rapidly around and through its powerful legs, the Kracken threw back its head and roared again. The cry came from deep within its barrel chest. It was part warning, part hunting cry, and territorial challenge. The sound let all other predators know that it was back and willing to fight for its domain.

The sunset and the jungle shadows grew dense over the thickening forest. The Kracken, not hampered by darkness, slowly and deliberately started down river.

Some distance away, the camp jumped with a start at the sound of the Kracken's roar then settled into a restless quiet as silence reclaimed the jungle.

"At least the drags won't be out tonight," Andrea spoke over the small campfire, the orange light flickering off her dark eyes.

The fire burned low, its smoldering embers glowed brightly against the otherwise dark night. The column of smoke rose lazily into the scarlet night sky as sparkling embers rode the hot current into the ruddy darkness. The camp was quiet and only a few muted conversations still floated on the breeze. Most of which consisted of the 'what ifs' and the 'what do you think it's gonna be likes' of freedom.

The younger children, overwhelmed by the day, had long ago fallen asleep. The older members sat in small circles solemnly contemplating both their past and their future. Suddenly, one of the younger girls sat up screaming, her eyes opened but not seeing, locked in a prison of her dreams. "The Kracken! It's coming after us. It's coming, it's coming," the girl repeated, kicking and clawing at the air.

Taking the girl in her arms, one of the older teens rocked her, trying to quiet her fears and coax her from her dream. Soon the child was back in the throes of a fitful sleep.

Looking at the girl, Mike again thought of Ted Waters and all the pain the one man had caused. He dared not think of what horror his own little girl had suffered before she died. His eyes burned with hatred, and he swore as tears stung his eyes.

"Excuse me," Jonas said, shaking Mike's shoulder. "Where are you buddy, we need you here with us now."

Mike turned and faced his friend, but did not speak.

"I know what you're feeling," Jonas began.

"No, you don't," Mike said in a harsh tone. "How could you? Did Waters murder your wife? Did he kill your children and blow up your home? Did he?"

"Well, no—"

"Then don't tell me that you know how I feel. Look at these children; they are here running and scared out of their wits because of one reason: Ted Waters." Mike stood up. "If it is the last thing I do, I'm gonna kill that man. I will make him pay for what he has done." He turned and walked into the darkness.

Skipp came over to Jonas. "I know how he feels," he said thinking of Julie's body in stasis onboard the Quest. "I think I finally have an inkling."

"But you know it's not right. You know Mary would not want him trying to avenge her; she didn't believe like that."

"Well, there's no use trying to tell him that now. I know you shared Mary's belief, doc. Maybe you should just pray for Mike because I don't see how anything you might say is going to make one bit of difference. I know talking is not gonna help." He stood. "I'm gonna get some sleep. Wake me in four hours."

"Yeah," Jonas said and settled back against a boulder to wait.

As morning broke over the jungle, Skipp was awakened by the sunlight piercing the dense canopy. Looking around, he saw Jonas still sitting by the now cold fire. "I said wake me in four hours," Skipp said angrily in spite of being rested or perhaps because he was so.

Jonas looked at him and grunted. "Is it morning already?"

"Where's Mike?"

"Still over by the river. He's been there all night."

"And you've been sitting here all night watching him?"

"No. More like watching over him. I took your advice and decided to pray."

Skipp became a little uncomfortable with the turn of topic, and he looked back toward the camp. "Jay up?"

Jonas laughed and got up himself, dusting off his pants. "Breakfast?"

After breakfast was completed, the group started off again, headed for the desert on the far side of the mountain to the safety of the Quest.

The sun shown in bright shafts as it broke through in patches of the canopy. Under foot, the ground was splotchy with greens, browns, and grays, covered with dead and dying plants. Bugs and other insects buzzed in and round the groups, some biting, drinking their blood, while others ate the salt accumulating on their skin.

As the bugs swarmed, so did the flocks of brightly colored birds feasting on the congregating cluster of flying insects. The squawks and cries soon filled the area echoing like the sounds of a busy street in the city. Low rumbles and high pitch wails cut back and forth in constant cry and response. The jungle was alive.

Strange colored birds swam through the air chasing bugs and drinking nectar from flowering plants high up in the trees, and beneath it, the group hurried quietly through the shadowed depths.

Skipp felt a presence beside him and turned to see Andrea matching his stride. After a moment and without looking at him or announcing herself, she simply began talking. "We'd been friends along time, you know, Monica and me." No pretense. No preamble.

Skipp remembered Andrea having begun telling him about her friend Monica, that she had been taken by the C-men and ravished.

"I'd known her since I was Rosemary's age." She took a shallow breath and held it for a long moment continuing.

Skipp realized she was not so much talking to him as much as she was sorting out her thoughts and feelings.

"We lived near each other in one of the projects back in Old City, New York." She looked at the ground as they walked, her voice just above a whisper. "It wasn't much of a homelife for us, I guess, but we were just kids. We didn't know we were poor or anything. So when I woke up in this place and saw a familiar face…well, naturally, we took comfort in that—and hung together."

All of a sudden, her mood seemed to darken. "When they came and took her, a part of me went with her." Sadness rolled across her face like heavy rain clouds in a prelude of a storm. Looking down, she continued her monologue. "When I lost her in that raid, I thought—I felt like a large portion of who I was broke off and died. As long as we were together we could talk, tell each other that one day we would be—that one day we would leave this place. That one day we would be free. But when they took her away…" Andrea's words drifted into silence, and for a long moment, there was only the sound of her crying.

Skipp walked beside her in silence. The hum of insects and the song of birds floated above the muted voices of the group lagging behind them.

Then as if nothing had happened she continued, "…all that just seemed to melt away."

As she spoke, her eyes fixed on the jungle. The pain of the memory etched itself in her face. She looked up catching and holding his gaze. "Even after you guys showed up, deep inside I felt that something would go wrong, and we would all be caught. That maybe you guys would turn out to be just like those other men."

Skipp grimaced.

She swallowed and dropped her face again. "And nothing would change."

Skipp knew she just needed to talk, so he let her, not interrupting with questions or offering solutions. Just listening. And through it all, he got a small glimpse of the burgeoning young woman that would be.

Before long, she had talked herself out, and they walked on in silence. It amazed Skipp that after all these children had endured just how vulnerable they really were, how open to trust and needful of love. The revelation made him feel more protective of them as a whole.

Chapter Twenty

Iona awoke from her self-induced hibernation to find the cockpit filling with an acrid blue haze and the nav-computer screaming. She was both surprised and happy to find that she had arrived at the planet a full eight hours ahead of her planned E.T.A.

Coughing to clear her throat, she increased power to life support and adjusted her position in the pilot's seat. "All I've got to do now is find exactly where they are in the midst of all this mess and manage to not get shot down in the process."

The onboard computer crackled to life. "Braced for atmospheric breach," it intoned.

The ship began to shake, breaking itself apart, as it bounced into the planet's upper atmosphere. Flexing her fingers to loosen and awaken them, Iona grabbed a hold of the helm and pulled back, hard.

The heat shields began to glow as they deflected energy from the ship's surface in a shower of flame and steam. Slowing her airspeed, Iona drove the ship through the stratopause and an instant later cleared the tropopause before leveling off just above the jungle canopy. Taking advantage of being in a one-man ship, Iona dove between the branches and maneuvered much closer to the planet's surface. Setting the scans for a wide sweep, she sat back, overwhelmed by the sheer number and variety of life forms that registered.

"Wow!" was all she said, focusing green eyes on the screen. It wasn't until she readjusted the setting for human life forms that she felt she had a chance to succeed.

Leaning forward, she pointed at the screen, noticing two separate groupings. One centered in the heart of the larger of the jungles moving west and the second smaller group, shadowing them, traveling around the perimeter of the central mountain. Acting on a hunch, she headed for the larger of the two groups, the one cutting through the heart of the jungle canopy.

Throttling up, the small ship cut through the jungle ceiling, ripping and tearing through it like a harvester cutting its way through a field of grain.

Fighting against the strain, the ship's engines began to whine under the increased burden and exertion of being flown above specs. *The ship can't keep this up much longer,* Iona thought to herself, *but with a little luck, it won't have to.*

Up ahead, the peak of the central mountain climbed over the horizon. The computer voice registered. 'Systems reaching critical. Automatic shutdown in 15 seconds."

"Override safety protocols." Iona countered.

The alarms fell silent. The cockpit filled with smoke. Panels exploded. The main screen went black.

"Extra power to the shields. Now!"

Vibrations increased. "Total power failure in two minutes."

Looking at the instrument panel, Iona knew the ship could not be saved. She reminded herself that she had known that fact coming in. "Thank you, God," she screamed as she broke through the canopy and saw the group of mostly children moving away from her. She continued. "I haven't done very much of this lately, praying I mean, but Albert says you've helped him out a couple of times, and if you would, Sir, I really would like your help on this one." With that finished, she began to hail the group on the ground.

"This is Iona Bowers calling the crew of the Quest." She used the ship's frequency Mary had given her. "If anyone is listening, please respond."

Silence.

Iona cried out, panic edging her voice. "Crew of the Quest, this is Iona Bowers. I have information for Mike Stone."

The ship began to vibrate; it would not hold together much longer.

"I repeat, I have information for Mike Stone. It is imperative that I deliver my message to Mike. Please come in."

The ship began to tear itself apart. Electrical fires burst from beneath the command panel, black smoke filling the cabin. Knowing she would not last under these conditions, Iona pulled the ripcord, blowing the canopy, and ejected.

The pilot's seat flipped and twisted violently before righting itself under the chute and began its slowed descent. Unable to put on a crash helmet before ejecting, the wind tore at Iona's face. Her long red hair caught in the gale, flowing freely behind her like a jet of flame.

"Mayday-mayday. Mike Stone, come in." Her voice cracked, "Mike Stone, I know you can hear me, now answer up!" Still there was no response.

She floated toward the jungle even as her ship crashed in the desert.

The wind rushed past her exposed face, the icy chill of the air drying out and chaffing her skin. She was coming down too fast.

One more time. "Mike Stone, this is Iona Bow—"

"Iona, redirect your descent by two degrees north by north west. Do it now," came Mike's stern voice over the open com.

"It's about time somebody down there answered me. I was beginning to get a little worried. Standby, I'm coming in."

She adjusted the booster pack on her pilot's seat to the coordinates Mike had given her. Thirty meters above the ground, she activated the chair's retro-boosters and slowed her descent, floating softly to the ground. Just before making contact, she released her harness and jumped free of the entanglement of the seat, executing a full tuck and spin, landing securely in a three-point stance.

Never having seen a full-grown woman, and especially one that looked like Iona, both Frankie and Peter stood with their mouths agape.

With the grace of a fighter, Iona walked up to the group near the edge of the dense jungle. She walked slowly knowing that if Mike or even Jay were not in a gracious mood, she might wind up dead where she stood. The realization that the last image they had of her was that of an enemy, she slowed her pace.

Still dressed in her trademark black bodysuit, although somewhat worn as a result of her emergency landing, she looked good.

She stood, not moving, knowing she was being assessed. She looked to Mike first. For a moment, time stopped when all she saw was him. All the old familiar feelings came flooding back. She steadied herself against them. Just looking at him was pleasurable; she fought to keep her feelings from showing in her face. "Aren't you gonna say hi to an old friend," she chanced.

Mike walked over, grabbed her upper arm and dragged her away from the crowd.

Rose tried to follow, but Jonas picked up the little girl. "Not this time, sweetheart."

She pouted, but she allowed Jonas to carry her back to the group.

When they were alone, Mike released Iona's arm and spun her to face him. "What do you want?" he demanded.

She was surprised that his reaction hurt her. She didn't know what she was hoping for, what she expected, but she had figured on the intensity of his anger. However, not at her. "I…" she began, but couldn't continue.

"Well!?"

For the briefest moment, she hoped he would look at her the way he had once, the way he felt about Mary now. She started to tell him that Mary and the kids were alive, but something held her back. He was still standing there, arms folding across his broad chest, deep chiseled features cut into his dark skin.

"I…" she started again, clearing her throat, "came here to warn you that Ted Waters knows you're here and has sent a small fleet out to intercept you." She could tell that he wasn't completely surprised by her news, that he had suspected something like this would happen.

Mike turned away and dropped his arms, then raised one hand rubbing his scalp roughly. "So why should I believe you? I know how you feel about Mary and me." He pointed a finger in her face. "Why should I believe you came all the way out here just to warn me?"

Iona started to deny what he had said but knew it had been true, and to some small degree, still was. She was still in love with him and probably always would be. She walked to him and reached a hand toward his muscular shoulder, but stopped just short of touching him. "God, Mike, you make this so hard," she said in frustration. "Yes, I still have feelings for you, but that's not the issue."

"Then what is?" He was toying with her and he knew it, but he had been hurt and wanted to hurt someone in return. She was the closest thing to Ted Waters around.

The wind blew again, and with it came that voice: *To the merciful, I will show myself merciful.*

Mike shook his head trying to rid himself of the effect of the voice. He looked at Iona, remembering that she had come out here in a one-way ship, appearing desperate to find him. "I'm sorry, maybe you didn't deserve that. I forget at times that Mary *was* your sister as well as my wife."

Her head snapped up at that. "Mike, Mary's alive."

He grabbed her by her arms, snatching her from her feet. "Don't play with me, woman. I saw the house explode; I was there, remember." Anger coursed through him, and it was all he could do to keep from throwing her to the ground.

Jay saw this from a distance and started toward them. He was not one to stand by and watch a woman, any woman, be beaten.

Mike could see that she was in pain, but he could not release her; his hands seemed to have a will of their own.

"Yes," she struggled. "I know you were there, but Mary and the kids weren't. They got away and went to Nonna's. They've been there ever since." She could see him fighting, trying to believe her.

Jay stepped between them. "Mike, let her go. This is not the way, mon." He placed a hand on Mike's chest and pressed softly.

"No, it's okay." Iona looked briefly at the large man.

Mike released her, and she began rubbing her arms where his fingers had been. He took a few steps away from them, stumbled and fell. "Alive? You're sure they're alive?" He buried his face in his hands and cried.

Iona went to him and laid a hand on his shoulders. She breathed in sharply and thought how many times she had wanted to hold him in her arms. Like a slow rising sun, it dawned on her that this was not one of her childhood games; he was not a prize to be fought for and won. He was her sister's husband. Her brother-in-law. She relaxed and slipped her arm around his shoulder, pulling him tighter, and together they cried, but perhaps for different reasons.

Jay stepped back, confused.

After a while, they returned to the group and shared the news of Mary and the children's escape to safety. As she sat apart from the gathering, Iona surveyed the camp. Looking into the children's faces, she was moved, tears stinging her eyes as she imagined the hellish situations they had been forced to endure. A second wave of emotion, anger, swept over her as she thought, *And this was the fate Paul Adams had intended for Albert...her Albert.*

"What's happened to you?" Mike asked simply.

She brushed away fresh tears and, with obvious effort, pulled her gaze from the children. "Well, it began with the raid at your home. When I saw Mary and the kids, my nephews and niece..." she choked up, but then was able to relay to him all that had happened, ending with her crash landing in the jungle.

"Wow," was all the men could say.

Standing to face him, Iona was no longer trying to hide her tears, her eyes already red and swollen. "I'm sorry for the way I acted. I was wrong about a great many things, and I admit it. Mary and I have already made our peace. Well...we've begun, and now it's our turn."

"Iona, I—" Mike began.

"No. Let me finish." She raised her hand, palm facing him. "I need to say this. It's true; I believed I loved you, but I know now that it wasn't meant to be. These last few weeks I've had a chance to get to know Mary again, and through her, get to know you. I see now that even if you had come to me, I would only have destroyed you. Destroyed what you were meant to be. Mary loves you, and you love her; that's plain." She took a deep breath and steadied herself. "Now all I want is to find that kind of love with somebody who will love me no matter what, and somebody I can love in return.

"Now with Albert in my life I have a start, and in time, I know I'll be all right." With that said, they hugged a warm embrace. A bitter war ended.

Jonas and the others stood by watching the exchange, not really sure what all was going on but happy nonetheless that these two had made their peace.

Between getting the children safe as far as they had, and Mike and Iona making peace, Jonas was beginning to believe that they would actually beat this planet, that God had actually heard his prayers.

Chapter Twenty-One

Trevino sat nervously on the bridge of the command ship, his Adam's apple rose and fell as great drops of sweat pooled around his bandaged, broken nose. He was nervous and for good reason. Ted Waters was not one to make idle threats, and he had most definitely threatened Trevino before his leaving.

Having been discovered and pulled from the tub by Waters himself, Trevino jumped at the chance to lead the fleet after Stone. His saving grace had been his convincing Waters that Iona had fled to warn Stone and that she, too, needed to be controlled. Rendezvousing with the fleet at the refueling stop, he replaced the commander, Captain Hanson, demoting him to the first officer's position.

Trevino was in command, but it did not bring him the feeling of comfort and security he had always dreamed it would. Looking over the command quad at a very professional crew in their white strap-collared uniforms, he felt unqualified to command. Military tactics were not his specialty.

"Status report," he called to no one in particular for the fourth time within the hour. He reasoned that through giving orders he could keep the crew too busy to notice his weaknesses. "What's our E.T.A., Mr. Hanson?" he demanded of the newly assigned first officer.

"Eighteen hours, fifteen minutes," the officer snapped, but added under his breath, "thirty minutes since the last time you asked." A seasoned spacefarer, former Captain Dirk Hanson, a twenty-seven-year veteran, had served on many military missions. He knew how to handle inexperienced commanders, and he knew that of all the wet-behind-the-ears, *I think I'm in charge* type officers he had dealt with over the course of his career, Trevino was the most inept.

Taking in the sight of Trevino sitting in his command chair filled him with loathing and disgust, but he was too much of a professional to allow any of that to show openly. Yes, he would perform his duty to the best of his abilities, but this was one mission he would not enjoy.

He walked over and stood beside the command console. "Sir, may I suggest a softer hand with the troops?" He spoke softly so only Trevino could hear. "It has been my experience that just before a possible engagement, a crew as fine as this performs better when given a little time to reflect on the things they may find important, sir."

With an anger born of impotence, Trevino turned on Hanson. "When I need your advice on how to run *my* command, I'll ask you. Understood, mister?" Trevino hissed, his voice too loud.

The crew pretended not to hear.

"But there is one thing I know I don't need," Trevino continued in his still too loud voice, "I don't need you hovering underfoot every time I turn around!" He stood so he could look down on Hanson. "Captain, you are dismissed. Go to your quarters. You are to remain there until I call for you. Is that understood?" He sat back down dismissing Hanson with a wave of his hand.

Captain Hanson was not rebuffed by Trevino's outburst; he suspected as much. He faced his commanding officer. Bringing himself to attention, he spoke crisply and with extreme control. "Sir, it is my duty to serve you and I will. But I have a larger responsibility to the men of this crew." He lowered his voice. "If I see you do anything that unnecessarily endangers their lives, I will stop you." With that, he saluted, turned on his heels, and left the command quad.

As he left the command deck, the crew all stopped working and looked to him, ready to take their cue at his signal. Hanson looked neither left nor right, but stepped smartly through the bridge doors as they slid apart.

"Are you threatening me, sir?" Trevino yelled toward the retreating silhouette.

Without turning, the deposed captain spoke over his shoulder, "Threatening you, sir? No, sir. That would be insubordination, now wouldn't it?" Sarcasm dripped from his words. With an echoing swoosh, the bridge doors slid shut behind him, and he was gone.

Trevino sat hard in the command chair. Raking his hands through sweat dampened hair, he was coming apart at the seams, and he knew it. "ETA?" he demanded again.

A crewman called out the response.

Trevino spun away from his crew. He faced forward, as if studying the giant screen that dominated the forward view. He was thankful that the bridge crew was all in the command quad behind him and couldn't see his face. "Come on, Trevino, pull yourself together," he muttered.

Rocking forward in his seat, he propped his elbows on his knees, rubbed his hands across his face again, and sighed. "Come on, T, you've worked too hard to get where you are to lose it now. Settle down. Settle down." His breathing was shallow and irregular, his heart rate accelerated. Sweat ran down his back and pooled at his belt. Knowing he should not have exploded at his first officer, especially in front of the crew, he cursed and stood, walking toward the screen. The pressure had gotten to him. *I still got eighteen hours.* He pinched the bridge of his nose between his thumb and index finger, his offhand drumming absently against his thigh.

Eighteen hours?

He still had time. Time to rest. Time to sort out the mess he'd gotten into. Wiping the sweat from his face and taking time to smooth out his appearance, he turned and faced his command crew. Speaking to his second officer, "I'll be in my quarters if you need me, but call only if it is an emergency." After giving his speech, Trevino walked with brisk steps, quickly exiting the quad, doing his best to show a face of confidence he was not feeling.

As the door closed behind him, he relaxed against the bulkhead. He knew no one on the crew would call him because no one on the crew needed him. In addition, for the next eighteen hours or so that was a reality with which he could live.

Chapter Twenty-Two

Rooaaar!

The throaty voice of the beast rang out through the jungle like a sustained thunderclap across a broken sky. The Kracken sniffed the air, seeking the odor of the ones who injured it. The human scent had been strong and not one that it would easily lose. It would leave its normal hunting grounds, it would cross the burning sands if need be, but it would not stop until the human creature had been forced from its territory.

The Kracken moved forward, coming to the falls that had been its prey's campsite the night before. Lowering its massive head, it scratched the dust refreshing the scent. A rippling snarl creased its face as it bared the 9-inch canines extruding from its upper jaw. A new scent. A new predator was hunting its prey. This new information drove the Kracken.

Anger spawned by the need to protect its territory, and the drive to remove the human threat was its fuel, and it would not be denied. Raising itself to its full height, the Kracken threw back its head and roared again. It was intended to let everything in its path know it was coming and to flee or be ready to fight.

Many of the larger predators of the planet had found the band of humans a tempting treat, but the warning had its desired effect. These particular humans were taken.

Studying the jungle, Jay turned to face Skipp. "What do you make of the absence of other animals here? I thought we'd be up to our armpits in drags by now."

"Oh, they're out there. Look," Skipp said, holding the notepad up for Jay to see, "For whatever reason, they're keeping their distance from us, but moving right along with us."

It was then that they heard the Kracken's roar. The entire camp came alive. Break was over. "Get those little ones together. Let's get out of here," Mike called. "It sounds like it's quite a ways behind us, but we have no way of knowing how fast it's moving."

"What was that thing?" Iona asked. Her eyes reflecting the fear she saw in the children's faces.

Mike stopped. "Skipp, get me a wide range scan. I want to know where that thing is."

"Already on it. I'll have the results in one."

"Will somebody tell me what's going on," Iona demanded.

"It's the Kracken," Rose said. "It's coming after us."

Skipp turned and scanned the surrounding jungle looking for the signs of the giant predator he knew was out there. It was a lot closer than he felt comfortable with, and judging from the ensuing roars, it was coming their way and fast.

The camp broke and began to run. Still not sure what was going on, Iona looked to Mike for an explanation, but he was busy trying to comfort and direct the children. Finding Jay, she grabbed a hold of his arm and stopped him. "What is a Kracken?"

For a brief moment, as their eyes met, they froze.

Jay shook himself. "W-what?" he said, buying time and then brought her up to speed.

Jonas pulled Andrea and Peter to one side as they ran. "Tell me everything you know about this Kracken; I need to know how we can fight it."

Fighting panic, the children tried to focus on the man's face. "You've seen it," Peter blurted out between breaths. "You can't beat it."

"The Kracken is the top predator. Even the C-men were afraid of it," Andrea added.

"It's too big to try and out climb, and you know it will come into the caves," Peter said, looking around. "The only place I know to go are the small caves where we camped or the deep desert," Peter finished, but without hope.

"The desert," Andrea said excitedly. "The C-men always said the Kracken doesn't like the desert, but I don't know why."

"Skipp," Jonas yelled over the noise, "head us toward the nearest edge of the desert, but we need deep desert not the shallow tracks we crossed earlier." Turning, he called out, "Mike, Jay, I've got a plan."

"Keep the line moving," Mike said to Iona.

"Not on your life, I'm coming with you." Then turning, she said, "Andrea, take the point. Keep them moving."

When they joined Mike, Jonas filled them in on the details of the plan.

"So," Mike said, "all we've got to do is get to the desert before the Kracken can get to us."

"But why won't the Kracken go out on the sand?" Jay asked. They waved the line of children passed them as they talked. "Keep going," Jay's bass voice rang out. "Somebody tell me why de Kracken won't go 'n the desert."

"I got it," Skipp called out.

"Yeah?" Mike turned to him.

"What?" Skipp answered distractedly. "No, no, the desert, I mean. It's about 1200 meters that way. That's the good news. The bad news is that the Kracken is coming, and it's moving fast. At our speed, it'll catch us before we make the sand."

Underfoot, many brightly colored bugs of varying sizes scurried by, rustled from their daytime leisure. Long snail-like creatures, leaving a slimy residue in their wake, gave off an offensive odor that burned and irritated the eyes of the travelers when they happened by too close. Giant earthworm-like creatures with offsetting scissored mandibles broke free of the earth and seemed to sense that this prey was too large and bored back beneath the rich loam to await a more manageable dinner.

Still, the constant roaring grew louder. Its ear-piercing scream served to remind the fleeing prey that it was coming. Though hampered by the dense undergrowth, the Kracken did not slacken its pace. Huge branches snapped and broke free as the massive body slammed through the trees. Large rocks and small boulders were kicked out of the way as easily as if they had been pebbles.

With a flare of its nostrils, the Kracken threw back its head again and let out a roar.

It was coming.

The group ran. The little ones were on the shoulders of those who could bear their weight. "I thought you said we couldn't outrun this Kracken and, if we can't fight him, what good will putting ourselves out on the open sand do?" Iona asked.

Running and carrying Rose, Mike found conversation difficult; he spoke as best he could. "We're not sure what effect...laser will have on it...so if we can't out run it...then we'll just have to outsmart it." He finished and took a deep breath.

Skipp ran on the opposite side of Iona. "If we can make it onto one of the larger rock formations, we might get some help from the planet itself."

Underfoot, grass and weeds gradually became sand and stone as they approached the desert. Behind them, the sound of the Kracken grew closer; it had come within a few hundred meters or so. Suddenly, they were clear of the jungle. Rolling dunes of yellow sand stretched out as far as the eye could see.

"There," Mike called, pointing to a large stone platform about a hundred meters into the sand.

Behind them, about 50 meters back, the Kracken broke into the clearing. It stopped and roared in triumph. The creature stood to its full height and reached out its clawed hands as if it would grab its prey from across the distance.

"Keep the line moving, I'll slow it down," Jay said, stopping and un-slinging the laser rifle.

"Not by yourself," Mike said, releasing Rose's hand and falling in beside Jay. Together they stood their ground while the children, led by Iona and Jonas, made their way across the sand to the relative safety of the stone.

"What did he mean by, 'help from the planet?'" Iona asked Jonas as the children fled by them.

"Yeah," Andrea said. "This place hasn't done anything good for us yet."

"Well, let's just wait and see, but for now, we need these kids moving faster, and get them as high up on that platform as they can get," Jonas answered.

Skipp noted that the group was moving due west into the desert, but still a few hours trek from the Quest. He had a plan, but needed to get the group up on the rocks before he could test his theory.

The Kracken stopped.

The jungle fell silent.

Mike raised his fist, signaling to stop. He and Jay stood abreast, leveling their weapons at the Kracken.

It studied them. Then the Kracken roared, but still it did not charge. It stomped, lifted its arms, and roared again. This time it stepped forward, a hesitant action.

Mike and Jay held their position.

The Kracken extended its jaws, snapping them in thunderous repetition. As the jaws slammed shut, a yellow spray of drool splashed from its razor sharp teeth.

The Kracken took another tentative step forward, slamming its huge clawed foot down.

The earth beneath them trembled.

The men stumbled but held their footing.

The Kracken took another measured step, and as its foot hit the ground a second time, the earth reverberated with the footfall. This time, however, the Kracken didn't stop, it roared, lowered its head, and charged.

Looking back, Skipp saw the Kracken begin its charge. He knew that Mike and Jay would not last long, matched against the creature. He could see the light from the laser rifles firing, but he could not hear the sound over the roar of the Kracken. Climbing to the top of the rock platform, he pulled open the notepad and set his plan into action.

Mike and Jay continued to fire, targeting what they believed to be the weaker areas of the Kracken's underbody. Only the

Kracken didn't appear to have any true vulnerable spots. However, the men's efforts did succeed in slowing the creature's attack. The smell of burnt hide permeated the mingled humid air of the jungle and the hot dry air hovering over the sand. The odor hung heavy like the smell of cattle at branding.

"Target its face," Mike screamed. "I'll try and drop that tree in front of it. Maybe we can make it out on the sand before it recovers. Now!" He shifted his point of aim.

Jay screamed and fired. The Kracken stumbled backwards just as the huge tree fell across its path. Temporarily distracted, the Kracken attacked the tree, releasing its fury.

"Run!" Mike screamed. Both men turned and made for the rock platform.

They ran, dragging themselves through the ever-deepening soft sand. It wasn't until they reached the stone platform that they realized the Kracken was no longer chasing them. It had stopped at the edge of the sand.

The children cheered.

Bellowing out in frustration over the desert emptiness the Kracken stomped its foot, kicking up a huge spray of sand. It roared again, this time gingerly placing its foot out on the sand. Repeatedly, the beast toyed at stepping out onto the golden dryness, and each time it retreated.

A sweaty silence ensued in which the two parties simply stared at each other, the beast from the edge of the jungle and the group from the rise of stone.

Then...

"It's coming," one of the children screamed and pointed. A fresh surge of panic rushed through the already stressed children. Then to everyone's utter vexation, they watched as the Kracken stepped out on the sand and started toward them.

There was nowhere for them to go.

Tentatively, the Kracken stepped out onto the yellow silt-like sand. Then lifting its massive head, it roared and charged.

Being slowed by the unfamiliar surface, the Kracken sunk to mid-calf in the sand, stumbled, fell, and fell again. This only added to its rage.

Reaching the plateau, Mike surveyed the surrounding desert. "Trapped," he said more to himself than to be heard. The platform was surrounded by open desert, and he knew there was no way they could outrun the Kracken even without the smaller children.

The Kracken closed the distance between it and its prey. It roared, throwing its head back in triumph and intimidation; it continued to close the gap.

Iona turned her eyes to the deep desert. "Where's this help from the planet," she said directing her ire toward Jonas.

Jonas also looked toward the desert, but mumbled as if he had not heard Iona's question. "Come on, come on, where are you?" he mouthed. "Don't disappoint me."

Looking at him like he'd lost his mind, Iona got into his face. "What are you doing? The Kracken is coming!" she yelled.

Jonas never broke eye contact with the sand, never bothered looking up. "Come on, baby; don't let this brute run through your house. Come on and set him right."

The children scurried to the far edge of the platform trying to put as much distance as possible between them and the Kracken. From the front edge, now joined by Skipp, the men continued firing at the animal.

The Kracken reached the base of the stone tower, its chest heaved as droplets of rancid saliva pooled at its feet. The beast slowed and approached with deliberate movements, knowing its quarry had nowhere else to run. The Kracken coiled, preparing to lunge itself upon its prey.

Just then, a cloud of dust and sand, yellows, reds and oranges, exploded from the desert floor. When it settled, the Kracken was gone.

The roar of the Kracken dragged their attention back to the floor of the desert. Locked in mortal combat with the Kracken was a giant brightly colored creature that looked to be part snake and part spider. Its huge segmented body gave way to a rough muscled tail. Attached on either side of the creature's upper body were four legs and on the foremost set of arms, a pair of pincers. The Kracken roared in pain as the pincers cut into the flesh of its muscled arm.

The creature wrapped its coils tightly around one arm and the torso of the Kracken, burying its fangs deep in the opposite shoulder of the Kracken. Both of the Kracken's arms were pinned useless. Dark, almost black blood poured from the wound on its shoulder.

The Kracken screamed in pain and began thrashing wildly. Rocks and stones became projectiles being dislodged and kicked up by the warring behemoths.

The Kracken managed to turn and return a bite along the serpent's spine. Bright orange blood burst from the taut skin and ran into the sand mixing with the blackened blood of the Kracken.

The giants fought.

"We can't stay here," Mike said fighting to maintain his balance. "Whoever wins that battle is gonna consider us the prize."

As the Kracken and the giant serpent battled on the far side of the stone platform, the roars and screams blending into one indecipherable shriek of pain and fury, Skipp slipped down and headed back toward the jungle.

"Run," Skipp yelled and headed back beneath the cover of the trees.

After only a moment of indecision, where they stood frozen with fear, the children leapt off the backside of the stone island and ran for the relative safety of the jungle. Taking advantage of the giants' distraction, the children and the five adults hurriedly made their way back under the canopy of the dense foliage toward safety of the Quest.

The two behemoths, both dominate predators, kept separate only by their habitats. The Kracken ruled the jungles, and the sand-serpent, the desert sands. The two had never met.

Swimming beneath the sand and coming up behind the Kracken, the serpent had coiled itself around the Kracken's chest, trying to crush it. The beasts rolled in the desert sand, the yellow silt clotting what might otherwise be potentially life-threatening injuries.

As the group disappeared into the jungle, the Kracken sank its teeth into the throat of the serpent. The sound of crushing vertebra exploded over the desert like the snapping of green tree limbs. The serpent thrashed violently and screamed, trying to free itself from the crushing vice.

The tail lashed back and forth, casting waves of the fine sand spraying through the air. Finally, the body relaxed and the red eyes bulged and went dark.

The Kracken stood to its full height, florescent orange blood dripping from its fangs and maw mingling with the dull burgundy blood from its own varied and many wounds. Grabbing the carcass of the serpent, the Kracken roared and flung it toward the boundary of the jungle and desert.

Chapter Twenty-Three

Seeing that the children were weary with fear and hunger, Skipp suggested that they at least take a break. Mike looked back through the jungle, back down the path they'd just fled, considered the possibilities, and dipped his chin agreeing.

Skipp began digging a fire pit when Iona joined him. Leaning down, she whispered to him. "You think we should be lighting a fire with that thing still behind us?" When Skipp didn't answer, she looked back toward the group of kids, her eyes pausing on Andrea before returning to Skipp. "I don't think your little friend likes me very much."

Andrea quickly turned her face away, pretending she hadn't been watching.

"Oh, that," he said sheepishly and looked back to the pit. "She's just being watchful is all. You did kind of just drop out of nowhere." He smiled and fixed her with his gaze.

She looked again and saw Andrea watching them. "Well, I'm no expert, but I think the young lady might have a crush on you," she laughed. "We girls know these things."

Skipp stopped what he was doing and looked up at her, his hazel-blue eyes reflecting the light from the fading sun. An easy silence settled between them. All around the camp the children began settling down, some falling asleep as soon as they sat or laid down.

Iona looked away. "I haven't had a chance to properly thank you for what you did back there, calling that snake thing, I mean. You saved us."

"It wasn't me. I mean, not really. I didn't call it or anything like that. Oh, I ran the scans earlier. I knew something huge was out there beneath the sand." Skipp broke eye contact, looking back toward the path. "I knew something, but I only hoped that whatever *it* was it would come in time and..." He left the sentence unfinished.

She sobered. For a long moment, neither spoke but only stared into the empty fire pit, pondering the other's thoughts. Iona looked away first. "I-I'm not sure," she stammered. "I don't know how much Mike has told you about me, but I really haven't been a very nice person." She paused. "What I'm trying to say is that I'm sorry. For everything."

Sensing that this was hard for her, Skipp reached out, laying a hand on her forearm. "You know, Mike never says a bad word about anybody," he encouraged.

Iona paused. She had not recoiled from his touch; she wondered why. She also knew he was lying about Mike not having spoken harshly about her, but she appreciated that Skipp had chosen not to bring it up. She swallowed, brushing loose strands of hair back from her face.

Iona was not as forgiving of her past as others might be. Feelings of guilt clawed at her spine, threatening to turn her stomach. She looked at Skipp again, looking into his eyes trying to see any duplicity that might be there. Deciding to take a chance, she settled down preparing to talk.

Mike stared toward the horizon. Above him, a red sun began setting in the purple sky. Yellow-tinged clouds floated like wisps of smoke across the arc of the heavens. He swore. Pacing back and forth, he drummed a fist against his thigh.

He cursed again. "We gotta get off this planet. We gotta get to the ship." He looked back toward the camp. *These kids need rest. Mary and the kids alive. I can't die on this rock.*

Mike stomped into the center of the group. "Skipp, take the older kids and gather fruits and nuts and berries for dinner. The kids will know what's good to eat. Don't go too far from the clearing."

"I'm on it." Skipp stood, pointing to five of the boys, overt in his pronouncement and obvious in his overlooking Andrea. Gathering the group, he turned and started toward the woods.

"Jay—" Mike began.

"Fire detail. I'm already on it," Jay said and grabbed Sally's hand. "Let's go crew." Like an oversized pied piper, he led the band of smaller kids into the near woods to gather kindling.

"Looks like maybe an hour or so before it's too dark to work," Jonas said, walking up beside Mike.

Mike watched as the sky shifted from a light purple to a deep shade of indigo and dipped his chin in silent agreement with his old friend. Turning, he saw Jonas looking at Iona gathering wood with Jay and the others. "What do you think?"

"I think we don't dare try making it through the jungle with these kids at night. Too easy for something to go wro—"

"What? Nhaa…Iona, man. What do you think about Iona showing up here?"

"You know me." Jonas paused and looked up at his friend for a moment before he answered. "Viola raised both those girls." He raised and dropped his shoulders. "Can there be that much difference between the two?"

Turning to face Jonas, Mike stared at his friend. "I thought you would try and find some way to give God the credit for all this—Iona showing up when she did." It was not so much as sarcasm in his voice, as willful doubt.

"Why state the obvious?" Jonas said and knelt down, stirring the pit fire and igniting the kindling. The blaze caught the small fire, suggesting more comfort than offering heat.

"Stating the obvious?" Mike asked incredulously. He harrumphed, and then with an effort, lifted himself from the ground and went to help gather wood.

The small dinner eaten, the need for sleep began to settle over the camp. Iona volunteered for first watch. Before long, the sound of deep breathing and lack of conversation told her that, for the moment, fatigue had finally overcome the group's fears and anxiety. Taking advantage of the quiet, Iona decided to study Jay's features as he slept beside the fire. A moment later, she decided she could see why some would think him beautiful.

Shadows from the fire played across the rich bronze tones of his skin and dark hair. Dancing fingers of shadows, cast by the soft light from the fire, streaked back and forth over his strong shoulders. His was a masculine face, not unlike Mike's hard chiseled features, but more rugged. A face accustomed with being outdoors, a warrior's face.

Musing, she played with the idea of her being in a serious relationship. The possibility would cause her at least to be willing to touch another's soul and to allow that soul to touch hers. She began shaking her head against the thought and, just as quickly, relaxed into it again.

She shifted and continued studying Jay's face and wondered at his character. She remembered her own and frowned. Looking away, she recalled the many casual trysts which had been a part of her past. Feeling the weight of her own history, she shook her head, tears escaping her eyes.

What would Mary do? She sighed defeated.

"She would say change. Go for it," Iona said softly. *In fact, that's exactly what I did with Mike.* She paused, lost in thought. But in her heart she knew it hadn't been the same.

"You like him, don't you?" a voice asked from the darkness. "What do you want with him anyway?" Andrea walked into the circle of light. Her voice had not been unkind, but challenging nonetheless.

At first, Iona was annoyed at being caught in her musings, but she recovered quickly. Looking at the girl—*the young lady*— Iona corrected her line of thinking and stood. She met the younger woman's gaze and realized that Andrea had been talking about Skipp who lay sleeping across the fire pit from where Jay slept.

Iona figured that whatever this young lady felt for Skipp, the feelings were real and needed to be respected and dealt with as such. She did not want or need a new enemy, even one as young as Andrea. Walking a short distance from the fire, Iona turned and found Andrea following her.

"You got a crush on Skipp?"

Andrea swallowed, but did not answer.

Iona stopped, then turned to face the girl. "He's a little old for you, isn't he?"

"But don't you…"

Iona smiled at the girl, inviting her to keep talking. "Hey, I'm probably not the best one to give you advice." She raised a hand and brushed the corner of her forehead. "Now my sister, Mary, she's the one to ask."

Andrea allowed her gaze to travel back to the sleeping Skipp before turning to look again at Iona.

Iona smiled a friendly knowing smile, intending to win the girl over. "Who knows what Skipp is feeling; I don't." She stopped, realizing she was perhaps saying too much.

"I only met him a few days ago myself," Andrea said finally, and it sounded like a confession.

The defensiveness was gone, Andrea now sounded like the teenager she was. She looked up shyly. "But he's so cute," Andrea added with a chuckle.

Iona returned the smile. "I know," she answered in a conspiratorial tone.

They both giggled like girls as they shared what had turned into a special moment. Once they had reigned in their jubilation, they found themselves laughing again at the idea of them talking over Skipp's head; a secret shared.

Inwardly, Iona smiled even broader as she studied the joy on Andrea's face. Warmed by memories of her and Mary flooded back to her mind. She was transported back to her own childhood and more innocent days. She realized this new life could be a lot of fun if she filled it with people like Andrea and perhaps Jay. The thought surprised her.

She smiled at the thought of having a life that included Jay and wondered what Albert would think of the possibility.

Later that night when Iona woke Skipp to take watch, she could not keep the smile from showing on her face.

"Mmmm," he yawned and rolled to his back. Then asked, "What?" when he saw the expression on Iona's face.

"Oh, nothing," she said and covered her head with her bedroll.

He turned when a giggle sounded from the far side of the fire, but he would have sworn Andrea was sound asleep.

"Look at them. This is one tough bunch of kids," Jonas remarked to Mike as they continued their trek the next morning.

"What do you make of that?" Mike said, tilting his head toward Jay and Iona walking together.

"Whooa," Jonas wondered out loud. The men looked at each other and smiled.

Soon it was Mike's turn to take up the rear and Iona lagged back to walk beside him. "Mike," she began, "can I have a moment?"

"Sure. What's on your mind?"

"It's about Mary and the kids. I didn't want to go into this earlier, but I think Waters is still after them."

A look of frustrated anger washed Mike's face.

"Just before I left, Trevino—one of Waters's henchmen—questioned me about Mary and Nonna. I never answered his questions which probably only made things worse." She looked at him, trying to judge his emotions.

"We've got to get off this planet," Mike said and slammed a fist into the palm of his hand, wishing instead that it was Waters he was hitting. He looked at the line of haggard children stretched out ahead of him. "I've got to get these kids out of here."

Iona stopped.

After taking a few steps, Mike turned and walked back to where she stood with her head down. He looked at her, not sure if he should prompt her or just wait.

"Mike," she swallowed and started again, "Mike, there are so many things that I am sorry for." She still hadn't looked up. "I just didn't want this to go any further without me saying that I'm so sorry for everything and to ask for—to ask for your forgiveness." She looked up and her eyes met his. She held her breath.

Mike turned and faced her full on. For a few moments, nothing happened. Around them, the jungle was coming awake with the morning. He sucked in a breath, holding it for an instant before he spoke. "You are my wife's sister; that makes us family. Of course, I forgive you. After all this, everything else seems kind of petty."

She reached out a hand, laying it on his forearm. Mike pulled her into a rough embrace. "Let's get these kids out of here and go save our family."

"What about Waters?"

He pushed back from her, and for a moment, his vision drifted into the far away. "I'll take care of Waters."

"Mike, I don—"

"Now," Mike said interrupting her, "what's going on with you and Jay?"

She flushed and turned away from him. "Miiiike," she said, elongating his name and sighed a dry lonely sound.

"Hey, there you are. I think we're here," Andrea shouted from up ahead.

Happy for the reprieve, Iona turned and ran to catch up with the group.

"You never answered my question," Mike called after her, a smile in his voice.

She turned and smiled, still not answering and then joined the group.

Mike looked back scanning the trail behind them, listening for the sounds of pursuit. Catching up to the group, he joined Jonas at the lead.

They broke out of the jungle and looked over a sea of yellow sand glowing orange in the warming light of the rising sun. Unlike the last vista, this view of the desert offered few, if any, rock outcroppings or stone platforms, just miles of windswept emptiness.

Chapter Twenty-Four

"Where's the ship?"

"There's no ship."

Several voices began in question all at once.

"Oh no! The C-men stole the ship!"

"We're never getting off this planet."

"Okay," Jay said, stepping to the front of the group, by virtue of his massive bulk drawing the group's attention. He smiled. "Skipp, give me that controller. I need to bring up my baby." Taking the notepad, Jay positioned himself so that he had a clear view of the sweeping sand. Almost immediately, a low rumble sounded from deep beneath the sand.

"A sand serpent!" someone shouted, and the children screamed, turned, and ran back toward the jungle.

Jonas stepped out in front of the group, his arms stretched out to his side. "Stop!"

The intensity of the roar increased until it became a whine. Then slowly, the chrome colored nose of the Quest broke free of its earthen tomb, reflecting the morning sun in dazzling brightness through cascading layers of sand.

As the ship continued to rise, all traces of dust and sand fell free, unable to stick to the ship's varying wave shields. Sunshine danced and leapt in fiery displays as curtains of sand slipped from the hull. In a matter of seconds, the Quest floated above the desert floor, rotating away from the group. Jay lowered it to the ground, presenting the main ingress port. Just a few meters of open sand now separated the group and the safety of the ship.

Jay's face was stern in concentration; he clinched the muscles of his forearms and shoulders as he focused on bringing the ship closer. The retrorockets fired, and the ship began to back toward the jungle's edge. "Just a bit closer, baby," he muttered beneath his breath. At barely ten meters from the confluence of desert and jungle, repulsor rockets came online and locked the Quest in a low hover just above the dusty sand.

The seal released with a snap as the boarding ramp opened, and air rushed in replacing the vacuum. Running lights came to life, blinking as if waking from a long sleep. With the rear ramp down, she presented a safe haven from the dangers on the ground and a way off the planet.

Jay turned to Mike and smiled. "She's all yours, skipper."

With a mock salute, Mike gave the order, "Board." Amongst cheers and screaming, the children ran for the ramp. With Iona and Skipp leading the way, Jonas followed close behind them carrying Sally on his shoulders. The children's fear of the jungle melted at seeing the open bay of the Quest. Still, they were somewhat skeptical about walking out on the sand despite the ship being so close.

Mike stood near the edge of the desert encouraging the children to make the short run across the sand to the Quest while Jonas beckoned them from atop the ramp.

As they entered the ship, Skipp and Iona directed them to the ship's commons.

"Fire her up, Jay," Mike called. "I want out of here as soon as that hatch is sealed."

Jay turned and ran for the conn.

Jonas yelled out to Mike. "We need to light a fire under these kids." Obviously relaxed, he was laughing. "Maybe you can call that Kracken and chase them up here."

Mike turned and surveyed the jungle. "You know what they say, be careful of what you wish for you may just get—"

The jungle exploded as the Kracken burst through the underbrush. Ripped and torn, it stood in total defiance; blood oozing from open wounds and smeared with the effulgent blood of the sand serpent.

The Kracken threw its head back and roared, not a simple roar of triumph, but of anger and open challenge. Its arms still seeped blood from where the giant ophidian had bitten it, and in its claws was the severed head of the defeated serpent; its black forked tongue dangling from it lifeless mouth.

The Kracken chucked the head of the serpent, and it rolled within yards of where Mike stood. Like a boulder in the path, it blocked Mike's view of the Kracken, and he had to adjust to keep the creature in his line of sight.

Unslinging his laser rifle, Jay started down the ramp. "Haven't we seen this movie already?"

"I told you to get to the conn."

Jay laughed, "Yeah, Skipp's got that for now. You need me more right here, right now."

Mike chanced a look at his friend, but then turned his gaze back toward the Kracken. "What's it doing?"

"Best guess, boss?"

The Kracken did not charge, instead it stood its ground; lowering its massive head, the maw slightly ajar, it stared at them.

Mike stared back. Taking short shallow breaths, Mike began backing toward the open hatch. Still, the Kracken did not move. "Let's go."

"I'm with ya on that."

Widening its stance, the Kracken bellowed again. Stomping and dragging its feet through the turf, it tore up large clumps of terrain, kicking them behind it. Crouching, it roared and pulled small trees from the earth and threw them onto the sand. Hissing, globs of yellowish-green spittle expelled from its lips. It roared again and shuffled forward. The message was clear, it was king; stay out of its territory.

Mike met Jonas at the bottom of the ramp and all three men backed into the hollow of the ship. "Get us some distance and altitude," Mike called over his shoulder.

Jay turned and ran.

Lifting, the Quest started slowly toward the desert and rose pirouetting until she faced the jungle and the Kracken. Entering the bridge, Mike took his seat at the conn. "Get us out of here."

Jay tapped Skipp on the shoulder. "I got it."

Skipp rose and moved back to his station. Iona stood behind him while looking over his shoulder at the multiple screen set.

Through the main viewer, they could see the Kracken roar one last time before turning and heading back into the heart of the jungle. Before long, its massive bulk disappeared beneath the emerald canopy.

Iona sighed. "It's over. Now for the hard part."

Chapter Twenty-Five

Minutes later, the Quest blasted free of the planet's atmosphere. "Planet's UGC, universal gravitational constant, approaching zero in 15 seconds," Skipp said without looking up from his station. With one last shudder, the Quest was free and heading toward the Terran system.

The connecting door opened, and Jonas came onto the bridge. "The kids are settling, but they could use some comforting."

"I'll go." Iona volunteered. "But before I do, Jonas, what was it that gave you the idea to run out onto the sand when the Kracken was chasing us?"

Taking a deep breath and leaning back against the nav-center, Jonas said, "Just an educated guess, really."

"A guess?" Mike exclaimed. "You mean you put us up on that, that dinner plate based on a guess?"

"Well, yes," he answered. "Kind of, anyway." He turned to his control panel and shifted the viewing screen filter to space-normal.

"You remember the scans Skipp took of the planet before we landed?" he asked, bringing them up on the viewing screen. "The Kracken is an alpha predator, right?" he asked rhetorically. Not expecting an answer, he continued without a pause. "So I figure the only reason it wouldn't go out on the sand was because that area belonged to another alpha." He smiled, satisfied with his explanation.

When no one seemed impressed, he added, "If you remember, the children said over and over again that they had never seen or even heard of the Kracken venturing out into the desert. Couple that, with these scans of the large life forms in the sand, it was the only reasonable explanation."

"Like you said, a guess," Jay laughed, looking over his shoulder.

From across the bridge, Mike watched Iona leave the bridge and tracked Jay's eyes as he noticed the big man watching her as well.

Mike surveyed the rest of his crew, taking special note of a growing shadow coming over Skipp's face. Mike shook his head. He could only imagine what being back on the Quest must mean for the younger man; it was here that Julie had died. Sighing, Mike stood and, for a minute, memories of the bombed out crater where his house once rested flooded back into his mind. With measured steps, Mike walked over to where Skipp sat and bent near his ear; speaking so only Skipp could hear. "You all right?"

Skipp knew he was talking about Julie. "Yeah, it's just that I really hadn't had time to think about her until now. She died protecting me. Man, I barely even knew her. Who dies for someone they barely even know." He sighed, resting his elbow on the console, allowing it to support him. Skipp shook his head like a man trying to erase a memory, then looked up at Mike. "But there was something about her. You know—"

Mike nodded, letting him talk. He couldn't miss the parallel of Julie's dying to save Skipp and what Mary always said about Jesus dying for the world; for him.

After a while, Mike asked, "What now?"

Skipp smiled and turned away. "So much has happened in such a short period of time."-He shook his head-"I don't know."

Mike cut him off. "All I'm saying is just don't give up— keep living. You owe her that much."

Mike and the crew took their places at their various duty stations and continued the in-flight sequencing. All systems checked green. Standing behind the helm, Mike laid his hand on his friend's broad back. "Jay, you're the pilot, get us out of here.

We've got a bunch of kids aboard who would like to see Earth again."

"Sol, here we come," Jay said and eased the stick back. The Quest seemed to stall and then with blinding acceleration climbed toward space. The ion trail streaked like a rend across the vault of the sky.

Looking back, Jay marveled that he could see the dense jungle greens and the contrasting flocks of colorful avian creatures moving like clouds through the sky.

Chapter Twenty-Six

"Sir, a ship is approaching from the planet surface. It matches the specs for the ship we're looking for," the crewman stated from helm control on the command ship.

"Has it seen us yet?" Hanson's voice came over the com.

"I don't think so, sir. Shall I notify the commander?"

"Not yet," Hanson said, fastening his uniform jacket. He stood and the desk lamp's illumination began to decrease as he moved away. "Hide the fleet in the gas ring of the third moon. Let the ship clear the planet's atmosphere, then we can simply trap them clear of the planet. The sooner we get this over, the sooner I can get that buffoon off my ship."

Hanson closed the channel and headed for the bridge. He would deal with Trevino and his orders later.

Taking position at the conn, Hanson studied the screen. "Open a channel to base," he ordered.

"We're on a time delay due to the gas interference, sir," came the officer's quick response.

"Belay that order," Trevino said, bursting onto the bridge. "I thought I told you to remain in your quarters."

Hanson vacated the conn, but remained standing beside it. "I felt that in this position you needed my expertise on the bridge."

Trevino stared at his second in command, studying the man. He knew Hanson didn't like him, but he was a good officer. Trevino knew if he was going to survive, he needed Hanson; he also knew that this was a fact of which Hanson was well aware.

"Scan that ship," Trevino ordered and turned away from Hanson, who still stood impassively beside the conn.

"She's faster than we are, sir. If she makes it into open space, we'll never catch her," Hanson said over Trevino's shoulder.

"Bring the fleet out. Block that ship in," Trevino ordered, as if the idea had been his. He knew his only chance was to corral it in and pound it into submission.

Proximity alerts rang out on the bridge of the Quest. "Evasive action!" Mike ordered needlessly.

Jay had already nosed the Quest down and away from The Company fleet closing in on them.

"Hey, we've got scared kids down here. What's going on up there?" Iona's anxious voice came over the intercom.

"It's that fleet you warned us about. Get up here." Mike's voice was clipped.

"On my way."

Just as Iona came through the access tunnel, the first blast landed.

"Shields holding, but we can't just sit here and take this," Jonas said from the engineering station.

"They're trying to box us in," Jay said, putting the ship through a series of dives, twists, and banking maneuvers. However, the fleet wasn't interested in pursuing, just in keeping them from escaping.

Every way the Quest turned, she faced a new combatant, a new wall of blaster fire. "They're larger and slower, but carrying significantly more firepower than the Quest," Jonas said from his station.

"Hey, mon," Jay said and grimaced as he initiated another turn. "I can do this all day, but it's only a matter of time before they wear down our shields."

The battering continued. The ship rocked and the light flickered before recovering.

"I will not let these children go back to that god forsaken planet," Mike said through gritted teeth. "Jay, find me a gap and get us through it. Either we're getting through or we're not, but there's no going back."

"I don't care about survivors, destroy that ship," Trevino ordered. He sat back in the command chair allowing a slight smile to play across his swarthy features. Rubbing the bruise on the side of his face and thinking of Iona, he thought he *would* have his revenge. He only wished she knew it had been on his order that she died.

The laser fire and cannon blasts came at them from every angle. The Quest rocked back and forth under the barrage of firepower assaulting her shields.

Jay flew evasive maneuvers, dodging as much of the assault as possible, as Skipp and Iona fired volley after volley of return fire. But they all knew this couldn't last much longer.

"Targeting stabilizers off line," Jonas called. "You're gonna have to site in manually guys."

A light blue smoke began to fill the bridge. Forced to target by the seat of their pants, Skipp and Iona managed to inflict a fair amount of damage to the opposing fleet in spite of themselves, but the numbers were against them, still outnumbered five to one.

Jay accelerated the Quest backwards and rolled into an inverted pivot, then dove for the planet's surface hoping to get a respite from the battering.

Anticipating this move, one of the ships moved in, blocking his path. He had no choice but to angle back up to the fleet. They were closing the trap.

Slashing from side to side and dodging incoming fire, Jay headed for the command ship. As he approached within 200,000 kilometers, he rolled the Quest over and fell back out of the attack run. "Full power to forward shields." He swallowed hard and dropped the ship into the line of incoming fire.

In mockery of his earlier maneuver against the fighter, Jay brought the Quest down across the bow of the command ship. Using the gravity field of the ship as a base, he fired the Quest's repulsor rockets. Bouncing off the energy wave, the Quest broke away at an angle otherwise not possible in the vacuum of space.

The pursuing ship did not have enough time to readjust its firing line and blasted its sister ship caught in the crossfire.

The blast hit the ship broadside and tore through its shields. The resulting explosion showered the area with debris and frozen atmosphere, the brilliance in stark contrast against the dark of space.

"Skipp," Mike called over the din, "you think those modifications—the one's you dabbled with in the alley—think they'll work with the ship's systems?"

Pulling himself up, Skipp answered, "Now is as good a time as any to find out."

Mike looked at his younger friend contemplating whether to use the new defense measure.

The ship rocked beneath another explosion. Lights flickered off and on again. Acrid smoke billowed and hung near the ceiling before the sump pumps dragged it from the air.

"I know I'm good guys, but the odds are not with us on this lasting much longer. Sooner or later one of those shots is going to get to us," Jay said, a grimace of concentration darkening his features.

A panel exploded, and bright yellow and red flames leapt from the gap on the board. Jonas swung around in his seat and slammed his palm down on a large black button on his console. The fire suppression system came online and sprayed mucousy blue foam from the hidden vents incasing the engulfed panel. The fire died leaving a lingering haze on the command deck.

The blaster fire intensified against the ship's hull. The Quest rocked beneath the barrage.

All eyes moved to Mike; it was his call. "Skipp, make it happen." Mike returned their gaze. He was looking at his crew, but he saw the faces of the children he had onboard and those of Mary and his own kids instead.

"I'll need a minute or two to bring it online," Skipp said, exchanging places with Jonas at the engineering station.

"In the meantime, Jay, keep us away from those ships," Mike ordered.

Skipp lowered himself to the deck and began pulling open panels. He looked up and saw Iona nod toward him in support. He wiped sweat from his face and shoved his hands back inside the electrical panel. After minutes that seemed like hours, Skipp finally gave the word. "On my mark, Jay, release the controls. Mark…five, four, three…"

"Destroy that ship," Trevino screamed, "I want nothing left but fragments and gas."

"What's going on?" Iona asked, her voice anxious.
Skipp: "…two, one. Mark!"

"All ships, open fire. I repeat open fire!" Trevino was standing now, sweat beading on his forehead and upper lip. He cursed and pumped his fist into the air. "I've got you now, I've won, I've won."

Jay released the controls.

Skipp shouted, "Hold on," and flipped the switch. Everything inside the ship stopped. Sound ceased. The lights blinked, and for a moment, the artificial gravity field surged.

Then with a shudder that reverberated through the deck, everything settled back down. The lights flickered and came back up; the sounds of a ship coming back online. Outside, what the fleet had seen, resembled a small sun going nova. The Quest's hull absorbed the laser fire and appeared to swell. Fingers of iridescent flame danced along its outer edge, and twisting tearing spires leapt free in every spectrum of visible light.

"Cease fire. Cease fire! Something's wrong. Pull back! Pull back! All ships cut attack and run!" Commander Hanson screamed through the intra-ship connect.

"Belay that," Trevino counter ordered. "Blast them! Destroy them! I want nothing left, nothing. You hear me!"

"Something's not right, sir, we need to vacate, and now." Hanson grabbed Trevino's arm. "Sir?"

"You will not deny me my victory, commander."

Hanson snatched Trevino around to face him. "Look, I don't care about you or the vendetta you have against that ship, but I am not going to stand by and watch you get my crew killed. Now give the order or so help me I will kill you where you stand and give it myself."

Trevino snatched his arm away and stumbled back against the conn. Seeing the fear and anger in Hanson's face, he relented. Sagging against the command chair, Trevino finally gave the order. It was too late.

"Pull back. All ships pull back."

Only those on the command deck ever heard it issued.

All at once, the Quest released the stored energy reflecting and amplifying it back against the armada from which it had come. The blast hit the attacking edge of the fleet like a tsunami; ship after ship tilted backwards, shuddering and exploding as blades of energy pierced their hulls and overloaded their systems. The energy wave continued spreading until it encased the entire fleet and then like the percussive blast of a bomb, breathed and then released its final mass of energy in a spreading ring of fire.

The energy released created a feedback in the fleet ships' electrical systems blowing them out, destroying all life support stations and freezing the controls. The ships engines overheated and began to blow. One by one, the ships exploded, ramming into one another then slowly fell toward Yargon, the giant yellow sun.

In the center of the inferno, quiet returned to space.

As the fire and debris cleared only two ships remained, the Quest and the command ship.

An eerie silence filled the bridge of the Quest. No one moved or spoke, wondering if they had survived. Seeing the command ship still on the main view screen, Mike said, "Open a channel to that ship."

For a moment nothing happened, and then a fuzzy picture came into view. On the screen, the bridge of the command ship was in disarray. Bodies lay strewn about the deck, some sat slumped at their workstations. Trevino sat lifeless at the conn, a single laser blast at his temple.

Iona gasped.

The face of Commander Hanson filled the viewer.

"This is Mike Stone commander of the spaceship Quest—" Mike began but got no further.

A worn, but proud voice interrupted him. "Mike Stone? I thought you were dead." There was a long pause. Then a resonant beeping began in the background.

Mike started to respond when he heard the man's raspy breathing and low mutterings. "It's over…the whole thing for not. I've given my entire life to this," Hanson said as if he had just awakened from a nightmare turned real. He focused back on Mike.

The ships drifted closer.

Hanson cleared his throat and adjusted what was left of his uniform. He laughed. "I've got nothing now and it's all your fault. It was all for naught," he repeated.

Mike turned. "Get us out of here, now!"

"Aren't we gonna try and help the survivors?" Jonas asked.

"Now!" Mike demanded. Jay pulled hard on the control, and the Quest leaped into hyperspace just ahead of the explosion. No sooner had the Quest disappeared, the blast engulfed that sector of space. The command ship had self-destructed.

Chapter Twenty-Seven

The Quest sped on its way back to the Terran sector, back to the place called home, and to Mike's great satisfaction back to the waiting arms of his beloved Mary. Rejecting his desire to hurry, Mike knew the responsibilities of command came first. "Slow ship's speed by one perc. Run diagnostics and let's get started on repairs. We have no idea what Waters will run at us once he discovers we're not dead."

Jonas walked up beside him. "Good idea. It'll give us time to wrap our minds around what just happened and—for the kids."—he motioned with his head—"for the kids to prepare themselves for a world that has..." He left the sentence unfinished.

"Yeah." Mike walked back to the commons and leaned against the bulkhead. He crossed his arms, watching as the children, yet again, begin to adapt. Only this time they would not be forced to accept the horror of their existence as the only real life they could know. This time they would have a choice—a chance.

"Mike, Mike," Rose screamed, breaking him from his reverie as she ran to him and jumping into his arms. Catching her, he spun her around.

"I was so scared," she said and began telling him about what happened during the battle. He laughed as she told her tale with excited gestures, flinging arms and contorted expressions. Mike glanced up and took in all the children as they looked on, yet holding their distance.

What am I going to do now, he thought to himself. *Somehow, these kids will need to fit into society.* He continued thinking as Rose talked while sitting on his knee.

Rose looked up. "Jonas!"

Jonas exhaled as he read Mike's expression and sat beside his friend. "It's a big job."

"What? Oh, yeah, don't I know. How we gonna do this, Jonas?" Mike asked distractedly, still looking at the children. He shooed Rose off his lap, who then ran off to play, seeing Sally on the far side of the room.

"I know you told me you didn't want to hear this, but God has gotten us this far. Don't you think you might want to try trusting Him just a little?" Jonas asked warily.

Mike did not answer, but just looked hard at Jonas, his face impassive.

Jonas inhaled sharply. "First, Mary and the kids…alive, and now that escape." He eyed his friend. "You can't think that was all just chance?"

Not answering, Mike turned his face back toward the playing children.

"We'll do fine," Jonas said, deciding on a different tact. "We've done well so far."

"We'll have to find homes for them back on Earth, places where they can just be kids," Mike said without turning.

Jonas leaned back. "The problem as I see it is still Ted Waters. He is not going to just let what we did back there go unchallenged."

"That's right," Mike said, slapping his thigh and standing. "We still have to somehow tie him to all this and expose him for what he is." He rubbed a hand across his head roughly, massaging his scalp, as if trying to force an idea to the surface.

"You mean, besides his being the most powerful man in our sector of space?" Jonas asked, a wry smile pulling at the corners of his mouth, but not touching his eyes.

"I know." Mike exhaled. "But we can't just walk away from this. Who's to say he doesn't have a dozen more planets just like the one back there."

"This is where God comes in, my friend." Jonas stood and faced Mike. "Like it or not, you need Him, and for whatever reason, it looks like He's chosen you to do this." Jonas rubbed his face, massaging his eyes. He was tired. "Go figure."

"Why's that?"

"The Lord has chosen you, and you're too proud or too stupid to even say thank you for the favors He's already done." He shook his head. "I've got to get back to work. That power board won't fix itself."

Mike sat and watched his friend leave and wondered about what he'd said. How many times had Mary called him on the question of his pride? "Too many times to count," he said rubbing his face. His eyes were tired and gritty like sand had collected at the corner just under the lids.

"What do you want from me?" he whispered to the unseen but ever present presence of Mary's God. He stood to get back to work when he heard the whisper again.

You.

Jonas sat near one of the few true windows watching the stars streaming past, his mind traveling just as fast, covering the distance to his own history. He sat remembering that day on patrol. How long had it been, one year? Two? Recalling the little girl.

He laughed aloud, interrupting his thoughts; he had forgotten her name. "Where do You fit into all this, God? Did You intend that I find that ship? Was it Your plan to get Mike back into space? Where is all this going?" He leaned his head against the cold plasti-glass and sighed.

He looked out again. *I can't even remember her name,* he said to himself. Then out loud, "I can't remember her name."

Jay and Iona worked in silence repairing the ship's electrical systems. They worked well together. Finishing the last task, she could feel Jay looking at her as she began closing panels and putting away her tools.

His eyes played over her long red hair that was pulled back from her face, revealing almost flawless skin. "Got a question for you," Jay said, clearing his throat.

"Yeah," Iona said, stopping but not looking at him.

"So, what's next for you? It's not like you can just go back to your old life. You're one of us now—an outcast."

Iona didn't answer him, but returned to the silence instead. After a while, she turned to face him, asking him a question instead, changing the direction of the conversation. "There *is* something I'd like to know."

"Single, never been married, and I prefer jerk pork to seafood."

"Not that," she said laughing to cover a sudden feeling of awkwardness.

"Oh." He feigned innocence.

"Back there…Skipp—how did he do that? The fleet had us surrounded; what *was* that? I've never seen anything like it." She turned to look fully at him, amazed.

Jay stopped and made to sit up, finding it difficult to maneuver his large frame in the confined space. He turned toward her and offered her a combination of one of his brightest smiles mingled with a look of apology. Trying hard to stay out of lecture mode, he briefed her on the events and happenings that led up to the critical moment. He told her about Skipp's fight in the alley, his moment of inspiration. And he told her about Julie.

Iona nodded, gaining insight into the somewhat moody Skipp.

Jay noticed her withdrawing into herself and stopped. He saw that she was no longer listening; her focus somewhere far away. Tentatively, he reached out and brushed her cheek with his knuckle, barely touching her skin. "I've wanted to do that for some time." He smiled.

She didn't move, neither encouraging nor discouraging him.

Jay pulled his hand away. The moment stretched out between them. The silence grew heavy. "What 'appened to you?"

Iona looked away.

After a moment, she slowly lifted her face, looking at him with strained haunted eyes. She stood gracefully, and without speaking, strolled away.

Jay watched her leave. He could see that she was in pain, but what he couldn't see was how to help her. He also knew he had never wanted anyone to find peace as much as he wanted it for Iona at that moment. He laid his head back against the open hatch and moaned from deep inside himself, the lights of the circuit boards above his face blinking on—off—on, unseen.

Iona had retreated to the bridge hoping to be alone. She hugged herself around the waist, furrowing her brow—too many new feelings too quick. She thought about Albert and then she thought about Jay's question. 'What 'appened to you?' *Too many things.* She sighed. *Too new.*

She looked deeper into herself and wondered if she could truly feel good about herself...feel clean again. She thought back to how—to what—she had been. She pressed her face into the coolness of the bulkhead. "Oh, Nonna, where are you when I need you," she asked into the silence. "What would you tell me now, I wonder."

You know what you've been, she began to berate herself. *Do you think God would love...would forgive you knowing the number of men you've been with, none of them meaning any more than the last.* She swore and slapped the bulkhead. Turning, she stalked away and collided into Mike.

"Hey, save some of that for Waters."

Shocked, she pushed against his chest causing him to step backwards. "Sorry. I didn't see you. I didn't know you were there," she said sheepishly. Her cheeks heating, she cocked her head toward him. "How long have you been standing there?"

"I was here when you came in," he said, smiling. "I didn't want to interrupt you. Looked like you wanted to be alone."

"I thought I was."

"Well, I figured you might want to talk about whatever it was that was bothering you, but that was before you started trying to destroy my ship."

She smiled, imagining what she must have looked like. "Sorry about that." She rubbed her hand across the wall where she had struck it.

"Want to talk?"

She paused and looked at him, searching his face. After a long moment, she turned her back to him, but as she did, her shoulders slumped. "Am I ruined, Mike? Is it too late for me?"

It was Mike's turn to be silent, and for a long while, he didn't answer her.

Finally, she turned to face him. "Well?" she asked sounding afraid.

In that moment, Mike began to see himself in a different light. His pride and arrogance. His self-determination to do everything on his own—a self-made man.

Iona laughed mirthlessly. "That bad, huh?"

Mike stammered, cleared his throat, and began again, "No, it's not that. It's just your question made me think about myself."

"What, you? What did you do? All this happened to you—to you and Mary and the kids."

Mike waved a hand interrupting her. "You know if we had had this conversation a few months ago…"—he smiled when he saw the expression on her face and started again—"providing we could have had this conversation a few months ago, I might have agreed with you then. Well, it's something Jonas said to me a little while ago. There's just too many things that have worked in our favor to be coincidental. Know what I mean?"

She was nodding her head. "Next to Nonna, I'd say you and Mary know me best; you know what I've been. You think God could want a woman like me? I mean, you didn't even want me." She dropped her eyes, suddenly ashamed and turned away from him.

He grabbed her by the shoulders and held her. "Is that what you thought?" He turned her to face him. "What is it Nonna's always saying, 'Judge not and you won't be judged'? Well, trust me, I have no room to point fingers at you or anyone else."

"Then why did you reject me?" she asked. She had not intended to ask him this question, but it was out now, and in spite of herself, she did want to know.

"Iona, I didn't reject you. I fell in love with your sister; I fell in love with Mary. We never meant to hurt you. We hadn't even planned on falling in love; we just did." He pulled her to him and let her cry. "Hey, if there's really anything to this whole God and Jesus thing maybe we'll find out for sure."

After a minute, she stepped back from Mike, composed now. She wiped the final few tears from her cheeks and turned to look again at the passing stars.

Iona looked up at Mike. "I bet Mary and Nonna are both driving God crazy praying for us right now. So we better not disappoint them by getting ourselves killed before we get home, what-da-ya-say?"

He smiled down at her and kissed the top of her head.

"Maybe there is something to that God and the second chance stuff Nonna is always talking about, huh?" She rested her face against the plasti-glass and fell again into silence.

"Yeah, maybe. Maybe."

Chapter Twenty-Eight

Jay tried again to focus on the sparking circuits and junctures hanging over his face. Picking up where he left off had been harder than he thought. He found himself distracted by thoughts of Iona.

From where his feet stuck out from under the workstation, a voice broke through the fog of Jay's jumbled thoughts. "What, you sleep under there?"

"What," Jay muttered, giving up on the board and scooting out to see his visitor.

Skipp stood, looking down on his friend. With oil streaks on his face and beads of sweat on his forehead, Jay looked more like a mechanic than a ship's pilot. "I've been standing here calling you for the last few minutes and not so much as a 'what, mon' from ya." Skipp pointed toward the panel. "Things that bad in there? Maybe I should take a look at it."

Jay looked up at the smaller man, his eyes asking the question that his mouth couldn't seem to say. *Where do I go from here?*

Skipp squatted down next to Jay's feet. Taking a towel from a pocket, he offered it to Jay and watched as Jay wiped oil and sweat from his face. When Jay was done, Skipp pulled a water decanter from another of his oversized pockets. He offered it to Jay and twisted the top off a second for himself. In response to Jay's unasked question, he said, "I saw the two of you—it looked like you'd been talking…a lot. I figured you might need some male bonding after all that." He finished with a smile.

"It's not like that...at least not yet." Jay said and twisted the top on his decanter, a spray of refrigerant spread between the double-walled liner instantly chilling the flavored liquid within. He held the cold of the bottle against his forehead. "I'm confused, I think?"

"Oooooh yeah, my friend."

They both laughed and took long drafts from their bottles.

Smacking his lips and wiping his mouth with the back of his hand, Skipp squeezed his eyes shut. "Good, ey?"

They tapped their bottles together.

"Very good, thanks." Sobering, Jay took a long drink and looked up at Skipp. "What do I do now? She's hurting, mon. She's working through a lot of stuff. She's not like any girl I've met before. S-she's special. Know what I mean? Sophisticated."

Skipp stood and offered Jay a hand, pulling him up to a standing position. "It's worse than I thought." He smiled. "Look out there," he said pointing to a view port. "Tell me, what do you see?"

"Stars?"

"Not just the stars, but worlds and each one different." He smiled like he'd made a point.

Jay gave him a "what in the world are you talking about" look.

Skipp exhaled and continued. "A woman is like a world, all full of mystery. We men are more like visitors coming to explore that world." He turned to look at Jay. "Take for instance the world we just left; it was beautiful but dangerous. When The Company found it, the place was beautiful; the animals lived in a balanced harmony. Not evil, not good just balanced. Nature.

"Waters and the C-men upset that balance. He made the Kracken something evil, a tool of destruction and abuse. Man scarred that planet."

Jay looked at Skipp, still confused.

Feeling like he might be losing his audience, Skipp hurried in an attempt to salvage his point. "We came along and removed the scar, now the planet's back in a place of balance, ready to heal itself," he finished and looked at his friend, satisfied.

Jay's face remained dark. "What in the world are you talking about...scars, planets, balance? If you've got a point, I sure wish you'd make it."

Skipp threw up his hands above his head, "Aahh, how can you be so dense? Yes, she's special, she's beautiful, and you know she's been messed over and messed with; so you can't go into this if you're not serious about it, man. Don't hurt her. How can you not see that? Don't be adding to her scars."

"Oh," Jay said sobering, "thanks."

With that, Skipp turned and walked away muttering to himself, leaving Jay to contemplate the planets as they sped by.

Jay wondered about the women he had known and asked himself, *of all the worlds he had visited, how many of them had he left scarred.*

Finished checking the charts, Jonas was determined to get some answers. He headed back to where the children were. He decided Andrea, Peter, and Frankie represented his best chance at discovering anything of true importance and headed to where the older kids sat gathered talking.

Jonas stopped short when he saw Iona sitting on the floor with two of the smaller girls, Rose and Sally. Seeing the impish grin on Rose's face, he decided to watch as the event unfolded.

With her hands folded in her lap, Iona leaned toward the girls, the light of her smile reflected in her eyes. "You girls ever play dress up or have tea parties when you were on the planet? My sister Mary and I played all kind of games when we were little girls at Nonna's."

Rose picked up a doll made of sticks and rags which lay on the floor in the space between where the three of them sat facing each other. "Oh, did you guys have fun, a lot of fun?"

"I bet you guys didn't have to worry about the Kracken or no bad C-men," Sally said in a matter fact voice.

A look of pain crossed Iona's face. "Let me teach you girl's a simple game Mary and I played, especially when it was too wet or cold to go outside."

The girls clapped their hands and bounced with anticipation to learn something new, but more so for having the undivided attention of this woman. This was the closest experience any of them remembered to having had a mother.

Iona held her left hand out in front of her, the palm facing up. "Okay," she began. "Take your other hand and make a fist."

The girls giggled, imitating her move for move.

With the fisted hand, Iona began tapping her open palm while counting, "1-2-3-4." On the count of four, she opened her hand and began to demonstrate a number of different configurations, explaining them as she did. "You see, when I curl my hand on the side and point one knuckle, that's called the laser. If I cup my hand and make the clapping sound, that's called the shield."

The girls laughed and struggled to fix their hands in the shapes demonstrated by Iona.

"Now the last one is the fusion-bomb, and you do that by putting the heel of your hand in the opened one and then opening your fingers like a fan." Iona showed the girls the various configurations explain how one beat out the other.

"I get it, I get it," Sally said.

"But what do you get if you win?" Rose asked.

Iona giggled in response to the girl's excitement. "That's where the fun part comes in. If you win, you get to ask a question of the other players, and they have to tell the truth."

The girls screamed and with a whoop of laughter, collapsed in their moment of joy.

"That'll be so much fun."

"Wow, fun-fun. Let's play."

After playing for some time, Iona found herself having as much fun as the girls. She thought back to her times playing with Mary. *Funny*, she thought to herself, *take a child half way across the galaxy and hide 'em down a hole for the most part of their lives, but give them a chance and they'll still be kids.* She smiled and hugged the girls to herself.

The game continued. One-two-three-four; they displayed their hands and Iona won the round.

"Hah, I won," Iona, squealed, genuinely enjoying herself.

"Ohhh" the girls moaned.

"Okay, go ahead and ask your question," Rose said, gathering her breath after laughing.

"Why, thank you," Iona said. In a moment of sudden inspiration, she cleared her throat and settled on her question. "I'd like to know how the first escape attempt came about?"

"Oh, that's easy. We were always talking about getting away from the C-men, but didn't know where to go. A group of the older kids decided they would rather die in space than continue living in the mines," Rose said.

"So they stole a ship," Sally finished.

The girls never stopped the game, but kept playing slapping their small fist into their opened palms.

Sensing a slight change in the atmosphere of the game, Iona proceeded carefully. She began telling the girls about the derelict spacecraft that Jonas had related to her.

From across the room Jonas leaned forward, interested in the turn the conversation had taken.

Iona was careful not to provide too much detail. But as the game lulled, she breathed and for reasons unknown looked up to see Jonas leaning against the bulkhead on the far side of the room. She saw Jonas looking at her. He nodded. When Iona mentioned the little girl Jonas had found alive, Sally suddenly stopped playing and lowered her head to the floor, her face in her hands.

Rose ignored Sally, but continued with the game. Iona could see Sally's shoulders shaking as the child cried.

Rose continued talking as if nothing had happened. "So, Iona, did you and your sister play a lot of different kinds of games?"

Iona stuttered, surprised by the girl's lack of reaction. "A-ah y-yes, but…" she stopped unable to complete her thought.

"How good?" Rose's voice was clear and precise. "That must have been so much fun for you two. Will you teach us more games?"

"Yes, I will be happy to." Iona looked at Jonas, silently asking for help.

Jonas moved as if to join her, then settled back against the wall. He motioned with his hand for Iona to continue.

Iona breathed. "About the little girl on the ship, she had blue eyes and—"

"I can't wait to learn more games," Rose said, interrupting her.

Iona looked at Rose. "Jonas described the girl to me; I imagined her face to have been heart shaped just like yours…"

"Stop it! Stop it! Stop it!" Sally screamed. She reached a hand to Rose, touching the back of her friend's down curled knuckles. When Rose didn't acknowledge her, she pulled her hands back and covered her ears. "Please stop it." She put her head back on the deck, her shoulders quaking.

The commons had gone silent, and the rest of the kids hurried around them. "I'm sorry," Iona said softly. "I was just asking about the little girl on the ship. I didn't know it would upset her so."

Jonas rushed over and gathered Sally into his arms. "I'm sorry," he said as he stroked her dark hair. He spoke in soft tones, "I'm sorry. I'm sorry. We didn't mean to upset you. Iona just wanted to know the girl's name. We won't talk about it anymore, okay."

Sally turned her face toward Rose. "Oh, Rose, I'm so sorry."

Jonas and Iona looked at Rose. The child hadn't moved but sat unmoving, her gaze unfocused.

A very bad feeling began to grow in Iona's gut, like worms crawling through her stomach. She looked at Jonas as understanding began to dawn in both of them. The other children had come and now stood over them, enclosing them in a protective circle.

A lone voice droned on through the heavy silence.

Drawn together at moments like these, the children drew strength from each other. Now was one of those times.

Still, Rose's voice, sounding small and tiny, carried on. "Oh, you and your sister must have had so much fun together…safe together."

As Jonas watched, Andrea knelt and wrapped an arm around Rose, "Rose...Rose...it's okay, Rose. It's okay."

Rose fell silent and then turned in a painfully slow transition to look into the older girl's face. Tears brimmed and then spilled down her small face. As she spoke, her lip quivering, more tears rushed down her face in a steady stream. "I m-miss her so much," she said, collapsing into Andrea's arms. "I miss her so much," she continued sobbing, her face buried at the breast of the older girl.

Rose lifted her face and tried to speak again, her voice barely a whisper. "Andrea, it...hurts...so...bad." Each word stressed by her grief and broken by sobs.

"I know, I know," Andrea said soothingly. We all miss her, Rose. We miss them all." She lifted the smaller girl up in her arms and headed back toward the sleeping quarters.

Another of the teen girls, Monica, put her arm around Iona, who was also crying. "Her name was Mickie; she was Rose's sister."

With red eyes, Iona looked up at the girl. "I'm so sorry. I didn't know. I'm so sorry." The crowd of children pressed in on Iona giving her their strength, accepting her into their circle. She cried. She cried for Rose. She cried for Mickie. She cried for herself.

The door opened, and Mike walked into the commons. "What's going on?" he asked, looking around.

The group slowly began to disperse, kids grouping together in sets of fours and fives. Peter volunteered and brought Mike up to speed, explaining what just happened.

Suddenly the intercom sounded: "Mike," came Skipp's excited voice.

"What now?" Mike said in exasperation. "A second attack fleet?"

"Mike, I've got Mary on the com-link. You might want to hurry."

Mike burst onto the bridge. He studied Skipp's face; not the joyous expression he anticipated. He passed him quickly and headed for the com-center, a swelling darkness settling in his gut.

Rushing in behind Mike, Iona leaned over his shoulder. Skipp gripped her around her shoulders and pulled her to one side. His face said it all even before he opened his mouth to speak.

Iona looked at Skipp and broke away from him. "It's Waters, isn't it? He has them." She sprinted back to stand beside Mike.

Mike's eyes were locked onto the screen. Veins bulged in his neck and forehead. This was not a happy message.

On the screen, Mary looked calm but stressed. To her credit, she held herself composed. Behind and to one side of Mary stood Ted Waters, his charcoal black suit matching the lifeless depth of his eyes. He wore on his face an expression of one in complete control.

His voice was low, monotone. He was not trying to impress or persuade. He was simply stating the facts as he wanted them to be. He was not bargaining. He did not even threaten. It was a simple statement of what was. "Michael, I have your family."

Behind Waters and Mary, Mike could see his boys and another child about the age of his sons playing on the floor.

Iona caught her breath.

For a moment, Waters's eyes traveled to Iona and then back to Mike.

"Where is my—"

"Your daughter is here," Waters said flatly.

Mike's blood ran cold.

Ted Waters placed a huge arm around Mary's shoulder and pulled her close to him. "I hope you can appreciate *your* position, Michael. I am not interested in banter; I have no interest in your children. But if you do not present yourself here to me within forty-eight hours, I will simply kill your family."

Waters lowered his arm and as it fell below the visual pickup range, the view shifted. Standing between his legs was Mike's daughter unaware of the danger just above her.

Waters spoke again, "You now have forty-seven hours and fifty-three minutes. Do not waste them." A smile crept across his face and the transmission ended.

Chapter Twenty-Nine

Ted Waters knew he was what the common people called, evil. He was okay with that. The laughter stopped and Waters began to play with the baby girl's hair. Mary slapped his hand away from her child and picked up her daughter and walked over to where the boys sat playing.

"Mrs. Stone, I would appreciate you refraining from any future violent outburst, or I will have to...reciprocate."

He eyed her coldly, and Mary hugged the baby to her chest. She felt exposed beneath his baleful gaze. Walking over to her, he reached out and touched her face. Permitting his hand barely to touch the baby's back, Waters allowed the back of his knuckle to brush Mary's breast.

She stepped away from him.

"Maybe later," he said. "But trust me, Mrs. Stone, I am a man accustomed to getting what I want, but that can wait until my business is completed with your husband."

"My daddy's gonna kill you," M2 shouted and ran to stand between Ted Waters and his mother.

"Impudence! I cannot abide an impudent child. I think my method for handling them is so much better." He turned his back on her and walked away. He called over his shoulder as he exited, "Please make yourselves at home. Your sister decorated it herself; this used to be her office."

The door closed behind him, and Mary could hear the electronic locks slide into place.

Mike squeezed the edge of the console until it creaked under the strain of his grip. *Ted Waters has my family.* Mike dropped his head to the work surface and screamed an agonized cry.

Forced to stand by and watch this man handle his family, the same man who had taken his life from him almost nine years earlier was about to do it again.

His crew wisely gave him time to gain his composure. When he stood, he was singularly possessed. He had only two goals: the first, to save his family and second, to kill Ted Waters.

He knew the burden was too large for him to carry; he knew he could not do it alone. Yes, he had his crew, but to do this, he needed more. Looking at his friends, his thoughts were elsewhere. *Okay, you win. All I ask is that you protect my family and that you let me kill Ted Waters.*

Turning to Jay, Mike asked, "How far out are we?"

Jay headed to the helm. "A better question would be, when do you want to get there? The flight plan says thirty-six hours, but computers lie."

"Good. Ted Waters gave me forty-seven hours. Get me back in thirty. That gives us close to a day to take care of these kids, find Waters, and put him out of business. Permanently. I can't ask that you guys come with me. I'm not sure I'll be coming back," Mike said, seating himself at the conn.

No one answered the implied question. Iona squeezed a hand on his shoulder before turning to join the crew as they settled to their duties. No words were spoken, none were needed; each filed off to their perspective stations. Mike watched them work and feelings of pride and gratitude washed over him.

"Watch the gauges, we're going hot," Jay called as Jonas and Skipp set to work. "I'm gonna need everything she's got." Jay pushed the Quest past red on the engines. The ship streaked through space at 101% of her rated energy output. They arrived in the Terran system four hours ahead of the planned E.T.A. Passing Sol, Jay began to slow. "Where to, boss?"

Mike sat forward, rubbing eyes strained from staring at the forward screen. "You remember where Mary's grandmother lives? You used to be able to get in and out of Earth's atmosphere without tripping detection satellites. Think you still can?"

"Piece a cake. Those things are set to pick up man-made objects. We'll come in nice and slow and on a low trajectory. They'll think we're just space-junk falling into the atmosphere."

An hour later, the Quest circled and landed in the wooded area about two miles from Nonna's house. They decided to go in on foot, just in case the house was being watched. Mike led Iona into the wood-framed house; then he gathered Nonna into his arms and hugged and kissed her wrinkled face. He told her about his plans to go after Mary and the kids.

"Pray for us, Nonna. We won't make it if your God doesn't help us."

"Like you'd even have to ask," she said, pushing his hands away. "Can't you see Him working already, child? He's got you and Iona together in my kitchen." She collected Iona into her arms, and for a long while, the two ladies, grandmother and granddaughter, stood locked in each other's embrace. Then after a long moment, Nonna stood back, grasping Iona's face in wrinkled hands. "Only the Lord knows how much I've missed you, child."

"I've missed you, too, Nonna, but I'm back now. I'm home."

Nonna smiled, looking at both Mike and Iona. "Now, don't you worry about me praying. Those are my babies that snake has in that glass tower of his. He may be a big man in this world, but he's no match for the angels of God. Now you go do what you have to do and bring my babies home."

A half hour later, the children were off the ship, secured at Nonna's, and the crew back on board the Quest. Mike sat in the center seat and contemplated the plan. He had fought Ted

Waters once before and failed. He quickly put the thought from his mind and focused on the battle at hand.

Taking the ship to just outside the city, Jay set her down in a quarry, safe from prying eyes and security scans.

Each took time alone to collect their thoughts, to center themselves before the approaching assault.

Iona sat on the edge of the stasis chamber from which they had earlier taken Julie's body for burial at Nonna's farm. Iona thought about how she had come to this point and the memories saddened her. She remembered having had her life given back to her after being loved by a little boy. Her heart was placed on ice for far too long while she tried to please a man, she admitted, she hadn't even liked.

She knew it would take their combined efforts and strength of will if they were to have any real hope of succeeding against Ted Waters. She inhaled and let her breath out slowly, deciding that no matter the outcome, she was glad to have a part in it.

Skipp wandered out on the wooded promontory and watched as the light reflected on the rolling surface of the ocean in the near distance. He stood, contemplating the events of the past few weeks and those that led to his life underground. He thought about the events that had reunited him with Mike and the impossible task that still lay before him.

He had to admit he had done it in the beginning just for the chance to take on The Company and Ted Waters, to beat Waters at his own game.

He had had many friends before Julie whose lives had been ground down by the machine of Ted Waters. But if he were honest, he had to admit that not even that had been enough to move him into action before.

"So what made the difference this time?" he asked of the night. *What made the difference?* It came down to one thing: Mike had asked him and that had been enough.

In with his beloved engines, Jay was totally at peace with himself. He had always hated Ted Waters, The Company, and what it stood for, and would have signed on just to fight against them. Getting to pilot the Quest again was just a bonus. He smiled in anticipation of the fight.

Armed with a name to go with the face he would never forget, Jonas realized his joining Mike was not a choice for him; he simply had to. His own emptiness had overwhelmed him. A life defined by work and professional accomplishments had left him empty inside. But then the little girl, Mickie, had been placed in his path. He remembered being a man broken, desperate, wandering out on a dark, cold and rainy night looking for one last chance to make his life count for something. He remembered trying to convince Mary and then Mike that this was the right thing to do, but now he realized it was himself that he had really been petitioning; his own life for which he had been fighting.

Mike sat alone at the conn. He sat forward looking at a copy of the Bible on the main screen, its text running in a slow scroll from bottom to top. He thought about his wife's faith in her God, and in him as her husband. He stared as line after line of the ancient text scrolled across the screen. "What is it about this book that you love so much, Mary?"

He thought about Nonna's comment: "He's working already…" *First Jonas, now Nonna.* Mike sighed and stood, turning his back to the screen and thought back to how it all started.

What seemed like not so long ago, he and Ted Waters were not so different, he had to admit. He remembered his early strivings and clawing his way up at any cost. The lives he'd ruined, the broken promises to Mary; and then came the Gliese System debacle. Only that had been a lie. The families had not been killed as reported, but pressed into slavery by Ted Waters, and the planet stripped for its resources. To make it worse, Waters had stolen even more children and shipped them in to prop up the scheme.

Mike sighed and stumbled when he thought how he had taken the blame, the responsibility; how he had taken the fall while Waters had risen in power until he became the beast that he was today.

Mike knew that just as he had been there at the beginning it was not a mistake that he was here now in what would be the end.

Chapter Thirty

An hour later, the crew began to filter back onto the command deck of the Quest. Mike looked around at the small but determined group and took in expressions of hope and resolution. "We need a plan, people."

Pushing her hair from her face, Iona spoke first. "The one thing we can't do is underestimate Ted Waters. He's no fool, Mike. He expects us to try something, but it's you he wants. What he won't expect is for you to just walk in and surrender." She looked around, pausing to look into each face. "I've worked with the man. I know how he thinks. If we hit him with anything less than brilliance, he'll serve it up cold and force-feed it to us."

Swiveling his chair, Jonas agreed. "But he has to have some weakness; after all, no man is invincible. He's not God."

"No, but he thinks he is," she replied.

"'He thinks he is...'" Mike said, jumping up from his seat, "and lady and gentlemen, that is his weakness." He smiled and kissed Iona on the cheek. "We're going to have to continue to allow him to believe that he has the absolute upper hand. That he's in complete control."

"Right now that's not too far from the truth," Jay said.

"That's the beauty of it, the truth to the lie," Mike exulted.

"Yeah, let him get sloppy," Skipp added, looking up from his notepad.

"I'd tell you what I'd like to do," Jay said through gritted teeth, "but there's a lady present."

Iona smiled. "On that, I think we all share your sentiment, but we have to beat him first." She tilted her head toward him in acknowledgement of Jay's statement.

"What's the one thing they'd never expect us to do?" Mike said turning to look at the tall building illuminated against the city horizon.

"Like Iona said, walk in through the front door, I guess," Skipp said absently.

"Yes," Mike said, pacing, "but if we did that, he'd be expecting a second or even a third angle strike. I say we give it to him, but—"

Jonas cut him off. "But with each plan having a viable chance to succeed. That way—"

"That way when he analyzes the attacks each will appear real and feed his ego, making him think he has outsmarted us at every turn," Mike concluded.

Iona leaned forward. "His confidence rises and his diligence slips."

"And that's where we come in," Skipp said, lifting his notepad and kissing it.

The crew turned to their stations and set to work on their plans, each working out individual details, each with one goal: Invade The Company and bring out Mary and the children alive.

With plans made, the time for action had come. Leaving the meager safety of the canyon, the Quest rose above the rim of the quarry. As Jay directed the Quest toward the midtown office, they separated themselves into teams of ones and twos.

Not much later, Mike approached the main doors of The Company on foot. The computer voice that greeted him was cordial, oblivious to the confrontation of powers about to happen, recognizing neither one side nor the other as evil or good. It simply served. The Company building, a monolith of glass, steel, and stone, stood in the heart of the planet's largest city, the new capital of Earth, New-New York. The inhabitants of the city largely took no notice of it while passing it daily, neither afraid nor thankful, but like ants, busy with their own lives, struggling to live in the city.

Rising only eighty-nine floors from the surface, The Company's main building was not the tallest structure in the city, but like its schemes, most of the building was underground, unseen.

"Please identify yourself," the male-patterned voice said. "Place the palm of your right hand on the vid-pad and look directly into the optical scanner please."

Mike looked around the elaborately appointed foyer and then placed his hand on the vid-pad. Leaning forward, he focused on the emerald beam of the optical scanner. As the infrared light danced across his eye, reading his retina pattern, Mike resisted the impulse to pull his face away; he'd always hated the device. It always made him feel as if it was taking more information than it said, like siphoning your soul through your eyeball.

The computer voice spoke again, snapping Mike's attention back to the business at hand. "Identification verified. Mike Stone, former employee of The Company terminated for violating company policies." The voice went quiet as if it were thinking; but in reality, it was searching its multitude of files. "You were terminated on 04-06:2589."

"We've already established the fact that I was fired, but if you're interested in the truth, I quit."

"Correction," the computer answered. "Mike Stone was assassinated on 04-06:2589 old reckoning. Mr. Stone, you are dead and cannot be allowed entry."

"Now, if I'm dead what difference does it make if I come in? A dead man can't cause any harm, can he?" Mike couldn't believe that he was having this conversation with a computer. When he'd agreed to allow Waters to make the false entry, he'd believed it was best for he and Mary if he just simply disappeared. Now he wasn't so sure it was the right or best thing to have done. But then again, he reasoned, the more invulnerable you think you are, the more chances you have to overlook the small things. It was one of these small things he was hoping to capitalize on in the computer's logic bank now.

"I'm waiting," he said to the computer.

The computer came back online. "I can find no reason to deny you entry. You do not exist."

Mike began to smile as a thought came to his mind. "So then, I guess," he began slowly, "since Mike Stone does not exist, it would be a waste of your time and energies to stop him or recognize his presence."

"Affirmative," the voice answered.

Trying a long shot, Mike said, "Computer, lock out all references to Mike Stone, bio-scan included. You are not to respond to him in any way. He does not exist."

The computer was silent. It was thinking again. "It is done," the voice simply said and then the panel went dark.

"Computer...computer...computer! Blasted thing," Mike grunted. His plan had worked too well. The computer had refused to acknowledge him once it accepted the lockout instruction. To the computer, Mike was simply a gray spot on the vid-lens, nothing more than a spec to be ignored, white noise.

Now all he had to do was wait for the door to open and then casually slip in. An hour passed, and Mike found himself still sitting on the stone bench in the solarium adjacent to the entryway. He was just about to look for another point of ingress when he saw two techs walking, deep in conversation, heading for the main door.

If he timed it just right, he should be able to make it in on their coattails, literally. He waited, he watched, he ran. The doors slid shut just as he cleared the path.

Once in the lobby, the computerized sentry scanned the men before allowing further admittance. The scan then reaffirmed the entrants' identities using bio-scans, and then registered their presence in the building. A secondary scan checked for weapons on incoming traffic and theft on those leaving. This was not a business built on trust.

The scan swept the first man, then the second and shut off. The first two looked curiously at the third. Mike pulled an old

ID from his pocket and passed it before the men's faces in a manner of which prevented them from reading it but made them feel as if they had.

The men exchanged a glance between each other, then turned and walked away saying nothing more.

"What good little boys," Mike spoke under his breath and then headed off to business of his own.

Chapter Thirty-One

Banking on the axiom that those on the bottom never really knew what was going on up top, Iona, with Jay hidden in the rear compartment, pulled her Company issued cruiser up to the parking attendant. The older man walked slowly over to where the transport hung, hovering just above the concrete ramp. "Can I help you, ma'am?" he asked in a kind but tired voice.

"Yes, you can," she said in a tone reminiscent of her former self. "You can get out of my way before I drive over you." Her voice was cold and hid the true emotion she felt in her heart. She would have to work on resolving the conflict she was beginning to feel. Her world had been cold and aloof, not one where the pains or feelings of others touched her. She winced as the older man jumped in response.

"Ah, yes, ma'am," was the weak reply. He turned and ambled back to his guard station and sat heavily.

Iona felt bad for how she had spoken to the man and decided that when this was all over, she would return and make it right.

Minutes later, Iona and Jay headed for the elevator and didn't notice that the old man no longer sat hunched over at the waist, nor was his voice weak or cracked with age. "They're inside, sir," he said in a crisp baritone. "Yes, sir. Iona Bowers and at least one black adult male just entering the elevator bank 23-C1…car number five, sir."

A muffled voice was his response.

"Yes, sir. It was Mike Stone." The man pulled the fake whiskers from his face and dropped them on top of the desk. Opening the drawer, he removed a laser pistol and strapped it on. He had been very careful to give a full description of the man who had entered with Iona. There would be no problem identifying, again, the man he had heard Iona refer to as Mike Stone.

The guard, confident he had been careful in the execution of his duties, was sure that he hadn't missed a detail of their description. "Sir, I could tell you the perfume that Bowers woman was wearing." He smiled, sensing Waters's approval.

The one detail he had missed however had been Skipp who, while Iona distracted the guard, had crawled out of the transport on the opposite side. Staying low and keeping the vehicle between him and the guard station, Skipp scooted into the maintenance bay. While the guard busied himself removing his disguise and relaying his report, Iona, rather conspicuously, shuffled Jay into the lift car; Skipp slid quietly into a service hatch and padded away.

Opening the access panel in the top of the elevator, Skipp lifted himself into the innards of the elevator. He began working his way through the cable and plumbing tunnels that honeycombed the entire structure of the building.

Removing his notepad from the pack slung over his shoulder, Skipp braced himself pressing his feet against the far wall with his back jammed against the opposite side, spanning the descending shaft between two walls. Flicking on a small lamp attached at the side of his face, he traced the cables reading the codes stamped on their casing. "There you go, baby. That's what I'm looking for." Slipping a connector cable from his bag, he inserted it into a juncture at the cable intersection. Tapping into the main computer, Skipp logged himself in as a building technician giving himself the freedom to move around virtually undetected.

Accessing The Company's own systems, Skipp was able to monitor all movement inside the building. Using the infrared setting, his job was to get an exact body count floor by floor and relay that information to the team as needed.

He continued working his way up through the building's innards, crawling and pulling himself along the narrow shoots and chimneys. Even though the building was state of the art, the brainchild of the Earth's greatest engineers, those same designers had not thought to add climate control to the maintenance tunnels. The tunnels were hot.

Beads of sweat rolled and dripped into Skipp's eyes, burning them, making it even more difficult in the low light to read the panel of his notepad. If things went off as planned, he knew it was only a matter of time before Iona and Jay were captured; and he needed to have control over the building's internal defense systems before that happened.

Iona and Jay entered the executive lobby outside her old office. "It's too quiet," Iona whispered.

"Well, we wanted them to expect us," Jay said, walking lightly beside her. The only sound came from the beeping and clicking of the computerized machinery performing any number of varied-timed tasks. The lights were dimmed and her office door was ajar.

"Well...shall we?" Jay nodded his head indicating the opened door.

"Yeah, I see it, but the question is, why?" Iona stopped by the doorjamb and peaked through the crack in the doorway. "This is probably a trap, but there are some things I need out of that office. I know Waters would have moved Mary and the kids, besides I don't hear the children."

Jay nodded his head, listening. "Then go in get what you need, and get back out here. I'll watch our six." He checked the charges on his weapons, and settled in for the wait. "I prefer a straight up fight anyway. Throw all your cards on the table, and let the best man win."

She smiled at him and ducked through the darkened doorway expecting to find a small army waiting inside. She rolled to her right and came up, weapon at the ready.

The office was empty.

The curtains were drawn casting the room into shadows. The air was fresh and the room cleaned.

Jay peaked in through the open door. "You have nice taste. Expensive, too."

Iona smiled. "I had an expense budget...Company money for that purpose. Wait here, I'll be right back." With that, she disappeared into the bathroom.

"How you doing in there?" Jay called out after more than a few minutes had passed.

"Just about done; working in the dark slows me a bit." Iona's voice floated back through the gray darkness.

"You know my opinion about that," Jay said, turning his face toward the opened bathroom door. "I prefer a plain fight up front; winner takes all."

The lights came on. "That is exactly what I had in mind. I mean the part about the winner taking it all." Ted Waters's voice seemed to come from everywhere at once. "You know what they say..." Water's voice continued, "Jay, it is Jay, is it not? Be careful what you ask for, you just might get it."

"You're the second person to tell me that lately."

"And how did the last ordeal workout for you?" Ted Waters asked.

"I'm here, ain't I. Bring it on!"

"Considering that you are not Michael Stone, I can only assume he is also somewhere inside my building." He paused, then the voice continued. "It's no matter. I will locate him and then none of you will leave here alive."

Jay paced around the office and chanced a glance back into the foyer. "Hurry up, Iona, we're about to have company."

And as if on cue, the doors to the office burst open as armed guards poured into the room.

Jay launched himself at the men swinging and kicking. He didn't trust shooting in such close quarters; not wanting to chance hitting Iona. Men continued rushing into the room. As fast as Jay and Iona could drop them, another rank replaced the first.

Booted heel and hammering fist met chin and temple and still the guards came. Iona completed the spin of a side thrust kick and had to duck as a second guard swung at her head. She leapt and grabbed the man's head, ramming it down against her rising knee. Blood cast off in a fine spray as the man crumpled at her feet.

Jay crouched and, with a roar, launched himself against three men attacking Iona's unguarded back. His snarl drew their attention as his elbow landed square against the jaw of the nearest man. Chattered teeth and blood spatter was his reward. Still they came.

Grabbing an ornamental fighting staff which was mounted on her office wall, Iona rolled the staff in her hands, spun it and slammed it to the floor. "Who's next?" She demanded.

The guards suddenly stopped the headlong dash into the room. They seemed to realize they had underestimated this twosome; the guards began to spread out readying the final assault.

A breath and the moment passed. The attack was on. Jay intercepted the first two with alternating blows that landed like bombs against the faces of the unlucky pair. Dazed and broken, they stumbled backwards and fell over their already downed comrade.

Lashing out with the boa staff, Iona added to the pile. Still, new guards came to replace those already fallen.

A blow caught Iona from her blindside and sent her crumbling to the floor. Distracted by Iona going down, Jay didn't see the fist until it was too late. He staggered and, before he could recover, multiple sets of hands secured him and a crushing blow landed to the side of his head.

The fight was over.

Mike had heard the alarm sound and knew Iona and Jay had been discovered. "Skipp," Mike spoke over the communicator, "you hear that? They've got Iona and Jay. The clock starts now. I need a location buddy; where's my family?"

"I'm on it. I need a minute." Skipp started.

"I don't have a minute. Waters knows we're in the building now; he'll kill my family!" Mike cursed and slapped a hand against the wall. "This is taking too long." He started down the hall.

"Mike, what are you doing? Stick to the plan," Skipp said just before the connection went dead.

Deciding to use a tactic he had learned from Jay, Mike found the nearest security video com, centered himself in front of it, and shouted, "Here I am. Come and get me. That's what you want isn't it. I'm here come and get me!"

Silence answered him.

Time passed.

Mike knew things were going bad when nothing happened. His fears were confirmed when the walls on either side of the hall flickered and shimmered and an image appeared beside and behind him. He could feel the bile at the back of his throat as he watched the screens. Lying in restraints and unconscious were the battered bodies of Iona and Jay. Both of their faces bruised and swollen, but they were alive, he reasoned, or they would not have been restrained. It would be a long hard road to recovery.

"You see, Michael." Ted Waters's voice greeted him from speakers imbedded in the walls and ceiling. "I have proven, once again, that there is nothing you have built that I cannot destroy. First your planet, then your family, and now your friends, but then again, maybe you should have picked smarter friends."

"What do you want?" Mike shouted, his posture slumping in defeat.

"You, of course. It is you that I want. Nothing more. That is…I want nothing more than your absolute and total destruction."

"Why? I left you alone. I gave you everything, didn't I?" Mike complained.

"But you know the truth, and I cannot have you out there with that kind of information, now can I?"

"Okay," he said in resignation. "Here I am. Just let my family and my friends go." Mike tried to focus on the voice—tried to think—tried to remember from where that voice might have originated.

"I do not think so, Michael."

The voice moved again.

Mike spun. "But why? I turned myself in."

"Why? Because I can, Michael."

Mike's mind worked furiously trying to find an angle—a way—anyway to get an advantage. "Please let my family go. They can't hurt you."

"Are you giving me directives now? I think you have it all wrong, Michael. Again, I give the orders. You are simply here for me to enjoy until I bore of you and then, Michael, I will kill you."

Mike ran, heading for the elevators.

"Do not be silly, Michael. There is no place for you to go. Besides, I am not ready for you yet. I need the others like you, those who would oppose me, to watch your destruction. After I finish with you, none will dare."

Waters was toying with him, and Mike knew it, but that didn't matter. As long as Waters was focused on him, he was not hurting his family or his crew, but he knew this wouldn't end well; it couldn't.

"And—" Waters's voice continued.

"And what?" Mike asked defiantly.

"Do not interrupt me!" He paused. "Now, as I was saying... And that they know the consequence for opposing me is always fatal."

As his final words hug like ice in the air, Ted Waters's mirthless laugh reverberated throughout the building.

Mike stood helpless; his arms limp at his sides, listening to that insidious voice. Powerless. Pressed against the wall, he allowed himself to slide down until he sat sprawled on the floor. Broken.

"God, help me. Help me, please."

For long moments, nothing happened. An eerie silence began to build, pressure intensifying. "Help me?" his voice rasped out, creating a moist fog on the tile floor.

Like a whisper, a thought brushed against his mind: *Mike, work the plan.*

Mike rolled onto his back, his face turned upward into the glare of the recessed lighting. Willing himself to concentrate on what had to be done. His thoughts slowly returned to Skipp. *Skipp, everything's up to you now.*

In his mind, he willed Skipp to succeed. He willed him strength.

"You see, Michael," Ted Waters began. The voice sounded from behind Mike, and he spun to face an empty hall.

"As I have said in the past, I am your master. It was true then, and it is true now."

Mike fell to his knees, crushed by feelings of helplessness. In raw frustration, he shook his fist and screamed as new images of Iona and Jay flickered and solidified on the wall turned video screens. At the end of the hall, a larger wall began to hum then flash with streaming video images of his family.

Mike buried his face in his hands. Tears brimmed and then overflowed his eyes—not of anguish or despair—but anger, barely contained rage. In that state of mind, Mike turned back to that still small voice. "Help me," he begged.

Work the plan.

"You want me to spare your friends, Michael?" Ted Waters's voice emanated from yet a different series of speakers. "Do you want me to spare your wife and the lives of your children, Michael?"

The voice paused.

"Yes? Then beg, Michael. Beg for their lives. Beg me, Michael, and maybe I'll kill them quickly."

Waters began to laugh and the screens went black.

Chapter Thirty-Two

Skipp reached out with his left hand. In his right, he held onto the ledge while trying not to drop his notepad. Sweat ran down his forehead and into his eyes; his muscles began to burn with the exertion; his fingers starting to cramp. But Skipp knew too much was riding on his success for him to consider giving up. He had no choice. He had to succeed.

With one last gasp, Skipp swung his legs and let go. He closed his eyes, and for a moment, there was nothing. Weightless, he floated across the gap, the shaft beneath him disappearing down into darkness. He landed with a thud on the far ledge. He lay there, not moving, just catching his breath. Fine silt-like dust billowed around him, clung to his skin, and stuck to his shirt. Sitting up, he checked to make sure his notepad had survived the landing and then began to wipe his brow with the back of his hand—then he froze.

He heard something.

A muffled noise floated upward to him out of the darkness. Straining and slowing his breathing, he listened. From somewhere, the sound of voices echoed along the walls of the concrete tube. Skipp leaned toward the sound, concentrating, trying to see through the semi-darkness. He ran a hand across his face and brought up the notepad to scan the area ahead of him, forcing himself to slow his pace, using time he did not have.

There should have been no one there, no one besides him, that is. Yet, still he could hear what sounded like...laughing.

Taking a breath, Skipp checked his chronometer. "I don't have time for this," he hissed through clenched teeth. He began making his way down the dark corridor. He had to gain control over the building's computer system if they were to have any chance of ever leaving this place alive.

Rounding the next bend, Skipp heard the sound of laughter again, unguarded and easy. "At least it's not guards…too relaxed. Too high toned." He stopped. "Is that a baby," he whispered. "It couldn't be. Is that Mary and the children?"

Peering through a vent in the corridor, Skipp saw that he was better than three meters above the floor in the room beneath him. However, what he could not see was how many people were in the room or if a guard was in the room with them.

Using a vision cord, Skipp snaked the fiber optic cable through the vent, setting it to climb along the ceiling. Soon the signal returned to his notepad and an image flickered and blossomed on the screen. He could see Mary lying on a low cot, the baby drowsing, fussy, beside her. All three boys played on the floor near her feet.

The only thing that gave him pause was that there was no guard in sight. He did not want to give himself away by being seen on camera exiting the ceiling vent. He had to discover the method of monitoring before risking contact.

Standard procedure was to have one guard stationed inside the room with at least two standing by, outside the room. Shifting the vision cord, Skipp scanned the rest of the room. Failing to capture a full visual of the space below him, he frowned and resisted the urge to curse. He pressed the side of his face to the grate, trusting his ears instead.

Nothing. No guard.

Preparing to risk it, Skipp prepared to lower himself into the room. Just as he positioned himself to lift the vent, the top of a man's head passed beneath him.

Just then, Mary looked up at the approaching guard and caught a glimpse of Skipp through the vent. Standing, she drew the guard's attention toward her. "You feeling pretty safe in here all by yourself with us criminals?" she asked sarcastically.

Very smart, Skipp thought and carefully lifted the grill. Grabbing the edge of the opening and in one smooth movement, he dropped and swung through the vent mouth.

The guard turned just in time to catch both of Skipp's booted heels in his face. He was unconscious before he fell.

Mary caught the unconscious man and lowered him to the floor. Hurriedly, she quieted the three boys who were about to cheer their rescuer.

"Quick," Mary said, "they're due to swap guards in about fifteen minutes. She pointed to the opposite corner. "What about the video? She picked up her daughter, pressed her to her breast, and patted the child's back.

"The active feed indicator's not on. I guess you're not considered much of a threat. So, no live feed. Help me put him on the cot. I have an idea."

Mary nodded at Skipp and passed Sissy to M2. "Keep her quiet."

The boy looked at his mother as if to say "with what?" but he shrugged and cradled his little sister as best he could.

Minutes later, the guard, gagged and bound, lay unconscious on the cot beneath a thin blanket.

"We better face him away from the camera just in case," Mary suggested. "I know there are at least two more guards outside this door, but beyond that I have no idea," she whispered.

"Got it covered," Skipp said, pointing to the opened vent. "We're going out the way I came in. You first, I'll pass the kids up to you."

Soon Mary was kneeling in the dusty work tunnel grabbing the kids as they were passed up, the baby first then the rest, one at a time from Skipp.

After climbing back up inside, Mary pulling him to keep the sound of his assertion down, Skipp carefully replaced the vent cover. "I tried to keep debris from falling to the floor, but it won't take a genius to figure out which way we went."

"But maybe it'll buy us some time. What now?" Mary asked, repositioning the now fussing toddler in her arms.

Irritated at being awakened and jostled, the child was beginning to cry in earnest. Like a locater beacon, the child's whiny-pitched cry echoed off the concrete walls and through the tunnel.

"This way." Skipp started down the corridor, leading them through a maze of tunnels and switchbacks. "Mary, quiet that baby. She'll lead them straight to us."

Mary frowned and fought back the cutting remark that tore at the edges of her already frayed nerves. *Lord help us. You've brought us this far; don't let us get caught now.*

The boys, at first, excited by the sense of adventure, now began to lag as fatigue set in, exasperated by the dusty dry heat. Finally, after several more minutes, even the boys were beginning to whine.

After several more minutes travel, Skipp stopped before a small door in the wall. Opening it, he led them into what appeared to be an abandoned workstation. "I found a few of these on my way up. Must have been used during construction, but I don't think anybody's been in here in years. No toilet, but there's a faucet and drain in the corner." He smiled awkwardly.

They closed the door behind them, and Mary finally grabbed and hugged Skipp in relief.

"Thank you, too, but this ain't over." He hugged her back.

"Thank God you came when you did," she said, releasing him. Feeling safe enough to speak, she peppered him with questions. "Where's Mike? Where's the crew? Is everyone here? How do we get out of here?"

Skipp raised his palms toward her. "Uh, that would be the bad news."

"We have to go after them!" Mary said.

"What about the children?" Skipp asked. "We can't just leave them here."

"Why not?" she said, surprising him. "They're safer here than they were back there in that cell."

Skipp looked at her and stepped back, stunned.

"Look!" Mary said, closing the gap he'd created. "If we don't get Mike and help the team, we're all gonna die in this place; you, me, and the children. I'm not gonna sit around playing the scared woman while that happens."

Pulling M2 aside, Mary stooped and spoke into her oldest son's face. "I'm gonna need you be a big-man. Can you do that for me?"

As M2 began nodding his head, Mary explained what she needed him to do.

When she finished, Skipp looked at the boys. "Okay, guys, your mom and me have to go after the bad guys, but we need you to stay here until we get back. M2, looks like you're in charge," Skipp said patting the boy on his head.

"What about me, I want to be in charge, too," Travist complained.

"No, you're too little," M2 said, puffing up his chest and standing a little taller.

"Wait, wait," Skipp interrupted. "Okay, M2, you're in charge. Albert you and Travist can take turns being the sergeant and the lieutenant, but you have to stay inside this room and you have to keep quiet."

Skipp went down on one knee in front of M2, looking him in the eyes. He gave him his orders. "Now, no matter what, you keep these guys inside this room and that door shut. Don't let anyone go out for any reason and lock that latch when your mom and I leave," he said, pointing to the simple thumb lock.

"Okay." M2's face was stern, determined.

Mary felt proud of her young sons, counting Albert as one of her own, but still felt the fear of a mother's love pulling at the edges of her heart. She looked at her daughter who sat on the dusty floor making small circles with her pudgy hand. It's not that there was a real argument, it was just that she felt awful leaving her children alone.

If it hadn't been for a small wall mounted lamp that was hard wired to the building, the children would have been left in complete darkness once the door was shut. As it was, the russet glow that filled the small room felt warm as Mary pulled the door closed behind her.

"We're far enough away from the core that any noise they make should go unheard," Skipp said trying to reassure Mary.

She nodded. "I just wish they would all just fall asleep and wake up to find this whole mess over with and behind us; a bad dream." Rising and stretching her back, Mary pulled her hair out of her face and fastened it in a single braid at the nape of her neck. "Let's go."

Carefully, Mary and Skipp made their way back out into the main ventilation tunnel. "Which way?" she asked, looking to Skipp.

Taking out his notepad, Skipp activated the scan and marked their present location into memory. "Don't want to not be able to find the kids," he answered Mary's unasked question. Not lifting his eyes from the screen, Skipp said, "I'm going to try and pick up on the low frequency noise generated by the mainframe refrigeration unit and use that to hone in on its location."

"The coolant system," Mary said, beginning to understand. "It's a long shot, but it could work."

They traced the sound through the tunnel, moving faster as the sound grew louder. Only a few minutes had passed when Skipp held up a hand, indicating they should stop. "We're here." Reaching their destination, Skipp removed the room's vent-screen. He lowered his head through the opening and looked around at what turned out to be a massive space.

"Be careful," Mary whispered.

Skipp smiled. "Not a soul in sight."

Just as he'd thought, the room was empty. The massive computer was self-sufficient and didn't require any real maintenance, just an occasional checkup once a quarter. As long as it had power and the temperature remained between seven and ten degrees Celsius, the computer could continue indefinitely.

Skipp sighed; the lower temperature in the room came as a welcomed relief after the dusty dry heat of the tunnels. They split up, deciding to cut their task in half.

Mary went up the left side of the cavernous room, heading toward the main wiring array. She knew that if Skipp couldn't reprogram the main computer, it would fall to her to disable the entire system.

Skipp found the main frame protected behind a wire mesh wall. He looked at the blaster on his hip and shook his head, reminding himself that they didn't want to destroy the computer; on the contrary, they wanted to use it. Reaching a hand toward the handle, Skipp yelped as a blue arc of energy leapt and bit at his fingertip. The fence was charged.

Wandering through an endless maze of wires and power cells, Mary was beginning to wonder if she would ever find the main power station. Rows of thick cords, like trunks of trees, covered the floor, ran up the wall and disappeared into dark openings. The shear current running through the giant synthetic vines caused hairs on her arms to stand up and sent a slight tickle along her skin. Stumbling around a last bend, she happened upon a console, dark with disuse and covered in a fine patina of dust. "Thank you, God," she whispered.

Checking the monitor, Mary found the power indicator nodule glowing faintly. "Good. It has power." Taking a breath and wiping sweat from her forehead, she flipped the main switch closed, powering up the unit.

Just then, a pair of glowing orbs caught her attention. She reached a hand tentatively toward them when the orbs moved.

The glow narrowed and came forward. Attached to the orbs was a set of razor sharp teeth and claws, the huge snout of an electrorodent. The giant rat-like creature had evolved from the wharf rats and fed mainly on electrical energy; but had no taboos against supplementing its diet with protein when available.

As the animal leapt, Mary screamed and jumped back, barely avoiding the attack. As she moved, the animal lashed out with its tail, slashing her across the cheek and leaving a bruise on her face and neck. The electrorodent landed with a heavy loud thud and just as quickly turned and hissed. The animal bared its teeth, a sound reminiscent of water gushing through a pipe buried beneath a wall or floor.

Mary pulled the knife from her belt that Skipp had given her *just in case* and braced herself for the attack. The rodent launched itself, knocking her back. She stumbled and fell across rows of giant cables. Before she could right herself, the animal's tail wrapped itself around her arm, forcing the knife down and away.

It launched at her again.

Mary caught the animal's throat in her free hand and held its snarling and snapping mouth away from her neck and face. The rear claws tore at her jacket, searching for flesh. She snatched her arm free and rammed the knife into the flank of the beast. Once. Twice. It yelped and jumped back, but did not retreat.

Mary scrambled to her feet and faced the animal. It circled her, looking for another opening. Mary flexed her hands and re-asserted her grip on the handle of the blade. Chancing a look around the small space, she spotted a metal handle of the auxiliary engine, the smaller engine used to prime the electrical charge if the main battery ever died.

Her glance away appeared to be the chance the large rat needed. With its fangs bared and claws extended, it leapt at her. Mary grabbed the heavy metal handle and sidestepped the animal's attack. As it passed her, Mary brought that pole down with both hands on the back of the rat's skull.

Rewarded with a resounding crack, she wasted no time celebrating, but jumped on the animal and buried the knife in its throat. A few minutes later, the giant rodent lay twitching on the floor, its dark red blood pooling then seeping away beneath coiled cables and disappearing into the floor.

"Mary," came Skipp's voice over the communicator, "you doing okay over there? I've run into a slight problem. The fence is electrified."

Mary sighed at the frustration she heard in Skipp's voice. "Electrified," she sighed under her breath, looking back at the large rat. She gasped. Already two other rats were making a meal of the fallen hunter. She eased back and away from the dark corner.

"Mary? You okay?"

"Yeah, just rats."

"Oh...that's all. Okay, let's get finished in here."

She quirked an eyebrow and made her way back to the main room and the monitor. Shining her flashlight around the room, she searched for reflective orbs before sitting down this time. "I've reached the unit and have begun the booting process," Mary said into the communicator. She looked around in appreciation for the massive cables running to and from the station and the amount of power it demanded. With a shuddering breath, she checked again for glowing eyes. Absentmindedly, she brushed loose strands of blond hair from her face and settled down to wait.

"Copy that," returned Skipp's whispered response.

"It's moments like these when I wish I had your computer savvy, Skipp," a bit of relief coloring her voice.

Settling in behind the desk, she activated the monitors. She sat forward. "What have we here?"

Skipp found the mainframe situated just beyond his reach, separated behind a wire mesh wall. The metal fencing ran the length of the wall and the gate. The low-level hum told him it was magnetically sealed, and the sting in his finger told him it was electrified.

Opening his bag, Skipp set out to deactivate the electrical charge and cut a hole in the wire mesh. Minutes later, the bluish-white light and the smell generated by the miniature arc blade seemed harsh in the low-level luminosity, but soon a man-size hole appeared in the center of the metal gate. Careful to avoid the edges that were still hot and still carrying an electrical charge, Skipp stepped through the hole and stood studying the computer access panel. He swore and slammed a fist against the surface.

"What's the problem over there?" came Mary's excited voice. "We got trouble?"

"No. There is no ingress point. I can't plug in. The unit's keyboard has been removed and all other ports fused shut. No," he grunted in frustration and sank down to the floor.

"Skipp?"

No answer.

Mary tried again. "Skipp, you there?" When he still didn't answer, Mary keyed her mic again. "Look, Skipp, you guys have come too far and through too much to think we're in this on our own. You continue to work and I'll pray. Okay? God will help us. I know He will."

Mary prayed.

Long minutes later, Skipp sat still staring at the computer mainframe. He hadn't moved. He ran a hand through his hair and let the ponytail slide across his open palm. "I've got no choice," he said to himself. He grunted and stood to his feet. "I didn't want to destroy the computer. I wanted to use it," he mumbled in frustration. Coming to a resolution, he stopped and keyed his mic. "Mary, cut the main line."

"What? I thought you said we needed the computer to make this plan work."

Skipp chuckled. "Well, you prayed and this is all I got. Cut the line."

He was rewarded with silence.

"Look, Mary, think of it this way, we won't have the use of the computers, but neither will Ted Waters.

After a moments delay, the computer console and the room itself slipped into darkness. A heartbeat later, the red glow of emergency backup lights began to glow and fill the room with an eerie warmth. Picking up his communicator, Skipp was just beginning his transmission when his beeper went off.

"Skipp, get over here!" Mary said excitedly. "I think you might want to see this."

A short while later, Skipp found himself sitting in front of the workstation Mary discovered, three screens still alive with activity.

"Wait!" Skipp said excitedly, his hazel-blue eyes locked in concentration on lines of binary code. "I've got it!" In quick manner, Skipp opened his bag and began pulling cords and cables from pockets and folds. "Mary, if I weren't afraid of your husband, I'd kiss you. I'm in. We own the computer." He jumped up and hugged Mary. "We've got 'em!"

Mary leaned her back against the wall and closed her eyes. *Thank you, Father, thank you.*

Chapter Thirty-Three

Jay awoke slowly and tried to wipe the sweat from his face, but found his arms restrained. His chest still hurt from the laser blast that had taken his consciousness and his mouth soured with the aftertaste of electrical surge that had accompanied the blast.

He swiveled his head trying to look around the small room and a wave of nausea pulled at his stomach, threatening vertigo. His head hurt—his back hurt—his legs hurt—he hurt all over.

Taking a breath, he waited, and after a while, his vision began to clear and his stomach settled. Lifting his head as far as he could, he chanced a second look at his surroundings. He saw Iona strapped to a table identical to his own, not more than four feet away.

She was unconscious. She looked hurt.

"Iona," he called to her. Determined to free himself, Jay began pulling against his bindings.

She did not respond.

Veins in his arms bulged as muscles flexed and rippled. Sweat pooled then dripped from his forehead with the efforts of his struggle. Concentrating on a single strap at a time, Jay pulled against the wrist restraint and was rewarded by the creak and groan of the metal-plast, the synthetic and natural metal alloy, beginning to break.

From up a small flight of stairs and outside the door, the sound of voices approached.

Jay stilled his movements, pretending to still be unconscious.

Two uniformed guards entered into the room speaking in hushed tones. "You see, they're both in here," the first voice said.

Looking through slitted eyelids, Jay studied the men and did not like the expressions he read on their faces.

The second guard was standing over him now. "He doesn't look so tough," he said. "From what I'd heard, I thought he'd be a monster."

Jay heard the sound just before the droplet of spit splattered in his face. He forced himself not to react.

"You can play with him all you want, but this is what I came here for." The first guard turned to look at the unconscious Iona. "I remember her strutting around here like she owned the place. Now she's just a nobody." He laughed. His voice had grown husky with lust. A smile played across the man's features, coloring them darkly. He looked back at his partner, who still stood over Jay. "You ready? I never thought I'd get a chance with her."

"I-I don't know, man. What if we get caught? This just doesn't seem right somehow," the second guard said, walking around to stand by him. "Roughing up the big guy, that's one thing, but this is…well this is…"

"What? Are you afraid?" The first guard exploded, "Who's going to file charges? What do you think, tomorrow Waters is going to give 'er her job back? He's gonna kill her, idiot." He turned and locked his gaze on Iona's unconscious form. "I'm going to pay her back for everything she ever did to me. This is my chance, and I'm taking it."

"You're talking about rape," the second guard said and began backing away.

"If you don't want to get in on this…go wait in the hall. I don't want you watching."

"I didn't know you were going to rape her. I thought you just wanted to slap the big guy around." Rushing back up the stairs, the man opened the door and slipped quickly outside, closing the door behind him.

The remaining guard turned his full attention back to Iona, appraising her with hungry intentions. He stretched out his hand haltingly and let it fall softly across her chest. His breath caught.

With trembling fingers, he unfastened Iona's blouse. Sliding his hand in against the skin of her stomach, closing his eyes, he let his hand rest there.

Looking down at her unconscious form, he leaned over to kiss her. In a husky voice, he whispered, "I'm gonna enjoy this. Too bad you won't."

"She'll enjoy it a lot more than you're going to." Jay ripped free of the broken wrist restraint. In one continuous and fluid motion, he slammed the metal bracket against the man's head.

With his hand still on Iona's stomach, the guard could only look as the metal-plast restraint crashed into his face. He fell where he had stood without so much as having gurgled.

"Never touch a woman without her permission," Jay said, still strapped to his cot from the waist down, the metal-plast restraints around his abdomen and legs. With his hands now free, he made quick work of the remaining restraints, and stepping over the fallen guard, he saw to Iona.

"Hey, you okay, Iona," he whispered as he undid the bindings. "Com'on wake up for ole Jay, now."

Iona rolled her head to the side and slowly began to focus on Jay's face. Then she looked down at her blouse and frowned.

"Hey now, none of that. Jay didn't do that to ya, but I did tell the guy thank you very much that did." He pointed to the unconscious man crumpled at the foot of the table. Jay helped her to stand. He made his way to the door and opened it with a slow careful motion.

"Ha, that was the fastest…" The guard never finished his statement.

Jay grabbed the man by his collar and snatched him into the room. The man's eyes grew wide with fear, his arms and legs snapping backward against the force. "Spit in my face, will ya," Jay said as he slammed his massive fist against the man's nose, bones crunching beneath the blow. Jay then turned and threw the man on the floor beside his unconscious partner.

Running back to Iona, who still looked dazed, Jay closed her shirt and helped steady her on her feet. Lifting her, he coaxed her back toward full consciousness.

She moaned in his arms and opened her eyes. Touching her face which was still swollen, she asked groggily, "What happened?"

"I'll tell ya on the way. We gotta be going."

Taking the weapons and key cards off the guards, Iona partly walking and partly carried by Jay, they made their way into the hall.

Chapter Thirty-Four

The screen flickered and came to life. Downloading codes from his notepad, Skipp hacked his way into the computer's hard drive. One by one, he brought up the security files. One by one, he downloaded information detailing Ted Waters's orchestration of the Gliese System Quadrant catastrophe and the use of child slave labor.

"Look," he said to Mary over his shoulder. "Here's the file on the jiyst production. He's been pumping this stuff into the streets for years now."

"Why would Waters want a narcotic on the streets?" Mary asked. "What's that?" Mary pointed to a flashing icon.

"I don't know, but we'd better download it now. We can study it later."

"Right," she agreed. "We need to find Mike and the others and get out of here."

"Time to re-write some command codes," Skipp said, smiling.

They exchanged thoughts about the files and decided it was time to put the final stage of the plan into effect.

"Let's update Mike, grab the kids, and head to the roof," Skipp said.

"Think we should risk using the com-link?" Mary asked.

"I think it's time we better."

Overhead in a high earth orbit, Jonas monitored his team from the conn of the Quest. When he agreed to let Jay go in with Iona in his place, it was only because he thought all the waiting would be too hard on the big man. But now it was Jonas's nerves that were wearing thin waiting for the signal that would tell him they were still alive.

For the fifth time in as many minutes, he checked the comboard for the message from either Mike or Skipp telling him it was time. He checked the hardcopy backup just in case he had not been paying attention when the message arrived. It, too, was blank.

Getting up from the center seat, Jonas walked around the bridge, consumed with concerns and pangs of guilt. Staring at the blue planet floating far beneath the Quest, Jonas exhaled deeply and willed himself to relax. "Okay, Lord, now that we've done all we know to do, we really do need You to do the rest. Get them out of there alive, please."

Dropping again into the center seat, Jonas rubbed his face and checked the screen again.

Still no change.

"If only I knew what was happening." He bursted up from the seat. "This is driving me nuts," he yelled to the walls. He felt a sudden surge of urgency. "It's been too long," he said to the emptiness and ran to the pilot's chair.

Taking the controls in his hands, Jonas began his descent.

Mike looked up at the blackened vid screens and checked his chronometer. The screens had been dark for some time now, and Waters had been quiet.

He thought to himself, *only one of two things could have happened: either Waters had carried out his threat and the others were already dead;* or… He jumped to his feet and said into the air, "Skipp, I love you. Come on guys, let's make this happen!"

Making his way to the stairwell, Mike headed for Waters's office. Opening his com-link, he gave the command, "Jonas, now."

"I'm already moving," came Jonas's terse reply.

Just as Mike closed the circuit, his com-link sounded again. "Yeah, Jonas, go," he answered automatically as the hall door slid shut behind him.

"Baby," Mary's voice greeted him.

He froze mid-step and slumped against the wall. "Mary?" he said unbelieving.

"Yes, baby, it's me." Mary's voice was strained, but sweet to his ear. She continued, "We're safe. Skipp found us and we're heading for the rendezvous. I just wanted you to know that we are okay." She paused. "I knew you would come for us."

Upon hearing her voice, Mike's heart raced. He tried but couldn't speak. When back on the planet Yargon and Iona first told him that his family was still alive, he barely allowed himself to believe it. Then when Ted Waters had stolen them, even before he had the chance to tell Mary he loved her, his heart had gone numb. Now upon hearing her voice, he felt truly alive for the first time since watching his home go up in flames.

"It's really me," she said again.

"Mary, I love you so much," Mike finally managed.

"Hey, excuse me for breaking in on you lovebirds," Skipp said, "but we do have business left."

Mike could hear the smile in Mary's voice and the sound of her moving away from the com-link. "Okay, okay, business first."

Skipp broke in. "We managed to get into the computer and rig a few surprises. I thought we'd head down to find Iona and Jay-"

"Negative," Mike said. "Get my family to the roof. I'll get Iona and Jay."

"Copy that," Skipp said hesitantly. "We'll meet you there."

"Mike…" Mary's voice broke through.

"I'll be careful," he answered her. "I lost you once, I don't intend on losing you again."

He closed the circuit and sat on the stair. Closing his eyes, he spoke to Mary's God, "Thank you." After a minute, Mike continued toward the roof with one stop first: Ted Waters's office. He still had a score to settle.

Chapter Thirty-Five

"How ya feelin'?" Jay asked, still half-holding and half-pulling Iona along with him.

"Better," came her quiet but stronger reply.

"Well, if it means anything, you still look nice." He smiled and took on more of her weight.

"Liar." She limped on. "Actually, I'm feeling a lot better. I just like you carrying me."

"In that case..." He stepped quickly away from her, but caught her before she stumbled.

"Jay," she began in a serious tone. "I don't know what happened back there, but I'm sure it had something to do with those two guards on the floor. I-I just wanted to say thank you."

She wasn't sure, but she thought she saw his cheeks grow warm. She didn't know exactly why, and probably never would, considering her past, but he had been overtly careful with her since escaping the cell.

"Well," she prompted.

He smiled, but he did not answer.

At her direction, they arrived at Paul Adams's old office.

"Why are we here?" Jay asked.

"Paul was a weasel, a great executive, but a weasel nonetheless. If I know him, he would have backed up everything he and Waters ever discussed. It'll be in his office somewhere."

They opened the door and nothing happened: no lights, no alarm, no sentry, another hole in the armor or another trap?

Walking into the room, the sensors registered their presence, and the lights slowly began to rise.

"Computer. Lights to twenty-five percent norm," Iona said, hoping the system still recognized her voice pattern.

The lights stalled and began to lower, halting. The computer voice rang out, "Lights at twenty-five percent."

"Let's get in and get out. We need to make our way to the roof," Jay said, urging Iona to work.

The first thing she did was go to the desk. Reaching under it, she retrieved a laser blaster. Holding it up, she smiled at Jay's quizzical expression and threw it to him. "Ours was not a trusting staff."

Activating the computer, Iona began inputting codes. The screen flashed: password—password.

"What is it," Jay whispered, catching the look on Iona's face.

"It's password protected. I can't get in," she said in obvious frustration.

"Did he have any children? pets? fetishes?" Jay asked, trying to encourage her.

"Yeah, himself," she muttered, pushing the chair back from the desk.

"Well, try it."

"Try what? You don't think he could have been that vain, do you?" She scooted back up to the desk.

"I don't know. He was your friend." Jay laughed and walked back to check the corridor.

Iona pulled the keyboard toward her and typed in P-A-U-L. The screen flashed and came to life. She turned and smiled at Jay and winced when the cut on her lip pulled.

"Now this is more like the Paul I knew," she said and began downloading files. "Go through his cabinets, anything locked, blast it open."

Jay was moving before she finished talking. He opened doors and pulled out drawers. "Nothing over here."

The sound of approaching troops drew their attention back toward the door.

"We've got trouble! Didn't we just leave this party?" Iona said, rushing and closing the door. "Quick, Jay, weld the door to the frame; it's a metal alloy."

Using the blaster, Jay melted the door to the frame. "How long do you think that will keep them out?" he asked.

"Longer than without it," she said, indicating their physical conditions.

"Can you breach the wrist-com link frequency using the desk's communication system?" Jay asked coming to stand by her.

"I don't know; I can try." Iona settled behind the desk again. She tried adjusting the frequencies, playing with the settings. "Skipp, this is Iona, can you hear me? Mike, Jonas—are you there?"

Nothing.

A whirring buzzing noise began to come from the door. The sound had started soft, but began to grow in intensity.

The guards, finding the door sealed, had set neuron bombs designed to attack the metal at a microscopic level, to weaken the metal making it brittle. Coupled to the small devices, about three inches in diameter, were wave amps that began emitting a continuing escalating noise until it rendered those exposed to the wave unconscious.

"They're coming in," Jay said. "Get behind me."

The noise level continued to increase and began overtaxing their neural pathways. Screaming and covering their ears, they dropped to their knees. Their vision began to blur, their hands trembling.

"They're using neuron bombs," Iona said. "Smart, no fight that way. We need to get out of here—fast."

Jonas's voice came over the opened channel. "Iona, Jay, do you read me?"

The noise level continued to climb.

Iona and Jay clung to each other on the floor, desperately trying to get away from the deafening, brain piercing noise.

The whine increased.

They weren't sure at first, but they thought they could hear someone calling for them. Straining to hear, Jay crawled to the desk. "Yeah," he screamed. "We hear ya."

"What's that noise?" Jonas asked and then answered his own question. "Neurons! Get down; I'll open a door for you."

Jay crawled back to Iona. Covering his ear with one hand, he dragged her with the other, pulling her toward the backroom. He wrapped her in his large arms, covering her with his body.

"I have your location on screen. Get down." Jonas's voice was barely audible over the increasing whine of the bomb.

Jonas closed the channel, shutting off the irritating noise of the neuron bomb. Pushing the nose of the Quest downward, Jonas increased acceleration and directed the Quest toward the origin of the open channel like it was a beacon. "Make weapons hot," Jonas directed the shipboard computer. "Shields up," he said in the same business tone.

The Quest dove into Earth's atmosphere at one-quarter jump speed, a brilliant rooster tail of flame and smoke fanning in its wake, slow enough to avoid incineration, but still too fast for orbital defenses to react. She came in low over the city's skyline and screamed to a hovering stop just outside the eighty-eighth floor of The Company.

The neuron bomb was fast reaching its zenith, and inside the office both Jay and Iona lay exhausted from their exposure.

The vibration increased, the whine intensified, and helmeted guards, breaking the weld, crashed through the office door, weapons at the ready.

Ion cannon fire erupted from the forward battery of the Quest. The blast tore into the office, washing the troops back into the hall like flotsam caught in the surf. The inner wall careened backwards, slamming into guards still heading through the door.

A spray of molten plexiglass, concrete, and steel blasted into the wall just over the bowed heads of Iona and Jay. As soon as the storm had begun, it ended. Internal klaxons and fire suppression units clicked into service. The dull red light emanating from glow rods, fixed at ceiling level, added a surreal blush to what was left of the office and adjoining corridor.

Freed from the assault on their nerves, both Jay and Iona lay spent and exhausted in the increasingly wet carpet. Struggling to his feet, Jay helped Iona to stand and, together, made their way back into the main office. Spotting the Quest through the hole, they waved and gave a thumbs up and pointed toward the roof.

The single blast had cleared out the entire security task unit, leaving Jay and Iona alone. Heading out the door, Iona looked back to where she and Jay had been huddled against the wall. The blast had torn open a safe that previously had been hidden in the wall behind a series of shelves. "Wait," she said and pulled away from Jay.

"Wait-what-why? What is it? We need to go." Jay leaned his massive hand against the wall, his arm trembling beneath his weight. Sighing, he followed her back into the nearly gutted office.

Iona reached into the shattered safe and retrieved a single data storage rod. "Bingo. Thank you, Paul."

Together, they hobbled out and headed to the roof. "I'm sure our friend Skipp will be able to tell us what's on this baby," Jay said, clearly teasing.

She smiled up at Jay, kissed the data rod, and dropped it into her pocket, pressing it close as she did.

Collecting weapons from among the wreckage, they set out through the eerily empty halls heading for the roof and for their scheduled pickup.

Outside, Jonas rotated the Quest while maintaining the hover. The team wasn't ready for pickup. Checking the scan, he found no hostile aircraft in the immediate area, but he knew they were coming. He fired the repulsor rockets, and the Quest rose quietly, executing a 180-degree turn and exploded upward in a muted surge. Rather than push his luck, he chose discretion, pulled back hard on the stick, headed back to high altitude, and began a slow arcing circle that kept him near the towering structure.

Chapter Thirty-Six

Mike paused and took a breath before continuing toward the door at the end of the hall. Just ahead of him, stood a twin set of oversized mahogany doors, the polished metal nameplate attached with brass rivets set off to one side displayed a single name, Ted Waters. As he approached, and as he had expected, with only the faint sound of moving air, the doors swung open on silent hinges. Inside the dimly lit office, Ted Waters sat calmly behind his large white desk.

"I suppose you think you have gained some kind of victory, Michael, but I assure you…it is not." Only Ted Waters mouth had moved; his hand clasped, and fingers interlaced on the desktop before him.

The fabric-covered walls of the room seemed to absorb the light as it flooded in through the wall-sized windows. The blood red carpet, in stark contrast against the almost pure white desk, appeared wet and alive. As he sat unmoving, Waters drew on the large cigar held between thin lips beneath a finely trimmed mustache. Wafts of gray smoke rose lazily above his head and collected near the ceiling before being drawn out by invisible vents.

The whole office seemed to generate a not so real feeling engineered to keep any visitor feeling off kilter.

"Come in, Michael. Have a seat."

He still hadn't moved. Even in the face of apparent defeat, Ted Waters presented himself as respected and powerful, in charge. "You never answered my question, Michael. Do you think you have won? Do you think you have beaten me?" He laughed. "You are wrong again. You have underestimated me. Again."

Mike walked forward until he stood over the desk, glaring down at Ted Waters. Standing over the man that had ruined his life and threatened his family, Mike's hands clenched and unclenched, his breaths coming in short, quick bursts. All the hatred he'd felt for this man boiled just beneath a barely controlled surface. Barely contained, like a membrane pulled taut, he waited. Just one impulse from erupting, and he knew that was just where Waters wanted him, angry—emotional—not thinking. He breathed and forced himself to relax.

Waters sat, unmoving, puffing on his cigar and locked his eyes onto Mike's.

"I said sit down, Michael. Do not be rude."

"There's only one person who has earned the right to call me Michael, and you're not her," Mike said.

Waters laughed again, but this time he did not sound as secure, as sure as he had earlier. He stood and walked around his desk. His steps were slow and measured as if sizing up Mike as he approached.

Now standing face to face, Waters exhaled a breath of cigar smoke.

Coughing, Mike reached up, pulled the cigar from Waters's mouth and threw it to the carpet, stamping on it, and said, "Now who's being rude? Besides"—Mike smiled—"smoke stinks."

Like a bear roused, Waters exploded. A blindly fast backhand caught Mike squarely on the side of his face, sending him crashing to the floor. Before Mike could regain his footing, Waters pounced on him, kicking and pounding him.

Unprepared for the attack, Mike was taken completely off guard. He covered his head with his arms, using them to take the brunt of the assault. Overwhelmed by the raw savagery, all Mike could do was try and absorb and deflect the attack. Blow after blow landed solidly against his body.

Backing against a wall, Mike managed to brace and then launch himself at Waters. The change in tactic gave him the small break he needed. Catching Waters just above the knees, Mike forced him backwards, both men collapsing to the floor.

Mike gained the top mount and straddled Waters chest, jamming his knees into his armpits and began to pummel him with a flurry of blows. With every punch, Mike recalled an injury or hurt Waters had inflicted. With mumblings and groans, which accented the force and effort placed into each strike, Mike hammered away at Waters's unguarded face.

Then, as easily as a child lifts a toy, Waters grabbed Mike's arm, and with seemingly little effort, he threw Mike across the floor. Dazed and winded, Mike raised blurry eyes and watched as Waters regained his feet.

To Mike's surprise, Waters showed no ill effect from the barrage of blows landed in his face. Startled, he lay unmoving as he watched Waters stand gracefully and start toward him.

Mike staggered to his feet, and when Waters was close enough, he punched. Waters's head snapped with the collision of knuckle and face, and then slowly turned his face back to stare at Mike.

Grabbing Mike again, Waters spoke softly. "Now do you finally begin to understand, Michael? You cannot defeat me."

Mike struck him again and again.

Waters stared at him. "Shall I end it now and put you out of your misery, Michael?" his voice was soft, sounding kind.

Mike hacked at Waters's arms which felt like he was slapping metal posts. Waters laughed and tossed him again across the room.

Desperate, Mike screamed and reached for his blaster. But before he could take the first shot, Waters jumped, clearing the short distance between them, trapping the blaster in Mike's hand.

Waters grabbed Mike by the wrist. He squeezed.

Mike screamed in pain, dropping to his knees at Waters's feet. Looking up into Ted Waters's impassive face, the truth finally settled on him. He was about to die.

But instead of delivering the blow that would have ended his life, Waters snatched Mike up from the floor and put him roughly into the chair in front of the white desk. "Earlier, I offered you a seat, and if you recall, I asked you not to be rude."

Waters walked back behind his desk. Casually taking out another cigar, he bit off the end, spat it into the recycle bin, and leaned back in his chair. Lighting the cigar, he took a long drag and released the smoke toward Mike. "You really should try one," he said, but made no move to offer.

"I told you before our..."—he paused—"un-pleasantries, Michael, and so I say again; you cannot defeat me."

Mike stared at Waters through swollen eyes. Every part of him hurting.

"Look at me, Michael! Do not pass out yet," Waters said in a patriarchal tone. "There are some things you still need to know."

Mike stirred and forced himself to sit up in the chair. "What do you want, Waters?" he managed through swollen lips.

"I have already answered that question, but that is not the question you should be asking," he answered in patient tones. "Do you not, instead, want to know why?"

"Why?" Mike echoed, confused. "Why, what?" he said and slipped in the chair. Readjusting himself, he focused on Waters. "Yes. Why the Gliese System sector? Why the children? Why me?" Mike's thoughts were disjointed, his head felt bruised and swollen.

"Very good," Waters said, standing. Adjusting the cuffs on his jacket, he started toward Mike. "The answer is simple really, Michael. I am The Company." He was standing over Mike now. "It is not just about the business markets or even terra farming new planets for *those pathetic* masses with their petty needs. Michael, I am surprised you do not understand it, really."

Waters stopped in front of Mike and looked down at him. "The reason you could never beat me, Michael, is that you are simply too small. Your concept of life is in complete error."

Taking the handkerchief from his pocket, Waters leaned forward and dabbed the line of blood trickling from Mike's mouth, and then readjusted him in the chair. "My dear, Michael, it is all about power. It is all about me. I will rule not only this city, Michael, but *everything*. There is simply no room for you, or your ancient God in my plan..."

Mike's mind began to swim as understanding dawned. All that had happened to him, being defamed and losing his career, his home and family being threatened, and even his involvement in trying to save the children. His attempt to undo his own mistakes had all happened because Waters saw him as a threat. *It was ironic*, Mike thought, that only now at the end, he truly had come to understand.

Waters believed Mike was a Christian.

Mike allowed his vision to blur as he thought back over the events in his life. His meeting, falling in love with and eventually marrying Mary, and all the times she told him about her God. His fall from power. The visit from Jonas. The children. His children. The thoughts came rushing at him faster than he could order them. He looked up at Waters and smiled.

Waters was standing and folding the blood stained handkerchief, and then dropped it on the desk.

Mike spoke in a voice, a little more than a whisper. "God, I've been a fool. Only now do I realize that it was You. I can finally see it now. I'm sorry."

"No, Michael, do not mumble. Speak plainly," Waters said, smiling.

It was while you were still a sinner that I died for you, Mike. My blood shed to cover your sins.

It was the voice again.

"Lord, forgive me," Mike forced through a swollen throat. "Forgive me…I believe."

"We will have none of that," Waters said, as he slapped Mike across his face. "And now, Michael," Waters said, reaching out for him, "it is time that you die."

Waters's hand closed around Mike's throat. With slow steady pressure, he began to squeeze.

Mike slapped at the vice-like grip, bright spots appearing in his vision. Gasping, he fought for breath that simply would not come. At his periphery, darkness closed in from the edges; he was passing out.

Images of Mary kneeling and praying by their bedside came rushing back into his mind. The sound of his children's voices as they recited prayers and scriptures cascaded over him like subtle showers.

Then, like a flash of lightning, Waters's calm face replaced the image and sounds of his family, and Mike knew then that he would die.

"Good-bye, Michael," Waters whispered softly.

The pressure increased, and Mike thrashed futilely against the constriction on his throat. Spots of red, yellow, and white lights flashed before his unseeing eyes. Mike felt his body begin to spasm and jerk, frog breathing.

At that moment, the voice returned. *Will you hear Me, son? Will you now accept My gift of grace?*

Pain washed over Mike, a burning suffocating constriction in his lungs, a desperate aching for breath. He could feel his hands and legs numb with cold.

The voice: *Will you yield?*

"Yes...yes! I am sorry...I've waited...until now...to call you Father. Forgive me." Mike was not sure if he actually said the words or if he just thought them.

He felt his knees crash into the carpet, and still, the pressure continued. He fought no longer; he knew he was dying, that maybe he was already dead. "Thank you, Father."

"And now, Michael," Waters said in a voice of finality, "good-bye."

Chapter Thirty-Seven

The blaster shot hit Ted Waters near the top of his right shoulder, tearing him backwards and breaking his grip from Mike's throat.

Mike fell like a wet rag dropping to the floor.

Jay ran into the room and inserted himself between Waters and the semiconscious Mike lying crumpled on the blood red carpet.

Waters stood and turned facing Jay and Mike, his shoulder smoldering where he'd taken the shot. He attacked.

Jay fired.

Waters stumbled backwards.

Jay held the blaster steady. "Get him out of here," he called over his shoulder to Iona, gesturing toward Mike.

Mike inhaled and tried to get up. "Don't, mon, let her help you. You're hurt pretty bad." Jay set his blaster by his feet in order to use both hands to steady Mike. "Just sit for a minute. Catch your breath."

Unseen and forgotten, Waters stirred, pushed up to his knees and then stood. Locking hate-filled eyes on Jay, he roared like a mad beast and charged.

Jay rolled to the side just as Mike grabbed the laser and fired. From across the room a second stream of energy followed the first. Iona stood, shoulders squared, just lowering her blaster.

This time the laser blast struck Waters just above the heart, exposing the wires and circuitry that controlled the android.

"You should not have done that," it said, as wafts of acrid smoke snaked upward from the gash and a viscous yellow fluid oozed out, dripping to the carpet.

Mike fired again. "An android?"

The machine stumbled, stepped backwards, then attacked again.

Both Mike and Iona held a sustained blast, hitting the machine in the exposed circuitry.

"Let's get out of here!" Jay yelled, frantically pointing toward the door.

The android Waters froze in mid-stride. Beginning to shake, it fell backwards, crashing onto the marble desk.

"Is that it?" Jay asked in unbelief. Looking around cautiously, he said, "That was too easy."

"I knew something was wrong with him," Mike said wheezing through a swollen throat. "He was way too strong."

Iona hefted Mike to his feet. "Come on, let's get out of here. We've got a ride waiting on the roof."

Clap-clap-clap.

The clapping sound erupted from hidden speakers. A slit appeared in the ceiling as an oversized holographic image of Ted Waters materialized in the center of the room. "Very good, gentlemen..." Then he added, almost as an afterthought, "and you too, madam."

The group looked from the holograph to each other, speechless. Then Mike stood and looked from the android to the image of the man, as if trying to determine which was real.

"I assure you," Ted Waters said, "that this is indeed me, Michael."

Mike exchanged glances with Iona and Jay.

"Why the android?" Waters asked. "A man never leaves himself without options, Michael. I needed a distraction. Thank you for volunteering." He smiled condescendingly.

"From the moment I lost control of the building's computer, I knew I must have miscalculated you to some small degree. A mistake I will not repeat; I assure you.

"Michael, you have not won. If you manage to survive the building, which I am not at all convinced you will, I will look forward to our next encounter. Remember, Michael, I am **The Company**."

The hologram shimmered and disappeared.

"We need to get out of here. Now!" Mike demanded, his voice barely audible. He headed toward the elevator.

"No!" Iona said, "he'll have those rigged. We'd better take the stairs."

They turned instead for the exit. Four flights to the roof.

Mike lifted his wrist, indicating his communicator and pointed to Jay. "Let Jonas know we're on our way," he whispered. "Make sure Mary and the kids are onboard."

In the ladder well, red and green lights flashed in opposition of each other. "The self-destruct has been activated," Iona said. "There's no way of knowing how much time we have."

Mike reached for his wrist-com. "Jonas, get that ship off the roof; the building is set to blow. Do you read?" Although he screamed the words, they still came out just over a whisper.

"You just get to the roof; let me do my job!" Jonas shouted back.

"We won't leave without you," Mary said over the opened channel. "Either we all go home or nobody goes home. Now get up here!"

"I think she means it," Jay said. He turned and looked at Iona. "She's your sister? I see it runs in the family."

Iona smiled. "Believe me, she means it."

A white smoke began to rise from the floors beneath them, swallowing the lower floors into a billowing invisibility.

"It's tetrafluoroethane," Iona shouted.

"What?" Jay asked, stopping to look down at the cloud.

"Coolant," Mike answered in his strained voice. "Mix R13a with a heat source and—"

"Boom! Mechanical explosion. Massive and easy to hide," Iona finished. "He must have been planning this all along."

From somewhere hidden in the cloud below, blaster fire erupted. Red and yellow bolts tore past them carving holes in the wall. Jay leveled his blaster, preparing to return fire.

"Don't," Mike yelled. "Boom, remember?"

Jay pulled the blaster back to his side and pressed his back to the wall. "Thanks."

Iona pointed at the massive vent hood mounted on the wall and nodded. Jay opened fire on that instead.

A few minutes later, the heavy metal box of valves, tubing, and coils went crashing, bouncing along the stairs and banging against the walls of the ladder well.

A short time later, the group burst out onto the roof. The Quest sat a short distance away with the ramp down and the rear door opened.

Blaster fire erupted as soon as they came through the door. Troops hidden behind anchored spacecrafts came out in mass, intent on stalling, if not stopping their escape.

"Get down!" Jay yelled.

Blaster fire furrowed the floor and gouged craters in the wall beside the door. Jay opened fire. Ducking, Mike and Iona returned fire as well at the advancing troops. They began to edge back to the relative shelter of the ladder well.

The rooftop lights started blinking in rapid succession and then abruptly shut off.

"We're out of time," Iona said. "Either we go now, or we don't go at all."

"Then that settles it," Jay said. Bursting through the door firing his blaster, he rushed the guards' position.

Directly over his head, a single beam of laser fire erupted from the Quest and tore into the hangared aircraft that had served as cover for the armed guards. One by one, the ships began to explode.

"Get in here. Hurry!" Mary yelled from the ship's ramp.

As they entered the Quest, the ramp began closing on their heels, blaster fire careening off the hull in halos of brilliant color.

Slapping the intercom, Skipp yelled, "They're onboard. Go! Go! Get us out of here!"

Jay rushed to the bridge and assumed the pilot's duties. "Thanks for the pickup, but I'll take her from here."

"With pleasure," Jonas said, vacating the seat.

Jay pulled hard on the helm and fired the boosters. The Quest jumped off the roof, positive g-forces pulling down against the bodies of the crew.

As soon as they had cleared the building, Mary ran and threw herself into Mike's arms, hugging him and covering his face with kisses.

Mike took his daughter and cradled her in his arms. He kissed the little face as she reached a pudgy hand against her daddy's bruised face. "Dadda, Dadda, Dadda."

Held in the crook of his arm, Mary continued to call his name softly in between kisses as they together settled onto the floor.

"Dad!

"Daddy!"

M2 and Travist squealed as the boys piled on top of their parents, hugging their father and just trying to be close to him.

"I thought I'd lost you...the kids," Mike whispered between squeals and kisses.

Mary kissed him again.

Mike buried his face in the crook of her neck, kissing her jaw line and holding her tightly to himself. "I thought I'd lost you. I thought I'd lost." Tears washed his bruised face.

"I know."

"I was so mad. Mad at Ted Waters. Mad at God."

Beside them, both boys were telling their own version of the events as the baby continued to touch and feel the discolored protrusions on her daddy's face.

Mike groaned and Mary softly kissed him. "Kiss me. I'm here now and we're together." She kissed him again.

Iona dropped to her knees in front of Albert, and the boy flung himself in to her arms. "I was so worried," he said.

"Yeah, me too," Iona managed around her tears. "Me too, but I came back just like I promised. Right?"

"Right," Albert said and hugged her tighter. "Now we can always be together."

A shadow passed over her, and Iona looked up to see Jay looking down at her. "Hi," he said approaching them.

"Looks like things are going..." Iona began.

Jay dropped down beside her and Albert. He extended a hand. "Hi, I'm Jay."

Albert stood and looked at Jay. "I know who you are, M2 and Travist told me. You helped Iona help us."

Jay laughed, his baritone voice rich and warm. "Yeah, I helped."

Just then, Travist ran over. "Hey, Albert, come meet my dad." He grabbed the boy by his hand and pulled him after him.

Iona stood slowly and faced Jay. She reached a hand up and touched a bruise on his face. She inhaled preparing to speak. "Look, I—"

Jay laughed aloud, pulled her into his embrace, and held her there, not invading, but giving her a safe place, someone to depend on besides herself.

They stood like that for a moment before Iona pushed him away and looked at him sternly, a trace of the old Iona flickering across her face. She did not speak, but only looked at him. The silence stretched into long pregnant moments.

Looking down, she looked toward where Albert stood playing with Mike and Mary's children. With one hand, she brushed loose strands of hair from her face, and with the other, she interlaced her fingers into Jay's. And in that moment, Iona thought she began to understand what her sister had come to know so long ago.

It began as a low rumble near the basement. The building, which had served as the earth's symbol of government and commerce, the icon of Ted Waters, imploded. A fiery halo highlighted the massive structure against an otherwise dull sky.

The building shuddered and, in an anticlimactic collapse, fell in on itself, collecting in a shapeless mass four miles square at the base. The resulting dust cloud rose several thousand feet into the air and mushroomed out for miles, casting the city and surrounding area into an unnatural twilight that would last for weeks.

Chapter Thirty-Eight

Mike and Mary walked silently, enjoying the nearness of each other and the quiet of Nonna's farm. Ahead of them, the boys ran back and forth, chasing each other and playing tag. Sissy toddled a few steps away from her parents before sitting hard in the soft grass. She raised her arms, and Mike reached forward and lifted her, holding her against his chest and enjoying hollow kisses from moist lips.

"You know"—he began looking at his wife—"it's ironic when you consider that all of this started because Waters thought I was a Christian and would hinder his plans for The Company. Wonder what he'd think if he found out that I only came to believe because of what he did?"

"Maybe it's like Nonna always says, 'God works in mysterious ways.' Like with Joseph."

"Joseph?" Mike looked at his wife, confusion on his face.

"You've got a lot to learn." She giggled, and he pulled her to him and kissed her deeply.

Sticky hands on the side of his face interrupted the kiss. "Kiss, Daddy," Sissy uttered and smiled. Mike kissed his daughter.

"So, who's Joseph?" he said, looking at Mary.

"You know, from the Bible. God allowed Joseph to get sold into slavery and eventually put into prison for a crime he didn't commit."

Mike turned so he could see her better. "That's the one where his brothers sold him, right?" He grabbed her hand and kissed her knuckles.

"Yep, and when it was all said and done, all that trouble got him right where God wanted him in the first place." She traced a finger around the line of his jaw, enjoying the contrast of her fair skin against the rich brown of his face.

He laughed. "That's me all right," he said, smiling at her. "Good old Joseph."

"Mike, Mary," Iona called from the house. "You guys might want to hear this." She waved them over as Albert ran past her to join the boys in their game.

Coming in through the screened door, they heard the news reporter's voice mid-sentence. "...the terrorists managed to break in and steal a number of classified files before setting off bombs and fleeing via a daring roof top escape."

The reporter stopped and looked off camera. "This just came in..." he continued. "Ladies and gentlemen, you may remember him from a scandal that happened almost sixteen years ago..."

A picture of Mike flashed on the screen; his name in bold print beneath it.

"...when he was arrested and charged for over five-hundred deaths associated with the failed Gliese System Planet Terra Farming Project. He is Michael Stone, a former employee of The Company."

The screen changed to a remote interview from the site of the explosion. An elegant blond reporter stood holding her left hand to her ear and a microphone to her mouth. She nodded as if she'd just agreed with something and looked into the camera. "This is Camille Saunders reporting live from the scene of the destroyed Company building."

The camera view changed, showing the rubble of heap still smoking and emergency vehicles moving the injured to area hospitals.

"Medical facilities are being swamped with injured at this hour; there is no telling just how high the death toll will get before this is over. Authorities are trying to piece together just what the terrorist were trying to accomplish."

The voice of the news anchor spoke over the image of the blond reporter. She put her hand to her ear again. "Camille, this is Dan Johnson at the news desk. We're hearing reports that the lead terrorists has been identified as former Company employee Michael Stone. Can you confirm this?

The blond nodded her head before she began speaking, "One minute, Dan, we have a witness who puts Mr. Stone here on the premises shortly before the alarms sounded. Here he comes now, the CEO of the Company, Ted Waters."

Ted Waters walked into the field of view. He still wore his trademark gray suit, but also wore a bandage around his head, a fresh bloodstain showing just over his right eye.

Placing his hand on the reporter's shoulder for balance, Waters looked into the camera lens. "Hello, Ms. Saunders, thank you for coming out."

"No, thank you, Mr. Waters. Can you tell our audience why the authorities have ID'd Michael Stone, a former employee here, of doing this?" She gestured toward the smoking debris pile.

"Yes, I found it hard to believe myself. I have always counted Mr. Stone as one of my close, personal friends. I can only imagine that he has never fully recovered from his ordeal from a few years back," Waters said.

"But why would he resort to this, almost 10 years after the fact?"

"Mr. Stone," Waters began soberly, "joined one of the ancient religious cults and since that time began making threats related to some of its supposed prophecies found in their holy book." He shook his head as if fighting off confusion. "But I never thought he would go this far."

"Do you have any idea how—" she began, but Waters cut her off.

"Let me say this," Waters said, turning to face the camera. "Mr. Stone may have dealt us a crippling blow, but we will not allow this to defeat us. We will rebuild. We will expand." He stepped toward the camera, his chin lowering as did the tone of his voice.

"Of course, I will not go into the details here, but suffice it to say, what we will become will hardly compare to what we were before this savage and unprovoked attack. I have already spoken with many of my friends at the governmental level and suggested a restriction on harmful religious groups like the one Stone is championing. It is my plan that the world will soon come together as one family under the banner of unity, and the society of humanity itself no longer fragmented by the archaic and superstitious beliefs of the past."

With that, Waters smiled, touched his bandaged head as if wincing with pain, and without another word, turned and walked away.

"Well, Dan, you heard it here. Not only have the authorities identified the man responsible for this act of cowardice, but Ted Waters just told us that he has determined to rebuild, making The Company bigger and better than it ever was."

Dan Johnson: "Any idea what that will look like, Camille?"

"Not really, Dan," the reporter said into her microphone after a short pause. "I guess we'll just have to wait along with the rest of the world to find out. But I can't imagine a better man than Ted Waters to lead us into that future, Dan. And if Ted Waters keeps his word, then this is one world citizen who can't wait to see what that future will be.

"For The Company News Network, this is Camille Saunders reporting from the bomb site."

The image changed back to the studio reporter. "Thanks for that report, Camille. Mr. Waters certainly has his work cut out for him. It's my understanding that he lost almost everything in that attack."

The reporter shifted in his seat, and turned to look into a different camera. Shuffling papers on his desk, he began, "In other news..."

Mary turned the monitor off. "Now what?" she asked, deflated.

Everyone looked to Mike. He stood and paced over to the screened window, his back to them. For long moments, no one spoke.

Running a hand over his scalp, Mike looked up watching clouds float with seeming aimless direction and released a long sigh. After releasing his breath, he turned to face the group. Holding up the memory rod in his hand that Iona had taken from Paul Adam's bombed out office, he waited until everyone focused on it. "Somewhere on this memory rod is the key to what Waters is up to. We start with this."

"But what do we do now—I mean, right now? You know Waters has men looking for us even as he did that interview," Iona said.

Mike smiled and then winked at Mary. "Now we pray," he said. "Now we pray."

...After

All the rescued children were placed in families, members of Nonna's underground church, all but one. Nonna decided to keep Rosemary with her on the farm. When asked why, all she would ever say is, "I have a soft spot for little girls."

The End.

Acknowledgement

In the course of any endeavor there comes a point where you realize you're gonna need friends for the journey. Dorothy had the Tin Man, Scare Crow, and the Lion and Jason had his Argonauts. I thank God that when that time came for me, I realized that those friends, my team, were already assembled and standing by. I would like to thank my team at NCC Publishing and the many invisible warriors that spent hours in prayer for Kracken.

And because this was actually the first manuscript I wrote, some 20 years ago, many of those people who helped birth Kracken have long since moved on to their own journeys. To all those, Pam J. and Linda T, and the others, I say thank you.

Lastly, to my church family here in Idaho: I say thank you for all the support, encouragement, and prayers. And most of all, to my Lord and Savior, Jesus Christ, who I hope to glorify in all that I am and do, thank you.

A Note From The Author

Thank you for reading *Kracken*. Now that you've finished this book, I would love to hear from you. You can email me with your thoughts on the book or become my friend on Facebook. You can even sign up for updates by joining my *Kracken* page, which will give you updates on upcoming releases and all the other craziness going on in my corner of the world.

If you would like to help this story succeed, please tell others about it. You can loan your copy to a friend and ask your local libraries and bookstores to order it.

In addition, if you could please post a review on amazon.com, or goodreads.com, it would be very helpful. Again, thank you.

My email address is:
rayellisauthor@gmail.com

You can download discussion questions or follow my blog entries at:
http://authorray.blogspot.com

Please visit my book page at:
https://www.facebook.com/groups/1410112512539597/

Follow me on Twitter at:
Twitter@RayEllisWriter

More By Ray Ellis

Notorious (A Nate Richards Mystery - Book One)
　Previously released as *N.H.I. (No Humans Involved)*

Dead List (A Nate Richards Mystery - Book Two)
　Previously released as *D.R.T. (Dead Right There)*

Insidious (A Nate Richards Mystery - Book Three)

"I" – A Short Story

About The Author

A veteran law enforcement officer, former United States Marine, and ordained Christian pastor, Ray's first novel, *NOTORIOUS*, previously released as N.H.I. *No Humans Involved*, was published in 2011. Since then, Ray has been selected as one of Idaho's Top 50 Authors for the year of 2011, and then as a Top 10 Idaho Author in 2012; and in 2014 he was selected as the ACFW Idaho branch Writer of the Year.

When not writing, Ray can be found still working as an active duty officer, speaking to student groups, or teaching Bible studies in his local community.

Would you like to receive notifications on free book giveaways, special discounts, or new book announcements from NCC Publishing? If so, you can "like" us on Facebook (NCC Publishing, L.L.C.), or send an email to:

specialoffers@nccpublishing.com

www.nccpublishing.com

If you enjoyed this book, you may enjoy some of the other publications available from NCC Publishing. The complete list of publications is available at:

www.nccpublishing.com/publications

www.ingramcontent.com/pod-product-compliance
Lightning Source LLC
Chambersburg PA
CBHW032134190626
46814CB00005BA/1691